Shadows on the Rock

The Willa Cather Scholarly Edition

General Editor:
Susan J. Rosowski

Editorial Board:
Frederick M. Link
Charles W. Mignon
John J. Murphy
David Stouck

Advisory Committee:
Joan S. Crane
Gary Moulton
Paul A. Olson
James Woodress

Edition Sponsored by:
University of
Nebraska–Lincoln

WILLA CATHER

Shadows on the Rock

Historical Essay by
JOHN J. MURPHY and
DAVID STOUCK

Explanatory Notes by
JOHN J. MURPHY and
DAVID STOUCK

Textual Editing by
FREDERICK M. LINK

University of Nebraska Press
Lincoln

DISCARDED

COMMITTEE ON
SCHOLARLY EDITIONS

AN APPROVED EDITION

MODERN LANGUAGE
ASSOCIATION OF AMERICA

The Committee on Scholarly Editions emblem means
that one of a panel of textual experts serving the Committee
has reviewed the text and textual apparatus of the printer's
copy by thorough and scrupulous sampling, and has approved
them for sound and consistent editorial principles employed
and maximum accuracy attained. The accuracy of the text
has been guarded by careful and repeated proofreading
according to standards set by the Committee.
Published by arrangement with Alfred A. Knopf, Inc.

Copyright © 2005 by the Board of Regents
of the University of Nebraska
All rights reserved
Manufactured in the United States of America

☉

Library of Congress Cataloging-in-Publication Data
Cather, Willa, 1873–1947.
Shadows on the rock / Willa Cather ; historical essay by John J.
Murphy and David Stouck ; explanatory notes by John J. Murphy
and David Stouck ; textual editing by Frederick M. Link.
p. cm. — (The Willa Cather scholarly edition)
Includes bibliographical references.
ISBN 0-8032-1532-0 (cl. : alk. paper)
1. Canada — History — To 1763 (New France) — Fiction.
2. Frontenac, Louis de Buade, comte de, 1620–1698 — Fiction.
3. Fathers and daughters — Fiction. 4. Québec (Québec) —
Fiction. 5. Pharmacists — Fiction. 6. Physicians — Fiction.
I. Murphy, John J. (John Joseph), 1933– II. Stouck, David, 1940–
III. Link, Frederick M. IV. Title.
PS3505.A875 S 2005
813'.52–dc22
2005005291

DISCARDED

CONTENTS

In Memory of
SUSAN J. ROSOWSKI
1942–2004

Preface

THE objective of the Willa Cather Scholarly Edition is to provide to readers—present and future—various kinds of information relevant to Willa Cather's writing, obtained and presented by the highest scholarly standards: a critical text faithful to her intention as she prepared it for the first edition, a historical essay providing relevant biographical and historical facts, explanatory notes identifying allusions and references, a textual commentary tracing the work through its lifetime and describing Cather's involvement with it, and a record of revisions in the text's various editions. This edition is distinctive in the comprehensiveness of its apparatus, especially in its inclusion of extensive explanatory information that illuminates the fiction of a writer who drew so extensively upon actual experience, as well as the full textual information we have come to expect in a modern critical edition. It thus connects activities that are too often separate —literary scholarship and textual editing.

Editing Cather's writing means recognizing that Cather was as fiercely protective of her novels as she was of her private life. She suppressed much of her early writing and

vii

dismissed serial publication of later work, discarded manuscripts and proofs, destroyed letters, and included in her will a stipulation against publication of her private papers. Yet the record remains surprisingly full. Manuscripts, typescripts, and proofs of some texts survive with corrections and revisions in Cather's hand; serial publications provide final "draft" versions of texts; correspondence with her editors and publishers helps clarify her intention for a work, and publishers' records detail each book's public life; correspondence with friends and acquaintances provides an intimate view of her writing; published interviews with and speeches by Cather provide a running public commentary on her career; and through their memoirs, recollections, and letters, Cather's contemporaries provide their own commentary on circumstances surrounding her writing.

In assembling pieces of the editorial puzzle, we have been guided by principles and procedures articulated by the Committee on Scholarly Editions of the Modern Language Association. Assembling and comparing texts demonstrated the basic tenet of the textual editor — that only painstaking collations reveal what is actually there. Scholars had assumed, for example, that with the exception of a single correction in spelling, *O Pioneers!* passed unchanged from the 1913 first edition to the 1937 Autograph Edition. Collations revealed nearly a hundred word changes, thus providing information not only necessary to establish a critical text and to interpret how Cather composed, but also basic to interpreting how her ideas about art changed as she matured.

Cather's revisions and corrections on typescripts and page proofs demonstrate that she brought to her own writing her extensive experience as an editor. Word changes demonstrate her practices in revising; other changes demonstrate that she gave extraordinarily close scrutiny to such matters as capitalization, punctuation, paragraphing, hyphenation, and spacing. Knowledgeable about production, Cather had intentions for her books that extended to their design and manufacture. For example, she specified typography, illustrations, page format, paper stock, ink color, covers, wrappers, and advertising copy.

To an exceptional degree, then, Cather gave to her work the close textual attention that modern editing practices respect, while in other ways she challenged her editors to expand the definition of "corruption" and "authoritative" beyond the text, to include the book's whole format and material existence. Believing that a book's physical form influenced its relationship with a reader, she selected type, paper, and format that invited the reader response she sought. The heavy texture and cream color of paper used for *O Pioneers!* and *My Ántonia*, for example, created a sense of warmth and invited a childlike play of imagination, as did these books' large, dark type and wide margins. By the same principle, she expressly rejected the anthology format of assembling texts of numerous novels within the covers of one volume, with tight margins, thin paper, and condensed print.

Given Cather's explicitly stated intentions for her works, printing and publishing decisions that disregard her wishes represent their own form of corruption, and an authoritative edition of Cather must go beyond the sequence of words and punctuation to include other matters: page format, paper stock, typeface, and other features of design. The volumes in the Cather Edition respect those intentions insofar as possible within a series format that includes a comprehensive scholarly apparatus. For example, the Cather Edition has adopted the format of six by nine inches, which Cather approved in Bruce Rogers's elegant work on the 1937 Houghton Mifflin Autograph Edition, to accommodate the various elements of design. While lacking something of the intimacy of the original page, this size permits the use of large, generously leaded type and ample margins — points of style upon which the author was so insistent. In the choice of paper, we have deferred to Cather's declared preference for a warm, cream antique stock.

Today's technology makes it difficult to emulate the qualities of hot-metal typesetting and letterpress printing. In comparison, modern phototypesetting printed by offset lithography tends to look anemic and lacks the tactile quality of type impressed into the page. The version of the Fournier typeface employed in the original edition of *Shadows*, were it available for phototypesetting, would hardly survive the transition. Instead, we have chosen Linotype Janson Text, a modern rendering of the type used by Rogers. The subtle adjustments of stroke weight in this reworking do much to retain the integrity of earlier metal versions. Therefore, without trying to replicate the design of single works, we seek to represent Cather's general preferences in a design that encompasses many volumes.

In each volume in the Cather Edition, the author's specific intentions for design and printing are set forth in textual commentaries. These essays also describe the history of the texts, identify those that are authoritative, explain the selection of copy-texts or basic texts, justify emendations of the copy-text, and describe patterns of variants. The textual apparatus in each volume — lists of variants, emendations, explanations of emendations, and end-of-line hyphenations — completes the textual story.

Historical essays provide essential information about the genesis, form, and transmission of each book, as well as supply its biographical, historical, and intellectual contexts. Illustrations supplement these essays with photographs, maps, and facsimiles of manuscript, typescript, or typeset pages. Finally, because Cather in her writing drew so extensively upon personal experience and historical detail, explanatory notes are an especially important part of the Cather Edition. By providing a comprehensive identification of her references to flora and fauna, to regional customs and manners, to the classics and the Bible, to popular writing, music, and other arts — as well as relevant cartography and census material — these notes provide a starting place for scholarship and criticism on subjects long slighted or ignored.

Within this overall standard format, differences occur that are informative in their own right. The straightforward textual history of *O Pioneers!* and *My Ántonia* contrasts with the more complicated textual challenges of *A Lost Lady* and *Death Comes for the Archbishop*; the allusive personal history of the Nebraska novels, so densely woven that *My Ántonia* seems drawn not merely upon Anna Pavelka but all of Webster County, contrasts with the more public allusions of novels set elsewhere. The Cather Edition reflects the individuality of each work while providing a standard of reference for critical study.

Susan J. Rosowski

Shadows on the Rock

WILLA CATHER

Contents

BOOK I

The Apothecary

Vous me demandez des graines de fleurs de ce pays. Nous en faisons venir de France pour notre jardin, n'y en ayant pas ici de fort rares ni de fort belles. Tout y est sauvage, les fleurs aussi bien que les hommes.

Marie de l'Incarnation

(LETTRE À UNE DE SES SŒURS)

Québec, le 12 août, 1653

The Apothecary

I

ONE afternoon late in October of the year 1697, Euclide Auclair, the philosopher apothecary of Quebec, stood on the top of Cap Diamant gazing down the broad, empty river far beneath him. Empty, because an hour ago the flash of retreating sails had disappeared behind the green island that splits the St. Lawrence below Quebec, and the last of the summer ships from France had started on her long voyage home.

As long as *La Bonne Espérance* was still in sight, many of Auclair's friends and neighbours had kept him company on the hill-top; but when the last tip of white slid behind the curving shore, they went back to their shops and their kitchens to face the stern realities of life. Now for eight months the French colony on this rock in the North would be entirely cut off from Europe, from the world. This was October; not a sail would come up that wide waterway before next July. No supplies; not a cask of wine or a sack of flour, no gunpowder, or leather, or cloth, or iron tools. Not a letter, even—no news of what went on at home. There might be new wars, floods, conflagrations, epidemics, but the colonists would never know of them until next summer. People sometimes said that if King Louis died, the Minister would send word by the English ships that came to New York all winter, and the Dutch traders at Fort Orange would dispatch couriers to Montreal.

The apothecary lingered on the hill-top long after his fellow townsmen had gone back to their affairs; for him this severance from the world grew every year harder to bear. It was a strange thing, indeed, that a man of his mild and thoughtful disposition, city-bred and most conventional in his habits, should be found on a grey rock in the Canadian wilderness. Cap Diamant, where he stood, was merely the highest ledge of that fortified cliff which was "Kebec,"—a triangular head-land wedged in by the joining of two rivers, and girdled about by the greater river as by an encircling arm. Directly under his feet was the French stronghold,—scattered spires and slated roofs flashing in the rich, autumnal sunlight; the little capital which was just then the subject of so much discussion in Europe, and the goal of so many fantastic dreams.

Auclair thought this rock-set town like nothing so

8

much as one of those little artificial mountains which were made in the churches at home to present a theatric scene of the Nativity; cardboard mountains, broken up into cliffs and ledges and hollows to accommodate groups of figures on their way to the manger; angels and shepherds and horsemen and camels, set on peaks, sheltered in grottoes, clustered about the base.

Divest your mind of Oriental colour, and you saw here very much such a mountain rock, cunningly built over with churches, convents, fortifications, gardens, following the natural irregularities of the headland on which they stood; some high, some low, some thrust up on a spur, some nestling in a hollow, some sprawling unevenly along a declivity. The Château Saint-Louis, grey stone with steep dormer roofs, on the very edge of the cliff overlooking the river, sat level; but just beside it the convent and church of the Récollet friars ran downhill, as if it were sliding backwards. To landward, in a low, well-sheltered spot, lay the Convent of the Ursulines . . . lower still stood the massive foundation of the Jesuits, facing the Cathedral. Immediately behind the Cathedral the cliff ran up sheer again, shot out into a jutting spur, and there, high in the blue air, between heaven and earth, rose old Bishop Laval's Seminary. Beneath it the rock fell away in a succession of terraces like a circular staircase; on one of these was the new Bishop's new Palace, its gardens on the terrace below.

Not one building on the rock was on the same level with any other, — and two hundred feet below them all was the Lower Town, crowded along the narrow strip of beach between the river's edge and the perpendicular face of the cliff. The Lower Town was so directly underneath the Upper Town that one could stand on the terrace of the Château Saint-Louis and throw a stone down into the narrow streets below.

These heavy grey buildings, monasteries and churches, steep-pitched and dormered, with spires and slated roofs, were roughly Norman Gothic in effect. They were made by people from the north of France who knew no other way of building. The settlement looked like something cut off from one of the ruder towns of Normandy or Brittany, and brought over. It was indeed a rude beginning of a "new France," of a Saint-Malo or Rouen or Dieppe, anchored here in the ever-changing northern light and weather. At its feet, curving about its base, flowed the mighty St. Lawrence, rolling north toward the purple line of the Laurentian mountains, toward frowning Cap Tourmente which rose dark against the soft blue of the October sky. The Île d'Orléans, out in the middle of the river, was like a hilly map, with downs and fields and pastures lying in folds above the naked tree-tops.

On the opposite shore of the river, just across from the proud rock of Quebec, the black pine forest came down to the water's edge; and on the west, behind the town, the forest stretched no living man knew how far. That was the dead, sealed world of the vegetable kingdom, an uncharted continent choked with interlocking trees, living, dead, half-dead, their roots in bogs and swamps, strangling each other in a slow agony that had lasted for centuries. The forest was suffocation, annihilation; there European man was quickly swallowed up in silence, distance, mould, black mud, and the stinging swarms of insect life that bred in it. The only avenue of escape was along the river. The river was the one thing that lived, moved, glittered, changed, — a highway along which men could travel, taste the sun and open air, feel freedom, join their fellows, reach the open sea . . . reach the world, even!

After all, the world still existed, Auclair was thinking, as he stood looking up the way by which *La Bonne Espérance* had gone out only an hour ago. He was not of the proper stuff for a colonist, and he knew it. He was a slender, rather frail man of about fifty, a little stooped, a little grey, with a short beard cut in a point, and a fair complexion delicately flushed with pink about his cheeks and ears. His blue eyes were warm and interested, even in reflection, — they often had a kindling gleam as if his thoughts were pictures. Except for this lively and inquiring spirit in his glance, everything about him was modest and retiring. He was clearly not a man of action, no Indian-fighter or explorer. The only remarkable thing about his life was that he had not lived it to the end exactly where his father and grandfather had lived theirs, — in a little apothecary shop on the Quai des Célestins, in Paris.

The apothecary at last turned his back to the river. He was glancing up at the sun to reckon the time of day, when he saw a soldier coming up the grassy slope of Cap Diamant by the irregular earth path that led to the redoubt. The soldier touched his hat and called to him.

"I thought I recognized your figure up here, Monsieur Euclide. The Governor requires your presence and has sent a man down to your shop to fetch you."

Auclair thanked him for his trouble and went down the hill with him to the Château. The Governor was his patron, the Count de Frontenac, in whose service he had come out to Canada.

The Apothecary

II

IT was late in the afternoon when Auclair left the
Château and made his way through the garden of the
Récollet friars, past the new Bishop's Palace, and down
to his own house. He lived on the steep, winding street
called Mountain Hill, which was the one and only thor-
oughfare connecting the Upper Town with the Lower.
The Lower Town clustered on the strip of beach at the
foot of the cliff, the Upper Town crowned its summit.
Down the face of the cliff there was but this one path,
which had probably been a mere watercourse when
Champlain and his men first climbed up it to plant the
French lilies on the crest of the naked rock. The watercourse was now a steep, stony street, with shops on one
side and the retaining walls of the Bishop's Palace on
the other. Auclair lived there for two reasons: to be
close at hand where Count Frontenac could summon
him quickly to the Château, and because, thus situated
on the winding stairway connecting the two halves of
Quebec, his services were equally accessible to the citizens of both.

On entering his door the apothecary found the front

shop empty, lit by a single candle. In the living-room behind, which was partly shut off from the shop by a partition made of shelves and cabinets, a fire burned in the fireplace, and the round dining-table was already set with a white cloth, silver candlesticks, glasses, and two clear decanters, one of red wine and one of white.

Behind the living-room there was a small, low-roofed kitchen, built of stone, though the house itself was built of wood in the earliest Quebec manner, — double walls, with sawdust and ashes filling in the space between the two frames, making a protection nearly four feet thick against the winter cold. From this stone kitchen at the back two pleasant emanations greeted the chemist: the rich odour of roasting fowl, and a child's voice, singing. When he closed the heavy wooden door behind him, the voice called: "Is it you, Papa?"

His daughter ran in from the kitchen, — a little girl of twelve, beginning to grow tall, wearing a short skirt and a sailor's jersey, with her brown hair shingled like a boy's.

Auclair stooped to kiss her flushed cheek. *"Pas de clients?"* he asked.

"Mais, oui! Beaucoup de clients. But they all wanted very simple things. I found them quite easily and made notes of them. But why were you gone so long? Is Monsieur le Comte ill?"

"Not ill, exactly, but there is troublesome news from Montreal."

"Please change your coat now, Papa, and light the candles. I am so anxious about the poulet. Mère Laflamme tried hard to sell me a cock, but I told her my father always complained of a cock." The daughter's eyes were shaped like her father's, but were much darker, a very dark blue, almost black when she was excited, as she was now about the roast. Her mother had died two years ago, and she made the ménage for her father.

Contrary to the custom of his neighbours, Auclair dined at six o'clock in winter and seven in summer, after the day's work was over, as he was used to do in Paris, — though even there almost everyone dined at midday. He now dropped the curtains over his two shop windows, a sign to his neighbours that he was not to be disturbed unless for serious reasons. Having put on his indoor coat, he lit the candles and carried in the heavy soup tureen for his daughter.

They ate their soup in appreciative silence, both were a little tired. While his daughter was bringing in the roast, Auclair poured a glass of red wine for her and one of white for himself.

"Papa," she said as he began to carve, "what is the

earliest possible time that Aunt Clothilde and Aunt Blanche can get our letters?"

Auclair deliberated. Every fall the colonists asked the same question of one another and reckoned it all anew. "Well, if *La Bonne Espérance* has good luck, she can make La Rochelle in six weeks. Of course, it has been done in five. But let us say six; then, if the roads are bad, and they are likely to be in December, we must count on a week to Paris."

"And if she does not have good luck?"

"Ah, then who can say? But unless she meets with very heavy storms, she can do it in two months. With this west wind, which we can always count on, she will get out of the river and through the Gulf very speedily, and that is sometimes the most tedious part of the voyage. When we came over with the Count, we were a month coming from Percé to Quebec. That was because we were sailing against this same autumn wind which will be carrying *La Bonne Espérance* out to sea."

"But surely the aunts will have our letters by New Year's, and then they will know how glad I was of my béret and my jerseys, and how we can hardly wait to open the box upstairs. I can remember my Aunt Blanche a little, because she was young and pretty, and used to play with me. I suppose she is not young now, any more; it is eight years."

"Not young, exactly, but she will always have high spirits. And she is well married, and has three children who are a great joy to her."

"Three little cousins whom I have never seen, and one of them is named for me! Cécile, André, Rachel." She spoke their names softly. These little cousins were almost like playfellows. Their mother wrote such long letters about them that Cécile felt she knew them and all their ways, their individual faults and merits. Cousin Cécile was seven, very studious, *bien sérieuse*, already prepared for confirmation; but she would eat only sweets and highly spiced food. André was five, truthful and courageous, but he bit his nails. Rachel was a baby, in the midst of teething when they last heard of her.

Cécile would have preferred to live with Aunt Blanche and her children when she should go back to France; but by her mother's wish she was destined for Aunt Clothilde, who had long been a widow of handsome means and was much interested in the education of young girls. The face of this aunt Cécile could never remember, though she could see her figure clearly, — standing against the light, she always seemed to be, a massive woman, short and heavy though not exactly fat, — square, rather, like a great piece of oak furniture; always in black, widow's black that smelled of dye, with gold rings on her fingers and a very white handkerchief in her hand. Cécile could see her head, too, carried well back on a short neck, like a general or a statesman sitting for his portrait; but the face was a blank, just as if the aunt were standing in a doorway with blinding sunlight behind her. Cécile was once more trying to recall that face when her father interrupted her.

"What are we having for dessert tonight, my dear?"

"We have the cream cheese you brought from market yesterday, and whichever conserve you prefer; the plums, the wild strawberries, or the gooseberries."

"Oh, the gooseberries, by all means, after chicken."

"But, Papa, you prefer the gooseberries after almost everything! It is lucky for us we can get all the sugar we want from the Count. Our neighbours cannot afford to make conserves, with sugar so dear. And gooseberries take more than anything else."

"There is something very palatable about the flavour of these gooseberries, a bitter tang that is good for one. At home the gooseberries are much larger and finer, but I have come to like this bitter taste."

"*En France nous avons tous les légumes, jusqu'aux dattes,*" murmured Cécile. She had never seen a date, but she had learned that phrase from a book, when she went to day-school at the Ursulines.

18

The Apothecary

Immediately after dinner the apothecary went into the front shop to post his ledger, while his daughter washed the dishes with the hot water left in an iron kettle on the stove, where the birch-wood fire was now smouldering coals. She had scarcely begun when she heard a soft scratching at the single window of her kitchen. Through the small panes of glass a face was looking in,—a terrifying face, but one that she expected. She nodded and beckoned with her finger. A short, heavy man shuffled into the kitchen. He seemed loath to enter, yet drawn by some desire stronger than his reluctance. Cécile went to the stove and filled a bowl.

"There is your soup for you, Blinker."

"Merci, ma'm'selle." The man spoke out of the side of his mouth, as he looked out of the side of his face. He was so terribly cross-eyed that Cécile had never really looked into his eyes at all,—this was why he was called Blinker. He took a half-loaf from his coat-pocket and began to eat the soup eagerly, trying not to make a noise. Eating was difficult for him,—he had once had an abscess in his lower jaw, it had suppurated, and pieces of the bone had come out. His face was badly shrunken on that side, under the old scars. He knew it distressed Cécile if he gurgled his soup; so he struggled between greed and caution, dipping his bread to make it easy chewing.

This poor mis-shapen fellow worked next door, tended the oven fires for Nicholas Pigeon, the baker, so that the baker could get his night's sleep. His wages were the baker's old clothes, two pairs of boots a year, a pint of red wine daily, and all the bread he could eat. But he got no soup there, Madame Pigeon had too many children to feed.

When he had finished his bowl and loaf, he rose and without saying anything took up two large wooden pails. One was full of refuse from the day's cooking, the other full of dish-water. These he carried down Mountain Hill, through the market square to the edge of the shore, and there emptied them into the river. When he came back, he found a very small glass of brandy waiting for him on the table.

"Merci, ma'm'selle, merci beaucoup," he muttered. He sat down and sipped it slowly, watching Cécile arrange the kitchen for the night. He lingered while the floor was swept, the last dish put in place on the shelves, the dish-towels hung to dry on a wire above the stove, following all these operations intently with his crooked eyes. When she took up her candle, he must go. He put down his glass, got up, and opened the back door, but his feet seemed nailed to the sill. He stood blinking with that incredibly stupid air, blinking out of the side of his face, and Cécile could not be sure that he saw her or anything else. He made a fumbling as if to button his coat, though there were no buttons on it.

"Bon soir, ma'm'selle," he muttered.

Since this happened every night, Cécile thought nothing of it. Her mother had begun to look out for Blinker a little before she became so ill, and he was one of the cares the daughter had inherited. He had come out to the colony four years ago, and like many others who came he had no trade. He was strong, but so ill-favoured that nobody wanted him about. Neighbour Pigeon found he was faithful and dependable, and taught him to stoke the wood fire and tend the oven between midnight and morning. Madame Auclair felt sorry for the poor fellow and got into the way of giving him his soup at night and letting him do the heavy work, such as carrying in wood and water and taking away the garbage. She had always called Blinker by his real name, Jules. He had a cave up in the rocky cliff behind the bakery, where he kept his chest, — he slept there in mild weather. In winter he slept anywhere about the ovens that he could find room to lie down, and his clothes and woolly red hair were usually white with ashes. Many people were afraid of him, felt that he must have crooked thoughts behind such crooked eyes. But the Pigeons and Auclairs had got used to him and saw no harm in him. The baker said he could never discover how the fellow made a living at home, or why he had come out to Canada. Many unserviceable men had come, to be sure, but they were usually adventurers who disliked honest work, — wanted to fight the Iroquois or traffic in beaver-skins, or live a free life hunting game in the woods. This Blinker had never had a gun in his hands. He had such a horror of the forest that he would not even go into the near-by woods to help fell trees for firewood, and his fear of Indians was one of the bywords of Mountain Hill. Pigeon used to tell his customers that if the Count went to chastise the Iroquois beyond Cataraqui, Blinker would hide in his cave in Quebec. Blinker protested he had been warned in a dream that he would be taken prisoner and tortured by the Indians.

Dinner was the important event of the day in the apothecary's household. The luncheon was a mere goûter. Breakfast was a pot of chocolate, which he prepared very carefully himself, and a fresh loaf which Pigeon's oldest boy brought to the door. But his dinner Auclair regarded as the thing that kept him a civilized man and a Frenchman. It put him in a mellow mood, and he and his daughter usually spent the long evening very happily without visitors. She read aloud to him, the fables of La Fontaine or his favourite Plutarch, and he corrected her accent so that she would not be ashamed when she returned home to the guardianship of that intelligent and exacting Aunt Clothilde. It was only in the evening that her father had time to talk to her. All day he was compounding remedies, or visiting the sick, or making notes for a work on the medicinal properties of Canadian plants which he meant to publish after his return to Paris. But in the evening he was free, and while he enjoyed his Spanish snuff their talk would sometimes lead far away and bring out long stories of the past. Her father would try to recall to her their old shop on the Quai des Célestins, where he had grown up and where she herself was born. She thought she could remember it a little, though she was only four years old when they sailed with the Count for the New World. It was a narrow wedge, that shop, built in next to the carriage court of the town house of the Frontenacs. Auclair's little chamber, where he slept from his sixth year until his marriage, was on the third floor, under the roof. Its one window looked out upon the carriage court

23

and across it to the front of the mansion, which had only a blind wall on the street and faced upon its own court.

When he was a little boy, he used to tell Cécile, nothing ever changed next door, except that after a rain the cobbles in the yard were whiter, and the ivy on the walls was greener. Every morning he looked out from his window on the same stillness; the shuttered windows behind their iron grilles, the steps under the porte-cochère green with moss, pale grass growing up between the stones in the court, the empty stables at the back, the great wooden carriage gates that never opened, — though in one of them a small door was cut, through which the old care-taker came and went.

"Naturally," Auclair would tell his daughter, "having seen the establishment next door always the same, I supposed it was meant to be like that, and was there, perhaps, to give a little boy the pleasure of watching the swallows build nests in the ivy. The Count had been at home when I was an infant in arms, and once, I believe, when I was three, but I could not remember. Imagine my astonishment when, one evening about sunset, a dusty coach with four horses rattled down the Quai and stopped at the carriage entrance. Two footmen sprang down from the box, rang the outer bell, and, as soon as the bar was drawn, began pulling and prying at the gates, which I had never seen opened in my life. It seemed to me that some outrage was being committed and the police should be called. At last the gates were dragged inward, and the coach clattered into the court. If anything more happened that night I do not recall it.

"The next morning I was awakened by shouting under my window, and the sound of shutters being taken down. I ran across my room and peeped out. The windows over there were not only unshuttered, but open wide. Three young men were leaning out over the grilles beating rugs, shaking carpets and wall-hangings into the air. In a moment a blacksmith came in his leather apron, with a kit of tools, and began to repair the hinges of the gates. Boys were running in and out, bringing bread, milk, poultry, sacks of grain and hay for the horses. When I went down to breakfast, I found my father and mother and grandparents all very much excited and pleased, talking a great deal. They already knew in which chamber the Count had slept last night, the names of his equerries, what he had brought with him for supper in a basket from Fontainebleau, and which wines old Joseph had got up from the cellar for him. I had scarcely ever heard my family talk so much.

"Not long after breakfast the Count himself came

25

into our shop. He greeted my father familiarly and began asking about the people of the Quarter as if he
had been away only a few weeks. He inquired for my
mother and grandmother, and they came to pay their
respects. I was pulled out from under the counter where
I had hidden, and presented to him. I was frightened
because he was wearing his uniform and such big boots.
Yes, he was a fine figure of a man forty years ago, but
even more restless and hasty than he is now. I remember he asked me if I wanted to be a soldier, and when I
told him that I meant to be an apothecary like my father, he laughed and gave me a silver piece."

Though Auclair so often talked to his daughter of the
past, it was not because there was nothing happening in
the present. At that time the town of Quebec had fewer
than two thousand inhabitants, but it was always full of
jealousies and quarrels. Ever since Cécile could remember, there had been a feud between Count Frontenac
and old Bishop Laval. And now that the new Bishop,
Monseigneur de Saint-Vallier, had just come back from
France after a three years' absence, the Count was quarrelling with him! Then there was always the old quarrel
between the two Bishops themselves, which had broken
out with fresh vigour upon de Saint-Vallier's return.
Everyone in the diocese took sides with one prelate or

the other. Since he landed in September, scarcely a week went by that Monseigneur de Saint-Vallier did not wreck some cherished plan of the old Bishop.

Before they went to bed, Auclair and his daughter usually took a walk. The apothecary believed this habit conducive to sound slumber. Tonight, as they stepped out into the frosty air and looked up, high over their heads, on the edge of the sheer cliff, the Château stood out against the glittering night sky, the second storey of the south wing brilliantly lighted.

"I suppose the Count's candles will burn till long past midnight," Cécile remarked.

"Ah, the Count has many things to trouble him. The King has not been very generous in rewarding his services in the last campaign. Besides, he is old, and the old do not sleep much."

As they climbed Mountain Hill, they passed in front of Monseigneur de Saint-Vallier's new episcopal Palace, and that, too, was ablaze with lights. Cécile longed to see inside that building, toward which the King himself had given fifteen thousand francs. It was said that Monseigneur had brought back with him a great many fine pieces of furniture and tapestry to furnish it. But he was not fond of children, as the old Bishop was, and his servants were very strict, and there seemed to be no way in which one could get a peep behind those heavy curtains at the windows.

Their walk was nearly always the same. On a precipitous rock, scored over with dark, uneven streets, there were not many ways where one could stroll with a careless foot after nightfall. When the wind was not too biting, they usually took the path up to the redoubt on Cap Diamant and looked down over the sleeping town and the great pale avenue of river, with black forest stretching beyond it to the sky. From there the Lower Town was a mere sprinkle of lights along the water's edge. The rock-top, blocked off in dark masses that were convents and churches and gardens, was now sunk in sleep. The only lighted windows to be seen were in the Château, in the Bishop's Palace, and on the top floor of old Bishop Laval's Seminary, out there on its spur overhanging the river. That top floor, the apothecary told his daughter, was the library, and likely enough some young Canadian-born Seminarians to whom Latin came hard were struggling with the Church Fathers up there.

The Apothecary

III

AUCLAIR did a good trade in drugs and herbs and remedies of his own compounding, but his pay was small, and very little of it was in money. Besides, people wasted a great deal of his time in conversation and thus interfered with his study of Canadian plants. Like most philosophers, he was not averse to discourse, but here much of the talk was gossip and very trivial. The colonists liked to drop in at his house upon the slightest pretext; the interior was like home to the French-born. On a heavy morning, when clouds of thick grey fog rolled up from the St. Lawrence, it cheered one to go into a place that was like an apothecary's shop at home; to glimpse the comfortable sitting-room through the tall cabinets and chests of drawers that separated without entirely shutting it off from the shop.

Euclide Auclair had come over with the Count de Frontenac eight years ago, as his apothecary and physician, and had therefore been able to bring whatever he liked of his personal possessions. He came with a full supply of drugs and specifics, his distilling apparatus, mortars, balances, retorts, and carboys, all the paraphernalia of his trade, even the stuffed baby alligator, brought long ago to Paris by some sailor from the West Indies and purchased by Auclair's grandfather to ornament the shop on the Quai des Célestins.

Madame Auclair had brought her household goods, without which she could not imagine life at all, and the salon behind the shop was very much like their old salon in Paris. There was the same well-worn carpet, made at Lyon, the walnut dining-table, the two large arm-chairs and high-backed sofa upholstered in copper-red cotton-velvet, the long window-curtains of a similar velvet lined with brown. The same candelabra and china shepherd boy sat on the mantel, the same colour prints of pastoral scenes hung on the walls. Madame had brought out to Canada the fine store of linen that had been her marriage portion, her feather beds and coverlids and down pillows. As long as she lived, she tried to make the new life as much as possible like the old. After she began to feel sure that she would never be well enough to return to France, her chief care was to train her little daughter so that she would be able to carry on this life and this order after she was gone.

Madame Auclair had kept upon her feet until within a few weeks of her death. When a spasm of coughing came on (she died of her lungs) and she was forced to lie down on the red sofa there under the window, she would beckon Cécile to the footstool beside her. After she got her breath again and was resting, she would softly explain many things about the ménage.

"Your father has a delicate appetite," she would murmur, "and the food here is coarse. If it is not very carefully prepared, he will not eat and will fall ill. And he cannot sleep between woollen coverlids, as many people do here; his skin is sensitive. The sheets must be changed every two weeks, but do not try to have them washed in the winter. I have brought linen enough to last the winter through. Keep folding the soiled ones away in the cold upstairs, and in April, when the spring rains come and all the water-barrels are full of soft rainwater, have big Jeanette come in and do a great washing; give the house up to her, and let her take several days to do her work. Beg her to iron the sheets carefully. They are the best of linen and will last your lifetime if they are well treated."

Madame Auclair never spoke of her approaching death, but would say something like this:

"After a while, when I am too ill to help you, you will perhaps find it fatiguing to do all these things alone, over and over. But in time you will come to love your duties, as I do. You will see that your father's whole happiness depends on order and regularity, and you will come to feel a pride in it. Without order our lives would be disgusting, like those of the poor savages. At home, in France, we have learned to do all these things in the best way, and we are conscientious, and that is why we are called the most civilized people in Europe and other nations envy us."

After such admonition Madame Auclair would look intently into the child's eyes that grew so dark when her heart was touched, like the blue of Canadian blueberries, indeed, and would say to herself: "*Oui, elle a beaucoup de loyauté.*"

During the last winter of her illness she lay much of the time on her red sofa, that had come so far out to this rock in the wilderness. The snow outside, piled up against the window-panes, made a grey light in the room, and she could hear Cécile moving softly about in the kitchen, putting more wood into the iron stove, washing the casseroles. Then she would think fearfully of how much she was entrusting to that little shingled head; something so precious, so intangible; a feeling about life that had come down to her through so many centuries and that she had brought with her across the wastes of obliterating, brutal ocean. The sense of "our way," — that was what she longed to leave with her daughter. She wanted to believe that when she herself was lying in this rude Canadian earth, life would go on almost unchanged in this room with its dear (and, to her, beautiful) objects; that the proprieties would be observed, all the little shades of feeling which make the common fine. The individuality, the character, of M. Auclair's house, though it appeared to be made up of wood and cloth and glass and a little silver, was really made of very fine moral qualities in two women: the mother's unswerving fidelity to certain traditions, and the daughter's loyalty to her mother's wish.

It was because of these things that had gone before, and the kind of life lived there, that the townspeople were glad of any excuse to stop at the apothecary's shop. Even the strange, bitter, mysterious Bishop Laval (more accusing and grim than ever, now that the new Bishop had returned and so disregarded him) used to tramp heavily into the shop for calomel pills or bandages for his varicose legs, and peer, not unkindly, back into the living-room. Once he had asked for a sprig from the box of parsley that was kept growing there even in winter, and carried it away in his hand, — though, as everyone knew, he denied himself all the comforts of the table and ate only the most wretched and unappetizing food.

33

In a corner, concealed from the shop by tall cabinets, and well away from the window draughts, stood M. Auclair's four-post bed, with heavy hangings. Underneath it was a child's bed, pulled out at night, where Cécile still slept in cold weather. Sometimes on a very bitter night, when the grip of still, intense cold tightened on the rock as if it would extinguish the last spark of life, the pharmacist would hear his daughter softly stirring about, moving something, covering something. He would thrust his night-cap out between the curtains and call:

"*Qu'est-ce que tu fais, petite?*"

An anxious, sleepy voice would reply:

"*Papa, j'ai peur pour le persil.*"

It had never frozen in her mother's time, and it should not freeze in hers.

IV

THE accident of being born next the Count de Frontenac's house in Paris had determined Euclide Auclair's destiny. He had grown up a studious, thoughtful boy, assisting his father in the shop. Every afternoon he read Latin with a priest at the Jesuits on the rue Saint-Antoine. Count Frontenac's irregular and unexpected returns to town made the chief variety in his life.

It was usually after some chagrin or disappointment that the Count came back to the Quai des Célestins. Between campaigns he lived at Île Savary, his estate on the Indre, near Blois. But after some slight at Court, or some difficulty with his creditors, he would suddenly arrive at his father's old town house and shut himself up for days, even weeks, seeing no one but the little people of the parish of Saint-Paul. He had few friends of his own station in Paris, — few anywhere. He was a man who got on admirably with his inferiors, — seemed to find among them the only human ties that were of any comfort to him. He was poor, which made him boastful and extravagant, and he had always lived far beyond his means. At Île Savary he tried to make as great a show as people who were much better off than he, — to equal them in hospitality, in dress, gardens, horses and carriages. But when he was in Paris, living among the quiet, faithful people of the quarter, he was a different man. With his humble neighbours his manners were irreproachable. He often dropped in at the pharmacy to see his tenants, the Auclairs, and would sometimes talk to the old grandfather about his campaigns in Italy and the Low Countries.

The Count had begun his military life at fifteen, and wherever there was fighting in Europe, he always managed to be there. In each campaign he added to his renown, but never to his fortune. When his military talents were unemployed, he usually got into trouble of some sort. It was after his Italian campaign, when he was recuperating from his wounds in his father's old house on the Quai, that he made his unfortunate marriage. Euclide's father could remember that affair very well. Madame de la Grange-Frontenac and her husband lived together but a short while, — and now they had been separated for almost a lifetime. She still lived in Paris, with a brilliant circle about her, — had an apartment in the old Arsenal building, not far from the Count's house, and when she received, he sometimes paid his respects with the rest of the world, but he never went to see her privately.

When Euclide was twenty-two, Count Frontenac was employed by the Venetians to defend the island of Crete against the Turks. From that command he returned with great honour, but poorer than ever. For the next three years he was idle. Then, suddenly, the King appointed him Governor General of Canada, and he quitted Europe for ten years.

During that decade Euclide's father and mother died.

36

He married, and devoted himself seriously to his profession. Too seriously for his own good, indeed. Although he was so content with familiar scenes and faces as to be almost afraid of new ones, he was not afraid of new ideas, — or of old ideas that had gone out of fashion because surgeons and doctors were too stupid to see their value. The brilliant reign of Louis XIV was a low period in medicine; dressmakers and tailors were more considered than physicians. Euclide had gone deep into the history of medicine in such old Latin books as were stuffed away in the libraries of Paris. He looked back to the time of Ambroise Paré, and still further back to the thirteenth century, as golden ages in medicine, — and he considered Fagon, the King's physician, a bigoted and heartless quack.

When sick people in his own neighbourhood came to Euclide for help, he kept them away from doctors, — gave them tisanes and herb-teas and poultices, which at least could do no harm. He advised them about their diet; reduced the surfeit of the rich, and prescribed goat's milk for the poorly nourished. He was strongly opposed to indiscriminate blood-letting, particularly to bleeding from the feet. This eccentricity made him very unpopular, not only with the barber-surgeons of the parish, but with their patients, and even estranged his own friends. Bleeding from the feet was very much in vogue just then; it made a sick man feel that the utmost was being done for him. At Versailles it was regularly practised on members of the King's household. Euclide's opposition to this practice lost him many of his patrons. His neighbours used to laugh and say that whether bleeding from the feet harmed other people or not, it had certainly been very bad for the son of their reliable old pharmacien, Alphonse Auclair.

Euclide's business contracted steadily, so that, with all his wife's good management and his own devotion to his profession, he scarcely knew where to turn; until one day the Count de Frontenac walked into the shop and put out his hand as if to rescue a drowning man. Auclair had never heard of the Count's difficulties with the Jesuits in Canada, and knew nothing about his recall by the King, until he appeared at the shop door that morning, ten years older, but no richer or better satisfied with the world than when he went away.

The Count was out of favour at Versailles, his estate on the Indre had run down during his absence in Canada, and he had not the means to repair it, so he now spent a good deal of time in the house next door. His presence there, and his patronage, eased the strain of the Auclairs' position. Moreover, he restored to Euclide the ten years' rent for the shop, which had been scrupulously paid to the Count's agent while he was away.

The Count was lonely in his town house. Many of his old acquaintances had accomplished their earthly period and been carried to the Innocents or the churchyard of Saint-Paul while he was far away in Quebec. His wife was still entertaining her friends at her apartment in the old Arsenal, and the Count occasionally went there on her afternoons at home. Time hung heavy on his hands, and he often sent for Euclide to come to him in a professional capacity, — a flimsy pretext, for, though past sixty, the Count was in robust health. Of an evening they would sometimes sit in the Count's library, talking of New France. Frontenac's thoughts were there, and he liked to tell an eager listener about its great lakes and rivers, the climate, the Indians, the forests and wild animals. Often he would dwell upon the explorations and discoveries of his ill-fated young friend Robert Cavelier de La Salle, one of the few men for whom, in his long life, he ever felt a warm affection.

Gradually there grew up in Auclair's mind the picture of a country vast and free. He fell into a habit of looking to Canada as a possible refuge, an escape from the evils one suffered at home, and of wishing he could go there.

This seemed a safe desire to cherish, since it was

impossible of fulfilment. Euclide was a natural city-dweller; one of those who can bear poverty and oppression, so long as they have their old surroundings, their native sky, the streets and buildings that have become part of their lives. But though he was a creature of habit and derived an actual pleasure from doing things exactly as he had always done them, his mind was free. He could not shut his eyes to the wrongs that went on about him, or keep from brooding upon them. In his own time he had seen taxes grow more and more ruinous, poverty and hunger always increasing. People died of starvation in the streets of Paris, in his own parish of Saint-Paul, where there was so much wealth. All the while the fantastic extravagances of the Court grew more outrageous. The wealth of the nation, of the grain lands and vineyards and forests of France, was sunk in creating the pleasure palace at Versailles. The richest peers of the realm were ruining themselves on magnificent Court dresses and jewels. And, with so many new abuses, the old ones never grew less; torture and cruel punishments increased as the people became poorer and more desperate. The horrible mill at the Châtelet ground on day after day. Auclair lived too near the prisons of Paris to be able to forget them. In his boyhood a harmless old man who lodged in their own cellar was tortured and put to death at the Châtelet for a petty theft.

One morning, in the summer when Cécile was four years old, Count Frontenac made one of his sudden reappearances in Paris and sent for Euclide. The King had again appointed him Governor General of Canada, and he would sail in a few weeks. He wished to take Auclair with him as his personal physician. The Count was then seventy years old, and he was as eager to be gone as a young man setting off on his first campaign.

Auclair was terrified. Indeed, he fell ill of fright, and neither ate nor slept. He could not imagine facing any kind of life but the one he had always lived. His wife was much the braver of the two. She pointed out that their business barely made them a livelihood, and that after the Count went away it would certainly decline. Moreover, the Count was their landlord, and he had now decided to sell his town property. Who knew but that the purchaser might prove a hard master, — or that he might not pull down the apothecary shop altogether to enlarge the stables?

V

I T was the day after *La Bonne Espérance* had set sail for
France. Auclair and his daughter were on their way
to the Hôtel Dieu to attend the Reverend Mother, who
had sprained her ankle. Quebec is never lovelier than
on an afternoon of late October; ledges of brown and
lavender clouds lay above the river and the Île d'Orléans, and the red-gold autumn sunlight poured over
the rock like a heavy southern wine. Beyond the Cathedral square the two lingered under the allée of naked
trees beside the Jesuits' college. These trees were cut
flat to form an arbour, the branches interweaving and
interlacing like basket-work, and beneath them ran a
promenade paved with flat flagstones along which the
dry yellow leaves were blowing, giving off a bitter per-
fume when one trampled them. Cécile loved that allée,
because when she was little the Fathers used to let her
play there with her skipping-rope, — few spots in Kebec
were level enough to jump rope on. Behind the avenue
of trees the long stone walls of the monastery — seven
feet thick, those walls — made a shelter from the wind;
they held the sun's heat so well that it was possible to

grow wall grapes there, and purple clusters were cut in September.

Behind the Jesuits' a narrow, twisted, cobbled street dropped down abruptly to the Hôtel Dieu, on the banks of the little river St. Charles. Auclair and his daughter went through the garden into the refectory, where Mother Juchereau de Saint-Ignace was seated, her sprained foot on a stool, directing the work of her novices. She was a little over forty, a woman of strong frame, tall, upright, with a presence that bespoke force rather than reserve; a handsome face, — the large, open features mobile and alert, perhaps a trifle masculine. She was the first Reverend Mother of the foundation who was Canadian-born, and she had been elected to that office when she was but thirty-four years of age. She was a religious of the practical type, sunny and very outright by nature, — enthusiastic, without being given to visions or ecstasies.

As the visitors entered, the Superior made as if to rise, but Auclair put out a detaining hand.

"I am two days late, Reverend Mother. In your mind you have been chiding me for neglect. But it is a busy time for us when the last ships sail. We have many family letters to write; and I examine my stock and make out my order for the drugs I shall need by the first boats next summer."

"If you had not come today, Monsieur Euclide, you would surely have found me on my feet tomorrow. When the Indians have a sprain, in the woods, they bind their leg tightly with deer thongs and keep on the march with their party. And they recover."

"Dear Mother Juchereau, the idea of such treatment is repugnant to me. We are not barbarians, after all."

"But they are flesh and blood; how is it they recover?"

As he pushed back her snow-white skirt a little and began gently to unwind the bandage from her foot, Auclair explained his reasons for believing that the savages were much less sensitive to pain than Europeans. Cécile fell to admiring the work Mother Juchereau had in hand. Her lap and the table beside her were full of scraps of bright silk and velvet and sheets of coloured paper. While she overlooked the young Sisters at their tasks, her fingers were moving rapidly and cleverly, making artificial flowers. She had great skill at this and delighted in it, — it was her one recreation.

"Yes, my dear," she said, "I am making these for the poor country parishes, where they have so little for the altar. These are wild roses, such as I used to gather when I was a child at Beauport. Oh, the wild flowers we have in the fields and prairies about Beauport!"

The Apothecary

When he had applied his ointment and bandaged her foot in fresh linen, the apothecary went off to the hospital medicine room, in charge of Sister Marie Domenica, whom he was instructing in the elements of pharmacy, and Cécile settled herself on the floor at Mother Juchereau's knee. Theirs was an old friendship.

The Reverend Mother (Jeanne Franc Juchereau de la Ferté was her proud name) held rather advanced views on caring for the sick. She did not believe in leaving everything to God, and had availed her hospital of Auclair's skill ever since he first came to Quebec. Quick to detect a trace of the charlatan in anyone, she felt confidence in Auclair because his pretensions were so modest. She addressed him familiarly as "Monsieur Euclide," scolded him for teaching his daughter Latin, and was keenly interested in his study of Canadian plants. Cécile had been coming to the Hôtel Dieu with her father almost every week since she was five years old, and Mother Juchereau always found time to talk to her a little; but today was a very unusual opportunity. The Mother was seldom to be found seated in a chair; when she was not on her knees at her devotions, she was on her feet, hurrying from one duty to another.

"It has been a long while since you told me a story, Reverend Mother," Cécile reminded her.

45

Mother Juchereau laughed. She had a deep warm-hearted laugh, something left over from her country girlhood. "Perhaps I have no more to tell you. You must know them all by this time."

"But there is no end to the stories about Mother Catherine de Saint-Augustin. I can never hear them all."

"True enough, when you speak her name, the stories come. Since I have had to sit here with my sprain, I have been recalling some of the things she used to tell me herself, when I was not much older than you."

While her hands flew among the scraps of colour, Mother Juchereau began somewhat formally:

"Before she had left her fair Normandy (*avant qu'elle ait quitté sa belle Normandie*), while Sister Catherine was a novice at Bayeux, there lived in the neighbourhood a *pécheresse* named Marie. She had been a sinner from her early youth and was so proof against all counsel that she continued her disorders even until an advanced age. Driven out by the good people of the town, shunned by men and women alike, she fell lower and lower, and at last hid herself in a solitary cave. There she dragged out her shameful life, destitute and consumed by a loathsome disease. And there she died; without human aid

46

and without the sacraments of the Church. After such a death her body was thrown into a ditch and buried like that of some unclean animal.

"Now, Sister Catherine, though she was so young and had all the duties of her novitiate to perform, always found time to pray for the souls of the departed, for all who died in that vicinity, whether she had known them in the flesh or not. But for this abandoned sinner she did not pray, believing, as did everyone else, that she was for ever lost.

"Twelve years went by, and Sister Catherine had come to Canada and was doing her great work here. One day, while she was at prayer in this house, a soul from purgatory appeared to her, all pale and suffering, and said:

"'Sister Catherine, what misery is mine! You commend to God the souls of all those who die. I am the only one on whom you have no compassion.'

"'And who are you?' asked our astonished Mother Catherine.

"'I am that poor Marie, the sinner, who died in the cave.'

"'What,' exclaimed Mother Catherine, 'were you then not lost?'

47

" 'No, I was saved, thanks to the infinite mercy of the Blessed Virgin.'

" 'But how could this be?'

" 'When I saw that I was about to die in the cave, and knew that I was abandoned and cast out by the world, unclean within and without, I felt the burden of all my sins. I turned to the Mother of God and cried to her: *Queen of Heaven, you are the last refuge of the ruined and the outcast; I am abandoned by all the world; I have no hope but you; you alone have power to reach where I am fallen; Mary, Mother of Jesus, have pity upon me!* The tender Mother of all made it possible for me to repent in that last hour. I died and I was saved. The Holy Mother procured for me the favour of having my punishment abridged, and now only a few masses are required to deliver me from purgatory. I beseech you to have them said for me, and I will never cease my prayers to God and the Blessed Virgin for you.'

"Mother Catherine at once set about having masses said for that poor Marie. Some days later there appeared to her a happy soul, more brilliant than the sun, which smiled and said: 'I thank you, my dear Catherine, I go now to paradise to sing the mercies of God for ever, and I shall not forget to pray for you.' "

Here Mother Juchereau glanced down at the young

listener, who had been following her intently. "And now, from this we see—" she went on, but Cécile caught her hand and cried coaxingly,

"*N'expliquez pas, chère Mère, je vous en supplie!*"

Mother Juchereau laughed and shook her finger.

"You always say that, little naughty! *N'expliquez pas!* But it is the explanation of these stories that applies them to our needs."

"Yes, dear Mother. But there comes my father. Tell me the explanation some other day."

Mother Juchereau still looked down into her face, frowning and smiling. It was the kind of face she liked, because there was no self-consciousness in it, and no vanity; but she told herself for the hundredth time: "No, she has certainly no vocation." Yet for an orphan girl, and one so intelligent, there would certainly have been a career among the Hospitalières. She would have loved to train that child for the Sœur Apothicaire of her hospital. Her good sense told her it was not to be. When she talked to Cécile of the missionaries and martyrs, she knew that her words fell into an eager mind; admiration and rapture she found in the girl's face, but it was not the rapture of self-abnegation. It was something very different,—almost like the glow of worldly pleasure. She was convinced that Cécile read altogether too much with her father, and had told him so; asking him whether he had perhaps forgotten that he had a girl to bring up, and not a son whom he was educating for the priesthood.

While her father and Mother Juchereau were going over an inventory of hospital supplies, Cécile went into the chapel to say a prayer for the repose of Mother de Saint-Augustin. There, in the quiet, she soon fell to musing upon the story of that remarkable girl who had braved the terrors of the ocean and the wilderness and come out to Canada when she was barely sixteen years old, and this Kebec was but a naked rock rising out of the dark forest.

Catherine de Saint-Augustin had begun her novitiate with the Hospitalières at Bayeux when she was eleven and a half years of age, and by the time she was fourteen she was already, in her heart, vowed to Canada. The letters and *Relations* of the Jesuit missionaries, eagerly read in all the religious houses of France, had fired her bold imagination, and she begged to be sent to save the souls of the savages. Her superiors discouraged her and forbade her to cherish this desire; Catherine's youth and bodily frailness were against her. But while she went about her tasks in the monastery, this wish, this hope, was always with her. One day when she was peeling vegetables in the novices' refectory, she cut her hand, and, seeing the blood flow, she dipped her finger in it and wrote upon the table:

Je mourrai au Canada
Sœur Saint-Augustin

That table, with its inscription, was still shown at Bayeux as an historic relic.

Though Catherine's desire seemed so far from fulfilment, she had not long to wait. In the winter of 1648, Père Vimont, from the Jesuit mission in Canada, came knocking at the door of the monastère at Bayeux, recruiting sisters for the little foundation of Hospitalières already working in Kebec. Catherine was told that she was too young to go, and her father firmly refused to give his permission. But in her eagerness the girl wrote petition after petition to her Bishop and superiors, and at last her request was brought to the attention of the Queen Mother, Anne of Austria. The Queen's intercession won her father's consent.

When, after a voyage of many months, unparalleled for storms and hardships, Catherine and her companions anchored under the rock of Kebec and were rowed ashore, she fell upon her knees and kissed the earth where she first stepped upon it.

Made Superior of the Hôtel Dieu at an early age, she died before she was forty. At thirty-seven she had burned her life out in vigils, mortifications, visions, raptures, all the while carrying on a steady routine of manual labour and administrative work, observing the full discipline of her order. For long before her death she was sustained by visions in which the spirit of Father Brébeuf, the martyr, appeared to her, told her of the glories of heaven, and gave her counsel and advice for all her perplexities in this world. It was at the direction of Father Brébeuf, communicated to her in these visions, that she chose Jeanne Franc Juchereau de la Ferté to succeed her as Superior, and trained her to that end. To many people the choice seemed such a strange one that Père Brébeuf must certainly have instigated it. Mother Catherine de Saint-Augustin was slight, nervous, sickly from childhood, yet from childhood precocious and prodigious in everything; always dedicating herself to the impossible and always achieving it; now getting a Queen of France to speak for her, now winning the spirit of the hero priest from paradise to direct and sustain her. And the woman she chose to succeed her was hardy, sagacious, practical, — a *Canadienne*, and the woman for Canada.

BOOK II

Cécile and Jacques

Cécile and Jacques

I

O N the last Friday of October Auclair went as usual to the market, held in front of Notre Dame de la Victoire, the only church in the Lower Town. All the trade in Quebec went on in the Lower Town, and the principal merchants lived on the market square. Their houses were built solidly around three sides of it, wall against wall, the shops on the ground floor, the dwelling-quarters upstairs. On the fourth side stood the church. The merchants' houses had formerly been of wood, but sixteen years ago, just after the Count de Frontenac was recalled to France, leaving Canada a prey to so many misfortunes, the Lower Town had been almost entirely wiped out by fire. It was rebuilt in stone, to prevent a second disaster. This square, which was the centre of commerce, now had a look of permanence and stability; houses with walls four feet thick, wide door-ways, deep windows, steep, slated roofs and dormers. *La Place*, as it was called, was an uneven rectangle, cobble-paved, sloping downhill like everything else in Quebec, with gutters to carry off the rainfall. In the middle was a grass plot (pitifully small, indeed), protected by an iron fence and surmounted by a very ugly statue of King Louis.

On market days the space about this iron fence was considered the right of the countrywomen, who trudged into Quebec at dawn beside the dogs that drew their little two-wheeled carts. Against the fence they laid out their wares; white bodies of dressed ducks and chickens, sausages, fresh eggs, cheese, butter, and such vegetables as were in season. On the outer edge of the square the men stationed their carts, on which they displayed quarters of fresh pork, live chickens, maple sugar, spruce beer, Indian meal, feed for cows, and long black leaves of native tobacco tied in bunches. The fish and eel carts, because of their smell and slimy drip, had a corner of the square to themselves, just at the head of La Place Street. The fishmongers threw buckets of cold water over their wares at intervals, and usually a group of little boys played just below, building "beaver-dams" in the gutter to catch the overflow.

This was an important market day, and Auclair went down the hill early. The black frosts might set in at any time now, and today he intended to lay in his winter supply of carrots, pumpkins, potatoes, turnips, beet-root, leeks, garlic, even salads. On many of the wagons there were boxes full of earth, with rooted lettuce plants growing in them. These the townspeople put away in their cellars, and by tending them carefully and cover-ing them at night they kept green salad growing until Christmas or after. Auclair's neighbour, Pigeon the baker, had a very warm cellar, and he grew little carrots and spinach down there long after winter had set in. The great vaulted cellars of the Jesuits and the Récollet friars looked like kitchen gardens when the world above ground was frozen stark. Careless people got through the winter on smoked eels and frozen fish, but if one were willing to take enough trouble, one could live very well, even in Quebec. It was the long, slow spring, March, April, early May, that tried the patience. By that time the winter stores had run low, people were tired of makeshifts, and still not a bud, not a salad except under cold-frames.

The market was full of wood doves this morning. They were killed in great numbers hereabouts, were sold cheap, and made very delicate eating. Every fall Auclair put down six dozens of them in melted lard. He had six stone jars in his cellar for that purpose, packing a dozen birds to the jar. In this way he could eat fresh game all winter, and, preserved thus, the birds kept their flavour. Frozen venison was all very well, but feathered creatures lost their taste when kept frozen a long while.

Auclair carried his purchases over to the cart of his butter-maker, Madame Renaude. Renaude-le-lièvre, she was called, because she had a hare-lip, and a bristling black moustache as well. She was a big, rough Norman woman, who owned seven cows, was extremely clean about her dairy, and quite the reverse in her conversation. In the town there was keen competition for her wares; but as she was rheumatic, she was more or less in thralldom to the apothecary, and seldom failed him.

"Good morning, Madame Renaude. Have you my lard for me this morning, as you promised? I must buy my wood doves today."

"Yes, Monsieur Auclair, and I had to kill my pet pig to get it for you, too; one that had slept under the same roof with me."

She spoke very loud, and the farmer at the next stall made an indecent comment.

"Hold your dirty jaw, Joybert. If I had a bad egg, I'd paste you." Old Joybert squinted and looked the other way. "Yes, Monsieur Auclair, you never saw such lard as he made, as sweet as butter. He made two firkins. Surely you won't need so much, — I can sell it anywhere."

"Yes, indeed, madame, I shall need every bit of it. Six dozen birds I have to put down, and I can't do with less."

"But, monsieur, what do you do with the grease after you take your doves out?"

"Why, some of it we use in cooking, and the rest I think my daughter gives to our neighbours."

"To that Blinker, eh? That's a waste! If you were to bring it back to me, I could easily sell it over again and we could both of us make something. The hunters who come up from Three Rivers in winter carry nothing but cold grease to fill their bellies. You forget you are not in France, monsieur. Here grease is meat, not something to throw to criminals."

"I will consider the matter, madame. Now that I am sure of my lard, I must go and select my birds. Good morning, and thank you."

After he had finished his marketing, Auclair put his basket down on the church steps and went inside to say a prayer. Notre Dame de la Victoire was a plain, solid little church, built of very hard rough stone. It had already stood through one bombardment from the water-side, and was dear to the people for that reason. The windows were narrow and set high, like the windows in a fortress, making an agreeable dusk inside. Occasionally, as someone entered to pray, a flash of sunlight and a buzz of talk came in from the Place, cut off when the door closed again.

While the apothecary was meditating in the hush and dusk of the church, he noticed a little boy, kneeling devoutly at one after another of the Stations of the Cross. He was at once interested, for he knew this child very well; a chunky, rather clumsy little boy of six, un-kept and uncared for, dressed in a pair of old sailor's breeches, cut off in the leg for him and making a great bulk of loose cloth about his thighs. His ragged jacket was as much too tight as the trousers were too loose, and this gave him the figure of a salt-shaker. He did not look at Auclair or the several others who came and went, being entirely absorbed in his devotions. His lips moved inaudibly, he knelt and rose slowly, clumsily, very carefully, his cap under his arm. Though all his movements were so deliberate, his attention did not wander, — seemed intently, heavily fixed. Auclair care-fully remained in the shadow, making no sign of recog-nition. He respected the child's seriousness.

This boy was the son of 'Toinette Gaux, a young woman who was quite irreclaimable. Antoinette was Canadian-born; her mother had been one of "the King's Girls," as they were called. Thirty years ago King

Cécile and Jacques

Louis had sent several hundred young Frenchwomen out to Canada to marry the bachelors of the disbanded regiment of Carignan-Salières. Many of these girls were orphans or poor girls of good character; but some were bad enough, and 'Toinette's mother proved one of the worst. She had one daughter, this 'Toinette, — as pretty and as worthless a girl as ever made eyes at the sailors in any seaport town in France. It once happened that 'Toinette fell in love, and then she made great promises of reform. One of the hands on *La Gironde* had come down with a fever in Quebec and was lying sick in the Hôtel Dieu when his ship sailed for France. After he was discharged from the hospital, he found himself homeless in a frontier town in winter, too weak to work. 'Toinette took him in, drove her old sweethearts away, and married him. But soon after this boy, Jacques, was born, she returned to her old ways, and her husband disappeared. It was thought that his shipmates had hidden him on board *La Gironde* and taken him home.

'Toinette and another woman now kept a sailors' lodging-house in the Lower Town, up beyond the King's warehouses. They were commonly called La Grenouille and L'Escargot, because, every summer, when the ships from France began to come in, they stuck in their window two placards: "FROGS," "SNAILS," to attract the hungry sailors, whether they had those delicacies on hand or not. 'Toinette, called La Grenouille, was still good to look at; yellow hair, red cheeks, lively blue eyes, an impudent red mouth over small pointed teeth, like a squirrel's. Her partner, the poor snail, was a vacant creature, scarcely more than half-witted, — and the hard work, of course, was put off on her.

This unfortunate child, Jacques, in spite of his bad surroundings, was a very decent little fellow. He told the truth, he tried to be clean, he was devoted to Cécile and her father. When he came to their house to play, they endeavoured to give him some sort of bringing-up, though it was difficult, because his mother was fiercely jealous.

It was two years ago, soon after her mother's death, that Cécile had first noticed Jacques playing about the market place, and begun to bring him home with her, wash his face, and give him a piece of good bread to eat. Auclair thought it natural for a little girl to adopt a friendless child, to want something to care for after having helped to care for her mother so long. But he did not greatly like the idea of anything at all coming from La Grenouille's house to his, and he was determined to deprive Cécile of her playfellow if he saw any signs of his bad blood. Observing the little boy closely, he had come to feel a real affection for him.

Cécile and Jacques

Once, not long ago, when the children were having their goûter in the salon, and the apothecary was writing at his desk, he overheard Jacques telling Cécile where he would kick any boy who broke down his beaver-dam, and he used a nasty word.

"Oh, Jacques!" Cécile exclaimed, "that is some horrible word you have heard the sailors say!"

Auclair, glancing through the partition, saw the child's pale face stiffen and his round eyes stare; he said nothing at all, but he looked frightened. The apothecary guessed at once that it was not from a sailor but from La Grenouille herself he had got that expression.

Cécile went on scolding him. "Now I am going to do what the Sisters at the convent do when a child says anything naughty. Come into the kitchen, and I will wash your mouth out with soap. It is the only way to make your mouth clean."

All this time Jacques said nothing. He went obediently into the kitchen with Cécile, and when he came back he was wiping his eyes with the back of his hand.

"Is it gone?" he asked solemnly.

This morning, as Auclair watched Jacques at his devotions, it occurred to him that the boatmen who brought the merchants up from Montreal to see the Count were doubtless staying with La Grenouille.

Likely enough something rowdy had gone on there last night, and the little boy felt a need of expiation. The apothecary went out of the church softly and took up his basket. All the way up the hill he wondered why La Grenouille should have a boy like that.

When he reached home, he called Cécile, who was busy in the room upstairs, where she slept until cold weather. As he gave her his basket, he asked her whether she had seen Jacques lately.

"No, I haven't happened to. Why, is anything the matter?"

"Oh, nothing that I know of. But I saw him in church just now, saying his prayers at the Stations of the Cross, and I felt sorry for him. Perhaps he is getting old enough to realize."

"Was he clean, Papa?"

The apothecary shook his head.

"Far from clean. I never saw him so badly off. His toes were sticking out of his shoes, and when he knelt I could see that he had no stockings on."

"Oh, dear, and I have never finished the pair I began for him! Papa, if you were to let me off from reading to you for a few evenings, I could soon get them done."

"But his shoes, daughter! It would be a mere waste to give the child new stockings. And shoes are very dear."

Cécile and Jacques

Cécile sat down for a moment and thought, while her father put on his shop apron. "Papa," she said suddenly, "would you allow me to speak to the Count? He is kind to children, and I believe he would get Jacques some shoes."

II

THAT afternoon Cécile ran up the hill with a light heart. She was always glad of a reason for going to the Château, — often slipped into the courtyard merely to see who was on guard duty. Her little friend Giorgio, the drummer boy, was at his post on the steps before the great door, and the moment he saw Cécile he snatched his drumsticks from his trousers pocket and executed a rapid flourish in the air above his drum, making no noise. Cécile laughed, and the boy grinned. This was an old joke, but they still found it amusing. Giorgio was stationed there to announce the arrival of the commanding officer, and of all distinguished persons, by a flourish on his drum. The drum-call echoed amazingly in the empty court, could be heard even in the apothecary shop down the hill, so that one always knew when the Count had visitors.

Cécile told the soldier on duty that she would like to see Picard, the Count's valet, and while she waited for him, she went up the steps to talk with Giorgio and to ask him if his cold were better, and when he had last heard from his mother.

The boy's real name was Georges Million; his family lived over on the Île d'Orléans, and his father was a farmer, Canadian-born. But the old grandfather, who was of course the head of the house, had come from Haute-Savoie as a drummer in the Carignan-Salières regiment. He played the Alpine horn as well, and still performed on the flute at country weddings. This grandson, Georges, took after him, — was musical and wanted nothing in the world but a soldier's life. When he was fifteen, he came into Quebec and begged the Governor to let him enter the native militia. He was very small for his age, but he was a good-looking boy, and the Count took him on as a drummer until he should grow tall enough to enlist. He put him into a blue coat, high boots, and a three-cornered hat, and stationed him at the door to welcome visitors. For some reason the Count always called him Giorgio, and that had become his name in Quebec.

Giorgio's life was monotonous; his duties were to keep clean and trim, and to stand perfectly idle in a draughty courtyard for hours at a time. There were very few distinguished persons in Quebec, and not all of those were on calling terms with Count Frontenac. The Intendant, de Champigny, came to the Château when it was necessary, but his relations with the Count were formal rather than cordial. Sometimes, indeed, he brought Madame de Champigny with him, and when they rolled up in their *carrosse*, Giorgio had a great opportunity. Old Bishop Laval, who would properly have been announced by the drum, had not crossed the threshold of the Château for years. The new Bishop had called but twice since his return from France. Dollier de Casson, Superior of the Sulpician Seminary at Montreal, was a person to be greeted by the drum, and so was Jacques Le Ber, the rich merchant. Sometimes Daniel du Lhut, the explorer in command of Fort Frontenac, came to Quebec, and, very rarely, Henri de Tonti, — that one-armed hero who had an iron hook in place of a hand. For all Indian chiefs and messengers, too, Giorgio could beat his drum long and loud. This form of welcome was very gratifying to the savages. But often the days passed one after another when the drummer had no one to salute but the officers of the fort, and life was very dull for him.

When a friendly soldier was on guard, Cécile would

often run in to give the drummer boy some cardamon
seeds or raisins from her father's shop, and to gossip
with him for a while. This afternoon their talk was cut
short by the arrival of the Count's valet, through whom
one approached his master. Picard had been with the
Count since the Turkish wars, and Cécile had known
him ever since she could remember. He took her by the
hand and led her into the Château and upstairs to the
Count's private apartment in the south wing.

The apartment was of but two rooms, a dressing-
cabinet and a long room with windows on two sides,
which was both chamber and study. The Governor was
seated at a writing-table in the south end, a considerable distance from his fireplace and his large curtained
bed. He was nearly eighty years old, but he had changed
very little since Cécile could remember him, except
that his teeth had grown yellow. He still walked, rode,
struck, as vigorously as ever, and only two years ago he
had gone hundreds of miles into the wilderness on one
of the hardest Indian campaigns of his life. When Picard spoke to him, he laid down his pen, beckoned Cécile with a long forefinger, put his arm about her familiarly, and drew her close to his side, inquiring about her
health and her father's. As he talked to her, his eyes took
on a look of uneasy, mocking playfulness, with a slightly

sarcastic curl of the lips. Cécile was not afraid of him. He had always been one of the important figures in her life; when she was little she used to like to sit on his knee, because he wore such white linen, and satin waist-coats with jewelled buttons. He took great care of his person when he was at home. Nothing annoyed him so much as his agent's neglecting to send him his supply of lavender-water by the first boat in the spring. It vexed him more than a sharp letter from the Minister, or even from the King.

After replying to his courtesies Cécile began at once:

"Monsieur le Comte, you know little Jacques Gaux, the son of La Grenouille?"

The old soldier nodded and sniffed, drooping the lid slightly over one eye, — an expression of his regard for a large class of women. She understood.

"But he is a good little boy, Monsieur le Comte, and he cannot help it about his mother. You know she neglects him, and just now he is very badly off for shoes. I am knitting him some stockings, but the shoes we cannot manage."

"And if I were to give you an order on the cobbler? That is soon done. It is very nice of you to knit stockings for him. Do you knit your own?"

"Of course, monsieur! And my father's."

The old Count looked at her from out his deep eye-sockets, and felt for the hard spots on her palm. "You are content down there, keeping house for your father? Not much time for play, I take it?"

"Oh, everything we do, my father and I, is a kind of play."

He gave a dry chuckle. "Well said! Everything we do is. It gets rather tiresome, — but not at your age, perhaps. I am very well pleased with you, Cécile, because you do so well for your father. We have too many idle girls in Kebec, and I cannot say that Kebec is exceptional. I have been about the world a great deal, and I have found only one country where the women like to work, — in Holland. They have made an ugly country very pretty." He slipped a piece of money into her hand. "That is for your charities. Get the Frog's son what he needs, and Picard will give Noël Pommier an order for his shoes. And is there nothing you would like for yourself? I have never forgot what a brave sailor you were on the voyage over. You cried only once, and that was when we were coming into the Gulf, and a bird of prey swooped down and carried off a little bird perched on one of our yard-arms. I wish I had some sweetmeats; you do not often pay me a visit."

"Perhaps you would let me look at your glass fruit," Cécile suggested.

Cécile and Jacques

The Count got up and led her to the mantelpiece. Between the tall silver candlesticks stood a crystal bowl full of glowing fruits of coloured glass: purple figs, yellow-green grapes with gold vine-leaves, apricots, nectarines, and a dark citron stuck up endwise among the grapes. The fruits were hollow, and the light played in them, throwing coloured reflections into the mirror and upon the wall above.

"That was a present from a Turkish prisoner whose life I spared when I was holding the island of Crete," the Count told her. "It was made by the Saracens. They blow it into those shapes while the glass is melted. Every piece is hollow; that is why they look alive. Here in Canada it reminds one of the South. You admire it?"

"More than anything I have ever seen," said Cécile fervently.

He laughed. "I like it myself, or I should not have taken so much trouble to bring it over. I think I must leave it to you in my will."

"Oh, thank you, monsieur, but it is quite enough to look at it; one would never forget it. It is much lovelier than real fruit." She curtsied and thanked him again and went out softly to where Picard was waiting for her in the hall. She wished that she could some time go there when the Count was away, and look as long as she pleased at the glass fruit and at the tapestries on the walls of the long room. They were from his estate at Île Savary and represented garden scenes. One could study them for hours without seeing all the flowers and figures.

III

THE next morning Auclair sent Cécile up to the Ursuline convent with some borax de Venise which the Mother Superior required, and a bottle of asafœtida for one of the Sisters who was ailing. At this time of year Cécile always felt a little homesick for the Sisters and her old life at the Ursuline school. She had left it so early, because of her mother's illness, and she never passed the garden walls without looking wistfully at the tree-tops which rose above them. From her walks on Cap Diamant she could look down into the rectangular courts and see, through the leafless boughs, the rows of dormer windows in the white roofs, each opening into a Sister's bare little room. One teacher she loved better than any of the others: Sister Anne de Sainte-Rose, who taught history and the French language. She was a niece of the Bishop of Tours, had been happily married, and had led a brilliant life in the great world. Only after the death of her young husband and infant son had she become a religious. She had charm and wit and the remains of great beauty — everything that would appeal to a little girl brought up on a rude frontier. Cécile still saw her when she went to the convent on errands, and she was always invited to the little miracle plays which Sister Anne had the *pensionnaires* give at Christmas-time, for the good of their French and their deportment. But her little visits with her teacher were very short, — stolen pleasures. The nuns were always busy, and if you once dropped out of the school life, you could not share it any more.

This morning she did not see Sister Anne at all; and after delivering her packages to Sister Agatha, the porteress, she turned away to enjoy the weather. It was on days like this that she loved her town best. The autumn fog was rolling in from the river so thick that she seemed to be walking through drifts of brown cloud. Only a few roofs and spires stood out in the fog, detached and isolated: the flèche of the Récollet chapel, the slate roof of the Château, the long, grey outline of Bishop Laval's Seminary, floating in the sky. Everything else was blotted out by rolling vapours that were constantly changing in density and colour; now brown, now amethyst,

73

now reddish lavender, with sometimes a glow of orange overhead where the sun was struggling behind the thick weather.

It was like walking in a dream. One could not see the people one passed, or the river, or one's own house. Not even the winter snows gave one such a feeling of being cut off from everything and living in a world of twilight and miracles. After loitering on her way, she set off for the Lower Town to look for Jacques.

Cécile never on any account went to his mother's house to find him. Sometimes, in searching for him, she went behind the King's warehouses, as far as the stone paving extended. Beyond the paving the strip of beach directly underneath Cap Diamant grew so narrow that there was room for barely a dozen houses to sit in a straight line against the foot of the cliff, and they were the slum of Quebec. Respectability stopped with the cobble-stones.

This morning she did not have to go so far; she found Jacques in a group of little boys who had kindled a fire of sticks at the foot of Notre Dame street, behind the church. Before she came up to the children, a light sprinkle began to fall. In a few seconds all the brownish-lilac masses of vapour melted away, leaving a lead-coloured sky, and the rain came down in streams, like water poured from a great height. Cécile caught Jacques by the arm and ran with him into the church, which had often been a refuge to them in winter. Not that the church was ever heated, but in there one was out of the wind, and perhaps the bright colours made one feel the cold less. This morning the church was empty, except for an old man and three women at their prayers. There were a few benches on either side of the nave, for old people who could not stand during mass, and the children slipped into one of these, sitting close together to keep warm.

"It's been a long time since we were in here together," Cécile whispered.

He nodded.

"But you come in to say your prayers, don't you, every day?"

"I think so," he answered vaguely.

"That is right. I like this church better than any other. Even in the chapel of the Ursulines I don't feel so much at home, though I used to be there every day when I was going to school. This is our own church, isn't it, Jacques?"

He glanced up at her and smiled faintly. This child never looked very well. He was not thin, — rather chunky, on the contrary, — but there was no colour in

75

his cheeks, or even in his lips. That, Cécile knew, was because he wasn't properly nourished.

"You might tell me about some nice saint," said Jacques presently. She began to whisper the story of Saint Anthony of Padua, who stood quite near them, ruddy and handsome, with a sheaf of lilies on one arm and the Holy Child on the other.

It chanced that this one church* in the Lower Town, near Jacques's little world, where he and Cécile had so often made rendezvous, was peculiarly the church of childhood. It had been renamed Notre Dame de la Victoire five years ago, after the Count had driven off Sir William Phips's besieging fleet, in recognition of the protection which Our Lady had afforded Quebec in that hour of danger. But originally it was called the Church of the Infant Jesus, and the furnishings and decorations which had been sent over from France were appropriate for a church of that name.

Two paintings hung in the Lady Chapel, both of Sainte Geneviève as a little girl. In one she sat under a tree in a meadow, with a flock of sheep all about her, and a distaff in her hand, while two angels watched her from

---

*The charm of this old church was greatly spoiled by unfortunate alterations in the lighting, made in the autumn of 1929.

a distance. In the other she was reading an illuminated scroll, — but here, too, she was in a field and surrounded by her flock.

The high altar was especially interesting to children, though it was not nearly so costly or so beautiful as the altar in the Ursulines' chapel with its delicate gold-work. It was very simple indeed, — but definite. It was a representation of a feudal castle, all stone walls and towers. The outer wall was low and thick, with many battlements; the second was higher, with fewer battle-ments; the third seemed to be the wall of the pal-ace itself, with towers and many windows. Within the arched gateway (hung with little velvet curtains that were green or red or white according to the day) the Host was kept. Cécile had always taken it for granted that the Kingdom of Heaven looked exactly like this from the outside and was surrounded by just such walls; that this altar was a reproduction of it, made in France by people who knew; just as the statues of the saints and of the Holy Family were portraits. She had taught Jacques to believe the same thing, and it was very com-forting to them both to know just what Heaven looked like, — strong and unassailable, wherever it was set among the stars.

Out of this walled castle rose three tall stone towers,

77

with holy figures on them. On one stood a grave Sainte Anne, regally clad like a great lady of this world, with a jewelled coronet upon her head. On her arm sat a little dark-skinned Virgin, her black hair cut straight across the back like a scholar's, her hands joined in prayer. Sainte Anne was noble in bearing, but not young; her delicately featured face was rather worn by life, and sad. She seemed to know beforehand all the sorrows of her own family, and of the world it was to succour.

On the central tower, which was the tallest and rose almost to the roof of the church, the Blessed Mother and Child stood high up among the shadows. Today, with the leaden sky and floods of rain, it was too dark up there to see her clearly; but the children thought they saw her, because they knew her face so well. She was by far the loveliest of all the Virgins in Kebec, a charming figure of young motherhood, — oh, very young, and radiantly happy, with a stately crown, and a long, blue cloak that parted in front over a scarlet robe. The little Jesus on her arm was not a baby, — he looked as if he would walk if she put him down, and walk very well. He was so intelligent and gay, a child in a bright and joyful mood, both arms outstretched in a gesture of welcome, as if he were giving a fête for his little friends and were in the act of receiving them. He was a little Lord indeed, in his gaiety and graciousness and savoir-faire.

Cécile and Jacques

The rain fell on the roof and drove against the windows. Outside, the ledges of bare rock and all the sloping streets were running water; everything was slippery and shiny with wet. The children sat contentedly in their corner, feeling the goodness of shelter. Jacques remarked that it would be nice if there were more candles. The tapers on the votive candle-stand were burning low, and nobody was coming in now because of the downpour. It was pleasanter, they agreed, when there were enough candles burning before Sainte Anne to show the gold flowers on her cloak.

"Why don't you light a candle, Cécile?" Jacques asked. "You do, sometimes."

"Yes, but this morning I haven't any money with me."

Jacques sighed. "It would be nice," he repeated.

"I wonder, Jacques, if it would be wrong for me to take a candle, and then bring the ten sous down later, when the rain stops."

Jacques brightened. He thought that a very good idea.

"But it's irregular, Jacques. Perhaps it would not be right."

"You wouldn't forget, would you?"

"Oh, no! But I might be struck by lightning or some-

79

thing on the way home. And then, I expect, I'd die in sin."

"But I would tell your father, and he would give me the ten sous to put in the box. I wouldn't forget."

She saw he wanted very much to light a candle. "Well, perhaps. I'll try it this once, and I'll light one for you, too. Only be sure you don't forget, if anything happens to me."

They went softly up to the feet of Sainte Anne, where the candles were burning down in the metal basin. Each of them took a fresh taper from the box underneath, lit it, and fitted its hollow base upon one of the little metal horns. After saying a prayer they returned to their bench to enjoy the sight of the two new bright spots in the brownish gloom. Sure enough, when the fresh tapers were burning well, the gold flowers on Sainte Anne's cloak began to show; not entire, but wherever there was a fold in the mantle, the gold seemed to flow like a glistening liquid. Her figure emerged from the dusk in a rich, oily, yellow light.

After a long silence Jacques spoke.

"Cécile, all the saints in this church like children, don't they?"

"Oh, yes! And Our Lord loves children. Because He was a child Himself, you know."

Cécile and Jacques

Jacques had something else in mind. In a moment he brought it out. "Sometimes sailors are fond of children, too."

"Yes," she agreed with some hesitation.

He sensed a reservation in her voice.

"And they're awful brave," he went on feelingly. "If it wasn't for the sailors, we wouldn't have any ships from France, or anything."

"That's true," Cécile assented.

Jacques relapsed into silence. He was thinking of a jolly Breton sailor who had played with him in the summer, and carved him a marvellous beaver out of wood and painted its teeth white. He had sailed away on *La Garonne* three weeks ago, nearly breaking Jacques's heart. With that curious tact of childhood, which fails less often than the deepest diplomacy, Jacques almost never referred to his mother or her house or the people who came there, when he was with Cécile and her father. When he went to see them, he left his little past behind him, as it were.

At last the fall of water on the roof grew fainter, and the light clearer. Cécile said she must be going home now. "Come along with me, Jacques. Never mind about your clothes," seeing that he hung back, "that will be all right. Perhaps my father will give you a bath while I am getting our déjeuner, and we will all have our chocolate together."

As they quitted their bench, someone entered the church; a very heavy, tall old man with wide, stooping shoulders and a head hanging forward. When he took off his shovel hat at the door, a black skull-cap still remained over his scanty locks. He carried a cane and seemed to move his legs with some difficulty under his long, black gown. It was old Bishop Laval himself, who had been storm-bound for an hour and more at the house of one of the merchants on the square. Cécile hurried up to him before he should have time to kneel.

"Excuse me, Monseigneur l'Ancien," she said respectfully, "but if it is quite convenient would you be so kind as to lend me twenty sous?"

The old man looked down at her, frowning. His eyes were large and full, but set deep back under his forehead. He had such a very large, drooping nose, and such a grim, bitter mouth, that he might well have frightened a child who didn't know him. With considerable difficulty he got a little black purse out from under his gown. There was not much in it.

"You see," Cécile explained, "the little boy and I wished to offer candles, and I had no money with me.

I was going up to my father's shop to get some, but I would rather not leave the church owing for the candles."

The old man nodded and looked slightly amused. He put two pieces in her hand, and she went to the front of the church to slip them in the box, leaving Jacques, who had got back against the wall as far as he could go, to bear the scrutiny of the Bishop's smouldering eyes. When she came back, she found them regarding each other in silence, but very intently; the old man staring down from his height, the little boy, his finger in his mouth, looking up at the Bishop shyly, but in a way that struck her as very personal. Cécile took him by the hand and led him to the door. Glancing back over her shoulder, she saw the Bishop sink heavily to his knees with something between a sigh and a groan.

Everything was glittering when they stepped out into the square; no sun yet, but a bright rain-grey light, silver and cut steel and pearl on the grey roofs and walls. Long veils of smoky fog were caught in the pine forests across the river. And how fresh the air smelled!

"Jacques," Cécile asked wonderingly, "do you know Monseigneur Laval? Did he ever talk to you?"

"I think once he did."

"What about?"

"I don't remember."

They went hand in hand up the hill.

He both did and did not remember; it came back to him in flashes, unrelated pictures, like a dream. Perhaps it was a dream. He could never have told Cécile about it, since it was hard for him to talk even about things he knew very well. But whenever he chanced to see old Bishop Laval, he felt that once, long ago, something pleasant had happened between them.

It had happened two years ago, when he was only four, before he knew the Auclairs at all. It was in January. A light, sticky snow had fallen irresolutely, at intervals, all day. Toward evening the weather changed; the sun emerged, just sinking over the great pine forest to the west, hung there, an angry ball, and all the snow-covered rock blazed in orange fire. The sun became a half-circle, then a mere red eyebrow, then dropped behind the forest, leaving the air clear blue, and much colder, with a pale lemon moon riding high overhead. There was no wind, it was a night of still moonlight, and within an hour after sunset the wet snow had frozen fast over roofs and spires and trees. Everything on the rock was sheathed in glittering white ice. It was a sight

84

to stir the dullest blood. Some trappers from Three Rivers were in town. They had supper with La Grenouille, and afterwards persuaded her to go for a ride in their dog-sledges up the frozen St. Lawrence. Jacques was in bed asleep. 'Toinette threw an extra blanket over him and put an armful of wood in the stove, then went off with the young men, taking L'Escargot with her. She meant to be out only an hour or two; but they had plenty of brandy along to keep them warm, and so they made a night of it. Dog-sledging by moonlight on that broad marble highway, with no wind, was fine sport.

After she had been gone a couple of hours, Jacques wakened up very cold and called for his mother. Presently he got up and went to look for her. He went to L'Escargot's bed, and that, too, was empty. The moonlight shone in brightly, but the fire had gone out, and all about him things creaked with the cold. He found his shoes and an old shawl and went out into the snow to look for his mother. The poor neighbour houses were silent. He went behind the King's storehouse and up Notre Dame street to the market square. The worthy merchants were long ago in bed, and all the houses were dark except one, where the mother of the family was very sick. The statue of King Louis, with a cloak and helmet of snow, looked terrifying in the moonlight.

Jacques already knew better than to knock at that solid, comfortable house where he saw a lighted window; he knew his mother wasn't well thought of by these rich people. Not knowing where to turn, he took the only forward way there was, up Mountain Hill.

Luckily, one other person was abroad that night. Old Bishop Laval, who never spared himself, had been down to the square to sit with the sick woman. He came toiling up the hill in his fur cloak and his tall fur cap, which was almost as imposing as his episcopal mitre, a cane in one hand, a lantern in the other. His valet followed behind. They were passing the new Bishop's Palace, now cold and empty, as Monseigneur de Saint-Vallier was in France. Just as they wound under the retaining wall of the terrace, they heard a child crying. The Bishop stopped and flashed his lantern this way and that. On the flight of stone steps that led up through the wall to the episcopal residence, he saw a little boy, almost a baby, sitting in the snow, crouching back against the masonry.

"Where does he belong?" asked the Bishop of his *donné*.

"Ah, that I cannot tell, Monseigneur," replied Houssart.

"Pick him up and bring him along," said the Bishop.

86

"Unbutton your coat and hold him against your body."
The lantern moved on.

The old Bishop lived in the Priests' House, built as a part of his Seminary. His private rooms were poor and small. All his silver plate and velvet and linen he had given away little by little, to needy parishes, to needy persons. He had given away the revenues of his abbeys in France, and had transferred his vast grants of Canadian land to the Seminary. He lived in naked poverty.

When they reached home, he commanded Houssart to build a fire in the fireplace at once (had he been alone he would have undressed and gone to bed in the cold) and to heat water, that he might give the child a warm bath.

"Is there any milk?" he asked.

Houssart hesitated. "A little, for your chocolate in the morning, Monseigneur."

"Get it and put it to warm on the hearth. Pour a little cognac in it, and bring any bread there is in the house."

One strange thing Jacques could remember afterwards. He was sitting on the edge of a narrow bed, wrapped in a blanket, in the light of a blazing fire. He had just been washed in warm water; the basin was still on the floor. Beside it knelt a very large old man with big eyes and a great drooping nose and a little black cap on his head, and he was rubbing Jacques's feet and legs very softly with a towel. They were all alone then, just the two of them, and the fire was bright enough to see clearly. What he remembered particularly was that this old man, after he had dried him like this, bent down and took his foot in his hand and kissed it; first the one foot, then the other. That much Jacques remembered.

When the servant returned, they gave the child warm milk with a little bread in it, and put him into the Bishop's bed, though Houssart begged to take him to his own.

"No, we will not move him. He is falling asleep already. I do not know if that flush means a fever or not."

"Monseigneur," Houssart whispered, "now that I have seen him in the light, I recognize this child. He is the son of that 'Toinette Gaux, the woman they call La Grenouille."

"Ah!" the old man nodded thoughtfully. "That, too, may have a meaning. Throw more wood on the fire and go. I shall rest here in my arm-chair with my fur coat over my knees until it is time to ring the bell." The Bishop got up at four o'clock every morning, dressed without a fire, went with his lantern into the church, and rang the bell for early mass for the working people. Many good people who did not want to go to mass at all, when they heard that hoarse, frosty bell clanging out under the black sky where there was not yet even a hint of daybreak, groaned and went to the church. Because they thought of the old Bishop at the end of the bell-rope, and because his will was stronger than theirs. He was a stubborn, high-handed, tyrannical, quarrelsome old man, but no one could deny that he shepherded his sheep.

When his *donné* had gone and he was left with the sleeping child, the Bishop settled his swollen legs upon a stool, covered them with his cloak, and sank into meditation. This was not an accident, he felt. Why had he found, on the steps of that costly episcopal residence built in scorn of him and his devotion to poverty, a male child, half-clad and crying in the merciless cold? Why had this reminder of his Infant Saviour been just there, under that house which he never passed without bitterness, which was like a thorn in his flesh? Had he been too much absorbed in his struggles with governors and intendants, in the heavy labour of founding and fixing his church upon this rock, in training a native priesthood and safeguarding their future?

Monseigneur de Laval had not always been a man of means and measures. Long ago, in Bernières's Hermitage at Caen, his life had been wholly given up to meditation and prayer. Not until he was sent out to Canada to convert a frontier mission into an enduring part of the Church had he become a man of action. His life, as he reviewed it, fell into two even periods. The first thirty-six years had been given to purely personal religion, to bringing his mind and will into subjection to his spiritual guides. The last thirty-six years had been spent in bringing the minds and wills of other people into subjection to his own, — since he had but one will, and that was the supremacy of the Church in Canada. Might this occurrence tonight be a sign that it was time to return to that rapt and mystical devotion of his earlier life?

In the morning, after he returned from offering early mass in the church, before it was yet light, the Bishop sent his man about over the hill, to this house and that, wherever there were young children, begging of one shoes, of another a little frock, — whatever the mother could spare from the backs of her own brood.

'Toinette Gaux had returned home meanwhile, and was frightened at missing her son. But she was ashamed to go out and look for him. Some neighbour would bring him back, she thought, — and, insolent as she was, she dreaded the moment. She got her deserts, certainly, when two long, black shadows fell upon the glistening snow before her door; the Bishop in his tall fur cap, prodding the icy crust with his cane, and behind him Houssart, carrying the little boy.

The Bishop came in without knocking, and motioned his man to put the child down and withdraw. He stood for some moments confronting the woman in silence. 'Toinette was no fool; she felt all his awfulness; the long line of noble blood and authority behind him, the power of the Church and the power of the man. She wished the earth would swallow her. Not a shred of her impudence was left her. Her tongue went dry. His silence was so dreadful that it was a relief when he began to thunder and tell her that even the beasts of the forest protected their young (*Les ourses et les louves protègent leurs petits*). He meant to watch over this boy, he said; if she neglected him, he would take the child and put him with the Sisters of the Congregation, not here, but in Montreal, to place him as far as possible from a worthless mother.

'Toinette knew that he would to it, too. When she was a little girl, she used to hear talk about just such a high-handed proceeding of the Bishop's. A rich man in Quebec had brought a girl over from France to work as a bonne in his family. The Bishop thought she did not come to mass often enough and was not receiving

91

proper religious training. So one day when he met her on the street, he took her by the hand and led her to the Ursuline convent and put her with the cloistered Sisters. There she stayed until the Governor gave her master a warrant to search the rock for his maid and take her wherever he found her. But 'Toinette knew that a woman of her sort, without money or good repute, had little chance of getting her boy back if once the Bishop took him away.

She kept Jacques in the house all the rest of the winter, and never went out herself except L'Escargot was there to watch him. It was not until the summer ships came, bringing new lovers and new distractions, that Jacques was allowed to go into the streets to play.

IV

CÉCILE was taking Jacques to Noël Pommier to be measured for his shoes. The cobbler lived halfway down Holy Family Hill, the steep street that plunged from the Cathedral down toward the St. Lawrence. There were other shoemakers in Quebec, but all persons of quality went to Pommier, unless they had had a short answer from him at some time. He would not hurry a piece of work for anybody, — not for the Count or the Intendant or the Bishop. If anyone tried to hurry him, he became surly and was likely to say something that a self-important person could not allow himself to overlook. It was rumoured that he had spoken unbecomingly to the valet of Monseigneur de Saint-Vallier, and had told him it would be better if his master had all his shoes made in Paris, where he spent so much of his time. Certainly the new Bishop had ceased to patronize him, which was a grief to Pommier's pious mother.

When the children entered the cobbler's door, they found him seated at his bench with a shoe between his knees, sewing the sole to the upper. Seeing that it was M. Auclair's daughter, he rose and put down his work. He was a thick-set man with stooped shoulders; his head was grown over with coarse black hair cut short like bristles, his fleshy face was dark red, and seamed with hard creases. The purple veins that spread like little roots about his nostrils suggested an occasional indulgence in brandy. When Pommier stood up, with his blackened hands hanging beside his leather apron, and his corded, hairy arms bare to the elbow, he looked like a black bear standing upright. His eyes, too, were small like a bear's, and somewhat bloodshot.

93

"Bonjour, Mademoiselle Cécile, what can I do for you?"

"If you please, Monsieur Pommier, I have brought little Jacques Gaux to be measured for his shoes. Has the Count's valet spoken to you about it?"

Pommier nodded. "Sit down there, little man, and let me see." He put Jacques down on a straw-topped stool (an old one his father had brought from Rouen, along with his bench and tools), took off the wretched foot-gear he had on, and began to study his feet and to make measurements.

While this was going on in deep silence, a door at the back of the house opened, and Pommier's mother, a thin, lively old woman with a crutch, came tapping lightly across the living-room and into the shop. She embraced Cécile with delight, and spoke very kindly to Jacques when he was presented to her.

"I have never seen this little fellow before, since I don't get about much, but I like to know all the children in Quebec. You will be very content with fine new shoes, my boy?"

"Oui, madame," Jacques murmured.

"And you have quite neglected me of late, Cécile. I know you are busy enough down there, but I have been looking for you every day since the ships sailed. My son

94

saw your father at the market yesterday and observed that he was laying in good supplies for you." Madame Pommier seated herself on one of the wooden chairs without backs and rested her crutch across her knees. She always came into the shop when there were clients, and she liked to know what her son was doing every minute of the day.

When Cécile was little, Madame Pommier used to come to see her mother very often. She was one of the first friends Madame Auclair made in Quebec, and had given her a great deal of help in her struggle to keep house in a place where there were none of the conveniences to which she was accustomed. The Pommiers themselves were old residents, had lived here ever since this Noël was a young lad, and his father had been the Count's shoemaker during his first governorship, twenty-odd years ago. Just about the time that Madame Auclair's health began to fail, Madame Pommier had fallen on the icy hill in front of her own door and broken her hip. The good chirurgien Gervais Beaudoin attended her, but though the bone knit, it came together badly and left one leg much shorter than the other. M. Auclair had made a crutch for her, and as she was slight and very active, she was soon able to get about in her own house and attend to her duties. Many a time Cécile had found her by her stove, the crutch under her left arm, handling her pots and casseroles as deftly as if she were not propped up by a wooden stick. Sometimes in winter she even got to mass. Her son had set an arm-chair upon runners, and in this he pushed her up the hill over the snow to the Cathedral.

After the cobbler had made his measurements and noted them down, he took up his work again and began driving his awl through the leather, drawing the big needle with waxed thread through after it. Tools of any sort had a fascination for Cécile; she loved to watch a shoemaker or a carpenter at work. Jacques, who had never seen anything of the kind before, followed Pommier's black fingers with astonishment. They both sat quietly, and the old lady joined them in admiringly watching her clever son. Suddenly she bethought herself of something, and pointed with her crutch to a little cabinet of shelves covered by a curtain. There ladies' shoes, sent in for repair or made to order, were kept, as being rather too personal to expose on the open shelves with the men's boots.

"*Tirez, tirez,*" whispered Madame Pommier. Cécile got up and drew back the curtain, and at once knew what the old lady wished her to see: a beautiful pair of red satin slippers, embroidered in gold and purple, with leather soles and red leather heels.

"Oh, madame, how lovely! To whom do they belong?"

"To Monseigneur l'Ancien. They are his house slippers. My son is to put new soles on them, — see, they are almost worn through. Houssart says he paces his chamber in the night when he is at his devotions, so that he will not be overcome by sleep."

"But these are so small, can he possibly wear them? And his walk is so heavy, too."

"Ah, that is because of his legs, which are bad. But he has a very slender foot, very distinguished. That is the Montmorency in him; he is of noble blood, you know."

Here Pommier himself reached up to a row of wooden lasts over his head and handed one of them to Cécile.

"That is his foot, mademoiselle."

Cécile took the smoothly shaped wood in her hands and examined it curiously. On the sole Noël had scratched with his awl: "Mgr. Lav'."

"And next it," said Madame Pommier, "you will find the Governor's. He, too, has a fine foot, very high in the arch, but large, as is needful for a soldier. And there to the left is the Intendant's, and Madame de Champigny's."

"Oh, Monsieur Pommier, you have the feet of all the great people here! Did you make them all yourself?"

97

"Ah, no! Some are from my father's time. Yes, you may look at them if it amuses you."

Cécile took them down one after another. To be sure, they all looked a good deal alike to her, but she could guess the original of each form from the awl scratches on the sole. On one she spelled the letters "R. CAV." She was trying to think whose that might be, when Pommier startled her a little by saying in a very peculiar tone of voice:

"That foot will not come back."

She could not tell whether he was angry or sorry, — there was something so harsh in his tone.

"But why, Monsieur Noël, why not?"

"It went too far," he replied with the same bitter shortness.

She stared at the letters. The old lady beckoned her and traced over the inscription with her finger. "That is my husband's marking; he always made capitals. It means Robert Cavelier de La Salle."

Cécile drew a deep breath. "Monsieur Noël believes he is really dead, then?"

Noël looked up from his black threads. "Everyone knows he is dead, mademoiselle. The people who say he will come back are fools. He was murdered, a thousand miles from here. Tonti brought the word. Robert de La

Salle has come into this shop many a time when I was a lad. He was a true man, mademoiselle, and nobody was true to him, except Monsieur le Comte; nor his own brother, nor his nephew, nor his King. It is always like that when there is a great one in a family. But I shall always keep his last. That foot went farther than any other in New France." He dropped his eyes and began driving his awl again.

Cécile knew it would be useless to question him, — such an outburst was most unusual from Pommier. But when she got home, she brought the matter up to her father and asked him whether it was true that the Abbé Cavelier had turned against his brother.

"I don't know, my dear. Nobody knows what happened down there. The Count blames him, but then, the Count always hated the Abbé."

V

I T was the afternoon of All Saints' Day, and Jacques had come up the hill through a driving sleet storm to put on his new shoes for the first time. When he had carefully laced them, he stood up in them and, looking from one to the other of his friends, smiled a glad,

surprised, soft smile. He was certainly not a handsome
child, but he had one beauty, — his baby teeth. When
his pale lips parted, his teeth showed like two rows of
pearls, really; even, regular, all the same size, lustrous
like those pearls that have just a faint shimmer of lilac.
The hard crusts, which were his fare for the most part,
kept them polished like veritable jewels. Cécile only
hoped that when his second teeth came in, they would
not be narrow and pointed, of the squirrel kind, like his
mother's.

When M. Auclair asked Jacques if the shoes were
comfortable, he looked up wonderingly and said: "Mais,
oui, monsieur," as if they could not possibly be otherwise.

The apothecary went back into his shop, where he
was boiling pine tops (*bourgeons des pins*) to make a
cough-syrup. Cécile told Jacques she had found in her
Lives of the Saints the picture of a little boy who looked
very much like him.

"I shall always keep it for a picture of you, Jacques.
Look, it is little Saint Edmond. He was an English
saint, and he became Archbishop of Cantorbéry. But he
died in France, at the monastery of Pontigny. Sit here
beside me, and I will read you what it says about him.

Cécile and Jacques

"Edmond était tout enfant un modèle de vertu, grâce aux tendres soins de sa pieuse mère. On ne le voyait qu'à l'école et à l'église, partageant ses journées entre la prière et l'étude, et se privant des plaisirs les plus innocents pour s'entretenir avec Jésus et sa divine Mère à laquelle il voua un culte tout spécial. Un jour qu'il fuyait ses compagnons de jeu, pour se recueillir intimement, l'Enfant Jésus lui apparaît, rayonnant de beauté et le regarde avec amour en lui disant: 'Je te salue, mon bien-aimé.' Edmond tout ébloui n'ose répondre et le divin Sauveur reprend: 'Vous ne me connaissez donc pas? — Non, avoue l'enfant, je n'ai pas cet honneur et je crois que vous ne devez pas me connaître non plus, mais me prenez pour un autre. — Comment, continue le petit Jésus, vous ne me reconnaissez pas, moi qui suis toujours à vos côtés et vous accompagne partout. Regardez-moi; je suis Jésus, gravez toujours ce nom en votre cœur et imprimez-le sur votre front et je vous préserverai de mort subite ainsi que tous ceux qui feront de même.' "

The little woodcut in Cécile's old book showed the boy saint very like Jacques indeed; a clumsy little fellow, abashed at the apparition, standing awkwardly with his finger in his mouth; his chin had no tip, because the old block from which he was printed was worn away. Beside him stood the Heavenly Child, all surrounded by rays, just Edmond's height, friendly like a playfellow, and treading on the earth, not floating in the air as visions are wont to do. Jacques bent over the book, his thumb on the page to keep it flat, and asked Cécile to read it over again, so that he could remember. When she finished, he drew a long, happy sigh.

"I wish the little Jesus would appear to me like that, standing on the ground. Then I would not be frightened," he murmured.

"I don't believe He ever does, in Canada, Jacques. Though perhaps He appears to the recluse in Montreal, she is so very holy. I know angels come to her. But I expect He is often near you and keeps you from harm, as He said to Saint Edmond; *moi qui suis toujours à vos côtés et vous accompagne partout.* Now you can look at the other pictures while I make our chocolate. Since this is All Saints' Day, we ought to think a great deal about the saints."

Left in the corner of the red sofa, Jacques held the book, but he did not turn the pages. He sat looking at the logs burning in the fireplace and making gleams on the china shepherd boy, the object of his especial admiration. He heard the sleet pecking on the window-panes and thought how nice it was to have a place like this to come to. When the chocolate began to give off its rich odour, his nostrils quivered like a puppy's. Cécile carried her father's cup to him in the shop, and then she and Jacques sat down at one corner of the table, where she had spread a napkin over the cloth.

Much as Jacques loved chocolate (in so far as he knew, this was the only house in the world in which that comforting drink was made), there was something he cared more about, something that gave him a kind of solemn satisfaction, — Cécile's cup. She had a silver cup with a handle; on the front was engraved a little wreath of roses, and inside that wreath was the name, "*Cécile*," cut in the silver. Her Aunt Clothilde had given it to her when she was but a tiny baby, so it had been hers all her life. That was what seemed so wonderful to Jacques. His clothes had always belonged to somebody else before they were made over for him; he slept wherever there was room for him, sometimes with his mother, sometimes on a bench. He had never had anything of his own except his toy beaver, — and now he would have his shoes, made just for him. But to have a little cup, with your name on it . . . even if you died, it would still be there, with your name.

More than the shop with all the white jars and mysterious implements, more than the carpet and curtains and the red sofa, that cup fixed Cécile as born to security and privileges. He regarded it with respectful, wistful admiration. Before the milk or chocolate was poured, he liked to hold it and trace with his finger-tips the letters that made it so peculiarly and almost sacredly hers. Since his attention was evidently fixed upon her cup, more than once Cécile had suggested that he drink his chocolate from it, and she would use another. But he shook his head, unable to explain. That was not at all what her cup meant to him. Indeed, Cécile could not know what it meant to him; she was too fortunate.

They had scarcely finished the last drop and the last crumb, when the shop door opened and they heard a woman's voice. Without a word Jacques slipped to the floor and began to take off his new shoes. Cécile sat still.

In the front shop Auclair was confronted by a vehement young woman, slightly out of breath, her head and shoulders tightly wrapped in a shawl, her cheeks reddened by the wind, and her fair hair curling about her forehead and glistening with water drops. The apothecary rose and said politely:

"Good day, 'Toinette, what will you have?"

She tossed her head. "None of your poisons, thank you! I believe my son is here?"

"I think so. He is in very good hands when he is here."

'Toinette struck an attitude, her hand on her hip. "Je suis mère, vous savez! The care of my son is my affair."

"Very true."

"What is this I hear about your getting shoes for him? I am his mother. I will get him shoes when I think it necessary. I am poor, it is true; but I want none of your money that is the price of poisons."

"Bien. I will take care that you get none of it. But I did not pay for the shoes. They were bought with the Governor's money."

'Toinette looked interested. Sharp points showed in her eyes, like the points of her teeth. "The Governor? Ah, that is different. The Governor is our protector, he owes us something. And the King owes something to the children of those poor creatures, like my mother, whom he sent out here under false pretences."

Auclair held up a warning finger. He was sorry for her, because he saw how ill at ease she was under her impertinence. "Do not quarrel with the Government, my girl. That can do you no good, and it might get you into trouble."

'Toinette loosened her shawl and then wound it tight. She wished she had been more civil; perhaps they would have offered her some chocolate. She called shrilly for

Jacques. He came at once, without saying a word, his new shoes in his hands, his old ones on his feet. His mother caught him by the shoulder with a jerk, — she could not cuff him in the apothecary's presence. "Au revoir, monsieur," she snapped, as Auclair opened the door for her. She went down the hill with her defiant stride, her head high, and Jacques walked after her as fast as he could, wearing an expression of intense gravity, blinking against the sleet, and carrying his new shoes, soles up, out in front of him in a most unnatural way, as if he were carrying a basin full of water and trying not to spill it.

Auclair thrust his head out and watched them round the turn, then closed the door. He looked in upon his daughter and remarked:

"She has shown her teeth; now she will not make any more trouble for a while. She will let him wear his shoes. She was pleased and was afraid of showing it."

"He pulled off his new stockings and stuffed them inside his shirt, Papa!"

Auclair laughed. "How often I have seen children and dogs, and even brave men, take on quick sly ways to protect themselves from an ill-tempered woman! I doubt whether she is very rough with him at home.

When she is among people who look down on her, she takes it out on him."

That night after dinner they did not go for their usual walk, since the weather was so bleak, but sat by the fire listening to the rattle of the sleet on the windows.

"Papa," said Cécile, "shall you have a mass said for poor Bichet this year, as always?"

"Yes, on the tenth of November, the day on which he was hanged."

This mass Auclair had said at the Récollets' chapel where Count Frontenac heard mass every morning.

"Please tell me about Bichet again, and it will be fresh in my mind when I go to the mass."

"It will not keep you awake, as it did the first time I told you? We must not grieve about these things that happened long ago, — and this happened when the Count was in Canada the first time, while your grandfather and grandmother were both living.

"Poor old Bichet had lodged in our cellar since I was a boy. He was a knife-grinder and used to go out every day with his wheel on his back, and he picked up a few sous at his trade. But he could never have kept himself in shoes, having to walk so much, if your grandfather had not given him his old ones. He paid us nothing for his lodging, of course. He had his bed on the floor in a dry corner of our cellar, where the sirops and elixirs were kept. In very cold weather your grandmother would put a couple of bricks among the coals when she was getting supper, and old Bichet would take these hot bricks down and put them in his bed. And she often saved a cup of hot soup and a piece of bread for the old man and let him eat them in the warm kitchen, for he was very neat and cleanly. When I had any spending-money, or when I was given a fee for carrying medicines to some house in the neighbourhood, I always saved a little for the old knife-grinder. He was reserved and uncomplaining and never inflicted his troubles upon us, though he must have had many. On Saturdays, when your grandmother cooked a joint and had a big fire, she used to heat a kettle of water for him, and he carried it down to his corner and washed himself. He was a Christian and went to mass. He was a kind man, gentle to creatures below him, — for there were those even worse off.

"Now, on the rue du Figuier stood a house that had long been closed, for the family had gone to live at Fontainebleau, and the empty coach-house was used as a store-room for old pieces of furniture. The care-taker was a careless fellow who went out to drink with his cronies and left the place unguarded. In the coach-house were two brass kettles which had lain there for many years, doing nobody any good. Bichet must have seen them often, as he went in and out to sharpen the care-taker's carving-knife.

"One night, when this fellow was carousing, Bichet carried off those two pots. He took them to an iron-monger and sold them. Nobody would ever have missed them; but Bichet had an enemy. Near us there lived a degenerate, half-witted boy of a cruel disposition. He tortured street cats, and even sparrows when he could catch them. Old Bichet had more than once caught him at his tricks and reproved him and set his victims at liberty. That boy was cunning, and he used to spy on Bichet. He saw him carrying off those brass kettles and reported him to the police. Bichet was seized in the street, when he was out with his grindstone, and taken to the Châtelet. He confessed at once and told where he had sold the pots. But that was not enough for the officers; they put him to torture and made him confess to a lifetime of crime; to having stolen from us and from the Frontenac house — which he had never done.

"Your grandfather and I hurried to the prison to speak for him. Your grandfather told them that a man so old and infirm would admit anything under fright and anguish, not knowing what he said; that a confession obtained under torture was not true evidence. This infuriated the Judge. If we would take oath that the prisoner had never stolen anything from us, they would put him into the strappado again and make him correct his confession. We saw that the only thing we could do for our old lodger was to let him pass quickly. Luckily for Bichet, the prison was overcrowded, and he was hanged the next morning.

"Your grandmother never got over it. She had for a long while struggled with asthma every winter, and that year when the asthma came on, she ceased to struggle. She said she had no wish to live longer in a world where such cruelties could happen."

"And I am like my grandmother," cried Cécile, catching her father's hand. "I do not want to live there. I had rather stay in Quebec always! Nobody is tortured here, except by the Indians, in the woods, and they know no better. But why does the King allow such things, when they tell us he is a kind King?"

"It is not the King, my dear, it is the Law. The Law is to protect property, and it thinks too much of property. A couple of brass pots, an old saddle, are reckoned worth more than a poor man's life. Christ would have forgiven Bichet, as He did the thief on the cross. We must think of him in paradise, where no law can touch him. I believe that harmless old man is in paradise long ago, and when I have a mass said for him every year, it is more for my own satisfaction than for his. I should like him to know, too, that our family remembers him."

"And I, Father, as long as I live, I will always have a mass said for Bichet on the day he died."

VI

O N All Souls' Day Cécile went to church all day long; in the morning to the Ursuline chapel, in the afternoon to the Hôtel Dieu, and last of all down to the Church of Notre Dame de la Victoire to pray for her mother in the very spot where Madame Auclair had always knelt at mass. All the churches were full of sorrowful people; Cécile met them coming and going, and greeted them with lowered eyes and subdued voice, as was becoming. But she herself was not sorrowful, though she supposed she was.

The devotions of the day had begun an hour after midnight. Old Bishop Laval had no thought that anyone should forget the solemn duties of the time. He was at his post at one o'clock in the morning to ring the

Cathedral bell, and from then on until early mass he rang it every hour. It called out through the intense silence of streets where there were no vehicles to rumble, but only damp vapours from the river to make sound more intense and startling, to give it overtones and singular reverberations.

> *"Priez pour les Morts,*
> *Vous qui reposez,*
> *Priez pour les tré-pas-sés!"*

it seemed to say, as if the exacting old priest himself were calling. One had scarcely time to murmur a prayer and turn over in one's warm bed, before the bell rang out again.

At twelve years it is impossible to be sad on holy days, even on a day of sorrow; at that age the dark things, death, bereavement, suffering, have only a dramatic value, — seem but strong and moving colours in the grey stretch of time.

On such solemn days all the stories of the rock came to life for Cécile; the shades of the early martyrs and great missionaries drew close about her. All the miracles that had happened there, and the dreams that had been dreamed, came out of the fog; every spire, every ledge and pinnacle, took on the splendour of legend. When one passed by the Jesuits', those solid walls seemed sentinelled by a glorious company of martyrs, martyrs who were explorers and heroes as well; at the Hôtel Dieu, Mother Catherine de Saint-Augustin and her story rose up before one; at the Ursulines', Marie de l'Incarnation overshadowed the living.

At Notre Dame de la Victoire one remembered the miraculous preservation for which it had been named, when this little church, with the banner of the Virgin floating from its steeple, had stood untouched through Sir William Phips's bombardment, though every heretic gun was aimed at it. Cécile herself could remember that time very well; the Lower Town had been abandoned, and she and her mother, with the other women and children, were hidden in the cellars of the Ursuline convent. Even there they were not out of gun range; a shell had fallen into the court just as Sister Agatha was crossing it, and had taken off the skirt of her apron, though the Sister herself was not harmed.

To the older people of Kebec, All Souls' was a day of sad remembrance. Their minds went back to churches and cemeteries far away. Now the long closed season was upon them, and there would be no letters, no word of any kind from France for seven, perhaps eight, months. The last letters that came in the autumn always brought disturbing news to one household or another;

word that a mother was failing, that a son had been wounded in the wars, that a sister had gone into a decline. Friends at home seemed to forget how the Canadians would have these gloomy tidings to brood upon all the long winter and the long spring, so that many a man and woman dreaded the arrival of those longed-for summer ships.

Fears for the sick and old so far away, sorrow for those who died last year — five years ago — many years ago, — memories of families once together and now scattered; these things hung over the rock of Kebec on this day of the dead like the dark fogs from the river. The cheerful faces were those in the convents. The Ursulines and the Hospitalières, indeed, were scarcely exiles. When they came across the Atlantic, they brought their family with them, their kindred, their closest friends. In whatever little wooden vessel they had laboured across the sea, they carried all; they brought to Canada the Holy Family, the saints and martyrs, the glorious company of the Apostles, the heavenly host.

Courageous these Sisters were, accepting good and ill fortune with high spirit, — with humour, even. They never vulgarly exaggerated hardships and dangers. They had no hours of nostalgia, for they were quite as near the realities of their lives in Quebec as in Dieppe or Tours. They were still in their accustomed place in the world of the mind (which for each of us is the only world), and they had the same well-ordered universe about them: this all-important earth, created by God for a great purpose, the sun which He made to light it by day, the moon which He made to light it by night, — and the stars, made to beautify the vault of heaven like frescoes, and to be a clock and compass for man. And in this safe, lovingly arranged and ordered universe (not too vast, though nobly spacious), in this congenial universe, the drama of man went on at Quebec just as at home, and the Sisters played their accustomed part in it. There was sin, of course, and there was punishment after death; but there was always hope, even for the most depraved; and for those who died repentant, the Sisters' prayers could do much, — no one might say how much.

So the nuns, those who were cloistered and those who came and went about the town, were always cheerful, never lugubrious. Their voices, even when they spoke to one through the veiled grille, were pleasant and inspiriting to hear. Most of them spoke good French, some the exquisite French of Tours. They conversed blithely, elegantly. When, on parting from a stranger, a Sister said pleasantly: "I hope we shall meet in heaven," that meant nothing doleful, — it meant a happy appointment, for tomorrow, perhaps!

Inferretque deos Latio. When an adventurer carries his gods with him into a remote and savage country, the colony he founds will, from the beginning, have graces, traditions, riches of the mind and spirit. Its history will shine with bright incidents, slight, perhaps, but precious, as in life itself, where the great matters are often as worthless as astronomical distances, and the trifles dear as the heart's blood.

VII

A HEAVY snowfall in December meant that winter had come, — the deepest reality of Canadian life. The snow fell all through the night of St. Nicholas' Day, but morning broke brilliant and clear, without a wisp of fog, and when one stepped out of the door, the sunlight on the glittering terraces of rock was almost too intense to be borne; one closed one's eyes and seemed to swim in throbbing red. Before noon there was a little thaw, the snow grew soft on top. But as the day wore on, a cold wind came up and the surface froze, to the great delight of the children of Quebec. By three o'clock a crowd of them were coasting down the steep hill named for the Holy Family, among them Cécile and her protégé. Before she and her father had finished their déjeuner, Jacques had appeared at the shop door, wearing an expectant, hopeful look unusual to him. Cécile remembered that she had promised to take him coasting on her sled when the first snow came. She unfastened his ragged jacket and buttoned him into an old fur coat that she had long ago outgrown. Her mother had put it away in one of the chests upstairs, not because she expected ever to have another child, but because all serviceable things deserve to be taken care of.

When they reached the coasting-hill, the sun was already well down the western sky (it would set by four o'clock), and the light on the snow was more orange than golden; the long, steep street and the little houses on either side were a cold blue, washed over with rose-colour. They went down double, —Jacques sat in front, and Cécile, after she had given the sled a running start, dropped on the board behind him. Every time they reached the bottom, they trudged back up the hill to the front of the Cathedral, where the street began.

When the sun had almost sunk behind the black ridges of the western forest, Cécile and Jacques sat down on the Cathedral steps to eat their goûter. While they sat there, the other children began to go home, and the air grew colder. Now they had the hill all to themselves, — and this was the most beautiful part of the afternoon. They thought they would like to go down once more. With a quick push-off their sled shot down through constantly changing colour; deeper and deeper into violet, blue, purple, until at the bottom it was almost black. As they climbed up again, they watched the last flames of orange light burn off the high points of the rock. The slender spire of the Récollet chapel, up by the Château, held the gleam longest of all.

Cécile saw that Jacques was cold. They were not far from Noël Pommier's door, so she said they would go in and get warm.

The cobbler had pulled his bench close to the window and was making the most of the last daylight. Cécile begged him not to get up.

"We have only come in to get warm, Monsieur Pommier."

"Very good. You know the way. Come here, my boy, let me see whether your shoes keep the snow out." He reached for Jacques's foot, felt the leather, and nodded. Cécile passed into the room behind the shop, called to Madame Pommier in her kitchen, and asked if they might sit by her fire.

Cécile and Jacques

"Certainly, my dear, find a chair. And little Jacques may have my footstool; it is just big enough for him. Noël," she called, "come put some wood on the fire, these children are frozen." She came in bringing two squares of maple sugar—and a towel for Jacques to wipe his fingers on. He took the sugar and thanked her, but she saw that his eyes were fixed upon a dark corner of the room where a little copper lamp was burning before some coloured pictures. "That is my chapel, Jacques. You see, being lame, I do not get to mass very often, so I have a little chapel of my own, and the lamp burns night and day, like the sanctuary lamp. There is the Holy Mother and Child, and Saint Joseph, and on the other side are Sainte Anne and Saint Joachim. I am especially devoted to the Holy Family."

Drawn out by something in her voice, Jacques ventured a question.

"Is that why this is called Holy Family Hill, madame?"

Madame Pommier laughed and stooped to pat his head. "Quite the other way about, my boy! I insisted upon living here because the hill bore that name. My husband was for settling in the Basse Ville, thinking it would be better for his trade. But we have not starved here; those for whom the street was named have looked out for us, maybe. When we first came to this country, I was especially struck by the veneration in which the Holy Family was held in Kebec, and I found it was so all out through the distant parishes. I never knew its like at home. Monseigneur Laval himself has told me that there is no other place in the world where the people are so devoted to the Holy Family as here in our own Canada. It is something very special to us."

Cécile liked to think they had things of their own in Canada. The martyrdoms of the early Church which she read about in her *Lives of the Saints* never seemed to her half so wonderful or so terrible as the martyrdoms of Father Brébeuf, Father Lalemant, Father Jogues, and their intrepid companions. To be thrown into the Rhone or the Moselle, to be decapitated at Lyon,— what was that to the tortures the Jesuit missionaries endured at the hands of the Iroquois, in those savage, interminable forests? And could the devotion of Sainte Geneviève or Sainte Philomène be compared to that of Mother Catherine de Saint-Augustin or Mother Marie de l'Incarnation?

"My child, I believe you are sleepy," said Madame Pommier presently, when both her visitors had been silent a long while. She liked her friends to be entertaining.

Cécile and Jacques

Cécile started out of her reverie. "No, madame, but I was thinking of a surprise I have at home, and perhaps I had better tell you about it now. You remember my Aunt Clothilde? I am sure my mother often talked to you of her. Last summer she sent me a box on *La Licorne:* a large wooden box, with a letter telling me not to open it. We must not open it until the day before Christmas, because it is a crèche; so, you see, we shall have a Holy Family, too. And we have been hoping that on Christmas Eve, before the midnight mass, Monsieur Noël will bring you to see it. You have not been in our house, you know, since my mother died."

"Noël, my son, what do you say to that?"

The cobbler had come in from the shop to light his candle at the fire.

"The invitation is for you too, Monsieur Noël, from my father."

The cobbler smiled and stood with the stump of candle in his hand before bending down to the blaze.

"That can be managed, and my thanks to monsieur your father. If there is snow, I will push my mother down in her sledge, and if the ground is naked, I will carry her on my back. She is no great weight."

"I shall like to see the inside of your house again, Cécile. I miss it. I have not been there since that time when your mother was ill, and Madame de Champigny sent her carriage to convey me."

Cécile remembered the time very well. It was after old Madame Pommier was crippled; Madame Auclair had long been too ill to leave the house. There was then only one closed carriage in Quebec, and that belonged to Madame de Champigny, wife of the Intendant. In some way she heard that the apothecary's sick wife longed to see her old friend, and she sent her *carrosse* to take Madame Pommier to the Auclairs'. It was a mark of the respect in which the cobbler and his mother were held in the community.

When Jacques and Cécile ran out into the cold again, from the houses along the tilted street the evening candlelight was already shining softly. Up at the top of the hill, behind the Cathedral, that second afterglow, which often happens in Quebec, had come on more glorious than the first. All the western sky, which had been hard and clear when the sun sank, was now throbbing with fiery vapours, like rapids of clouds; and between, the sky shone with a blue to ravish the heart, — that limpid, celestial, holy blue that is only seen when the light is golden.

"Are you tired, Jacques?"

"A little, my legs are," he admitted.

"Get on the sled and I will pull you up. See, there's the evening star — how near it looks! Jacques, don't you love winter?" She put the sled-rope under her arms, gave her weight to it, and began to climb. A feeling came over her that there would never be anything better in the world for her than this; to be pulling Jacques on her sled, with the tender, burning sky before her, and on each side, in the dusk, the kindly lights from neighbours' houses. If the Count should go back with the ships next summer, and her father with him, how could she bear it, she wondered. On a foreign shore, in a foreign city (yes, for her a foreign shore), would not her heart break for just this? For this rock and this winter, this feeling of being in one's own place, for the soft content of pulling Jacques up Holy Family Hill into paler and paler levels of blue air, like a diver coming up from the deep sea.

VIII

On the morning of the twenty-fourth of December Cécile lay snug in her trundle-bed, while her father lit the fires and prepared the chocolate. Although the heavy red curtains had not yet been drawn back, she

knew that it was snowing; she had heard the crunch
of fresh snow under the Pigeon boy's feet when he
brought the morning loaf to the kitchen door. Even
before that, when the bell rang for five o'clock mass, she
knew by its heavy, muffled tone that the air was thick
with snow and that it was not very cold. Whenever she
heard the early bell, it was as if she could see the old
Bishop with his lantern at the end of the bell-rope, and
the cold of the church up there made her own bed seem
the warmer and softer. In winter the old man usually
carried a little basin as well as his lantern. It was his
custom to take the bowl of holy water from the font in
the evening, carry it into his kitchen, and put it on the
back of the stove, where enough warmth would linger
through the night to keep it from freezing. Then, in the
morning, those who came to early mass would not have
a mere lump of ice to peck at. Monseigneur de Laval
was very particular about the consecrated oils and the
holy water; it was not enough for him that people
should merely go through the forms.

Cécile did not always waken at the first bell, which
rang in the coldest hour of the night, but when she did,
she felt a peculiar sense of security, as if there must be
powerful protection for Kebec in such steadfastness,
and the new day, which was yet darkness, was beginning

as it should. The punctual bell and the stern old Bishop who rang it began an orderly procession of activities and held life together on the rock, though the winds lashed it and the billows of snow drove over it.

With the sound of the crackling fire a cool, mysterious fragrance of the forest, very exciting because it was under a roof, came in from the kitchen, — the breath of all the fir boughs and green moss that Cécile and Blinker had brought in yesterday from the Jesuits' wood. Today they would unpack the crèche from France, — the box that had come on *La Licorne* in midsummer and had lain upstairs unopened for all these months.

Auclair brought the chocolate and placed it on a little table beside his daughter's bed. They always breakfasted like this in winter, while the house was getting warm. This morning they had finally to decide where they would set out the crèche. Weeks ago they had agreed to arrange it in the deep window behind the sofa, — but then the sofa would have to be put on the other side of the room! This morning they found the thought of moving the sofa, where Madame Auclair used so often to recline, unendurable. It would quite destroy the harmony of their salon. The room, the house indeed, seemed to cling about that sofa as a centre.

125

There was another window in the room, — seldom uncurtained, because it opened directly upon the side wall of the baker's house, and the outlook was uninteresting. It was narrow, but Auclair said he could remedy that. As soon as his shop was put in order, he would construct a shelf in front of the window-sill, but a little lower; then the scene could be arranged in two terraces, as was customary at home.

Cécile spent the morning covering the window and the new shelf with moss and fir branches until it looked like a corner in the forest, and at noon she waylaid Blinker, just getting up from his bed behind the baker's ovens, and sent him to go and hunt for Jacques.

When Blinker returned with the boy, he himself looked in through the door so wistfully that Cécile asked him to come and open the box for her in the kitchen. There were a great number of little figures in the crate, each wrapped in a sheath of straw. As Blinker took them one at a time out of the straw and handed them to Cécile, he kept exclaiming: "Regardez, ma'm'selle, un beau petit âne!" ... "Voilà, le beau mouton!" Cécile had never seen him come so far out of his shell; she had supposed that his shrinking sullenness was a part of him, like his crooked eyes or his red hair. When all the figures were unwrapped and placed on the dining-table in the salon,

Blinker gathered up the straw and carried it with the crate into the cellar. She had thought that would be the last of him, but when he came back and stood again in the doorway, she hadn't the heart to send him away. She asked him to come in and sit down by the fire. Her mother had never done that, but today there seemed no way out of it. The fête which she meant so especially for Jacques, turned out to be even more for Blinker.

Jacques, indeed, was so bewildered as to seem apathetic, and was afraid to touch anything. Only when Cécile directed him would he take up one of the figures from the table and carry it carefully to the window where she was making the scene. The Holy Family must be placed first, under a little booth of fir branches. The Infant was not in His Mother's arms, of course, but lay rosy and naked in a little straw-lined manger, in which he had crossed the ocean. The Blessed Virgin wore no halo, but a white scarf over her head. She looked like a country girl, very naïve, seated on a stool, with her knees well apart under her full skirt, and very large feet. Saint Joseph, a grave old man in brown, with a bald head and wrinkled brow, was placed opposite her, and the ox and the ass before the manger.

"Those are all that go inside the stable," Cécile explained, "except the two angels. We must put them behind the manger; they are still watching over Him."

"Is that the stable, Cécile? I think it's too pretty for a stable," Jacques observed.

"It's a little *cabine* of branches, like those the first missionaries built down by Notre Dame des Anges, when they landed here long ago. They used to say the mass in a little shelter like that, made of green fir boughs."

Jacques touched one of the unassorted figures on the table with the tip of his finger. "Cécile, what are those animals?"

"Why, those are the camels, Jacques. Did you never see pictures of them? The three Kings came on camels, because they can go a long time without water and carry heavy loads. They carried the gold and frankincense and myrrh."

"I don't think I know about the Kings and the Shepherds very well," Jacques sighed. "I wish you would tell me."

While she placed the figures, Cécile began the story, and Jacques listened as if he had never heard it before. There was another listener, by the fireplace behind her, and she had entirely forgotten him until, with a sniffling sound, Blinker suddenly got up and went out through the kitchen, wiping his nose on his sleeve. Then Jacques noticed how dusky it had grown in the room; the window behind the sofa was a square of dull grey, like a hole in the wall of the house. He caught up his cap and ran out through the shop, calling back: "Oh, I am late!"

Jacques had been gone only a few minutes when Giorgio, the drummer boy from the Château, came in to see the crèche, and to bid Cécile good-bye for three days, as the Count had let him off to go home to his family on the Île d'Orléans. He had left his drum in the guard-house, and already he felt free. He would walk the seven miles up to Montmorency (perhaps he would be lucky enough to catch a ride in some farmer's sledge for part of the way), then cross the river on the ice. The north channel had been frozen hard for several weeks now. He would have a long walk after he got over to the island, too; but even if the night were dark, he knew the way, and he would get there in time to hear mass at his own paroisse. After mass his family would make réveillon, — music and dancing, and a supper with blood sausages and pickled pigs' feet and dainties of that sort.

"And before daybreak, mademoiselle, my grandfather will play the Alpine horn. He always does that on Christmas morning. If you were awake, you would hear it even over here. Such a beautiful sound it has, and the old man plays so true!"

Georges bought some cloves and bay-leaves for his

mother (he had just been paid, and rattled the coins in his pocket), then started up the hill with such a happy face that Cécile wished she were going with him, over those seven snowy miles to Montmorency.

"He will almost certainly catch a ride," her father told her. "Even on the river there will be sledges coming and going tonight."

IX

THAT evening, soon after the dinner-table was cleared, the Auclairs heard a rapping at the shop door and went out to receive Madame Pommier in her chair on runners, very like the sledges in which great ladies used to travel at home. Her son lifted her out in all her wrappings and carried her into the salon, where the apothecary's arm-chair was set for her. But before she would accept this seat of honour, she must hobble all over the house to satisfy herself that things were kept just as they used to be in Madame Auclair's time. She found everything the same, she said, even to Blinker, having his sip of brandy in the kitchen.

After they had settled down before the fire to wait for the Pigeons, who were always late, Jacques Gaux came hurrying in through the shop, looking determined and excited. He forgot to speak to the visitors and went straight up to Cécile, holding out something wrapped in a twist of paper, such as the merchants used for small purchases.

"I have a surprise for you," he said. "It is for the crèche, for the little Jesus."

When she took off the paper, she held in her hand Jacques's well-known beaver.

"Oh, Jacques, how nice of you! I don't believe there was ever a beaver in a crèche before." She was a little perplexed; the animal was so untraditional — what was she to do with him?

"He isn't new," Jacques went on anxiously. "He's just my little old beaver the sailor made me, but he could keep the baby warm. I take him to bed with me when I'm cold sometimes, and he keeps me warm."

Madame Pommier's sharp ears had overheard this conversation, and she touched Cécile with the end of her crutch. "Certainly, my dear, put it there with the lambs, before the manger. Our Lord died for Canada as well as for the world over there, and the beaver is our very special animal."

Immediately Madame Pigeon and her six children arrived. Auclair brought out his best liqueurs, and the

Pommiers and Pigeons, being from the same parish in Rouen, began recalling old friends at home. Cécile was kept busy filling little glasses, but she noticed that Jacques was content, standing beside the crèche like a sentinel, paying no heed to the Pigeon children or anyone else, quite lost in the satisfaction of seeing his beaver placed in a scene so radiant. Before the evening was half over, he started up suddenly and began looking for his coat and cap. Cécile followed him into the shop.

"Don't you want your beaver, Jacques? Or will you leave him until Epiphany?"

He looked up at her, astonished, a little hurt, and quickly thrust his hands behind him. "Non, c'est pour toujours," he said decisively, and went out of the door.

"See, madame," Madame Pommier was whispering to Madame Pigeon, "we have a bad woman amongst us, and one of her clients makes a toy for her son, and he gives it to the Holy Child for a birthday present. That is very nice."

"C'est ça, madame, c'est ça," said matter-of-fact Madame Pigeon, quite liking the idea, now that her attention was called to it.

By eleven o'clock the company had become a little heavy from the heat of the fire and the good wine from the Count's cellar, and everyone felt a need of the crisp out-of-doors air. The weather had changed at noon, and now the stars were flashing in a clear sky, — a sky almost over-jewelled on that glorious night. The three families agreed that it would be well to start for the church very early and get good places. The Cathedral would be full to the doors tonight. Monseigneur de Saint-Vallier was to say the mass, and the old Bishop would be present, with a great number of clergy, and the Seminarians were to sing the music. Monseigneur de Saint-Vallier would doubtless wear the aube of rich lace given him by Madame de Maintenon for his consecration at Saint-Sulpice, in Paris, ten years ago. In one matter he and the old Bishop always agreed; that the services of the Church should be performed in Quebec as elaborately, as splendidly, as anywhere else in the world. For many years Bishop Laval had kept himself miserably poor to make the altar and the sacristy rich.

After everyone had had a last glass of liqueur, Madame Pommier was carried out to her sledge and tucked under her bearskin. The company proceeded slowly; pushing the chair up the steep curves of Mountain Hill and around the Récollet chapel, over fresh snow that had not packed, was a little difficult. When they reached the top of the rock, many houses were alight.

133

Across the white ledges that sloped like a vast natural stairway down to the Cathedral, black groups were moving, families and friends in little flocks, all going toward the same goal, — the doors of the church, wide open and showing a ruddy vault in the blue darkness.

BOOK III

The Long Winter

BOOK THREE

The Long Winter

I

ONE morning between Christmas and New Year's
Day a man still young, of a handsome but unstable countenance, clad in a black cassock with violet piping, and a rich fur mantle, entered the apothecary shop, greeted the proprietor politely, and asked for four boxes of sugared lemon peel.

It was not the young Bishop's custom to do his shopping himself; he sent his valet. This was the first time he had ever come inside the pharmacy. Auclair took off his apron as a mark of respect to a distinguished visitor, but replied firmly that, much to his regret, he had only three boxes left, and one of them he meant to send as a New Year's greeting to Mother Juchereau, at the Hôtel Dieu. He would be happy to supply Monseigneur de Saint-Vallier with the other two; and he had several boxes of apricots put down in sugar, if they would be of any use to him. Monseigneur declared they would do very well, paid for them, and said he would carry them away himself. Auclair protested that he or his little daughter could leave them at the Palace. But no, the Bishop insisted upon carrying his parcel. As he did not leave the shop at once, Auclair begged him to be seated.

Saint-Vallier sat down and threw back his fur mantle. "Have you by any chance seen Monseigneur de Laval of late?" he inquired. "I am deeply concerned about his health."

"No, Monseigneur, I have not seen him since the mass on Christmas Eve. But the bell has been ringing every morning as usual."

Saint-Vallier's arched eyebrows rose still higher, and he made a graceful, conciliatory gesture with his hand. "Ah, his habits, you know; one cannot interfere with them! But his valet told mine that the ulcer on his master's leg had broken out again, and that seems to me dangerous."

"I am sorry to hear it," said Auclair. "It is hardly dangerous, but painful and distressing."

"Especially so, since he will not remain in bed, and conceals the extent of his suffering even from his own Seminarians." The Bishop paused a moment, then continued in a tone so confidential as to be flattering. "I have been wondering, Monsieur Auclair, whether, provided we could obtain his consent, you would be willing to try a cauterization of the arm, to draw the inflammation away from the affected part. This was done with great success for Père La Chaise, the King's confessor, who had an ulcer between the toes while I was in office at Versailles."

"That was probably a form of gout," Auclair observed. "Monseigneur de Laval's affliction is quite different. He suffers from enlarged and congested veins in the leg. Such ulcers are hard to heal, but they are seldom fatal."

"But why not at least try the simple remedy which was so beneficial in the case of Père La Chaise?" urged the Bishop. There was a shallow brilliance in his large fine eyes which made Auclair antagonistic.

"Because, Monseigneur," he said firmly, "I do not believe in it; and because it has been tried already. Two years ago, when you were in France, Doctor Beaudoin made a cauterization upon Monseigneur de Laval, and he has since told me that he believes it was useless."

The Bishop looked thoughtfully about at the white jars on the shelves. "You are very advanced in your theories of medicine, are you not, Monsieur Auclair?"

"On the contrary, I am very old-fashioned. I think the methods of the last century better than those of the present time."

"Then you do not believe in progress?"

"Change is not always progress, Monseigneur." Auclair spoke quietly, but there was meaning in his tone. Saint-Vallier made some polite inquiry about the condition of old Doctor Beaudoin, and took his leave. His call, Auclair suspected, was one of the overtures he occasionally made to people who were known partisans of old Bishop Laval.

During the stay in France from which he had lately returned, Monseigneur de Saint-Vallier had induced the King to reverse entirely Laval's system for the training and government of the Canadian clergy, thus defeating the dearest wishes of the old man's heart and undoing the devoted labour of twenty years. Everything that made Laval's Seminary unique and specially fitted to the needs of the colony had been wiped out. His system of a movable clergy, sent hither and thither out among the parishes at the Bishop's discretion and always returning to the Seminary as their head and centre, had been changed by royal edict to the plan of appointing curés to permanent livings, as in France, — a method ill fitted to a new, wild country where within a year the population of any parish might be reduced by half. The Seminary, which Laval had made a thing of power and the centre of ecclesiastical authority, a chap-

ter, almost an independent order, was now reduced to
the state of a small school for training young men for
the priesthood.

These were some of the griefs that made the old
Bishop bear so mournful a countenance. The wilfulness
of his successor (chosen by himself, he must always bitterly remember!) went even further; Saint-Vallier had
taken away books and vases and furniture from the Seminary to enrich his new Palace. It was whispered that he
had made his Palace so large because he intended to take
away the old Bishop's Seminarians and transfer them to
the episcopal residence, to have them under his own
eye. If this were done, Bishop Laval would be left living
in the Priests' House, guarding a lofty building of long,
echoing corridors and empty dormitories, round a de-
serted courtyard where the grass would soon be growing between the stones. Monseigneur Laval's friends
could but hope that de Saint-Vallier would be off for
France again before he carried out this threat.

Saint-Vallier was a man of contradictions, and they
were stamped upon his face. One saw there something
slightly hysterical, and something uncertain, — though
his manner was imperious, and his administration had
been arrogant and despotic. Auclair had once remarked
to the Count that the new Bishop looked less like a

churchman than like a courtier. "Or an actor," the
Count replied with a shrug. Large almond-shaped eyes
under low-growing brown hair and delicate eyebrows, a
long, sharp nose — and then the lower part of his face
diminished, like the neck of a pear. His mouth was large
and well shaped, but seldom in repose; his chin narrow,
receding, with a dimple at the end. He had a dark skin
and flashing white teeth like an Italian, — indeed, his
face recalled the portraits of eccentric Florentine nobles. He was still only forty-four; he had been Bishop of
Quebec now twelve years, — and seven of them had
been spent in France!

Auclair had never liked de Saint-Vallier. He did not
doubt the young Bishop's piety, but he very much
doubted his judgment. He was rash and precipitate, he
was volatile. He acted too often without counting the
cost, from some dazzling conception, — one could not
say from impulse, for impulses are from the heart. He
liked to reorganize and change things for the sake of
change, to make a fine gesture. He destroyed the old
before he had clearly thought out the new. When he
first came to Canada, he won all hearts by his splendid
charities; but he went back to France leaving the Seminary many thousand francs in debt as the result of his
generous disbursements, and the old Bishop had to pay

this debt out of the Seminary revenues. For years now, he had seemed feverishly determined to undo whatever he could of the old Bishop's work. This was the more galling to the old man because he himself had gone to France and chosen de Saint-Vallier and recommended him to Rome. Saint-Vallier had at first exhibited the most delicate consideration for his aged predecessor, but this attitude lasted only a short while. He was as changeable and fickle as a woman. Indeed, he had received a large part of his training under a woman, though by no means a fickle or capricious one.

When Jean Baptiste de la Croix de Chevrières de Saint-Vallier came to Court in the capacity of the King's almoner, Madame de Maintenon was past the age of youthful folly, — if indeed she had ever known such an age. (A poor girl from the West Indies, landing penniless in France with all her possessions in a band-box, she had little time for follies, except such as helped her to get on in the world.) The young priest who was one day to be the second Bishop of Quebec knew her only after she had become the grave and far-seeing woman who so greatly influenced the King for the last thirty years of his reign.

Saint-Vallier was the seventh child of a noble family of Dauphiné. His eldest brother, Comte de Saint-

Vallier, was Captain of the King's Guard, and secured
for the young priest the appointment of *Aumônier ordinaire* to the King when he was but twenty-three years
of age. He retained that office for nearly ten years,
and was constantly in accord with Madame de Maintenon in emptying the King's purse for worthy charities. Saint-Vallier was by no means without enemies at
Court. The clergy and even the Archbishop of Paris
disliked him. They considered that he made his piety
too conspicuous and was lacking in good taste. His oval
face, with the bloom of youth upon it, his beautiful eyes,
full of humility and scorn at the same time, were seen
too much and too often. He had a hundred ways of
making himself stand out from the throng, and his exceptional piety was like a reproach to those of the
clergy who were more conventional and perhaps more
worldly. He obtained from the King special permission
to wear at Court the long black gown, which at that
time was not worn by the priests at Versailles. So at-
tired, he was more conspicuous than courtiers the most
richly apparelled. His fellow abbés found de Saint-
Vallier's acts of humility undignified, and his brother,
the Captain of the Guard, found them ridiculous. One
day the Captain met the Abbé following the Sacrament
through the street, ringing a little hand-bell. The Cap-

tain awaited his brother's return to the Palace and told him angrily that his conduct was unworthy of his family, and that he had better retire to La Trappe, where his piety would be without an audience. But to be without an audience was the last thing the young Abbé desired.

Nevertheless, in his own way he was a sincere man. He refused the rich and honourable bishopric of Tours, repeatedly offered him by the King, and accepted the bishopric of Quebec, — the poorest and most comfortless honour the Crown had to offer.

By the time de Saint-Vallier made his third trip back to France, the King knew very well that he was not much wanted in Canada; every boat brought complaints of his arrogance and his rash impracticality. The King could not unmake a bishop, once he was consecrated, but he could detain him in France, — and that he did, for three years. During de Saint-Vallier's long absences in Europe his duties devolved upon Monseigneur de Laval. There was no one else in Canada who could ordain priests, administer the sacrament of confirmation, consecrate the holy oils. Though in the performance of these duties the old Bishop had to make long journeys in canoes and sledges, very fatiguing at his age, he undertook them without a murmur. He was glad to take up again the burdens he had once so gladly laid down.

II

AFTER Epiphany, Auclair was away from home a great deal. The old chirurgien Gervais Beaudoin was ill, and the apothecary went to see him every afternoon, leaving Cécile to tend the shop. When he was at home, he was much occupied in making cough-syrups from pine tops, and from horehound and honey with a little laudanum; or he was compounding tonics, and liniments for rheumatism. The months that were dull for the merchants were the busiest for him. He and his daughter seldom went abroad together now, but their weekly visit to the Hôtel Dieu they still managed to make. One evening at dinner, after one of these visits, Cécile spoke of an incident that Mother Juchereau had related to her in the morning.

"Father, did you ever hear that once long ago, when an English sailor lay sick at the Hôtel Dieu, Mother Catherine de Saint-Augustin ground up a tiny morsel of bone from Father Brébeuf's skull and mixed it in his gruel, and it made him a Christian?"

Her father looked at her across the table and gave a perplexing chuckle.

"But it is true, certainly? Mother Juchereau told me only today."

"Mother Juchereau and I do not always agree in the matter of remedies, you know. I consider human bones a very poor medicine for any purpose."

"But he was converted, the sailor. He became a Christian."

"Probably Mother de Saint-Augustin's own saintly character, and her kindness to him, had more to do with the Englishman's conversion than anything she gave him in his food."

"Why, Father, Mother Juchereau would be horrified to hear you! There are so many sacred relics, and they are always working cures."

"The sacred relics are all very well, my dear, and I do not deny that they work miracles, — but not through the digestive tract. Mother de Saint-Augustin meant well, but she made a mistake. If she had given her heretic a little more ground bone, she might have killed him."

"Are you sure?"

"I think it probable. It is true that in England, in every apothecary shop, there is a jar full of pulverized human skulls, and that terrible powder is sometimes dispensed in small doses for certain diseases. Even in France it is still to be found in many pharmacies; but it was never sold in our shop, not even in my grandfather's time. He had seen a proof made of that remedy. A long while ago, when Henry of Navarre was besieging Paris, the people held out against him until they starved by hundreds. I have heard my grandfather tell of things too horrible to repeat to you. The famine grew until there was no food at all; people killed each other for a morsel. The bakers shut their shops; there was not a handful of flour left, they had used all the forage meant for beasts; they had made bread of hay and straw, and now that was all gone. Then some of the starving went to the cemetery of the Innocents, where there was a great wall of dry bones, and they ground those bones to powder and make a paste of it and baked it in ovens; and as many as ate of that bread died in agony, as if they had swallowed poison. Indeed, they had swallowed poison."

"But those were ordinary bones, maybe bones of wicked people. That would be different."

"No bones are good to be taken into the stomach, Cécile. God did not intend it. The relics of the saints may work cures at the touch, they may be a protection worn about the neck; those things are outside of my knowledge. But I am the guardian of the stomach, and I would not permit a patient to swallow a morsel of any human remains, not those of Saint Peter himself. There

are enough beautiful stories about Mother de Saint-
Augustin, but this one is not to my liking."

Cécile could only hope it would never happen that
her father and Mother Juchereau would enter into any
discussion of miraculous cures. Her father must be
right; but she felt in her heart that what Mother Juchereau told her had certainly occurred, and the English
sailor had been coverted by Father Brébeuf's bone.

III

"MA'M'SELLE, have you heard the news from
Montreal?"

Blinker had just come in for his soup, and Cécile saw
that he was greatly excited.

No, she had heard nothing; what did he mean?

"Ma'm'selle, there has been a miracle at Montreal.
The recluse has had a visit from the angels, — the night
after Epiphany, when there was the big snow-storm.
That day she broke her spinning-wheel, and in the
night two angels came to her cell and mended it for her.
She saw them."

"How did you hear this, Blinker?"

"Some men got in from Montreal this morning, in

dog-sledges, and they brought the word. They brought letters, too, for the Reverend Mother at the Ursulines'. If you go there, you will likely hear all about it."

"You are sure she saw the angels?"

He nodded. "Yes, when she got up to pray, at midnight. They say her wheel was mended better than a carpenter could do it."

"The men didn't say which angels, Blinker?"

He shook his head. He was just beginning his soup. Cécile dropped into one of the chairs by the table. "Why, one of them might have been Saint Joseph himself; he was a carpenter. But how was it she saw them? You know she keeps her spinning-wheel up in her workroom, over the cell where she sleeps."

"Just so, ma'm'selle, it is just so the men said. She goes into the church to pray every night at midnight, and when she got up on Epiphany night, she saw a light shining from the room overhead, and she went up her little stair to see what was the matter, and there she found the angels."

"Did they speak to her?"

"The men did not say. Maybe the Reverend Mother will know."

"I will go there tomorrow, and I will tell you everything I hear. It's a wonderful thing to happen, so near us — and in that great snow-storm! Don't you like to know that the angels are just as near to us here as they are in France?"

Blinker turned his head, glancing all about the kitchen as if someone might be hiding there, leaned across the table, and said to her in such a mournful way:

"Ma'm'selle, I think they are nearer."

When he had drunk his little glass and gone away for the last time, Cécile went in and told her father the good news from Montreal. He listened with polite interest, but she had of late begun to feel that his appreciation of miracles was not at all what it should be. They were reading Plutarch this winter, and tonight they were in the middle of the life of Alexander the Great, but her thoughts strayed from the text. She made so many mistakes that her father said she must be tired, and, gently taking the book from her, continued the reading himself.

Later, while she was undressing, her father filled the kitchen stove with birch logs to hold the heat well through the night. He blew out the candles, and himself got ready for bed. After he had put on his night-cap and disappeared behind his curtains, Cécile, who had feigned to be asleep, turned over softly to watch the dying fire, and with a sigh abandoned herself to her thoughts. In her mind she went over the whole story of the recluse of Montreal.

Jeanne Le Ber, the recluse, was the only daughter of Jacques Le Ber, the richest merchant of Montreal. When she was twelve years old, her parents had brought her to Quebec and placed her in the Ursuline convent to receive her education. She remained here three years, and that was how she belonged to Quebec as well as to Ville-Marie de Montréal. Sister Anne de Sainte-Rose saw at once that this pupil had a very unusual nature, though her outward demeanour was merely that of a charming young girl. The Sister had told Cécile that in those days Jeanne was never melancholy, but warm and ardent, like her complexion; gracious in her manner, and not at all shy. She was at her ease with strangers, — all distinguished visitors to Montreal were entertained at her father's house. But underneath this exterior of pleasing girlhood, Sister Anne felt something reserved and guarded. While she was at the convent, Jeanne often received gifts and attentions from her father's friends in Quebec; and from home, boxes of sweets and dainties. But everything that was sent her she gave away to her schoolmates, so tactfully that they did not realize she kept nothing for herself.

Jeanne completed her studies at the convent, returned home to Montreal, and was in a manner formally introduced to the world there. Her father was fond of society and lavish in hospitality; proud of his five sons, but especially devoted to his only daughter. He loved to see her in rich apparel, and selected the finest stuffs brought over from France for her. Jeanne wore these clothes to please him, but whenever she put on one of her gay dresses, she wore underneath it a little haircloth shirt next her tender skin.

Soon after Jeanne's return from school her father and uncle gave to the newly-completed parish church of Montreal a rich lamp of silver, made in France, to burn perpetually before the Blessed Sacrament. The Le Bers' house on Saint Paul street was very near the church, and from the window of her upstairs bedroom Jeanne could see at night the red spark of the sanctuary lamp showing in the dark church. When everyone was asleep and the house was still, it was her custom to kneel beside her casement and pray, the while watching that spot of light. "*I will be that lamp,*" she used to whisper. "*I will be that lamp; that shall be my life.*"

Jacques Le Ber announced that his daughter's dowry would be fifty thousand gold écus, and there were many pretendants for her hand. Cécile had often heard it said that the most ardent and most favoured of these was

Auclair's friend Pierre Charron, who still lived next door to the Le Bers in Montreal. He had been Jeanne's playfellow in childhood.

Jeanne's shining in the *beau monde* of Ville-Marie de Montréal was brief. For her the only real world lay within convent walls. She begged to be allowed to take the vows, but her father's despair overcame her wish. Even her spiritual directors, and that noble soldier-priest Dollier de Casson, Superior of the Sulpician Seminary, advised her against taking a step so irrevocable. She at last obtained her parents' consent to imitate the domestic retreat of Sainte Catherine of Siena, and at seventeen took the vow of chastity for five years and immured herself within her own chamber in her father's house. In her vigils she could always look out at the dark church, with the one constant lamp which generous Jacques Le Ber had placed there, little guessing how it might affect his life and wound his heart.

Upon her retirement Jeanne had explained to her family that during the five years of her vow she must on no account speak to or hold communication with them. Her desire was for the absolute solitariness of the hermit's life, the solitude which Sainte Marie l'Égyptienne had gone into the desert of the Thebais to find. Her parents did not believe that a young girl, affectionate and gentle from her infancy, could keep so harsh a rule. But as time went on, their hearts grew heavier. From the day she took her vow, they never had speech with her or saw her face, — never saw her bodily form, except veiled and stealing down the stairway like a shadow on her way to mass. Jacques Le Ber no longer gave suppers on feast-days. He stayed more and more in his counting-room, drove about in his sledge in winter, and cruised in his sloop in summer; avoided the house that had become the tomb of his hopes.

Before her withdrawal Jeanne had chosen an old serving-woman, exceptional for piety, to give her henceforth such service as was necessary. Every morning at a quarter to five this old dame went to Jeanne's door and attended her to church to hear early mass. Many a time Madame Le Ber concealed herself in the dark hallway to see her daughter's muffled figure go by. After the return from mass, the same servant brought Jeanne her food for the day. If any dish of a rich or delicate nature was brought her, she did not eat it, but fasted.

She went always to vespers, and to the high mass on Sundays and feast-days. On such occasions people used to come in from the neighbouring parishes for a glimpse of that slender figure, the richest heiress in Canada, clad in grey serge, kneeling on the floor near the altar, while her family, in furs and velvet, sat in chairs in another part of the church.

At the end of five years Jeanne renewed her vow of seclusion for another five years. During this time her mother died. On her death-bed she sent one of the household to her daughter's door, begging her to come and give her the kiss of farewell.

"Tell her I am praying for her, night and day," was the answer.

When she had been immured within her father's house for almost ten years, Jeanne was able to accomplish a cherished hope; she devoted that *dot*, which no mortal man would ever claim, to build a chapel for the Sisters of the Congregation of the Blessed Virgin. Behind the high altar of this chapel she had a cell constructed for herself. At a solemn ceremony she took the final vows and entered that cell from which she would never come forth alive. Since that time she had been known as la recluse de Ville-Marie.

Jeanne's entombment and her cell were the talk of the province, and in the country parishes where not much happened, still, after two years, furnished matter for conversation and wonder. The cell, indeed, was not one room, but three, one above another, and within them the solitaire carried on an unvarying routine of life. In the basement cubicle was the grille through which she spoke to her confessor, and by means of which she was actually present at mass and vespers, though unseen. There, through a little window, her meagre food was handed to her. The room above was her sleeping-chamber, constructed by the most careful measurements for one purpose; her narrow bed against the wall was directly behind the high altar, and her pillow, when she slept, was only a few inches from the Blessed Sacrament on the other side of the partition.

The upper cell was her atelier, and there she made and embroidered those beautiful altar-cloths and vestments which went out from her stone chamber to churches all over the province: to the Cathedral at Quebec, and to the poor country parishes where the altar and its ministrant were alike needy. She had begun this work years before, in her father's house, and had grown very skilful at it. Old Bishop Laval, so sumptuous in adorning his Cathedral, had more than once expressed admiration for her beautiful handiwork. When her eyes were tired, or when the day was too dark for embroidering, she spun yarn and knitted stockings for the poor.

In her work-room there was a small iron stove with a heap of faggots, and in the most severe cold of winter the recluse lit a little fire, not for bodily comfort, but because her fingers became stiff with the cold and lost their cunning, — indeed, there were sometimes days on which they would actually have frozen at their task. Every night at midnight, winter and summer, Jeanne rose from her cot, dressed herself, descended into her basement room, opened the grille, and went into the church to pray for an hour before the high altar. On bitter nights many a kind soul in Montreal (and on the lonely farms, too) lay awake for a little, listening to the roar of the storm, and wondered how it was with the recluse, under her single coverlid.

She bore the summer's heat as patiently as the winter's cold. Only last July, when the heat lay so heavy in her chamber with its one small window, her confessor urged her to quit her cell for an hour each day after sunset and take the air in the cloister garden, which her window looked out upon.

She replied: *Ah, mon père, ma chambre est mon paradis terrestre; c'est mon centre; c'est mon élément. Il n'y a pas de lieu plus délicieux, ni plus salutaire pour moi; point de Louvre, point de palais, qui me soit plus agréable. Je préfère ma cellule à tout le reste de l'univers.*

For long after the night when Cécile first heard of the angels' visit to Mademoiselle Le Ber, the story was a joy to her. She told it over and over to little Jacques on his rare visits. Throughout February the weather was so bad that Jacques could come only when Blinker (who was always a match for 'Toinette) went down and brought him up Mountain Hill on his back. The snows fell one upon another until the houses were muffled, the streets like tunnels. Between the storms the weather was grey, with armies of dark clouds moving across the wide sky, and the bitter wind always blowing. Quebec seemed shrunk to a mere group of shivering spires; the whole rock looked like one great white church, above the frozen river.

By many a fireside the story of Jeanne Le Ber's spinning-wheel was told and re-told with loving exaggeration during that severe winter. The word of her visit from the angels went abroad over snow-burdened Canada to the remote parishes. Wherever it went, it brought pleasure, as if the recluse herself had sent to all those families whom she did not know some living beauty, — a blooming rose-tree, or a shapely fruit-tree in fruit. Indeed, she sent them an incomparable gift. In the long evenings, when the family had told over their tales of Indian massacres and lost hunters and the almost human intelligence of the beaver, someone would speak the name of Jeanne Le Ber, and it again gave out fragrance.

The people have loved miracles for so many hundred years, not as proof or evidence, but because they are the actual flowering of desire. In them the vague worship and devotion of the simple-hearted assumes a form. From being a shapeless longing, it becomes a beautiful image; a dumb rapture becomes a melody that can be remembered and repeated; and the experience of a moment, which might have been a lost ecstasy, is made an actual possession and can be bequeathed to another.

I V

ONE night in March there was a knock at the apothecary's door, just as he was finishing his dinner. Only sick people, or strangers who were ignorant of his habits, disturbed him at that hour. Peeping out between the cabinets, Cécile saw that the visitor was a thick-set man in moccasins, with a bearskin coat and cap. His long hair and his face covered with beard told that he had come in from the woods.

"Don't you remember me, Monsieur Auclair?" he asked in a low, sad voice. "I am Antoine Frichette; you used to know me."

"It is your beard that changes you, Antoine. Sit down."

"Ah, it is more than that," the man sighed.

"Besides, I thought you were in the Montreal country, — out from the Sault Saint-Louis, wasn't it?"

"Yes, monsieur, I went out there, but I had no luck. My brother-in-law died in the woods, and I got a strain that made me no good, so I came back to live with my sister until I am cured."

"Your brother-in-law? Not Michel Proulx, surely? I am grieved to hear that, Antoine. He cannot well be spared here. We have few such good workmen."

"But you see, monsieur, no building goes on in Kebec in the winter, and there was the chance to make something in the woods. But he is dead, and I am not much better. I got down from Montreal only today, — we had a hard fight coming in this snow. I came to you because I am a sick man. I tore something loose inside me. Look, monsieur, can you do anything for that?" He stood up and unbuttoned his bearskin jacket. A rupture, Auclair saw at once, — and for a woodsman that was almost like a death-sentence.

Yes, he told Frichette, he could certainly do something for him. But first they would be seated more comfortably, and have a talk. He took the poor fellow back into the sitting-room and gave him his own arm-chair by the fire.

"This is my daughter, Cécile, Antoine; you remember her. Now I will give you something to make you feel better at once. This is a very powerful cordial, there are many healing herbs in it, and it will reach the sorest spot in a sick man. Drink it slowly, and then you must tell me about your bad winter."

The woodsman took the little glass between his thick fingers and held it up to the fire-light. "*C'est jolie, la couleur,*" he observed childishly. Presently he slid off his fur jacket and sat in his buckskin shirt and breeches. When he had finished the cordial, his host filled his glass again, and Antoine sighed and looked about him. "*C'est tranquille, chez vous, comme toujours,*" he said with a faint smile. "I bring you a message, monsieur, from Father Hector Saint-Cyr."

"From Father Hector? You have seen him? Come, Cécile, Antoine is going to tell us news of our friend." Auclair rose and poured a little cordial for himself.

"He said he will be here very soon, God willing, while the river is still hard. He had a letter from the new Bishop telling him to come down to Kebec. He asked me to say that he invited himself to dinner with you. He is a man in a thousand, that priest. We have been through something together. But that is a long story."

"Begin at the beginning, Frichette, my daughter and

The Long Winter

I have all evening to listen. So you and Proulx went into the woods, out from the Sault?"

"Yes, we went early in the fall, when the hunting was good, and we took Joseph Choret from Three Rivers. We put by plenty of fish, as soon as it was cold enough to freeze them. We meant to go up into the Nipissing country in the spring, and trade for skins. The Nipissings don't come to the settlements much, and I know a little of their language. We made a good log house in the fall, good enough, but you know what a man my brother-in-law was for hewing; he wasn't satisfied. When the weather kept open, before Christmas, he wanted to put in a board floor. I cannot say how it happened. You know yourself, monsieur, what a man he was with the ax, — he hewed the beams for Notre Dame de la Victoire when he was but a lad, and how many houses in Kebec didn't he hew the beams and flooring for? He could cut better boards with his ax than most men can with a saw. He was not a drinking man, either; never took a glass too much. Very well; one day out there he was hewing boards to floor our shack, and something happens, — the ax slips and lays his leg open from the ankle to the knee. There is a big vein spouting blood, and I catch it and tie it with a deer-gut string I had in my pocket. Maybe that gut was poisoned some

163

way, for the wound went bad very soon. We had no linen, so I dressed it with punk wood, as the Indians do. I boiled pine chips and made turpentine, but it did no good. He got black to the thigh and began to suffer agony. The only thing that eased him was fresh snow heaped on his leg. I don't know if it was right, but he begged for it. After Christmas I saw it was time to get a priest.

"It was three days' journey in to the Sault mission, and the going was bad. There wasn't snow enough for snowshoes, —just enough to cover the roots and trip you. I took my snowshoes and grub-sack on my back, and made good time. The second day I came to a place where the trees were thin because there was no soil, only flint rock, in ledges. And there one big tree, a white pine, had blown over. It hadn't room to fall flat, the top had caught in the branches of another tree, so it lay slanting and made a nice shelter underneath, like a shanty, high enough to stand in. The top was still fresh and green and made thick walls to keep out the wind. I cleared away some of the inside branches and had a good sleep in there. Next morning when I left that place, I notched a few trees as I went, so I could find it when I brought the priest back with me. Ordinarily I don't notch trees to find my way back. When there is no sun, I can tell directions like the Indians."

Here Auclair interrupted him. "And how is that, Antoine?"

Frichette smiled and shrugged. "It is hard to explain, — by many things. The limbs of the trees are generally bigger on the south side, for example. The moss on the trunks is clean and dry on the north side, — on the south side it is softer and maybe a little rotten. There are many little signs; put them all together and they point you right.

"I got to the mission late the third night and slept in a bed. Early the next morning Father Hector was ready to start back with me. He had two young priests there, but he would go himself. He carried his snowshoes and a blanket and the Blessed Sacrament on his back, and I carried the provisions — smoked eels and cold grease — enough for three days. We slept the first night in that shelter under the fallen pine, and made a good start the next day. That was Epiphany, the day of the big snow all over Canada. When we had been out maybe two hours, the snow began to fall so thick we could hardly see each other, and I told Father Hector we better make for that shelter again. It took us nearly all day to get back over the ground we had covered in two hours before the storm began. By God, I was glad to see that thin place in the woods again! I was afraid I'd lost it. There was our tree, heaped over with snow, with the opening to the south still clear. We crept in and got our breath and unrolled our blankets. A little snow had sifted in, but not much. It had packed between the needles of that pine top until it was like a solid wall and roof. It was warm in there; no wind got through. Father Hector said some prayers, and we rolled up in our blankets and slept most of the day and let the storm come.

"Next day it was still snowing hard, and I was afraid to start out. We ate some lard, and an eel apiece, but I could see the end of our provisions pretty soon. We were thirsty and ate the snow, which doesn't satisfy you much. Father Hector said prayers and read his breviary. When I went to sleep, I heard him praying to himself, very low, — and when I wakened he was still praying, just the same. I lay still and listened for a long while, but I didn't once hear an Ave Maria, and not the name of a saint could I make out. At last I turned over and told Father Hector that was certainly a long prayer he was saying. He laughed. 'That's not a prayer, Antoine,' he says; 'that's a Latin poem, a very long one, that I learned at school. If I am uncomfortable, it diverts my mind, and I remember my old school and my comrades.'

" 'So much the better for you, Father,' I told him. 'But a long prayer would do no harm. I don't like the look of things.'

"The next day the snow had stopped, but a terrible bitter wind was blowing. We couldn't have gone against it, but since it was behind us, I thought we'd better get ahead. We hadn't food enough to see us through, as it was. That was a cruel day's march on an empty belly. Father Hector is a good man on snowshoes, and brave, too. My pack had grown lighter, and I wanted to carry his, but he would not have it. When it began to get dark, we made camp and ate some cold grease and the last of our eels. I built a fire, and we took turns, one of us feeding the fire while the other slept. I was so tired I could have slept on into eternity. Father Hector had to throw snow in my face to waken me.

"Before daylight the wind died, but the cold was so bitter we had to move or freeze. It was good snowshoeing that day, but with empty bellies and thirst and eating snow, we both had colic. That night we ate the last of our lard. I wasn't sure we were going right, — the snow had changed the look of everything. When Father Hector took off the little box he carried that held the Blessed Sacrament, I said: 'Maybe that will do for us two, Father. I don't see much ahead of us.'

" 'Never fear, Antoine,' says he, 'while we carry that, Someone is watching over us. Tomorrow will bring better luck.'

"It did, too, just as he said. We were both so weak we made poor headway. But by the mercy of God we met an Indian. He had a gun, and he had shot two hares. When he saw what a bad way we were in, he made a fire very quick and cooked the hares, — and he ate very little of that meat himself. He said Indians could bear hunger better than the French. He was a kind Indian and was glad to give us what he had. Father Hector could speak his language, and questioned him. Though I had never seen him before, he knew where our shack was, and said we were pointed right. But I told him I was tired out and wanted a guide, and I would pay him well in shot and powder if he took us in.

"We got back to our shack six days after we left the mission, and they were the six worst days of the winter. My brother-in-law was very bad. He died while Father Hector was there, and had a Christian burial. The Indian took Father Hector back to the mission. Soon after that I got this strain in my side, and I lost heart. I left our stores for Joseph Choret to trade with, and I went down to the Sault and then to Montreal. I found a sledge party about to come down the river, and they brought me to Kebec. Now I am here, what can you do for me, Monsieur Auclair?"

The apothecary's kindly tone did not reassure Frichette. He looked searchingly into his face and asked:

"Will it grow back, my inside, like it was?"

Auclair felt very sorry for him. "No, it will not grow back, Antoine. But tomorrow I will make you a support, and you will be more comfortable."

"But not to carry canoes over portages, I guess? No? Nor to go into the woods at all, maybe?" He sank back in the chair. "Then I don't know how I'll make a living, monsieur. I am not clever with tools, like my brother-in-law."

"We'll find a way out of that, Antoine."

Frichette did not heed him. "It's a funny thing," he went on. "A man sits here by the warm fire, where he can hear the bell ring for mass every morning and smell bread baked fresh every day, and all that happened out there in the woods seems like a dream. Yet here I am, no good any more."

"*Courage, mon bourgeois,* I am going to give you a good medicine."

Frichette shook his head and spread his thick fingers apart on his knees. "There is no future for me if I cannot paddle a canoe up the big rivers any more."

"Perhaps you can paddle, Antoine, but not carry."

Antoine rose. "In this world, who paddles must carry, monsieur. Good night, Mademoiselle Cécile. Father Hector will be surprised to see how you have grown. He thinks a great deal about that good dinner you are going to give him, I expect. You ask him if it tastes as good as those hares the Indian cooked for him when he was out with Frichette."

V

FATHER Hector Saint-Cyr was not long in following his messenger. On the day of his arrival in Kebec he stopped at the apothecary shop, but, Auclair being out, he saw only Cécile, and they arranged that he should come to dinner the following evening.

He came after hearing vespers at the Cathedral, attended to the door of the pharmacy by a group of Seminarians, who always followed him about when he was in town. This was his first meeting with Auclair, and there was a cordial moisture in the priest's eyes as he embraced his old friend and kissed him on both cheeks.

"How many times on my way from Ville-Marie I have enjoyed this moment in anticipation, Euclide," he declared. "Only solitary men know the full joys of friendship. Others have their family; but to a solitary and an exile his friends are everything."

Father Hector was the son of a noted family of Aix-en-Provence; his good breeding and fine presence were by no means lost upon his Indian parishioners at the Sault. The savages, always scornful of meekness and timidity, believed that a man was exactly what he looked. They used Father Hector better than any of his predecessors because he was strong and fearless and handsome. If he was humble before Heaven, he was never so with his converts. He took a high hand with them. If one were drunk or impertinent, he knocked him down. More than once he had given a drunken Indian a good beating, and the Indian had come and thanked him afterwards, telling him he did quite right.

Cécile thought it a great honour to entertain a man like Father Hector at their table, and she was much gratified by his frank enjoyment of everything; of the fish soup with which she had taken such pains, and the wood doves, cooked in a casserole with mushrooms and served with wild rice. Her father had brought up from the cellar a bottle of fine old Burgundy which the Count had sent them for New Year's. She scarcely ate at all herself, for watching their guest.

When Auclair said that this dinner was to make up to Father Hector for the one he missed on Epiphany, he laughed and protested that on Epiphany he had dined very well.

"Smoked eels and cold lard — what more does a man want in the woods? It was on the day following that we began to feel the pinch, — and the next day, and the next. Frichette made a great fuss about it, but certainly it was not the first time either he or I had gone hungry. If one had not been through little experiences of that kind, one would not know how to enjoy a dinner like this." He reached out and put his hand lightly on Cécile's head. "How I wish you could keep her from growing up, Euclide!"

She blushed with joy at the touch of that large, handsome hand which the Indians feared.

"Yes," he went on, looking about him, "these are great occasions in a missionary's life. The next time I am overtaken by a storm in the woods, the recollection of this evening will be food and warmth to me. I shall see it in memory as plainly as I see it now; this room, so like at home, this table with everything as it should be; and, most of all, the feeling of being with one's own kind. How many times, out there, I shall live over this evening again, with you and Cécile." Father Hector tasted his wine, inhaling it with a deep breath. "Very clearly, Euclide, it was arranged in Heaven that I should be a missionary in a foreign land. I am peculiarly susceptible to the comforts of the fireside and to the charm of children. If I were a teacher in the college at home, where I have many young nieces and nephews, I should be always planning for them. I should sink into nepotism, the most disastrous of the failings of the popes."

Auclair had to remind Cécile when it was time to bring in the dessert. She had quite forgot where they were in the dinner, so intent was she upon Father Hector's talk, upon watching his brown face and white forehead, with a sweep of black hair standing out above it.

"And now, Cécile," said her father, "shall we tell Father Hector our secret? Next autumn the Count expects to return to France, and we go with him. We think you have been a missionary long enough; that it is time for you to become a professor of rhetoric again. We expect you to go back with us, — or very soon afterwards."

Father Hector smiled, but shook his head. "Ah, no. Thank you, but no. I have taken a vow that will spoil your plans for me. I shall not return to France."

Auclair had put his glass to his lips, but set it down untasted. "Not return?" he echoed.

"Not at all, Euclide; never."

"But when my wife was here, you both used to plan — "

"Ah, yes. That was my temptation. Now it is vanquished." He sat for a moment smiling. Then he began resolutely:

"Listen, my friend. No man can give himself heart and soul to one thing while in the back of his mind he cherishes a desire, a secret hope, for something very different. You, as a student, must know that even in worldly affairs nothing worth while is accomplished except by that last sacrifice, the giving of oneself altogether and finally. Since I made that final sacrifice, I have been twice the man I was before."

Auclair felt disturbed, a little frightened. "You have made a vow, you say? Is it irrevocable?"

"Irrevocable. And what do you suppose gave me the strength to make that decision? Why, merely a good example!" At this point Father Hector glanced at Cécile and saw that she had almost ceased to breathe in her excitement; that her eyes, in the candlelight, were no longer blue, but black. Again he put out his hand and touched her head. "See, she understands me! From the beginning women understand devotion, it is a natural grace with them; they have only to learn where to direct it. Men have to learn everything.

"There was among the early missionaries, among the martyrs, one whom I have selected for my especial reverence. I mean Noël Chabanel, Euclide. He was not so great a figure as Brébeuf or Jogues or Lalemant, but I feel a peculiar sympathy for him. He perished, you remember, in the great Iroquois raid of '49. But his martyrdom was his life, not his death.

"He was a little different from all the others, — equal to them in desire, but not in fitness. He was only thirty years of age when he came, and was from Toulouse, that gracious city.

"Chabanel had been a professor of rhetoric like me, and like me he was fond of the decencies, the elegancies of life. From the beginning his life in Canada was one long humiliation and disappointment. Strange to say, he was utterly unable to learn the Huron language, though he was a master of Greek and Hebrew and spoke both Italian and Spanish. After five years of devoted study he was still unable to converse or to preach in any Indian tongue. He was sent out to the mission of Saint Jean in the Tobacco nation, as helper to Father Charles Garnier. Father Garnier, though not at all Chabanel's equal in scholarship, had learned the Huron language so thoroughly that the Indians said there was nothing more to teach him, — he spoke like one of themselves.

"His humiliating inability to learn the language was only one of poor Chabanel's mortifications. He had no love for his converts. Everything about the savages and their mode of life was utterly repulsive and horrible to

175

him; their filth, their indecency, their cruelty. The very
smell of their bodies revolted him to nausea. He could
never feel toward them that long-suffering love which
has been the consolation of our missionaries. He never
became hardened to any of the privations of his life, not
even to the vermin and mosquitos that preyed upon his
body, nor to the smoke and smells in the savage wig-
wams. In his struggle to learn the language he went and
lived with the Indians, sleeping in their bark shelters,
crowded with dogs and dirty savages. Often Father
Chabanel would lie out in the snow until he was in
danger of a death self-inflicted, and only then creep
inside the wigwam. The food was so hateful to him that
one might say he lived upon fasting. The flesh of dogs
he could never eat without becoming ill, and even cornmeal boiled in dirty water and dirty kettles brought on
vomiting; so that he used to beg the women to give him
a little uncooked meal in his hand, and upon that he
subsisted.

"The Huron converts were more brutal to him than
to Father Garnier. They were contemptuous of his
backwardness in their language, and they must have
divined his excessive sensibility, for they took every occasion to outrage it. In the wigwam they tirelessly per-
petrated indecencies to wound him. Once when a hunt-

ing party returned after a long famine, they invited him to a feast of flesh. After he had swallowed the portion in his bowl, they pulled a human hand out of the kettle to show him that he had eaten of an Iroquois prisoner. He became ill at once, and they followed him into the forest to make merry over his retchings.

"But through all these physical sufferings, which remained as sharp as on the first day, the greatest of his sufferings was an almost continual sense of the withdrawal of God. All missionaries have that anguish at times, but with Chabanel it was continual. For long months, for a whole winter, he would exist in the forest, every human sense outraged, and with no assurance of the nearness of God. In those seasons of despair he was constantly beset by temptation in the form of homesickness. He longed to leave the mission to priests who were better suited to its hardships, to return to France and teach the young, and to find again that peace of soul, that cleanliness and order, which made him the master of his mind and its powers. Everything that he had lost was awaiting him in France, and the Director of Missions in Quebec had suggested his return.

"On Corpus Christi Day, in the fifth year of his labours in Canada and the thirty-fifth of his age, he cut short this struggle and overcame his temptation. At the mission of Saint Matthias, in the presence of the Blessed Sacrament exposed, he made a vow of perpetual stability (*perpetuam stabilitatem*) in the Huron missions. This vow he recorded in writing, and he sent copies of it to his brethren in Kebec.

"Having made up his mind to die in the wilderness, he had not long to wait. Two years later he perished when the mission of Saint Jean was destroyed by the Iroquois, — though whether he died of cold in his flight through the forest, or was murdered by a faithless convert for the sake of the poor belongings he carried on his back, was not surely known. No man ever gave up more for Christ than Noël Chabanel; many gave all, but few had so much to give.

"It was perhaps in memory of his sufferings that I, in my turn, made a vow of perpetual stability. For those of us who are unsteadfast by nature, who have other lawful loves than our devotion to our converts, it is perhaps the safest way. My sacrifice is poor compared with his. I was able to learn the Indian languages; I have a house where I can, at least, pray in solitude; I can keep clean, and am seldom hungry, except by accident in the journeys I have to make. But Noël Chabanel — ah, when your faith is cold, think of him! How can there be men in France this day who doubt the existence of God, when for the love of Him weak human beings have been able to endure so much?"

Cécile looked up at him in bewilderment. "Are there such men, Father?" she whispered.

"There are, my child, — but it is the better for you if you have never heard of them."

Presently it was time that Father Hector should get back to Monseigneur de Saint-Vallier's Palace, where he was lodged during his stay in Quebec.

"And your books, Father Hector? Will you not take them back to the Sault with you? If I leave Canada before you visit Quebec again, what shall I do with them?" Auclair opened a cabinet and pointed to a row of volumes bound in vellum. Father Hector's eyes brightened as he looked at them, but he shook his head.

"No, I shall not take them this time. If you go away, give them to Monseigneur l'Ancien to keep for me. If they could be eaten, or worn on the back, he would give them to the poor, certainly. But Greek and Latin texts will be safe with him. I will not say good-bye, for I shall come tomorrow to lay in a supply of medicines for my mission."

After Auclair had disappeared behind his bed-curtains that night, he lay awake a long while, regretting that a man with Father Hector's gifts should decide to live and die in the wilderness, and wondering whether there had not been a good deal of misplaced heroism in the Canadian missions, — a waste of rare qualities which did nobody any good.

"Ah, well," he sighed at last, "perhaps that is the box of precious ointment which was acceptable to the Saviour, and I am like the disciples who thought it might have been used better in another way."

This solution allowed him to go to sleep.

VI

ABOUT the middle of March, soon after Father Hector's visit, the weather went sick, as it were. The air suddenly grew warm and springlike, and for three days there was a continuous downpour of rain. The deep snow drank it up like a thirsty sponge, but never melted. Not a patch of ground showed through, even on the hill-sides. But the snow darkened; everything grew grey like faintly smoked glass. The ice in the river broke up before Quebec, and olive-green water carried grey islands of ice and snow slowly northward. The great pine forests, across the river and on the western sky-line, were no longer bronze, but black. The only colours in the world were black and white and grey, — bewildering variations of clouded white and grey. The Laurentian mountains, to the north, sometimes showed a little blue in their valleys, when the fogs thinned enough to let them be seen. After the interval of rain everything froze hard again and stayed frozen, — but no fresh snow fell. The white winter was gone. Only the smirched ruins of winter remained, mournful and bleak and impoverished, frozen into enduring solidity.

Behind the Auclairs' little back yard and the baker's, the cliff ran up to the Château in a perpendicular wall, and the face of it was overgrown with wild cherry bushes and knotty little Canadian willows. It was up there that one looked, from the back door, for the first sign of spring. But all through April those stumps and twigs were so forbidding, so black and ugly, that Cécile often wondered whether anything short of a miracle of the old-fashioned kind could ever make the sap rise in them again.

A great many people in the town were sick at this time, and Cécile herself caught a cold and was feverish. Her father wrapped her in blankets and made her sit with her feet in a hot mustard bath while she drank a great quantity of sassafras tea. Then he put her to bed and entertained her with an account of the cures his father and grandfather had effected with sassafras. It was one of the medicinal plants of the New World in which he had great faith. It had been first brought to Europe by Sir Walter Raleigh, he said, and had been for a time a very popular remedy in France. Even when it went out of fashion, the pharmacy on the Quai des Célestins had remained loyal to it, and continued to use sassafras after it became expensive because of infrequent supply. His father got it from London, where it still came in occasional shipments from the Virginia colony.

Cécile was kept in bed for three days, — in her father's big bed, with the curtains drawn back, while her father himself attended to all the household duties. He was an accomplished cook, and continual practice in making medicines kept his hand expert in handling glass and earthenware and in regulating heat. He debated the advisability of sending for Jeanette, the laundress, or of asking Madame Pigeon to come in and help him. "*Mais non, nous sommes plus tranquilles comme ça,*" he decided. That was the important thing — tranquillity. In the evenings he read aloud to his daughter; and even when he was in the shop, she could hear everything his clients had to say, so she was not dull. If her father was disengaged for a moment, he came in to chat with her. They talked about Father Hector, and of how soon they could hope for green salads in the market, and of whether it could be true that Pierre Charron was home from the Great Lakes already, since there was a rumour that he had been seen in Montreal.

It was a pleasant and a novel experience to lie warm in bed while her father was getting dinner in the kitchen, and to feel no responsibility at all; to listen to the drip of the rain, to watch the grey daylight fade away in the salon, and the firelight grow redder and redder on the old chairs and the sofa, on the gilt picture-frames and the brass candlesticks. But her mind roamed about the town and was dreamily conscious of its activities and of the lives of her friends; of the dripping grey roofs and spires, the lighted windows along the crooked streets, the great grey river choked with ice and frozen snow, the never-ending, merciless forest beyond. All these things seemed to her like layers and layers of shelter, with this one flickering, shadowy room at the core.

They dined on the little table beside the bed (as they so often breakfasted even when she was well), and after dinner her father closed the door so that she would not be disturbed by the noise he made in washing the dishes, or even by Blinker's visit. It was while he was thus alone in the kitchen that he had, one evening, a strange interview with Blinker.

When Blinker had finished his tasks, he asked timidly if monsieur would please give him a little of that medicine again, to make him sleep.

Auclair looked at him doubtfully.

"How long is it you have not been sleeping?"

"Oh, a long time! Please, monsieur, give me something."

"Sit down, Jules. What is the matter? You are strong and healthy. You do not overeat. I cannot understand why you have this trouble. Perhaps you have something on your mind."

"Perhaps."

"That will often keep one awake. I am not a man to meddle, but if you told me what worries you, I should know better what to do for you."

Blinker's head drooped. He looked very miserable.

"Monsieur, I am an unfortunate man. If I told you, you might put me out."

"You have told your confessor?"

"It was not a sin. Not what they call a sin. It was a misfortune."

"Well, we will never put you out, Jules, be sure of that."

Blinker, with his hands knotted on his knees, seemed to be trying to bring something up out of himself. "Monsieur," he said at last, "I am unfortunate. I was brought up to a horrible trade. I was a torturer in the King's prison at Rouen."

Auclair started, but he caught himself quickly.

"Well, Jules," he said quietly, "that, too, is the King's service."

"*Sale service, monsieur,*" the poor wretch exclaimed bitterly, "*sale métier!* It was my father who did those things, — he was under the chief, he had to do it. I was afraid of him, for he was a hard man. I had no chance to learn another trade. Nobody wanted the prison folks about. In the street people would curse us. My father gave me brandy when he made me help him, all I could hold. He said it was right to punish the wicked, but I could never get used to it. Then something dreadful happened." Blinker was shivering all over.

Auclair poured him a glass of spirits and put some more wood into the stove. "You had better get it out, my boy. That will help you," he told him.

Hard as it was for Blinker to talk, he managed to tell his story. In Rouen there was a rough sort of woman who lived down near the river and did washing. She was honest, but quarrelsome; her neighbours didn't like her.

She had a little son who was a bad boy, and she often thrashed him. When he grew older, he struck back, and they used to fight, to the great annoyance of the neighbours. One summer this boy disappeared. A search was made for him. His mother was examined, and contradicted herself. The neighbours remembered hearing angry shouts and a smashing of bottles one night; they began to say she had done away with him. Someone made an accusation. The laundress was taken before the examiners again, but was sullen and refused to talk. She was put to the torture. After half an hour she broke down and confessed that she had killed her son, had put his body into a sack with stones and dragged it to the river. A few weeks later she was hanged.

Not long afterwards Blinker began to have trouble with his lower jaw, some decomposition of the bone; pieces of bone came out through his cheek. For weeks he never lay down, but walked the floor all night. Sometimes when he was full of brandy, he could doze in a chair for half an hour.

But he had another misery, harder to bear than his jaw. This was the first time he had ever suffered great pain, and ghosts began to haunt him. The faces of people he had put to torture rose before him, faces he had long forgotten. When everybody else was asleep, he could think of nothing but those faces. He told himself it was the law of the land and must be right; someone had to do it. But they never gave him any peace.

The suppuration in his jaw stopped at last. The scars on his face had begun to heal, when that murdered boy came back, — walked insolently in the streets of Rouen. The truth came out. After his quarrel with his mother he had hidden himself away on a boat tied up to the wharf, had got to Le Havre undiscovered, and there shipped as *mousse* on a bark bound for the West Indies. He made the voyage and came home.

Blinker began to walk the floor at night again, just as when his jaw was at its worst. How many of the others had been innocent? He could never get the big washer-woman's screams out of his ears. He would have made away with himself then, but he was afraid of being punished after death. If he dropped asleep from exhaustion, he would dream of her. He had only one hope; that miserable boy's adventure had put a thought into his head. If he could get away to a new country, where nobody knew him for the executioner's son, perhaps he would leave all that behind and forget it. That was why he had come to Kebec. But sometimes, he never knew when or why, these things would rise up out of the past . . . faces . . . voices . . . even words, things they had said.

"They are inside me, monsieur, I carry them with me." Blinker closed his eyes and slowly dropped his head forward on his hands.

"Your sickness was a good chance for you, my poor fellow. Suffering teaches us compassion. There are some in Kebec, in high places, who have not learned that yet. If Monseigneur de Saint-Vallier had ever known chagrin and disappointment, he would not cross the old Bishop as he does. I will give you something to make you sleep tomorrow, but afterwards you will not need anything. When God sent you that affliction in your face, he showed his mercy to you. And, by the way, who is your confessor?"

"Father Sébastien, at the Récollets'. But I have wanted to tell you, monsieur, ever since All Souls' Eve. I came back late with my buckets, and the door there was a little open, — you were telling ma'm'selle about the old man who stole the brass pots. I wanted to make away with myself — but you said something. You said the law was wrong, not us poor creatures. Monsieur, I never hurt an animal to amuse myself, as some do. I was brought up to that trade." Blinker stopped and wiped the sweat out of his eyes with his sleeve.

The poor fellow had begun to give off a foul odour, as creatures do under fear or anguish. Auclair watched with amazement the twisted face he saw every day above an armful of wood, — grown as familiar to him as an ugly piece of furniture, — now become altogether strange; it brought to his mind terrible weather-worn stone faces on the churches at home, — figures of the tormented in scenes of the Last Judgment. He hastened to measure out a dose of laudanum. After Blinker had gone out of the kitchen door, he made the sign of the cross over his own heart before he blew out the candle and went in to his daughter.

Cécile was flushed and excited; she had been crying, he saw.

"Oh Father, why were you so long with Blinker, and what was he telling you? He sounded so miserable!"

Her father put her head back on the pillow and smoothed her hair. "He was telling me all his old troubles, my dear, and when you are well again, I will tell them to you. We must be very kind to him. Your mother was right when she said there was no harm in him. Tomorrow I will go to Father Sébastien, and between us we will cure his distress."

"Then it was not a crime? You know some people say he was in the galleys in France."

"No, he was never in the galleys. He was one of the unfortunate of this world. You remember, when Queen

Dido offers Æneas hospitality, she says: *Having known misery, I have learned to pity the miserable.* Our poor wood-carrier is like Queen Dido."

The next morning Cécile's recovery began. As soon as she had drunk her chocolate, her father brought a pair of woollen stockings and told her to put them on. When she looked up at him wonderingly, he said:

"I have something to show you."

He wrapped her in a blanket, took her up in his arms, and carried her into the kitchen, where the back door stood open.

"Look out yonder," he said, "and presently you will see something."

She looked out at the dreary cliff-side with its black, frozen bushes and dirty snow, and long, grey icicles hanging from the jagged rocks. She wondered if there could be yellow buds on the willows, perhaps; but they were still naked, like stiff black briars.

Suddenly there was a movement up there, a flicker of something swift and slender in the grey light, against the grey, granulated snow, — then a twitter, a scolding anxious protest. Now she knew why her father had smiled so confidently when he lifted her out of bed.

"Oh, Papa, it is our swallow! Then the spring is coming! Nothing can keep it back now." She put her head down on his shoulder and cried a little. He pretended not to notice it, but stood holding her fast, patting her back, so muffled in folds of blanket.

"She is hunting her old nest, up among the crags. I cannot see whether it is still there. But if it has been blown away, she can easily build herself another. She can get mud, because there is a thaw every day now about noon, and the dead leaves are sticking up wherever the snow melts."

"Is she the only one? Is she all alone?"

"She is the only one here this morning, but her friends will be close behind. Listen, how she scolds!"

"Father," said Cécile suddenly, "where has she been, our swallow? Where, do you think?"

"Oh, far away in the South! Somewhere down there where Robert de La Salle was murdered. By the Gulf of Mexico, perhaps."

"And in France where do the swallows go in winter?"

"Very far. Across the Mediterranean to Algérie, where the oranges grow."

"Has our swallow been where there are oranges? Do they grow by the Gulf of Mexico? Oh, Papa, I wish I could see an orange, on its little tree!"

"You will see them when we go home. There are fine

old orange-trees growing under glass in our own parish, and they are brought out into the courtyards in summer."

"But couldn't we possibly grow one here in Quebec? The Jesuits have such great warm cellars; I am sure they could, if they tried."

Her father laughed as he carried her back to bed. "I am afraid not even the Jesuits could do that! Now I am going to leave you for a little while. I will put a card on the door announcing that we are closed until noon. You are so much better, that I can make my visit to the Hôtel Dieu this morning."

"And on your way, Papa, will you stop and tell Monseigneur l'Ancien that our swallow has come? For his book, you know."

Ever since he first came out to Canada, old Bishop Laval had kept a brief weather record, noting down the date of the first snowfall, when the river froze over, the nights of excessive cold, the storms and the great thaws. And for nearly forty years now he had faithfully recorded the return of the swallow.

Pierre Charron

BOOK FOUR

Pierre Charron

I

IT was the first day of June. Before dawn a wild calling and twittering of birds in the bushes on the cliff-
side above the apothecary's back door announced clear
weather. When the sun came up over the Île d'Orléans,
the rock of Kebec stood gleaming above the river like
an altar with many candles, or like a holy city in an old
legend, shriven, sinless, washed in gold. The quickening of all life and hope which had come to France in
May had reached the far North at last. That morning
the Auclairs drank their chocolate with all the doors and
windows open.

Euclide was at his desk, making up little packets of
saffron flowers to flavour fish soups, when a slender
man in buckskins, with a quick swinging step, crossed
the threshold and embraced him before he had time to
rise. He was not a big fellow, this Pierre Charron, hero
of the fur trade and the coureurs de bois, not above
medium height, but quick as an otter and always sure of

195

himself. When Auclair, after returning his embrace with delight, drew back to look at him and asked him how he was, he threw up his chin and answered:

"*Je me porte bien, comme toujours.*"

"And have you had a good winter, Pierre?"

"But yes. I always have a good winter, monsieur. I see to it."

"And how do you happen to be down so early?"

Charron's face changed. He frowned. "That is not so good. My mother was ailing. They brought me word, out to Michilimackinac, so I returned to Montreal in March. She was better; the Sisters of the Congregation had been taking care of her. But I did not leave her again. No one can nurse her so well as I. I stayed at home and let the other fellows have my spring trade this year. I can afford it."

"But I must hear about your mother's ailment, my son; and first let me call Cécile. She will not want to lose even a minute of your visit."

Auclair went back to the kitchen, and Cécile ran in without stopping to take off her *tablier.* It flashed across Pierre that she was perhaps growing too tall to be kissed. But she was quicker than his thought, threw her arms about his neck, and gave him the glad kiss of welcome.

Pierre Charron

"Oh, Pierre Charron, I am delighted at you, Pierre Charron!"

He stood laughing, holding both her hands and swinging them back and forth in a rhythm of some sort, so that though they were standing still, they seemed to be dancing. Cécile was laughing, too, as children do where they never have been afraid or uncertain. "Oh, Pierre, have you been to the great falls again, and Michilimackinac?"

"Everywhere, everywhere!" He swung her hands faster and faster.

"And you will tell me about the big beaver towns?"

"Gently, Cécile," her father interposed. "Pierre's mother has been ill, and he will tell us first about her. What was it like this time, my boy, a return of her old complaint?" The one long journey Auclair had ever made away from Quebec since he landed here was to go up to Montreal in Pierre's shallop to examine and prescribe for Madame Charron.

From his first meeting with him, Auclair had loved this restless boy (he was a boy then) who shot up and down the swift rivers of Canada in his canoe; who was now at Niagara, now at the head of Lake Ontario, now at the Sault Sainte Marie on his way into the fathomless forbidding waters of Lake Superior. To both Auclair

197

and Madame Auclair, Pierre Charron had seemed the type they had come so far to find; more than anyone else he realized the romantic picture of the free Frenchman of the great forests which they had formed at home on the bank of the Seine. He had the good manners of the Old World, the dash and daring of the New. He was proud, he was vain, he was relentless when he hated, and quickly prejudiced; but he had the old ideals of clan-loyalty, and in friendship he never counted the cost. His goods and his life were at the disposal of the man he loved or the leader he admired. Though his figure was still boyish, his face was full of experience and sagacity; a fine bold nose, a restless, rather mischievous mouth, white teeth, very strong and even, sparkling hazel eyes with a kind of living flash in them, like the sunbeams on the bright rapids upon which he was so skilful.

Pierre's father, a soldier of fortune from Languedoc, had done well in the fur trade and built himself a comfortable dwelling in Montreal, on Saint Paul street, next the house of Jacques Le Ber. Pierre was almost exactly the same age as Le Ber's daughter, Jeanne; the two children had been playmates and had learned their catechism together. After Pierre's father was drowned in a storm on Lake Ontario, Jacques Le Ber took the son into his employ to train him for the fur business. Of all the suitors for Mademoiselle Le Ber's hand Pierre was thought to have the best chance of success, and the merchant would have liked him for a son-in-law. At the time when Mademoiselle Le Ber, then fifteen, came home from her schooling in Quebec, Pierre was her father's clerk and was often at the house. She had seemed favourably disposed toward him. It was an old story in Montreal that after Jeanne took her first vow and immured herself in her father's house, disappointment had driven young Charron into the woods. He had learned the Indian languages as a child, and the Indians liked and trusted him, as they had liked his father. All along the Great Lakes, as far as Michilimackinac, he had a name among them for courage and fair dealing, for a loyal friend and a relentless enemy. Every year he gave half the profits of his ventures to his mother; the rest he squandered on drink and women and new guns, as his comrades did. But in Montreal his behaviour was always exemplary, out of respect to his mother.

After accepting Auclair's invitation to come to supper that evening, Charron said he must go to Noël Pommier to order a pair of hard boots, — he was wearing moccasins. "And will you come along, little monkey?"

he asked, making a face. When Cécile was little, he had always called her his *petit singe*.

She glanced eagerly at her father. He nodded. "Run along, and give my respects to Madame Pommier."

Cécile slipped her hand into Charron's, and they went out into the street. Across the way, they saw Monseigneur de Saint-Vallier in his garden, directing some workmen who were apparently building an arbour for him.

"I see your grand neighbour has come home," Pierre observed.

"Oh yes, last September. But you must have heard? People say he brought such beautiful things for his house; furniture and paintings and tapestry and silver dishes. Wouldn't you love to see the inside of his Palace?"

"Not a bit! He is too French for me." Charron threw up his chin.

Cécile laughed. "But my father is French, and so is Father Hector; you like them."

"Oh, that is different. But the man over there goes against me. He smells of Versailles. The old man is my Bishop. But I could do without any of them."

"Hush, Pierre Charron! You are foolish to quarrel with the priests. I love Father Hector. You can't say he isn't a brave man."

Pierre shrugged. "Oh, he is brave enough. All the same, he's a little too Frenchified for me. You and I are Canadians, monkey. We were born here."

"Why, I wasn't at all! You know that."

"Well, if you weren't, you couldn't help it. You got here early. You were very little when I first saw you with your mother. Cécile, every autumn, before I start for the woods, I have a mass said at the *paroisse* in Ville-Marie for madame your mother."

Cécile pressed his hand softly and drew closer to him. Whenever Charron spoke of her mother, or of his own, his voice lost its tone of banter; he became respectful, serious, simple. It was clear enough that for him the family was the first and final thing in the human lot; and it was so engrafted with religion that he could only say: "Very well; religion for the fireside, freedom for the woods."

As they passed the end of the long Seminary building, the door of the garden stood open, and within they saw Bishop Laval, walking up and down the sanded paths, his breviary open in his hand. It was a very small garden; a grass plot in the centre, a row of Lombardy poplars along the wall, some lilac bushes, now in bloom, a wooden seat with no back under a crooked quince-tree. The old man caught sight of Pierre, though he walked so noiselessly, — beckoned to him and called out his name. The Bishop knew everyone along the river so well that it was said he could recognize a lost child by the family look in its face.

Pierre snatched off his cap and they went inside the garden door. Monseigneur inquired after the health of Madame Charron, and of the aged nun Marguerite Bourgeoys. And had Pierre heard whether Mademoiselle Le Ber was in health?"

Not directly. He supposed she was as usual; he had heard nothing to the contrary.

The Bishop breathed heavily, like a tired horse. "All the sinners of Ville-Marie may yet be saved by the prayers of that devoted girl," he said with a certain meaning in his tone. "And you, my son, have you been to your confessor since your return from the woods?"

Pierre said respectfully that he had. The Bishop then turned to Cécile and placed his hand upon her head, with the rare smile which always seemed a little sad on his grim features.

"And here we have a child who borrows money, — and of a poor priest, too! Why did you never come to pay me back my twenty sous?"

"But Monseigneur l'Ancien, I gave them to Houssart, the very day after!"

"I know you did, my child, but I should have liked it better if you had come to me when you paid your debt. You are not afraid of me?"

"Oh, no, Monseigneur! But you are always occupied, and I did not know whether you liked to have children come."

"I do. I like it very much. Make me a visit here in my garden some morning at this hour, and I will share my lilacs with you; they are coming on now. Bring the little boy, if you like. I hear from the Pommiers that you and your father are making a good boy of him, and that is very commendable in you."

During the rest of the short walk to the cobbler's, Pierre asked what the Bishop meant by the twenty sous, but he seemed to pay little attention to the story; he was rather overcast, indeed. It was not until he greeted Madame Pommier that he recovered his high spirits.

II

For Charron, that evening, the apothecary brought up from his cellar some fiery Bordeaux, proper for a son of Languedoc, and the hours flew by. After Cécile had said good-night and gone upstairs to her summer

bed-room, the two men talked on until after midnight;
of the woods, of the state of the fur trade, of the results of the Count's last Indian campaign, and the in-
gratitude of the King, who had rewarded his services so
inadequately.

Pierre lost his reserve after a bottle or two of fine
Gaillac, and the conversation presently took a very personal turn. Auclair, in speaking of Madame Charron's
illness, remarked that it was fortunate she had such
nurses at hand as the Sisters of the Congregation.

"Oh, yes, they took good care of her, to be sure,"
Pierre admitted. "And why not? By Heaven, they owe
me something, those women! Fifty thousand gold écus,
perhaps!"

"Charron," said his host reprovingly, "you do yourself wrong to pretend that you are chagrined at having
lost that dowry. You are not a mean-spirited man. You
have never cared much about money."

"Perhaps not, but I care about defeat. If the venerable Bourgeoys had not got hold of that girl in her
childhood and overstrained her with fasts and penances, she would be a happy mother today, not sleeping
in a stone cell like a prisoner. There are plenty of girls,
ugly, poor, stupid, awkward, who are made for such a
life. It was bad enough when she was shut up in her

father's house; but now she is no better than dead. Worse."

"Still, if it is the life she desires, and if her father can bear it — "

"Oh, her father, poor man! I do not like to meet him on the street, — and he does not like to meet me. I recall to him the days when she first came home from Quebec and used to be at her mother's side, at the head of a long table full of good company, always looking out for everyone, saying the right thing to everyone. It did his eyes good to look at her. He was never the same man after she shut herself away. I was in his employ then, and I know. He used to talk to me and say: 'It is like a fever; it will burn itself out in time. We shall all be happy again.' This went on three years, and he was always hoping. But not I. I saw her before I broke away to the woods, though. I made sure."

Pierre took out a pouch of strong Indian tobacco, pulverized it in his brown palm, and put it into his pipe. He drew the smoke in deep, like a man overwrought. Auclair had meant to bring out some old brandy to flavour their talk, but he thought: "No, better not." Aloud he said:

"You mean that you had an interview with Mademoiselle Le Ber after she went into retreat?"

"Call it an interview. I made sure." Charron took the pipe out of his mouth and spoke rapdily. "It was in the fourth year of her retreat. I had lost hope, but I wanted to know. She always went out of the house to early mass. One morning in the spring, when it gets light early, I went to the narrow allée between her garden and the church and waited there under an apple-tree that hung over the wall. When she came along with her old servant, I stepped out in front of her and spoke. Ah, that was a beautiful moment for me! She had not changed. She did not shrink away from me or reproach me. She was gracious and gentle, as always, and at her ease. She put back her grey veil as we talked, and looked me in the eyes. There was still colour in her cheeks, — not rosy as she used to be, but her face was fresh and soft, like the apple blossoms on that tree where we stood. She had no hard word for me. She said she was glad of a chance to see me again and to bid me farewell; she meant to renew her vows when the five years were over, and we should never meet again. When I began to cry, — I was young then, — and knelt down before her, she put her hand on my head; she did not fear me or the few people who hurried past us into the church, — they seemed frightened enough at such a sight, but she was calm. She told me it would be better if I left her father, and that I must marry. *I will always pray for you,* she said, *and when you have children, I will pray for them. As long as we are both in this world, you may know I pray for you every day; that God may preserve you from sudden death without repentance, and that we may meet in heaven."*

Charron sat silent for a moment, then bent over the candle and lit his pipe, which had gone out. "You know, monsieur, three times in the woods my comrades have thought it was all over with me; a powder explosion, my canoe going down under me in the rapids, and then the gunshot wound I had in the Count's last campaign. I have remembered that promise; for I have certainly been delivered from sudden death. I remember, too, her voice when she said those words, — it was still her own voice, which made people love to go to her father's house, and one felt gay if she but spoke one's name. And now it is harsh and hollow like an old crow's — terrible to hear!"

Auclair began to wonder whether Pierre might have had anything to drink before he came to dinner. "Now you are talking wildly, my boy. We cannot know what her voice is like now."

"I know," said Charron sullenly. He crossed the room to the door of the enclosed staircase, and examined it to see that it was shut. "The little one cannot hear, up there? No?" He sat down and leaned forward, his elbows on the table. "I know. I have heard her. I have seen her."

"Pierre, you have not done anything irreverent, that the nuns will never forgive?" Auclair was alarmed by the very thought that the sad solitaire, who asked for nothing on this earth but solitude, had perhaps been startled.

Charron was too much excited and too sorry for himself at that moment to notice his friend's apprehensions.

"It was like this," he went on presently. "You know, because of my mother, this year I got back to Montreal early, months before my time. There is not much to do there, God knows, except to be a pig, and I never behave like dirt in my mother's town. We live so near the chapel of the Congregation that I can never get the recluse out of my mind. You remember there were two weeks of terrible cold in March, and it made me wretched to think of her walled up there. No, don't misunderstand me!" Charron's eyes came back from their far-away point of vision and fixed intently, distrustfully, on his friend's face. "All that is over; one does not love a woman who has been dead for nearly twenty years. But there is such a thing as kindness; one wouldn't like to think of a dog that had been one's playfellow, much less a little girl, suffering from cold those bitter nights. You see, there are all those early memories; one cannot get another set; one has but those." Pierre's voice choked, because something had come out by chance, thus, that he had never said to himself before. The candles blurred before Auclair a little, too. God was a witness, he murmured, that he knew the truth of Pierre's remark only too well.

After he had relit his pipe and smoked a little, Charron continued. "You know she goes into the church to pray before the altar at midnight. Well, I hid myself in the church and saw her. It is not difficult for a man who has lived among the Indians; you slide into the chapel when an old sacristan is locking up after vespers, and stay there behind a pillar as long as you choose. It was a long wait. I had my fur jacket on and a flask of brandy in my pocket, and I needed both. God's Name, is there any place so cold as churches? I had to move about to keep from aching all over, — but, of course, I made no noise. There was only the sanctuary lamp burning, until the moon came round and threw some light in at the windows. I knew when it must be near midnight, you get to have a sense of time in the woods. I hid myself behind a pillar at the back of the church. I felt a little nervous, sorry I had come, perhaps. — At last I heard a latch lift,—you could have heard a rabbit breathe in that place. The iron grille beside the altar began to move outward. She came in, carrying a candle. She wore a grey gown, and a black scarf on her head, but no veil. The candle shone up into her face. It was like a stone face; it had been through every sorrow."

Charron stopped and crossed himself. He shut his eyes and dropped his head in his hands. "My friend, I could remember a face!—I could remember Jeanne in her little white furs, when I used to pull her on my sled. Jacques Le Ber would have burned Montreal down to keep her warm. He meant to give her every joy in the world, and she has thrown the world away. . . . She put down her candle and went toward the high altar. She walked very slowly, with great dignity. At first she prayed aloud, but I scarcely understood her. My mind was confused; her voice was so changed,—hoarse, hollow, with the sound of despair in it. Why is she unhappy, I ask you? She is, I know it! When she prayed in silence, such sighs broke from her. And once a groan, such as I have never heard; such despair—such resignation and despair! It froze everything in me. I felt that I would never be the same man again. I only wanted to die and forget that I had ever hoped for anything in this world.

"After she had bowed herself for the last time, she took up her candle and walked toward that door, standing open. I lost my head and betrayed myself. I was well hidden, but she heard me sob.

"She was not startled. She stood still, with her hand on the latch of the grille, and turned her head, half-facing me. After a moment she spoke.

"*Poor sinner,* she said, *poor sinner, whoever you are, may God have mercy upon you! I will pray for you. And do you pray for me also.*

"She walked on and shut the grille behind her. I turned the key in the church door and let myself out. No man was ever more miserable than I was that night."

III

EVER since Cécile could remember, she had longed to go over to the Île d'Orléans. It was only about four miles down the river, and from the slopes of Cap Diamant she could watch its fields and pastures come alive in the spring, and the bare trees change from purple-grey to green. Down the middle of the island ran a wooded ridge, like a backbone, and here and there along its flanks were cleared spaces, cultivated ground where the islanders raised wheat and rye. Seen from the high points of Quebec, the island landscape looked as if it had been arranged to please the eye, — full of folds and wrinkles like a crumpled table-cloth, with little fields twinkling above the dark tree-tops. The climate was said to be more salubrious than that of Quebec, and the soil richer. All the best vegetables and garden fruits in the market came from the Île, and the wild strawberries of which Cécile's father was so fond. Giorgio, the drummer boy, had often told her how well the farmers lived over there; and about the great eel-fishings in the autumn, when the islanders went out at night with torches and seined eels by the thousand.

Pierre Charron had a friend on the island, Jean Baptiste Harnois, the smith of Saint-Laurent, and he meant to go over and pay him a visit this summer, before he went back to Montreal. He had promised to take Cécile along, — every time he came to the shop, he reminded her that they were to make this excursion. One fine morning in the last week of June he dropped in to say that the wind was right, and he would start for the island in about an hour, to be gone for three days.

Very well, Auclair told him, Cécile would be ready.

"But three days, Father!" she exclaimed; "can you manage for yourself so long? You bought so many things at the market for me to cook."

"I can manage. You must go by all means. You may not have such a chance again."

"Good," said Pierre. "I will be back in an hour. And she must bring a warm coat; it will be cold out on the water."

Cécile had never gone on a voyage before,—had never slept a night away from home, except during the Phips bombardment, when she and her mother had taken refuge at the Ursuline convent, along with the other women and children from the Lower Town.

"What shall I take with me, Father? I am so distracted I cannot think!"

"The little valise that was your mother's will hold your things. You will need a night-gown, and a pair of stockings, and a clean cotton blouse, and some handkerchiefs; I should think that would be all. And I will give you a package of raisins as a present for Madame Harnois."

She ran upstairs and began to pack her mother's bag, finding it hard to assemble her few things in her excitement.

"Are you ready, Cécile?" her father presently called from the foot of the stairs.

"I am not sure, Father—I think so. I wish I had known yesterday."

"Then you would not have slept all night. Come along, and I will put the raisins in your valise."

Pierre was waiting, seated on the long table that served as a counter. Her father looked into her bag to see that she had the proper things, then handed it to him. Cécile put on her cap and coat. Auclair kissed her and wished them *bon voyage*. "Take good care of her, Pierre."

Pierre touched his hand to his black forelock. "As you would yourself, monsieur." He pushed Cécile out of the door before him.

"Papa," she called back, "you will not forget to keep the fire under the soup? It has been on only an hour."

Pierre's boat was a light shallop with one sail. He rowed out far enough to catch the breeze and then sat in the stern, letting the wind and current carry them. He had made a change in his clothes during the hour he was absent from the shop, Cécile noticed (later in the day she wondered why!), had put on a white linen shirt and knotted a new red silk neckerchief about his throat. He soon took off his knitted cap, lit his pipe, lounged at his ease. On one shore stretched the dark forest, on the other the smiling, sunny fields that ran toward Beaupré. Behind them the Lower Town grew smaller and smaller; the rock of Kebec lost its detail until they could see only Cap Diamant, and the Château, and the spires of the churches. The sunlight on the river made a silver glare all about the boat, and from the water itself came a deep rhythmic sound, like something breathing.

"Think of it, Pierre, in all these years I have never been on the river before!" Such a stretch of lost opportunity as life seemed just then!

Pierre smiled. "Not so many years, at that! Your father is over-cautious, maybe, but squalls come up suddenly on this river, and most of these young fellows had as lief drown as not. I'd rather you never went with anyone but me. If you like it, you can go with me any time."

"But I'd like to go the other way, — to Montreal, and up those rivers that are full of rapids. I want to go as far as Michilimackinac."

"Some time, perhaps. We'll see how you like roughing it."

Cécile asked what he had in the stone jug she saw in the bow, along with his blanket and buckskin coat.

"That is brandy, for the smith. But it will come back full of good country wine. He makes it from wild grapes. The wild grapes on the island are the best in Canada; Jacques Cartier named it the Île de Bacchus because he found such fine grapes growing in the woods. That ought to please you, with all your Latin!"

215

"Are you like Mother Juchereau, do you think it wrong for a girl to know Latin?"

"Not if she can cook a hare or a partridge as well as Mademoiselle Auclair! She may read all the Latin she pleases. But I expect you won't like the food at the Harnois', *à la campagnarde,* you know, — they cook everything in grease. As for me, it doesn't matter. When you can go to an Indian feast and eat dogs boiled with blueberries, you can eat anything."

Cécile shuddered. "I don't see how you can do it, Pierre. I should think it would be easier to starve."

"Oh, do you, my dear? Try starving once; it's a long business. I've known the time when dog meat cooked in a dirty pot seemed delicious! But the worst food I ever swallowed was what they call *tripe de roche.* I went out to Lac la Mort with some Frenchmen early in the spring once. They were a green lot, and they let most of our provisions get stolen on the way. As soon as we reached the lake, we were caught in a second winter; a heavy snow, and everything frozen. No game, no fish. We had to fall back on *tripe de roche.* It's a kind of moss that grows on the rocks along the lake, something like a sponge; the cold doesn't kill it, when everything else is frozen hard as iron. You gather it and boil it, and it's not so bad as it goes down, — tastes like any boiled weed.

But afterwards—oh, what a stomach-ache! The men sat round tied up in a knot. We had about a week of that stuff. We scraped the hair off our bear skins and roasted them, that time. But it's a truth, monkey, I wouldn't like a country where things were too soft. I like a cold winter, and a hot summer. My father used to boast that in Languedoc you were never out of sight of a field or a vineyard. That would mean people everywhere around you, always watching you! No hunting,—they put you in jail if you shoot a partridge. Even the fish in the streams belong to somebody. I'd be in prison in a week there."

The settlement at Saint-Laurent was Pierre's destination. After he had passed the point at Sainte-Pétronille and turned into the south channel, a sweet, warm odour blew out from the shore, very like the smell of ripe strawberries. Each time the boat passed a little cove, this fragrance grew stronger, the air seemed saturated with it. All the early explorers wrote with much feeling about these balmy odours that blew out from the Canadian shores,—nothing else seemed to stir their imagination so much. That fragrance is really the aromatic breath of spruce and pine, given out under the hot sun of noonday, but the early navigators believed it was the smell of luscious unknown fruits, wafted out to sea.

When Pierre had made a landing and tied his boat, they went up the path to the smith's house, to find the family at dinner. They were warmly received and seated at the dinner-table. The smith had no son, but four little girls. After dinner Cécile went off into the fields with them to pick wild strawberries. She had never seen so many wild flowers before. The daisies were drifted like snow in the tall meadow grass, and all the marshy hollows were thatched over with buttercups, so clean and shining, their yellow so fresh and unvarying, that it seemed as if they must all have been born that morning at the same hour. The clumps of blue and purple iris growing in these islands of buttercups made a sight almost too wonderful. All the afternoon Cécile thought she was in paradise.

The little girls did not bother her much. They were timid with a guest from town and talked very little. Two of them had been to Quebec, and even to her father's shop, and they asked her about the stuffed baby alligator, where it came from. They wanted to know, too, why her father bought so many pigs' bladders in the market. Did he eat them, or did he fill them with sausage meat? Cécile explained that he washed and dried them, and when people were sick, he filled the bladders with hot water and put them on the sore place, to ease the pain.

The little girls wore moccasins, but no stockings, and their brown legs were badly marked by brier scratches and mosquito bites. When they showed her the pigs and geese and tame rabbits, they kept telling her about peculiarities of animal behaviour which she thought it better taste to ignore. They called things by very unattractive names, too. Cécile was not at all sure that she liked these children with pale eyes and hay-coloured hair and furtive ways.

At supper she was glad to see Pierre and the genial blacksmith again, but the kitchen where they ate was very hot and close, for Madame Harnois shut all the doors and windows to keep out the mosquitos. There were mosquitos at home, on Mountain Hill, too, but her father drove them away by making a smudge of herbs, which were sent to him from France every year.

The family went to bed early, and after darkness had shut off the country about them, and bedtime was approaching, Cécile felt uneasy and afraid of something. Pierre had brought his own blanket, and said he would sleep in the hayloft. She wished she could follow him, and with a sinking heart heard him go whistling across the wagon-yard.

There were only three rooms in this house, the kitchen and two bedrooms. In one of these slept the smith and his wife. In the other was a wide, low bed made of split poles, and there slept all the four daughters. There, Cécile soon gathered, she too must sleep! The mother told them to give Cécile the outside place in the bed, for manners. Slowly she undressed and put on her night-gown. The little Harnois girls took off their frocks and tumbled into bed in their chemises,— they told her they only wore night-gowns in winter. When they kicked off their moccasins, they did not stop to wash their legs, which were splashed with the mud of the marsh and bloody from mosquito bites. One candle did not give much light, but Cécile saw that they must have gone to bed unwashed for many nights in these same sheets. The case on the bolster, too, was rumpled and dirty. She felt that she could not possibly lie down in that bed. She made one pretext after another to delay the terrible moment; the children asked whether she said so many prayers every night. At last the mother called that it was time to put out the candle. She blew it out and crept into the bed, spreading a handkerchief from her valise down on the bolster-cover where she must put her head.

She lay still and stiff on the very edge of the feather bed, until the children were asleep and she could hear the smith and his wife snoring in the next room. His snore was only occasional, deep and guttural; but his wife's was high and nasal, and constant. Cécile got up very softly and dressed carefully in the dark. There was only one window in the room, and that was shut tight to keep out mosquitos. She sat down beside it and watched the moon come up, — the same moon that was shining down on the rock of Kebec. Perhaps her father was taking his walk on Cap Diamant, and was looking up the river at the Île d'Orléans and thinking of her. She began to cry quietly. She thought a great deal about her mother, too, that night; how her mother had always made everything at home beautiful, just as here everything about cooking, eating, sleeping, living, seemed repulsive. The longest voyage on the ocean could scarcely take one to conditions more different. Her mother used to reckon Madame Pigeon a careless housekeeper; but Madame Pigeon's easy-going ways had not prepared one for anything like this. She tried to think about the buttercups in the marsh, as clean as the sun itself, and the long hay-grass with the star-white daisies.

Cécile sat there until morning, through the endless hours until daylight came, careful never to look back at the rumpled bed behind her. When Madame Harnois stuck her head in at the door to waken her children,

she complimented Cécile upon being up so early. All
the family washed in a wooden basin which stood on a
bench in the kitchen, and they all wiped their faces on
the same towel. The mother got breakfast in her night-
cap because she had not taken time to arrange her hair.
Cécile did not want much breakfast; the bread had so
much lard in it that she could not eat it. She had sagamite and milk.

When they got up from the table, Pierre announced
that he was going fishing, and he did not even suggest
taking her along. The little girls were expected to help
their mother in the morning, so Cécile got away unob-
served into the nearest wood. She went through it, and
climbed toward the ridge in the middle of the island. At
last she came out on a waving green hayfield with a
beautiful harp-shaped elm growing in the middle of it.
The grass there was much taller than the daisies, so that
they looked like white flowers seen through a driving
grey-green rain. Cécile ran across the field to that sym-
metrical tree and lay down in the dark, cloud-shaped
shadow it threw on the waving grass. The tight feeling
in her chest relaxed. She felt she had escaped for ever
from the Harnois and their way of living. She went to
sleep and slept a long while. When she wakened up in
the sweet-smelling grass, with the grasshoppers jump-

ing over her white blouse, she felt rested and happy,—though unreal, indeed, as if she were someone else. She was thinking she need not go back to the smith's house at all that day, but could lunch on wild strawberries, when she heard the little girls' voices calling her, "Cé-cile, Cé-cile!" rather mournfully, and she remembered that she ought not to cause the family anxiety. She looked for a last time at the elm-tree and the sunny field, and then started back through the wood. She didn't want the children to come to that place in their search for her. She hoped they had never been there!

After dinner she escaped into the fields again, but this time the girls went with her. They had a grape-vine swing in the wood; as she had never had a swing when she was little, she found it delightful. These children were nicer when they played at games and did not stand staring at one.

But as the sunlight began to grow intensely gold on the tree-tops and the slanting fields, dread and empti-ness awoke in Cécile's breast again, a chilling fear of the night. The mother had found her handkerchief spread out on the bolster and had put on a clean bolster-slip. But that made little difference. She couldn't possibly lie in that bed all night, not even if the children had taken a bath before they got into it. As soon as they were asleep, she got up and sat by the window as on the first night.

At breakfast Pierre Charron noticed that Cécile did not look at all like herself. When they left the table, he asked her to go down to the spring with him, and as soon as they were alone, inquired if she were not feeling well.

"No, I don't feel well, and truly I can't stay here any longer. Please, please, Pierre, take me home today!"

Pierre had never seen her cry before, and he was greatly surprised. "Very good. There is not much wind, and perhaps we had better go today, anyhow. Get your things, and I'll tell the smith I've changed my mind."

Cécile ran swiftly back to the house. She knew she had not been a very satisfactory visitor, and she felt remorseful. She gave the little girls all the handkerchiefs she had brought with her, — they hadn't any, but wiped their sweaty faces on their sleeves or their skirts. Several of her handkerchiefs had come from her aunts, and she was very fond of them, but she parted with them gladly and only wished she had more things to give the children.

She could scarcely believe in her good fortune when Pierre's boat actually left the shore and he began pulling out into the river, while the Harnois children stood waving to them from the cove.

"We needn't hurry, eh?" Pierre asked.

"Oh, no! I love being on the river," she replied unsteadily. He asked no further questions, but handled his oars, singing softly to himself. Of course, she thought sadly, he would never want to take her anywhere again. She used to dream that one day he might take her to Montreal in his boat, perhaps even to see the great falls at Niagara.

As soon as they were out of the south channel and had cleared the point of the island, they could see the rock of Kebec and the glare of the sun on the slate roofs. Cécile began to struggle with her tears again. It was as if she were home already. For a long while it did not grow much plainer; then it rose higher and higher against the sky.

"Now I can see the Château, and the Récollet spire," she cried. "And, oh, Pierre, there is the Seminary!"

"Yes? It's a fine building, but I never had any particular affection for it." He saw that she was much too happy to notice his banter.

Soon they could see the spire of Notre Dame de la Victoire — and then they were in the shadow of the rock itself. When she stepped upon the shore, Cécile remembered how Sister Catherine de Saint-Augustin, when she landed with her companions, had knelt down and kissed the earth. Had she been alone, she would have loved to do just that. They went hand in hand up La Place street, across the market square, down Notre Dame street beside the church, and into Mountain Hill. It was wonderful that everything should be just the same, when she had been away so long! Pierre did not bother her with questions, but she knew he was watching her closely. She was ashamed, but it couldn't be helped; some things are stronger than shame.

When they burst in upon her father, he was seated at his desk, rolling pills on a sheet of glass.

"What, back already?" He did not seem so overjoyed as Cécile had thought he would be.

"Yes, monsieur," Pierre replied carelessly, "we were a little bored in the country, both of us."

How grateful she was for that "*tous les deux*"! She might have known Pierre would not betray her.

"Father," she said as she kissed him again, "please ask Pierre Charron to come to dinner tonight. I want to make something very nice for him. I've given him a lot of trouble."

After Pierre was gone, and she had peeped into the salon and the kitchen to see that everything was as she had left it, Cécile came back into the shop.

"Father, Pierre took it on himself, but it was my fault we came home. I didn't like country life very well. I was not happy."

"But aren't they kind people, the Harnois? Haven't they kind ways?"

"Yes, they have." She sighed and put her hand to her forehead, trying to think. They had kind ways, those poor Harnois, but that was not enough; one had to have kind things about one, too. . . .

But if she was to make a good dinner for Pierre, she had no time to think about the Harnois. She put on her apron and made a survey of the supplies in the cellar and kitchen. As she began handling her own things again, it all seemed a little different, — as if she had grown at least two years older in the two nights she had been away. She did not feel like a little girl, doing what she had been taught to do. She was accustomed to think that she did all these things so carefully to please her father, and to carry out her mother's wishes. Now she realized that she did them for herself, quite as much. Dogs cooked with blueberries — poor Madame Harnois' dishes were not much better! These coppers, big and little, these brooms and clouts and brushes, were tools; and with them one made, not shoes or cabinet-work, but life itself. One made a climate within a climate; one made the days, — the complexion, the special flavour, the special happiness of each day as it passed; one made life.

Suddenly her father came into the kitchen. "Cécile, why did you not call me to make the fire? And do you need a fire so early?"

"I must have hot water, Papa. It is no trouble to make a fire." She wiped her hands and threw her arms about him. "Oh, Father, I think our house is so beautiful!"

BOOK V

The Ships from France

BOOK FIVE

The Ships from France

I

AT four o'clock in the morning Cécile was sitting by her upstairs window, dressed and wide awake. Across the river there was already a red and purple glow above the black pines; but overhead spread the dark night sky, like a tent with its flap up, letting in a new day, — the most important day of the year.

Word had come down by land that five ships from France had passed Tadoussac and were beating up the river against head winds. During the night the wind had changed; Cécile had only to hold her handkerchief outside her window and watch it flutter, to reassure herself that a strong breeze was blowing in from the east, and the ships would be in today. She wondered how her father could go on sleeping. Nicholas Pigeon and Blinker had been up all night, making a great deal of noise as they turned out one baking after another to feed the hungry sailors. The smell of fresh bread was everywhere, very tempting to one who had been awake so long.

At last she heard a door below open softly, and she ran down the stairs to the salon and out into the kitchen, where her father was just beginning to make his fire.

"Oh, Father, the wind is right! I knew it would come! Yesterday all the nuns at the Ursulines' were praying for the wind to change. How soon do you suppose they will get in? You remember last year it rained all day when the first ships came. But today will be beautiful. I expect Kebec will look very fine to them."

"No better than they will to us, certainly. But there is no hurry. They will not be along for hours yet."

Cécile told him she had been awake nearly all night and was very hungry, so would he please hurry the chocolate. She herself ran out through the board fence that divided their back yard from the Pigeons', to get a loaf from Blinker, as it was not nearly time for the baker's boy to come on his rounds.

They had just sat down to their breakfast when they heard the front door open, and heavy, rapid little steps crossed the bare floor of the shop. Jacques came in, his pale eyes so round that he looked almost frightened.

"Hurry, Cécile, they're coming!" he called. Then, remembering where he was, he snatched off his cap and murmured: "Pardon, monsieur. Bonjour, monsieur. Bonjour, Cécile."

Cécile sprang up. "You mean they are in sight, Jacques?"

"People say they are, nearly," he answered vaguely.

"What nonsense, Cécile! You are as foolish as the little boy. You know the cannon would be sounding and the whole town shouting if the ships were in sight. Sit down and calm yourselves, both of you. Jacques, here is some chocolate for you."

"Thank you, monsieur." He sat down on the edge of the chair and took the cup carefully in both hands, at the same time glancing at the clock. "But we must not be late," he added fearfully.

"We shall not be. The ships cannot possibly pass this end of the island before noon."

"Which ones do you think they will be, monsieur?"

"They will probably be old friends, that have come to us often before."

"Jacques means he hopes one of them will be *La Garonne*, with the nice sailor who made our beaver," Cécile explained.

Jacques blushed and looked up at her trustfully. But his anxiety was too strong for him. In a few moments he stole another glance at the clock and resolutely put down his cup.

"If you please, monsieur, I think I will go now."

233

Auclair laughed. "You may both go! You are as rest-less as kittens. I can do nothing with either of you about. I will follow you in an hour or two. You will have a long wait."

The children agreed they wouldn't mind that, and they ran out into the early sunshine and down the hill hand in hand.

"Oh, look at the market square, Jacques, look! I have never seen so many carts before."

Since long before daybreak the country people had been coming into town, bringing all they could carry in their carts and on their backs; fresh pork, dressed rab-bits and poultry, butter and eggs, salad, green beans, leeks, peas, cucumbers, wild strawberries, maple sugar, spruce beer. The sailors, after two or three months on salt meat and ship's bread, would sell their very ear-rings for poultry and green vegetables. All the market-women, and the men, too, were dressed in their best, in whatever was left of the holiday costume they used to wear at home, in their native town. A sailor would al-ways make straight for the head-dress or bonnet or jacket of his own *pays*.

The children found there was already a crowd at the waterside, and while they ran about, hunting for an advantageous post of observation, people kept streaming down Mountain Hill. The whole of the Upper Town was emptying itself into the Lower. The old people, who almost never left the house, came with the rest, and babies at the breast were carried along because there was no one at home to leave them with. Not even on great feast-days did one see so many people come together. Bishop Laval and his *donné* came down the hill and took their places in the crowd. Giorgio, the drummer boy, and Picard, the Count's valet, were sitting on one of the cannon that guarded the landing-place. Noël Pommier and his friend the wagon-maker came carrying old Madame Pommier between them, and a boy followed bringing her chair. There were even new faces: a company of Montreal merchants, who had been staying at the Château for several days, awaiting the ships.

All the poor and miserable were on the water front, as well as the great. 'Toinette was moving about in the crowd, looking fresh and handsome in a clean dress and a new kerchief. Her partner, the Snail, with her hair curled very tight and her hands hidden under her apron, was standing among the poor folk over by the King's warehouse. Jacques was careful to keep out of his mother's way; but she had no wish to be bothered with him and was blind to his presence in the crowd. The Count did not come down the hill, but he was in plain view on the terrace in front of the Château, and with him were the Intendant and Madame de Champigny, and a group of officers with their wives. Everyone in Kebec, Cécile believed, except the cloistered nuns, was out today. Even Monseigneur de Saint-Vallier, though he was so proud, had a chair placed in the highest part of his garden and sat there looking down over the roofs, watching for the ships.

The hours dragged on. Babies began to cry and old people to murmur, but nobody went away. Giorgio and Picard made a place for Jacques between them on the cannon. By the time her father arrived, Cécile was beginning to wonder whether she could possibly stand any longer. But very soon a shout went up — something flashed in the south channel against the green fields of the Île d'Orléans. Cécile held her breath and gripped her father's hand. It dipped, it rose again, a gleam of white. There could be no doubt now; larger and larger, the canvas of sails set full, with the wind well behind them. Soon the whole rigging rose above the rapidly dropping shore, then the full figure of a square-rigged ship emerged, passed the point of the island, and glided into the broad, undivided river. The cannon on the redoubt boomed the Governor's salute, and all the watchers on the waterside shouted a great welcoming cry, waving their caps, kerchiefs, aprons, anything at hand. Women, and men, too, cried for joy. Cécile hid her face on her father's shoulder, and Jacques stood up on the cannon, waving his little cap.

"*Les Deux Frères, Les Deux Frères!*" people began to shout, while others laughed at them. She was not near enough for anyone to be sure, but the townspeople knew those carrying boats by heart, held their lines and shape in mind all year. Sure enough, as the vessel bore up the river toward the rock, everyone agreed that it was *Les Deux Frères,* from Le Havre. Her anchor-chains had scarcely begun to rattle when the sound was drowned by new shouts; a second set of sails was sighted between the green fields and the pine-clad shore.

"*Le Profond, Le Profond!*" the people cried, and again the ordnance thundered from the redoubt.

Within half an hour the Captain of *Les Deux Frères* came ashore in a little boat, bringing dispatches for the Governor. But before he could make his way up to the Château, he had to stop to greet old friends and to answer the questions of the crowd that pressed about him.

The King was well, and Monsieur le Dauphin was in good health. The young Duc de Bourgogne — the King's grandson — was married to a little Princess of

Savoie, only twelve years old, *mais bien sage*. The war was at a standstill; but of that they would hear later, — he tapped his dispatch-case. The wheat-harvest had been good last year, the vintage one of the best within memory. Of the voyage he had no time to speak; they had got here, hadn't they? That was the important thing.

The Captain made his way up the hill, and Bishop Laval went into the church of Notre Dame de la Victoire to thank God for preserving the King's health.

Sometimes, owing to bad weather and high winds, the ships of the first fleet came in four or five days apart; but this year they came in close succession. By sunset five vessels were anchored in the roadstead before Quebec: *Les Deux Frères, Le Profond, La Reine du Nord, La Licorne, Le Faucon.* They stood almost in a row, out in the river. Worn, battered old travellers they looked. It brought tears to the eyes to think how faithful they were, and how much they had endured and overcome in the years they had been beating back and forth between Canada and the Old World. What adverse winds those sails had been trimmed to, what mountains of waves had beaten the sides of those old hulls, what a wilderness of hostile, never-resting water those bows had driven through! Beaten southward, beaten backward, out of their course for days and even weeks together; rolling helpless, with sails furled, water over them and under them, — but somehow wearing through. On bad voyages they retraced their distance three and five times over, out-tiring the elements by their patience, and then drove forward again — toward Kebec. Sometimes they went south of Newfoundland to enter the Gulf, sometimes they came south of Labrador and through the straits of Belle Île; always making for this rock in the St. Lawrence. Cécile wondered how they could ever find it, — a goal so tiny, out of an approach so vast.

Many a time a boat came in wracked and broken, and it took all summer to make repairs, before the captain dared face the sea again. And all summer the hardships and mischances of the fleet were told over and over in Quebec. The greater part of the citizens had made that voyage at least once, and they knew what a North Atlantic crossing meant: little wooden boats matched against the immensity and brutality of the sea; the strength that came out of flesh and blood and goodwill, doing its uttermost against cold, unspending eternity. The colonists loved the very shapes of those old ships. Here they were again, in the roadstead, sending off the post-bags. And tomorrow they would give out of their insides food, wine, cloth, medicines, tools, fire-arms, prayer-books, vestments, altars for the missions, everything to comfort the body and the soul.

II

THE next few days were like a continual festival, with sailors overrunning the town, and drinking and singing in the Place half the night. Every day was market day, and both Blinker and his master worked double shifts, trying to bake bread enough for five crews. The waterside was heaped with merchandise and casks of wine. The merchants employed every idle man and boy to help them store their goods, and all the soldiers were detailed to receive the supplies for the Château and the forts. Even the churches and the priests were busier than usual. The sailors, though they might indulge in godless behaviour, were pious in their own way; went to confession soon after they got into port, and attended mass. They lived too near the next world not to wish to stand well with it. Nobody begrudged them their rough pleasures; they never stole, and they seldom quarrelled. Even the strictest people, like Bishop Laval, recognized that men who were wet and cold and poorly fed for months together, who had to climb the rigging in the teeth of the freezing gales that blew down from Labrador, must be allowed a certain licence during the few weeks they were on shore. The colony owed its life to these fellows; whatever else they did, they got the ships to Quebec every year.

Cécile was allowed to take Jacques for an escort and go down to the waterside in the morning to watch the unloading, — until the third day, when Auclair's own goods, from the old drug house in the parish of Saint-Paul, were brought ashore from *Le Profond.* In a few hours the orderly shop, and the salon behind it, were full of bales and boxes. M. Auclair said they must begin unpacking at once, as with this confusion there was no room for customers to come and go. Jacques had followed the carriers up the hill, and he decided that he would rather stay and see these boxes opened than share in the general excitement on the waterside.

The apothecary took off his coat and set to work with his hammer and chisel. Blinker, very curious to see everything that came out of the boxes, ran in between bakings to carry the lumber and straw down into the cellar. One by one the white jars on the shelves, and the drawers of the cabinets, were filled up again; with powders, salts, gums, blue crystals, strong-smelling spices, bay-leaves, lime flowers, camomile flowers, senna, hyssop, mustard, dried plants and roots in great variety. There was the usual crate of small wooden boxes containing fruits conserved in sugar, very costly and much prized in Quebec. These boxes could not be opened, of course, as they were the most expensive articles in Auclair's stock, but it delighted the children to read the names on the covers: figs, apricots, cherries, candied lemon rind, and crystallized ginger.

While Cécile and Jacques were counting over these boxes of sweetmeats and wondering who would buy such luxuries, Auclair told them he was much more interested in a jar labelled *"Bitumen — oleum terræ"* than in the conserves. It contained a dark, ill-smelling paste which looked like wagon grease; a kind of petroleum jelly that seeped out of the rocks in a certain cairn on the island of Barbados and was carried from thence to France. He had great need for it here in Canada; he purified it, added a small amount of alcohol and borax, and prepared a remedy for snow-blindness, with which hunters and trappers and missionaries were so cruelly afflicted in winter. So far, no cure had been discovered that gave such relief. A physician in Montreal had tried a similar treatment, using goose grease and lard instead of the *oleum terræ*, with very bad results. This, Auclair explained to the children, was because all animal fat contained impurities, and this "Barbados tar," as it was vulgarly called, might be regarded as a mineral fat. He went on to say that in general he distrusted remedies made of the blood or organs of animals, though he must admit that some were of exceptional value. For a hundred years and more the Breton fishermen, who went as far as Newfoundland and Labrador for their catch, had been making a medicinal oil from the fat livers of the codfish, and had an almost fanatical faith in its benefits. He himself had used it in Quebec for cases of general decline, and found it strengthening.

"But I detest all medicines made from lizards and serpents," he concluded his lecture, "even viper broth."

"Viper broth, Father? I have never heard of that. Is it an Indian medicine?"

"My dear, at the time when we came out to Canada, it was very much the fashion at home. Half the great ladies of France were drinking a broth made from freshly killed vipers every morning, instead of their milk or chocolate, and believed themselves much the better for it. Medicine is a dark science, as I have told you more than once."

"Yes, but everything here in our shop is good for people. We know that, don't we, Jacques? You shouldn't speak against medicines, Father, when our new ones have just come and we are feeling so happy to have them. You always worry, you know, when any of the jars are nearly empty."

"Oh, we do what we can, my dear! We can but try." Her father took up his chisel again and began to pry the lid from another box. "The perplexing thing is that honest pharmaciens get such different results from the same remedy. Your grandfather, all his life, believed that he had helped many cases of epilepsy with pow-dered unicorn's horn, which he got from Africa at great expense; while I have so low an opinion of it that I never keep it in my shop."

"But your cough-sirops, Papa, both kinds, help ev-eryone. And Madame Renaude says she could never milk her cows in the morning if she did not put your rheumatism ointment on her hands at night."

Auclair laughed. "You are your mother over again. No matter on whom I tried a new remedy, she was always the first to feel its good effects. But what is this, Cécile? A package addressed to you, and in Aunt Blanche's handwriting, here among my Arabian spices! Why, she must have taken it to the pharmacie and per-suaded Monsieur Neuillant to pack it with his drugs, to ensure quick delivery. Now we shall have something of whose goodness there can be no doubt. No, you must open it yourself. Jacques and I will look on."

Night-gowns, with yokes beautifully embroidered by Aunt Blanche herself; a pair of stockings knit by the little cousin Cécile; a woollen dressing-gown; two jerseys, one red and one blue; a blue silk dress, all trimmed with velvet bands, to wear to mass; a gold brooch and a string of coral beads from Aunt Clothilde. Cécile unfolded them one after another and held them up to view. Never had a box from home brought such fine things before. What did it mean?

"It means that you are growing up now and must soon dress like a young lady. The aunts bear that fact in mind, — more than I, perhaps." Auclair sighed and became thoughtful.

Jacques clasped his two hands together and looked up at Cécile with his slow, utterly trustful and self-forgetful smile.

"Oh, Cécile," he breathed, "you will look so beautiful!"

III

P IERRE Charron had come down from Montreal and was giving a supper party for his friend Maître Pondaven, captain of *Le Faucon*. Cécile and her father were the only guests invited, though Pierre had said they might bring Jacques along to see the Captain's parrot. It was to be a party in the open air, down by the waterside, under the full moon.

Cécile had no looking-glass upstairs — the only one in the house was in the salon — so she always dressed by feeling rather than by sight. This afternoon she put on the blue silk dress with black velvet bands, walked about in it, then took it off and spread it out on her bed, where she smoothed it and admired it. It was too different from anything she had ever worn before, too long and too grand — quite right to wear to mass or to a wedding, perhaps, but not for tonight. She slipped on one of her new jerseys and felt like herself again. The coral beads she would wear; they seemed appropriate for a sailor's party. She left the beautiful dress lying on her bed and went down to see that her father had brushed his Sunday coat, and to give Jacques's hands a scrubbing. She and the little boy sat down on the sofa to wait for Pierre, while Auclair was arranging his shop for the night. To Cécile the time dragged very slowly. She was thinking, not about the novelty of having supper by moonlight, or of the *tête de veau* they were promised, or of the celebrated Captain Pondaven, but of his parrot.

All her life she had longed to possess a parrot. The

idea of a talking bird was fascinating to her — seemed to belong with especially rare and wonderful things, like orange-trees and peacocks and gold crowns and the Count's glass fruit. Her mother, she whispered to Jacques, had often told her about a parrot kept in one of the great houses at home, which saw a servant steal silver spoons and told the master. Then there was the imprisoned princess who taught her parrot to say her lover's name, and her cruel brothers cut out the bird's tongue. Magpies were also taught to speak, but they could say only a word or two.

At last she heard Pierre's voice at the front door.

"All ready, Monsieur Euclide?"

Cécile jumped up from the sofa and ran into the shop.

"We have been ready a long while, Pierre. I thought you had forgotten us."

"Little stupid!" Pierre pinched her ear.

Auclair now looked at his daughter for the first time. "But I supposed you would wear the new dress from Aunt Blanche?"

Cécile coloured a little. "I feel better like this. You don't mind, Pierre Charron?"

"Not a bit! This is a picnic, not a dinner of ceremony. Monsieur Auclair, will you be kind enough to bring some of those herbs you burn to keep off mosquitos?"

"Certainly, that is a good idea. I will fill my pockets."
The apothecary put on the large beaver hat which he
wore only to weddings and funerals, and they set off
down the hill, the two men before, Cécile and Jacques
following.

Down on the water-front, at some distance behind
the church of Notre Dame de la Victoire, a row of
temporary cabins were put up each summer, where hot
food was served to the sailors on shore leave. In one of
these Renaude-le-lièvre, the butter-woman, and an old
dame from Dinan sold fresh milk and butter and Breton
pancakes to the seamen from that part of the world.
Tonight they had prepared a special supper for the
Captain, of whom all the Bretons were proud; he had
come up from a *mousse* and had made his own way in the
world. Pierre had ordered things he knew the Captain
liked; a dish made of three kinds of shell-fish, a *tête de
veau*, which la Renaude did very well, a roast capon with
a salad, and for dessert Breton pancakes with honey and
preserves.

When the party arrived, their table was waiting for
them, with a white cloth, and a lantern hung from a
pole — already lit, though it was not yet dark and a pale
moon was shining in a clear evening sky. While Pierre
was giving instructions to the cooks, Captain Pondaven

was being rowed ashore by two of his crew. He came up from the landing, his parrot on his shoulder, dressed as no one there had ever seen him before, in his Breton holiday suit, which he carried about the world with him in his sailor's chest; a black jacket heavily embroidered in yellow, white knee-breeches, very full and pleated at the belt, black cloth leggings, and a broad-brimmed black hat with a shallow crown. He was a plain, simple man, direct in his dealings as in his glance, and he came from Saint-Malo, where the grey sea breaks against the town walls.

At first Cécile thought him a little sombre and solemn, but after a mug of Jamaica rum he was more at his ease, and as the supper went on he grew very companionable. She had hoped he would begin to tell at once about his voyages and the strange countries he had seen, but he seemed to wish to talk of nothing but his own town and his family. He had four boys, he said, and one little girl.

"And she is the only one who was born when I was at home. I am always a little anxious about her. The boys are strong like me and can take care of themselves, but she is more delicate,—not so sturdy as mademoiselle here, though perhaps mademoiselle is older."

"I was thirteen last month," Cécile told him.

249

"And she will be eleven in December. I am nearly always at home for her birthday."

Auclair asked him whether by home he meant Le Havre or Saint-Malo. The seaman looked surprised.

"Saint-Malo, naturally. I was born a Malouin."

"I know that. But since you take on your cargo at Le Havre, I thought you perhaps lived there now."

"Oh, no! One is best in one's own country. I run back to Saint-Malo after my last trip, and tie up there for the winter."

"But that must add to your difficulties, Monsieur Pondaven."

"It is nothing to me. I know the Channel like my own town. All my equipage are glad to get home. They are all Malouins. I should not know how to manage with men from another part."

"You Malouins stick together like Jesuits," Pierre declared. "Yet by your own account you were not so well treated there that you need love the place."

Captain Pondaven smiled an artless smile. "Perhaps that is the very reason! He means, Monsieur Auclair, that the town brought me up like a stepmother. My father was drowned, fishing off Newfoundland, and my mother died soon afterwards. With us, when an orphan boy is twelve years old, he is given a suit of clothes and a chest and is sent to sea as a *mousse*. They sent me out with a hard master my first voyage. But when I came back from Madagascar and showed how my ears were torn and my back was scarred, the townspeople took up my case and got my papers changed. My townspeople did not do so badly by me. When I was ready for a command, they saw that I had my chance. They put their money behind me, and I have been half-owner in my boat for five years now."

Though she liked the Captain very much and gave polite attention to his talk, Cécile's mind was on the parrot. He sat forgotten on the back of the chair, attached to his master's belt by a long cord. He seemed of a sullen disposition — there was nothing gay and bird-like about him. Neither was he so brilliant as she had expected. He was all grey, except for rose-coloured tail-feathers, and his plumage was ruffled and untidy, for he was moulting. He gave no sign of his peculiar talent, but sat as silent as the stuffed alligator at home, never moving except to cock his head on one side. When the leek soup put a temporary stop to conversation, she ventured a question.

"And what is your parrot's name, if you please, Monsieur Pondaven?"

The Captain looked up from his plate and smiled at

her. "His name is Coco, mademoiselle, and he will make noise enough presently. He is a little shy with strangers, not seeing many on board."

Then the shell-fish came on, and Auclair asked the Captain what people at home thought of the King's peace with the English.

He said he did not know what the inland people thought. "But with us on the coast it will make little difference. The King cannot make peace on the sea. Our people will take an English ship whenever they have a chance. They are looking for good plunder this summer. We must have our revenge for the ships they took from us last year."

"They are fine seamen, the English," Pierre Charron declared. Cécile had noticed that he was in one of his perverse moods, when he liked to tease and antagonize everyone a little.

The Captain answered him mildly. "Yes, they are good sailors, but we usually get the better of them. They are a blasphemous lot and have no respect for good manners or religion. That never pays."

Auclair reminded him that last summer the English had captured one of the boats bound for Canada.

"I remember well, *Le Saint-Antoine*, and the Captain is a friend of mine. They took the boat into Plymouth and sold her at auction. Many of our merchants lost heavily. Your Bishop, Monseigneur de Saint-Vallier, had sent some things for the missions over here by *Le Saint-Antoine*. Some bones of the saints and other holy relics were packed in an oak chest, and the Captain, out of respect, put it in his own cabin. The English, when they plundered the ship, came upon this chest and supposed it was treasure. When they opened it, they were furious. After committing every possible sacrilege they took the relics to the cook's galley and threw them into the stove where their dinner was cooking."

Cécile asked whether no punishment had come upon those sailors.

"Not at the time, mademoiselle, but I shouldn't like to put to sea with such actions on my soul, — and I am no coward, either."

"*Sales cochons anglais, sales cochons!*" said another voice, and she realized that at last the parrot had spoken. Jacques put his hand over his mouth to stifle a cry. Pierre and her father laughed, and applauded the parrot, but Cécile was much too startled to laugh. She had supposed that the speech of parrots called for a good deal of imagination on the part of the listener, like the first efforts of babies. But nobody could possibly mistake what this bird said. Had he been out of sight, in the shed kitchen with Mère Renaude, she would have thought some queer old person was in there, talking in a vindictive tone.

"Oh, monsieur, isn't he wonderful!" she gasped.

The Captain was pleased. "You find him amusing? Yes, he is a clever bird; you will see. Now let us all clink our cups together, — you, too, little man, — and perhaps he will say something else."

They rattled their pewter mugs several times, and the bird came out with: "*Vive le Roi, vive le Roi!*" Jacques began jumping up and down with excitement.

"He is a loyal subject of the King," said Pondaven. "He has been taught to say that when the cups clink. But for the most part, I don't teach him; he picks up what he likes."

"And do you always take him to sea with you, monsieur?"

"Nearly always, mademoiselle. My men believe he brings us good luck; they like to have him on board. I have his cage swung in my cabin, and when the ship pitches badly, I tie it down."

"But how does he endure the cold?" Auclair asked. "These are tropical birds, after all."

"Yes, his brother died of a chill on his first voyage — I had two of them. But this one seems to stand it. When

254

he begins to shiver, I give him a little brandy in warm water — he is very fond of it — and I put a blanket over him. He will live to be a hundred if I can keep him from taking cold."

Conscious that he was the centre of attention, the parrot began to croon softly: "*Bon petit Coco, bon petit Coco. Ici, ici!*"

Jacques and Cécile left their places and stood behind the Captain's chair to watch the bird's throat. Pondaven explained that he was an African parrot, and that was why he had so many tones of voice, harsh and gentle, for the African birds have a much more sensitive ear than the West Indian.

"Should you like to hear him whistle a tune, mademoiselle? He can, if he will. We will try to have a little concert." He put the parrot on his knee, took a piece of maple sugar from the table, and held it before the un-blinking yellow eyes. Then the Captain began to whistle a song of his own country:

> *A Saint-Malo, beau port de mer,*
> *Trois gros navires sont arrivés,*

After a few moments the bird repeated the air perfectly — his whistle was very musical, sounded somewhat like a flute. He was given the sugar, and stood on one foot while he fed himself with the other. The company now became interested in the *tête de veau*, but Jacques and Cécile scarcely tasted the dish for watching Coco. They were both wishing they could carry him off and keep him in the apothecary shop for ever.

"Has Coco a soul, Cécile?" Jacques whispered.

"I wonder! I will ask the Captain after a while, but we must listen now."

Captain Pondaven was relating some of the wonderful happenings in his own town. Presently he told them the story of how a great she-ape, brought to Saint-Malo as a curiosity by the Indian fleet, had one day broken her chain and run about the town. She dashed into a house, snatched a baby from its cradle, and ran up to the housetops with it, — and in Saint-Malo, he reminded them, the houses are four and even five storeys high. While all the terrified neighbours gathered in the street, the mother fell on her knees, shut her eyes, and appealed to the Blessed Virgin. The ape clambered along the roofs until she came to a house where an image of Our Lady stood in a little alcove up under the eaves. Into this recess the beast thrust the baby, and left it there, as safe as if it were with its own mother.

The children and the apothecary thought this a charming story, but Pierre sniffed. "Oh, you have nothing over us in the way of miracles!" he told the

256

Captain. "Here we have them all the time. Every Friday the beaver is changed into a fish, so that good Catholics may eat him without sin. And why do you look at me like that, Mademoiselle Cécile?"

"Everyone knows he is not changed, Pierre. He is only considered as a fish by the Church, so that hunters off in the woods can have something to eat on Fridays."

"And suppose in Montreal some Friday I were to consider a roast capon as a fish? I should be put into the stocks, likely enough!"

Captain Pondaven smiled and shook his head. "Mademoiselle has the better of you, Charron. A man can make fun of the angels, if he sets out to. But I was going to tell the little boy here that in our town, when a child is naughty, we still tell him the she-ape will get him; and the children are as much afraid of that beast as if she were alive."

The time had come for story-telling; Pondaven and Pierre Charron began to entertain each other with tales of the sea and forest, as they always did when they got together.

At about ten o'clock Father Hector Saint-Cyr came out from the Château, where he had been to lay before Count Frontenac a petition from the Christianized Indians of his mission at the Sault. He lingered on the terrace to enjoy the prospect, — he got to Quebec but seldom. The moon was high in the heavens, shining down upon the rock, with its orchards and gardens and silvery steeples. The dark forest and the distant mountains were palely visible. This was not the warm white moonlight of his own Provence, certainly, which made the roads between the mulberry-trees look like rivers of new milk. This was the moonlight of the north, cold, blue, and melancholy. It threw a shimmer over the land, but never lay in velvet folds on any wall or tower or wheat-field. Out in the river the five ships from France rode at anchor. Some sailors down in the Place were singing, and when they finished, their mates on board answered them with another song.

Why, the priest wondered, were these fellows always glad to get back to Kebec? Why did they come at all? Why should this particular cliff in the wilderness be echoing tonight with French songs, answering to the French tongue? He recalled certain naked islands in the Gulf of the St. Lawrence; mere ledges of rock standing up a little out of the sea, where the sea birds came every year to lay their eggs and rear their young in the caves and hollows; where they screamed and flocked together and made a clamour, while the winds howled around them, and the spray beat over them. This headland was scarcely more than that; a crag where for some reason human beings built themselves nests in the rock, and held fast.

Down yonder by the waterside, before one of the rustic booths, he could see a little party seated about a table with lanterns. He could not see who they were, but he felt a friendliness for that company. A little group of Frenchmen, three thousand miles from home, making the best of things, — having a good dinner. He decided to go down and join them.

IV

THE apothecary, in his shirt-sleeves, was standing on a wooden bench, taking down from the shelves of a high cabinet large sheets of paper, to which dried plants were attached by narrow strips of muslin gummed down with gum Arabic. This was his herbarium, his collection of medicinal Canadian plants which he meant to take back to France. Cécile, busily knitting, had been watching him for a long while. When at last he got down and began assorting the piles of paper, she spoke to him.

"Papa, what will become of Jacques when we go back to France?"

Her father was engaged with a plant of the milkweed kind, which the French colonists called *le cotonnier.* He did not look up.

"Ah, my dear, I have the Count's perplexities and my own, — I cannot arrange a future for your little protégé."

"But, Father, how can we leave him, with no one to look after him? I shall always be thinking of him, and it will make me very unhappy."

"You will soon have your little cousins for companions; Cécile, and André, and Rachel. Cousin André will fill Jacques's place in your heart."

"No, Papa. My heart is not like that."

She spoke quickly, almost defiantly, in a tone she had never used to her father before. He did not notice it; he was trying to decide which of two gentians was the better preserved. For a month now he had been distracted and absent-minded. Cécile went quietly into the salon. She almost hated that little André who was so fortunate, who had a wise and charming mother to watch over him, a father to provide for him, and a rich aunt to give him presents. Laying aside her knitting, she put on her cap and went out to walk about the town.

This was the first week of October. The autumn had been warm and sunny, — but rather sad, as always. After the gay summer, came the departures. First Pierre

The Ships from France

Charron had gone back to Montreal. Then Captain Pondaven, who had been coming to the apothecary shop so often that he seemed like a familiar friend, had suddenly set sail for his old town where the grey sea beat under the castellated walls. Three new ships had come in during September: *La Garonne, Le Duc de Bretagne, Le Soleil d'Afrique.* But *La Garonne* did not bring the Breton sailor Jacques waited for, and his mates reported that he had shipped on a boat in the West India trade.

None of the ships brought the word Cécile's father and the Governor were so impatiently expecting. A dark spirit of discontent and restlessness seemed to be sitting in the little salon behind the shop. All peace and security had departed. The very furniture looked ill at ease, as if it did not believe in its own usefulness any more. Perhaps the sofa and the table and the curtains had overheard her father say that he could not take them home with him, but must leave them to be scattered among the neighbours. Cécile wished that she could be left and scattered, too. She stayed out of doors and away from the house as much as possible. Her father cared little about his dinner now — sometimes forgot to go to market. So why should she spend the golden afternoons indoors?

The glorious transmutation of autumn had come on: all the vast Canadian shores were clothed with a splendour never seen in France; to which all the pageants of all the kings were as a taper to the sun. Even the ragged cliff-side behind her kitchen door was beautiful; the wild cherry and sumach and the blackberry vines had turned crimson, and the birch and poplar saplings were yellow. Up by Blinker's cave there was a mountain ash, loaded with orange berries.

In the Upper Town the grey slate roofs and steeples were framed and encrusted with gold. A slope of roof or a dormer window looked out from the twisted russet branches of an elm, just as old mirrors were framed in gilt garlands. A sharp gable rose out of a soft drift of tarnished foliage like a piece of agate set in fine goldsmith's work. So many kinds of gold, all gleaming in the soft, hyacinth-coloured haze of autumn: wan, sickly gold of the willows, already dropping; bright gold of the birches, copper gold of the beeches. Most beautiful of all was the tarnished gold of the elms, with a little brown in it, a little bronze, a little blue, even — a blue like amethyst, which made them melt into the azure haze with a kind of happiness, a harmony of mood that filled the air with content. The spirit of peace, that acceptance of fate, which used to dwell in the pharmacy on Mountain Hill, had left it and come abroad to dwell in the orchards and gardens, in the little stony streets where the leaves blew about. Day after day Cécile had walked about those streets trying to capture that lost content and take it home again. She felt almost as if she no longer had a home; often wished she could follow the squirrels into their holes and hide away with them for the winter.

This afternoon she saw that her father scarcely cared at all for those they would leave behind, — the only friends she had ever known. She was miserable, too, because she had spoken angrily to him. All the way up the hill her heart grew heavier, and the neat garden of the Récollets, where she was always welcome, seemed so full of sadness that she could not stay. She went into the Cathedral, found a dark corner behind the image of Saint Anthony, and knelt to pray. But she could only hide her face and cry. Once giving way to tears, she wept bitterly for all that she had lost, and all that she must lose so soon. Her mother had had the courage to leave everything she loved and to come out here with her father; she in turn ought to show just that same courage about going back, but she could not find it in her heart. "*O ma mère, je suis faible! Je n'ai pas l'esprit fort comme toi!*" she whispered under her sobs.

263

Bishop Laval, who was kneeling in the recess of a chapel, heard a sound of smothered weeping. He rose, turned about, and regarded her for some moments. Without saying a word he took her hand and led her out through the sacristy door into the garden of the Priests' House, where his poplar-trees were all yellow and the ground was covered with fallen leaves. He made her sit down beside him on a bench and waited until she had dried her tears.

"We are old friends, little daughter," he said kindly. "Your mother was a woman of exemplary piety. Have you been to your spiritual director with your troubles?"

"Oh, excuse me, Monseigneur l'Ancien! I am sorry to give way like this. I did not know it was coming on me."

"Can I help you in any way, my child?"

Cécile thought perhaps he could. At any rate, she felt a longing to confide in him. She had never been intimidated by his deep-set, burning eyes or his big nose. She always felt a kind of majesty in his grimness and poverty. Seventy-four years of age and much crippled by his infirmities, going about in a rusty old cassock, he yet commanded one's admiration in a way that the new Bishop, with all his personal elegance, did not. One believed in his consecration, in some special authority won from fasting and penances and prayer; it was in his face, in his shoulders, it was he.

The Ships from France

Cécile turned to him and told him in a low voice how she and her father expected to leave Quebec very soon and go back to France, and how hard it would be for her to part from her friends. "And what troubles me most is the little boy, Jacques Gaux. You have been so kind as to ask about him sometimes, mon père, and perhaps after we are gone you will not forget him. I wish someone would bear him in mind and look after him a little."

"You must pray for him, my child. It is to such as he that our Blessed Mother comes nearest. You must unceasingly recommend him to her, and I will not forget to do so."

"I shall always pray for him," Cécile declared fervently, "but if only there were someone in this world, here in Quebec — Oh, Monseigneur l'Ancien," she turned to him pleadingly, "everyone says you are a father to your people, and no one needs a father so much as poor Jacques! If you would bid Houssart keep an eye on him, and when he sees the little boy dirty and neglected, to bring him here, where everything is good and clean, and wash his face! It would help him only to sit here with you — he is like that. Madame Pommier would look after him for me, but she cannot get about, and Jacques will not go to her, I am afraid. He is shy. When he is very dirty and ragged, he hides away."

"Compose yourself, my child. We can do something. Suppose I were to send him to the Brothers' school in Montreal, and prepare him for the Seminary?"

She shook her head despondently. "He could never learn Latin. He is not a clever child; but he is good. I don't think he would be happy in a school."

"Schools are not meant to make boys happy, Cécile, but to teach them to do without happiness."

"When he is older, perhaps, Monseigneur, but he is only seven."

"I was only nine when I was sent to La Flèche, and that is a severe school," said the Bishop. Perhaps some feeling of pity for his own hard boyhood, the long hours of study, the iron discipline, the fasts and vigils that kept youth pale, rose in his heart. He sighed heavily and murmured something under his breath, of which Cécile caught only the words: " . . . *domus* . . . *Domine.*"

She thanked him for his kindness and curtsied to take her leave. He walked with her to the garden door. "I will not forget what you have confided to my care, and I will seek out this child from time to time and see what can be done for him. But our Blessed Mother can do more for him than you or I. Never omit to present him to her compassion, my daughter."

266

The Ships from France

Cécile went away comforted. Merely sitting beside the Bishop had given her an escape from her own thoughts. His nature was so strong of its kind, and different from that of anyone else she knew. She was hurrying home with fresh courage when she met Jacques himself, coming up the hill to look for her.

"I went to your house," he said, "but monsieur your father was occupied, so I came away."

"That was right. Have you had a bite of anything?"

He shook his head.

"Neither have I. If my father is busy with his plants, we should only bother him. Let us get a loaf from Monsieur Pigeon and take it up by the redoubt, and watch the sun go down."

By the time they had called at the baker's and climbed to the top of Cap Diamant, the sun, dropping with incredible quickness, had already disappeared. They sat down in the blue twilight to eat their bread and await the turbid afterglow which is peculiar to Quebec in autumn; the slow, rich, prolonged flowing-back of crimson across the sky, after the sun has sunk behind the dark ridges of the west. Because of the haze in the air the colour seems thick, like a heavy liquid, welling up wave after wave, a substance that throbs, rather than a light.

That crimson flow, that effulgence at the solemn twilight hour, often made Cécile think about the early times and the martyrs — coming up, as it did, out of those dark forests that had been the scene of their labours and their fate. The rainbow, she knew, was set in the heavens to remind us of a promise that all storms shall have an ending. Perhaps this afterglow, too, was ordained in the heavens for a reminder.

"Jacques," she said presently, "do you ever think about the martyrs? You ought to, because they were so brave."

"I don't like to think about them. It makes me feel bad," he murmured. He was sitting with his hands on his knees, looking vaguely into the west.

Cécile squeezed his arm. "Oh, it doesn't me! It makes me feel happy, as if I could never be afraid of anything again. I wish you and I could go very far up the river in Pierre Charron's canoe, and then off into the forests to the Huron country, and find the very places where the martyrs died. I would rather go out there than — anywhere." Rather than go home to France, she was thinking.

But perhaps, after she grew up, she could come back to Canada again, and do all those things she longed to do. Perhaps some day, after weeks at sea, she would find herself gliding along the shore of the Île d'Orléans and would see before her Kebec, just as she had left it; the grey roofs and spires smothered in autumn gold, with the Récollet flèche rising slender and pure against the evening, and the crimson afterglow welling up out of the forest like a glorious memory.

BOOK VI

The Dying Count

The Dying Count

I

C OUNT Frontenac sat at the writing-table in his long room, driving his quill across sheets of paper. He was finishing a report to Pontchartrain, the Minister, which was to go by *Le Soleil d'Afrique*, sailing now in three days. Auclair stood by the fireplace, where the birch logs were smouldering, — it was now the end of October. He was remarking to himself that his master, often so put about by trifles, could bear with calmness a crushing disappointment.

All summer the Count had been waiting for his release from office, had confidently expected a letter summoning him to return to France to fill some post worthy of his past services.

When the King had sent him out here nine years ago, it had been to save Canada — nothing less. The fur trade was completely demoralized, and the Iroquois were murdering French colonists in the very outskirts of Montreal. The Count had accomplished his task. He had chastised the Indians, restored peace and order, secured the safety of trade. He was now in his seventy-eighth year, and although he had repeatedly asked for his recall to France, the King had made no recognition of his services beyond sending him the Cross of St. Louis last autumn.

It was sometimes hinted that there was a personal reason for the King's neglect. There was an old story that because Madame de Montespan had been Count Frontenac's mistress before she became King Louis's, His Majesty disliked the sight of the Count. But Madame de Montespan had long ago fallen out of favour; she had been living in retirement for many years and never came to Court. The King himself was no longer young. Auclair doubted whether one old man would remember an affair of youthful gallantry against another old man, — when the woman herself was old and long forgotten.

He was thinking of this as he stood by the fire, awaiting his master's pleasure. At last the Governor pushed back his papers and turned to him.

"Euclide," he began, "I am afraid I cannot promise you much for the future. When the last ships came in, I had no doubt that I should go home on one of them, — and you and your daughter with me. By *La Vengeance*

the Minister sends me a letter concerning the peace of
Rijswijk, but ignores my petition for recall. He assures
me of His Majesty's esteem, and of his desire to reward
my services more substantially in the future. The future, for a man of my age, is an inconsiderable matter.
His Majesty prefers that I shall die in Quebec."

The Count rose and walked to the window behind
his desk, where he stood looking down at the ships anchored in the river, already loading for departure. As
he stood there lost in reflection, Auclair thought he
seemed more like a man revolving plans for a new
struggle with fortune than one looking back upon a life
of brilliant failures. The Count had the bearing of a
fencer when he takes up the foil; from his shoulders to
his heels there was intention and direction. His carriage
was his unconscious idea of himself, — it was an armour
he put on when he took off his night-cap in the morning, and he wore it all day, at early mass, at his desk, on
the march, at the Council, at his dinner-table. Even his
enemies relied upon his strength.

"I have never been a favourite," he said, turning
round suddenly. "I have not the courtier's address.
Without that, a military man cannot go far nowadays.
Perhaps I offended His Majesty by trying to teach him
geography. Nothing is more unpopular at Court than

the geography of New France. They like to think of Quebec as isolated, French, and Catholic. The rest of the continent is a wilderness, and they prefer to disregard it. Any advance to the westward costs money — and Quebec has already cost them enough."

The Count returned to his desk, sat down, and went on talking in the impersonal, remote tone which he often adopted with his apothecary. Indeed, Auclair's chief service to his patron was not to administer drugs, but to listen occasionally, when the Governor felt lonely, to talk of places and persons, — talk which would have been incomprehensible to anyone else in Kebec.

"After my reappointment to Canada I had two audiences with His Majesty. The first was at Versailles, when he was full of a project to seize New York and the Atlantic seaports from the English. I was not averse to such an enterprise, but I explained some of the difficulties. With a small fleet and a few thousand regulars, I would gladly have undertaken it.

"My second audience was at Fontainebleau, shortly before we embarked from La Rochelle. The King received me very graciously in his cabinet, but he was no longer in a conqueror's mood; he had consulted the treasury. When I referred to the project he had advanced at our previous meeting, he glanced at the clock over his fireplace and remarked that it was the hour for feeding the carp. He asked me to accompany him. An invitation to attend His Majesty at the feeding of the carp is, of course, a compliment. We went out to the carp basins. I like a fine pond of carp myself, and those at Fontainebleau are probably the largest and fiercest in France. The pages brought baskets of bread, and His Majesty threw in the first loaves. The carp there are monsters, really. They came grunting and snorting like a thousand pigs. They piled up on each other in hills as high as the rim of the basin, with all their muzzles out; they caught a loaf and devoured it before it could touch the water. Not long before that, a care-taker's little girl fell into the pond, and the carp tore her to pieces while her father was running to the spot. Some of them are very old and have an individual renown. One old creature, red and rusty down to his belly, they call the Cardinal.

"Well, after the ravenous creatures had been fed by the royal hand, the King accompanied me a little way down the chestnut avenue. He wished me God-speed and said adieu. I took my departure by the great gate, where my carriage waited, and the King went back to the carp pond. That was my last interview with my royal master. That was the end of his bold project to

277

snatch the seaports from the English and make this continent a French possession, as it should be. I sailed without troops, without money, to do what I could. Unfortunately for you, I brought you with me." The Count unlocked a drawer of his desk. He took out a leather bag and dropped it on his pile of correspondence. From its weight and the sound it made, Auclair judged it contained gold pieces.

"When I persuaded you to come out here," the Governor continued, "I promised you a return. I have already seen the captain of *Le Soleil d'Afrique* and bespoken his best cabin in case I have need of it. As you know, I am always poor, but in that sack there is enough for you to begin a modest business at home. If I were in your place, I should get my belongings together and embark the day after tomorrow."

"And you, Monsieur le Comte?"

"It is just possible that I may follow you next year. If not, Kebec is as near heaven as any place."

"Then I prefer to wait until next year also." Auclair spoke quietly, but without hesitation. "I came to share your fortunes."

The Governor frowned. "But you have your daughter's future to consider. At the present moment, I can in some degree assure you another start in the world. But if I terminate my days here, you will be adrift, and I doubt if you will ever get home at all. You are not very adept in practical matters, Euclide."

Auclair flushed faintly. "I have made my choice, patron. I remain in Kebec until you leave it. And I have no need for that," indicating the leather bag. "You pay me well for my services."

When the apothecary left the chamber, the Count looked after him with a shrug, and a smile in which there was both contempt and kindness. He remembered an incident very long ago: He had just come home from the foreign wars, and had nearly ruined himself providing a new coach and horses and liveries to make a suitable re-entrance in the world. The first time he went abroad in his new carriage, to pay calls in the fashionable part of Paris, the occupants of every coach he passed either were looking the other way, or saluted him carelessly, as if they had seen him only the day before. Not even a driver or a footman glanced twice at his fine horses. The gate-keepers and equerries at the houses where he stopped were insolently indifferent. Late in the afternoon, when he was crossing the Pont-Neuf at the crowded hour, in a stream of coaches, he saw among the foot-passengers the first admirers of his splendour: an old man and a young boy, gazing up

279

and following his carriage with eager eyes — the grandfather and grandson who lived in the pharmacy next his
stables and were his tenants.

I I

THE Count de Frontenac awoke suddenly out of a
curious dream — a dream so vivid that he could
not at once shake it off, but lay in the darkness behind
his bed-curtains slowly realizing where he was. The
sound of a church-bell rang out hoarse on the still air:
yes, that would be the stubborn old man, Bishop Laval,
ringing for early mass. He knew that bell like a voice.
He was, then, in Canada, in the Château on the rock of
Kebec; the St. Lawrence must be flowing seaward beneath his windows.

In his dream, too, he had been asleep and had suddenly awakened; awakened a little boy, in an old farm-
house near Pontoise, where his nurse used to take him
in the summer. He had been awakened by fright, a sense
that some danger threatened him. He got up and in his
bare feet stole to the door leading into the garden,
which was ajar. Outside, in the darkness, stood a very
tall man in a plumed hat and huge boots — a giant, in

fact; the little boy's head did not come up to his boot-tops. He had no idea who the enormous man might be, but he knew that he must not come in, that everything depended upon his being kept out. Quickly and cleverly the little boy closed the door and slid the wooden bar, — he had no trouble in finding it, for he knew the house so well. But there was the front door, — he was sleeping in the wing of the cottage, and that front door was three rooms away. Still barefoot, he went softly and swiftly through the kitchen and the living-room to the hallway behind that main door, which could be fastened by an iron bolt. It was pitch-dark, but he did not fumble, he found the bolt at once. It was rusty, and stuck. He felt how small and weak his hands were — of that he was very conscious. But he turned the bolt gently back and forth in its hasp to loosen the rust-flakes, and coaxed it into the iron loop on the door-jamb which made it fast. Then he felt suddenly faint. He wiped the sweat from his face with the sleeve of his night-gown, and waited. That terrible man on the other side of the door; one could hear him moving about in the currant bushes, pulling at the rose-vines on the wall. There were other doors — and windows! Every nook and corner of the house flashed through his mind; but for the moment he was safe. The broad oak boards and the iron bolt were

281

between him and the great boots that must not cross the threshold. While he stood gathering his strength, he awoke in another bed than the one he had quitted a few moments ago, but he was still covered with sweat and still frightened. He did not come fully to himself until he heard the call of the old Bishop's bell-clapper. Then he knew where he was.

Of all the houses he had slept in all over the world, in Flanders, Holland, Italy, Crete, why had he awakened in that one near Pontoise, and why had he remembered it so well? His bare feet had avoided every unevenness in the floor; in the dark he had stepped without hesitation from the earth floor of the kitchen, over the high sill, to the wooden floor of the living-room. He had known the exact position of all the furniture and had not stumbled against anything in his swift flight through the house. Yet he had not been in that house since he was eight years old. For four summers his nurse, Noémi, had taken him there. It was her property, but on her son's marriage the daughter-in-law had become mistress, according to custom. Noémi had taken care of him from the time he was weaned until he went to school. His own mother was a cold woman and had little affection for her children. Indeed, the Count reflected, as he lay behind his bed-curtains recovering from his dream, no woman, probably, had ever felt so much affection for him as old Noémi. Not all women had found him so personally distasteful as his wife had done; but not one of his mistresses had felt more than a passing inclination for him. Tenderness, uncalculating, disinterested devotion, he had never known. It was in his stars that he was not to know it. Noémi had loved his fine strong little body, grieved when he was hurt, watched over him when he was sick, carried him in her arms when he was tired. Now, when he was sick indeed, his mind, in sleep, had gone back to that woman and her farm-house on the Oise.

It struck him that a dream of such peculiar vividness signified a change in himself. A change had been coming on all summer — during the last few months it had progressed very fast. When from his windows he saw the last sail going out between the south shore and the Île d'Orléans, he knew he would never live to see those boats come back. Now, after this dream, he decided to make his will before another night fell.

Of late the physical sureness and sufficiency he had known all his life had changed to a sense of limitation and uncertainty. He had no wish to prolong this state. There was no one in this world whom he would be sorry to leave. His wife, Madame de la Grange Frontenac, he had no desire to see again, though he would will to her the little property he had, as was customary. Once a year she wrote him a long letter, telling him all the gossip of Paris and informing him of the changes which occurred there. From her accounts it appeared that the sons of most of his old friends had turned out badly enough. He could not feel any very deep regret that his own son had died in youth, — killed in an engagement in the Low Countries many years ago.

The Count himself was ready to die, and he would be glad to die here alone, without pretence and mockery, with no troop of expectant relatives about his bed. The world was not what he had thought it at twenty — or even at forty.

He would die here, in this room, and his spirit would go before God to be judged. He believed this, because he had been taught it in childhood, and because he knew there was something in himself and in other men that this world did not explain. Even the Indians had to make a story to account for something in their lives that did not come out of their appetites: conceptions of courage, duty, honour. The Indians had these, in their own fashion. These ideas came from some unknown source, and they were not the least part of life.

In spiritual matters the Count had always accepted

the authority of the Church; in governmental and military matters he stoutly refused to recognize it. He had known absolute unbelievers, of course; one, a witty and blasphemous scapegrace, the young Baron de La Hontan, he had sheltered here in the Château, under the noses of two Bishops. But it was for his clever conversation, not for his opinions, that the Count offered La Hontan hospitality.

When the grey daylight began to sift through the hangings of his bed, Count Frontenac rang for Picard to bring his coffee.

"I shall not get up today, Picard," he remarked. "You may shave me in bed. Afterwards, go to the notary and fetch him here to transact some business with me. Stop at the apothecary shop on your way, and tell Monsieur Auclair I shall not need him until four o'clock."

When Auclair arrived in the afternoon, he found his patron still in bed, in his dressing-gown. To his inquiries the Count replied carelessly:

"Oh, I do very well indeed! I find myself so comfortable that I have almost decided to stay in bed for the rest of my life. I have been making my will today, and that reminded me of a promise I once gave your daughter. That bowl of glass fruit on the mantel: do not forget to take it to her when you go home tonight, with my

285

greetings. She has always admired it. And there is another matter. In the leather chest in my dressing-room you will find a large package wrapped in brown Holland. It is table linen that I brought out from Île Savary. Tonight, when you will not be observed, I wish you to take it home with you for safe keeping. Upon Cécile's marriage, you will present it to her from me. Why do you look sober, Euclide? You know very well that I must soon change my climate, as the Indians say, and this Château will be in other hands. I merely arrange to dispose of my personal belongings as I wish."

"Monsieur le Comte, if you would permit me to try the remedy I suggested yesterday — "

"Tut-tut! We will have no more remedies. A little repose and comfort. The machine is worn out, certainly; but if we let it alone, it may go a little longer, from habit. When you come up tonight, you may bring me something to make me sleep, however. These long hours of wakefulness do a man no good. Draw up a chair and sit down by the fire, where I can speak to you without shouting. If you are to be in constant attendance here, you cannot be forever standing."

Picard was called to put more wood on the fire, and after he withdrew the Governor lay quiet for a time. The grey light of the rainy afternoon grew so pale that

286

Auclair could no longer see his patient's face, and supposed he had fallen asleep. But suddenly he spoke.

"Euclide, do you know the church of Saint-Nicholas-des-Champs, out some distance?"

"Certainly, Monsieur le Comte. I remember it very well."

"Many of my family are buried there; a sister of whom I was fond. I shall be buried here, in the chapel of the Récollets, but I should like my heart to be sent back to France, in a box of lead or silver, and buried near my sister in Saint-Nicholas-des-Champs. I have left instructions to that effect in my will, but I prefer to tell you, as I suppose you will have to attend to it. That is all we need say on the subject.

"Monseigneur de Saint-Vallier called here today, but as I was engaged with the notary, he left word that he would make his visit of ceremony tomorrow. I should be pleased if some indisposition were to keep him at home. If he looks for any apologies or recantations from me, he will be disappointed. The old one will not bother me with civilities." Auclair heard the Count chuckle. "The old one knows where he stands, at least, and never bends his neck. All the same, a better man for this part of the world than the new one. Saint-Vallier belongs at the Court — where he came from."

The Count fell into reflection, and his apothecary sat silent, waiting for his dismissal. Both were thinking of a scene outside the windows, under the low November sky — but the river was not the St. Lawrence. They were looking out on the Pont-Marie, and the hay-barges tied up at the Port-au-Foin. On an afternoon like this the boatmen would be covering the hay-bales with tarpaulins, Auclair was thinking, and about this time the bells always rang from the Célestins' and the church of Saint-Paul.

When the fire fell apart and Auclair got up to mend it, the Count spoke again, as if he knew perfectly well what was in the apothecary's mind. "The Countess de Frontenac writes me that the Île Saint-Louis has become a very fashionable quarter. I can remember when it was hardly considered a respectable place to live in, — when they first began building there, indeed!"

"And my grandfather could remember when it was a wood-pile, patron; before the two islands were joined into one. He was never reconciled to the change, poor man. He always thought it the most convenient place for the wood-supply of our part of Paris."

The Dying Count

III

ONE dark afternoon in November Cécile was sitting in the front shop, knitting a stocking. She sat
in her own little chair, placed beside her father's tall
stool, on which she had put a candle, as the daylight was
so thick. Though the street outside was wet and the fog
brown and the house so quiet, and though the Count
was ill up in the Château, she was not feeling dull, but
happy and contented. As she knitted and watched the
shop, she kept singing over Captain Pondaven's old
song, about the three ships that came

> *A Saint-Malo, beau port de mer,*
> *Chargés d'avoin', chargés de bléd.*

No more boats from France would come to Quebec as late as this, even her father admitted that, and
his herbarium had been put back on the high shelves of
the cabinet, where it belonged. As soon as those dried
plants were out of sight, the house itself changed; everything seemed to draw closer together, to join hands,
as it were. Cécile had polished the candlesticks and
pewter cups, rubbed the table and the bed-posts and the
chair-claws with oil, darned the rent in her father's

289

counterpane. A little more colour had come back into the carpet and the curtains, she thought. Perhaps that was only because the fire was lit in the salon every evening now, and things always looked better in the fire-light. But no, she really believed that everything in the house, the furniture, the china shepherd boy, the casseroles in the kitchen, knew that the herbarium had been restored to the high shelves and that the world was not going to be destroyed this winter.

A life without security, without plans, without preparation for the future, had been terrible. Nothing had gone right this fall; her father had not put away any wood doves in fat, or laid in winter vegetables, or bought his supply of wild rice from the Indians. "But we will manage," she sometimes whispered to her trusty poêle when she stuffed him with birch and pine.

Cécile tended the shop alone every afternoon now. A notice on the door requested messieurs les clients to be so good as to call in the morning, as the pharmacien was occupied elsewhere in the afternoon. Nevertheless clients came in the afternoon, especially country people, and her father placed all the most popular remedies on one shelf and marked them clearly, so that Cécile could dispense them when they were called for.

This afternoon, just as she was about to go for another candle, she thought she heard her father coming home; but it proved to be Noël Pommier, the cobbler, who wanted a mixture of rhubarb and senna that M. Auclair sometimes made up for his mother.

Cécile sprang up and told him it was ready at hand, plainly marked. *"Et préféreriez-vous les pilules, ou le liquide, Monsieur Noël?"*

"Les pilules, s'il vous plaît, mademoiselle. Et votre père?"

"He is always at the Château after three o'clock. The Governor has been indisposed for two weeks now."

"Everyone knows that, mademoiselle," said the cobler with a sigh. "Everyone is offering prayers for his recovery. It will be bad for all of us if anything goes wrong with the Count."

"Never fear, monsieur! My father is giving him every care, and he grows a little stronger each day."

"God grant it, mademoiselle. Picard is very much discouraged about his master. He says he cannot shave himself any more and does not look like himself. Picard thinks he ought to be bled."

"Oh, Monsieur Pommier, I wish you could hear what my father has to say to that! And what does Picard know about medicine? But he is not the only one. Other people have tried to persuade my father to bleed the Governor, but he is as firm as a rock."

"I have no doubt Monsieur Auclair knows best, Mademoiselle Cécile; but people will talk at such times, when a public man is ill."

Pommier had scarcely gone when her father came in, with a dragging step and a mournful countenance.

"Papa," said Cécile as she brought him his indoor coat, "I know you are tired, but the dinner will soon be ready. Sit down by the fire and rest a little. And, Father, won't you try to look a little more confident these days? The people watch you, and when you have a discouraged air, they all become discouraged."

"You think so?" He spoke anxiously.

"I am sure of it, Papa. I can tell by the things they say when they call here in your absence. You must look as if the Governor were much, much better."

"He is not. He is failing all the time." Her father sighed. "But you are right. We must put on a better face for the public."

Cécile kissed him and went into the kitchen. Just as she was moving the soup forward to heat, she heard a sharp knock at the shop door. Her father answered it, and Bishop de Saint-Vallier entered. Auclair hurriedly brought more candles into the shop and set a chair for his visitor. After preliminary civilities the Bishop came to the point.

The Dying Count

"I have called, Monsieur Auclair, to inquire concerning the Governor's condition. Do you consider his illness mortal?"

"Not necessarily. If he were ten years younger, I should not consider it serious. However, he has great vitality and may very easily rally from this attack."

The Bishop frowned and stroked his narrow chin. He was clearly in some perplexity. "When I called upon the Comte de Frontenac some days ago, he stated that his recovery would be a matter of a week, at most. In short, he refused to consider his indisposition seriously, though to my eyes the mark of death was clearly upon him. Does he really believe he will recover?"

"Very probably. And that is a good state of mind for a sick man."

"Monsieur Auclair," Saint-Vallier spoke up sharply, "I feel that you evade me. Do you yourself believe that the Count will recover?"

"I must ask your indulgence, Monseigneur, but in a case like the Count's a medical adviser should not permit himself to believe in anything but recovery. His doubts would affect the patient. If the Count still has the vital force I have always found in him, he will recover. His organs are sound."

Saint-Vallier seemed to pay little heed to this reply.

His eyes had been restlessly sweeping the room from floor to ceiling and now became fixed intently upon one point—on the stuffed alligator, as it happened. He began to speak rapidly, with gracious rise and fall of the voice, but in his most authoritative manner.

"If the Governor's illness is mortal, and he does not realize the fact, he should be brought to realize it. He has a great deal to put right with Heaven. He has used his authority and his influence here for worldly ends, rather than to strengthen the kingdom of God in Septentrional France!" For the first time he flashed a direct glance at the apothecary.

Auclair bowed respectfully. "Such matters are beyond me, Monseigneur. The Governor does not discuss his official business with me."

"But there is always open discussion of these things! Of the Governor's stand on the brandy traffic, for example, which is destroying our missions. I have denounced his policy openly from the pulpit, and on occasions when I noted that you were present in the church. You cannot be ignorant of it."

"Oh, upon that subject the Governor has also spoken publicly. Everyone knows that he considers it an unavoidable evil."

Saint-Vallier drew himself up in his chair and adopted

294

an argumentative tone. "And why unavoidable? You doubtless refer to his proposition that the Indians will sell their furs only to such traders as will supply them with brandy?"

"Yes, Monseigneur; and since the English and Dutch traders give them all the brandy they want, and better prices for their skins as well, we must lose the fur trade altogether if we deny them brandy. And our colony exists by the fur trade alone."

"That is our unique opportunity, Monsieur l'apothicaire, to sacrifice our temporal interests for the glory of God, and impress by our noble example the Dutch and English."

"If Monseigneur thinks the Dutch traders can be touched by a noble example — " Auclair smiled and shook his head. "But these things are all beyond me. I know only what everyone knows, — though I have my own opinions."

"If the Count's illness is as serious as it seems to me, Monsieur Auclair, he should be given an opportunity to acknowledge his mistakes before the world as well as to Heaven. Such an admission might have a salutary influence upon the administration which will follow his. Since he relies upon you, it is your duty to apprise him of the gravity of his condition."

Auclair met Saint-Vallier's glittering, superficial glance and plausible tone rather bluntly.

"I shall do nothing to discourage my patient, Monseigneur, any more than I shall bleed him, as many good people urge me to do. The mind, too, has a kind of blood; in common speech we call it hope."

The Bishop flushed — his sanguine cheeks were apt to become more ruddy when he was crossed or annoyed. He rose and gathered the folds of his cloak about him. "It is time your patient dropped the stubborn mask he has worn so long, and began to realize that none of his enterprises will benefit him now but such as have furthered the interests of Christ's Church in this Province. I have seen him, and I believe he is facing eternity."

Auclair expressed himself as much honoured by the Bishop's visit and accompanied him to the door, holding it open that the light might guide him across the street to the steps of his episcopal Palace. When he returned to the salon, Cécile was bringing in the soup.

"I began to think Monseigneur de Saint-Vallier would never go, Papa. How people do bother us about everything since the Count is ill! I am glad we can keep them away from him, at least."

Her father sat down and took a few spoonfuls of

soup. "Why, I find I am quite hungry!" he declared. "And when I came home, I did not think I could eat at all. For some reason, our neighbour's visit seems to have made me more cheerful."

"That is because you were so resolute with him, Father!"

He smiled at her between the candles.

"What restless eyes he has, Cécile; they run all over everything, like quicksilver when I spill it. He kept looking in again and again at your glass fruit, there on the mantel. Do you know, I believe he drew some conclusion from that; he has seen it at the Château, of course. These men who are trained at Court all become a little crafty; they learn to put two and two together. I have always believed that is why our patron never got advancement at Versailles: he is too downright."

IV

IT was late afternoon, and Cécile was alone — as she was nearly always now. The Count had died last night. Today her father had gone to the Château to seal his heart up in a casket, so that it could be carried back to France according to his wish. It was already arranged that Father Joseph, Superior of the Récollets, should take the casket to Montreal, then to Fort Orange, and down the river to New York, where the English boats came and went all winter. On one of those boats he would go to England, cross over to France, and journey to Paris with the Count's heart, to bury it in the Montmort chapel at Saint-Nicholas-des-Champs.

Auclair had been gone all the afternoon, and Cécile knew that he would come home exhausted from sorrow, from his night of watching, and from the grim duty which had taken him today to the Count's death-chamber. Cécile regarded this rite with awe, but not with horror; autopsies, she knew, must be performed upon kings and queens and all great people after death. That was the custom. Her father would have the barber-surgeon to help him, — though they were not very good friends, because they disagreed about bleeding people. The barber complained that the meddlesome apothecary took the bread out of his mouth.

Many times that afternoon Cécile went out to the door-step and looked up at the Château. A light snow was falling, and the sky was grey. It was very strange to look up at those windows in the south end, and to know that there was no friend, no protection there. She felt as if a strong roof over their heads had been swept away.

The Dying Count

She was not sure that they would even have a livelihood without the Count's patronage. Their sugar and salt and wine, and her father's Spanish snuff, had always come from the Count's storehouses. The colonists paid very little for their remedies; if they brought a basket of eggs, or a chicken, or a rabbit, they thought they were treating their medical man very handsomely. But what she most dreaded was her father's loneliness. He had lived under the Count's shadow. The Count was the reason for nearly everything he did, — for his being here at all.

About four o'clock, as the darkness began to close in, Cécile put more wood on the fire in the salon and set some milk to warm before it. There was very little to eat in the house. Her father had not been to market for a week. Running to the door every few minutes, she at last saw him coming down the hill, with his black bag full of deadly poisons. He looked grey and sick as she let him in. Before he threw his black bag into the cupboard, he took out of it a lead box, rudely soldered over. She looked at it solemnly.

"Yes," he said, "it is all we have left of him. Father Joseph will set out for France in two days. I am in charge of this box until it starts upon its journey."

He placed it in the cabinet where he kept his medical

299

books, then went into the salon and sank down in his chair by the fire. Cécile knelt on the floor beside him, resting her arms upon his knee. He bent and leaned his cheek for a moment on her shingled brown hair.

"So it is over, my dear," he sighed softly. "It has lasted a lifetime, and now it is over. Since I was six years old, the Count has been my protector, and he was my father's before me. To my mother, and to your mother, he was always courteous and considerate. He belonged to the old order; he cherished those beneath him and rendered his duty to those above him, but flattered nobody, not the King himself. That time has gone by. I do not wish to outlive my time."

"But you wish to live on my account, don't you, Father? I do not belong to the old time. I have got to live on into a new time; and you are all I have in the world."

Her father went on sadly: "The Count and the old Bishop were both men of my own period, the kind we looked up to in my youth. Saint-Vallier and Monsieur de Champigny are of a different sort. Had I been able to choose my lot in the world, I would have chosen to be like my patron, for all his disappointments and sorrows; to be a soldier who fought for no gain but renown, merciful to the conquered, charitable to the poor, haughty to the rich and overbearing. Since I could not be such a

man and was born in an apothecary shop, it was my
good fortune to serve such a man and to be honoured by
his confidence."

Cécile slipped quietly away to pour the warm milk
into a cup, and with it she brought a glass of brandy.
Her father drank them. He said he would want no dinner tonight, but that she must prepare something for
herself. Without noticing whether she did so or not, he
sat in a stupor of weariness, dreaming by the fire. The
scene at the Château last night passed again before his
eyes.

The Count had received the Sacrament in perfect
consciousness at seven o'clock. Then he sank into a sleep
which became a coma, and lay for three hours breathing
painfully, with his eyes rolled back and only a streak of
white showing between the half-open lids. A little after
ten o'clock he suddenly came to himself and looked
inquiringly at the group around his bed; there were two
nursing Sisters from the Hôtel Dieu, the Intendant and
Madame de Champigny, Hector de Callières, Auclair,
and Father Joseph, the Récollets' Superior, who had
heard the Count's confession and administered the last
rites of the Church. The Count raised his eyebrows
haughtily, as if to demand why his privacy was thus
invaded. He looked from one face to another; in those

faces he read something. He saw the nuns upon their knees, praying. He seemed to realize his new position in the world and what was now required of him. The challenge left his face, — a dignified calm succeeded it. Father Joseph held the crucifix to his lips. He kissed it. Then, very courteously, he made a gesture with his left hand, indicating that he wished every one to draw back from his bed.

"This I will do alone," his steady glance seemed to say.

All drew back.

"Merci," he said distinctly. That was the last word he spoke. While the group of watchers stood four or five feet away from the bed, wondering, they saw that his face had become altogether natural and lost all look of suffering. He breathed softly for a few moments, then breathed no more. One of the nuns held a feather to his lips. Madame de Champigny got a mirror and put it close to his mouth, but there was no cloud on it. Auclair laid his head down on his patron's chest; there all was still.

As Auclair was returning home after midnight, under the glitter of the hard bright northern stars, he felt for the first time wholly and entirely cut off from France; a helpless exile in a strange land. Not without reason, he told himself bitterly as he looked up at those stars, had the Latin poets insisted that thrice and four times blessed were those to whom it befell to die in the land of their fathers.

While Auclair sat by the fire thinking of these things, numb and broken, Cécile was lying on the sofa, wrapped up in the old shawl Madame Auclair had used so much after she became ill. She, too, was thinking of what they had lost. They would indeed have another winter in Quebec; but everything was changed almost as much as if they had gone away. That sense of a strong protector had counted in her life more than she had ever realized. To be sure, they had not called upon the Count's authority very often; but to know that they could appeal to him at any moment meant security, and gave them a definite place in their little world.

The hours went by. Her father did not speak or move, not even to fix the fire, which was very low. For once, Cécile herself had no wish to set things right. Let the fire burn out; what of it?

At last there came a knock at the door, not very loud, but insistent, — urgent, as it were. Auclair got up from his chair.

"Whoever it is, send him away. I can see no one tonight." He went into the kitchen and shut the door behind him.

Cécile was a little startled, — death made everything strange. She took a candle into the shop, set it down on the counter, and opened the door. Outside there, against the snow, was the outline of a man with a gun strapped on his back. She had thrown her arms around him before she could really see him, — the set of his shoulders told her who it was.

"Oh, Pierre, Pierre Charron!" She began to cry abandonedly, but from joy. Never in all her life had she felt anything so strong and so true, so real and so sure, as that quick embrace that smelled of tobacco and the pine-woods and the fresh snow.

"*Petite tête de garçon!*" he muttered, running his hand over her head, which lay on his shoulder. "There, don't try to tell me. I know all about it. I started for Kebec as soon as I heard the Count was sinking. Today, on the river, I passed the messengers going to Montreal; they called the word to me. And your father?"

"I don't know what to do, Pierre. It is worse with him than when my mother died. There seems to be no hope for us."

"I understand," he stroked her soothingly. "I knew this would be a blow to him. I said to myself in Ville-Marie: 'I must be there when it happens.' I came as quickly as I could. Never did I paddle so fast. The breeze was against me, there was no chance of a sail. I had only a half-man to help me — Antoine Frichette, you remember? That poor fellow for whom your father made the belly-band. He did his best, but since his hurt he has no wind. I'm here at last, to be of any use I can. Command me." He had loosed the big kerchief from his neck, and now he gently wiped her cheeks dry with it. Turning her face about to the candlelight, he regarded it intently.

"I wish you would go to him, Pierre. He is in the kitchen."

He kissed her softly on the forehead, unslung his gun, and went out into the kitchen. He, too, closed the door behind him. In the few moments while she was left alone in the shop, Cécile opened the outer door again and looked up toward the Château. The falling snow and the darkness hid it from sight; but she had once more that feeling of security, as if the strong roof were over them again; over her and the shop and the salon and all her mother's things. For the first time she realized that her father loved Pierre for the same reason he had loved the Count; both had the qualities he did not have himself, but which he most admired in other men.

When they came in from the kitchen, Charron had his arm over Auclair's shoulder.

"*Cécile,*" he called, "*je n'ai pas de chance.* Evidently I am too late for supper, and I have not had a morsel since I broke camp before daybreak."

"Supper? But we have had no supper here tonight. We had no appetite. I will make some for you, at once. There is not much in the house, I am afraid; my father has not been to market. Smoked eels, perhaps?"

Charron made a grimace. "Detestable! Even I can do better than that. I shot a deer for our supper in the forest last night, and I brought a haunch along with me, — outside, in my bag. What else have you?"

"Not much." Cécile felt deeply mortified to confess this, though it was not her fault. "We have some wild rice left from last year, and there are some carrots. We always have preserves, and of course there is soup."

"Excellent; all that sounds very attractive to me at the moment. You attend to everything else, but by your leave I will cook the venison in my own way. It's enough for us all, and there will be good pickings left for Blinker."

When Charron went out to get his game-bag, Auclair whispered to his daughter: "Are we really so destitute, my child? Do the best you can for him. I will open a box of the conserves from France."

He now seemed very anxious about his dinner, and

she could not forbear a reproachful glance at the head of the house, who had been so neglectful of his duties.

"And you, Monsieur Euclide," said Pierre, when he came back with the haunch in his hand, "you ought to produce something rather special from your cellar for us."

"It shall be the best I have," declared his host.

The supper lasted until late. After the dessert the apothecary opened a bottle of heavy gold-coloured wine from the South.

"This," he said, "is a wine the Count liked after supper. His family was from the South, and his father always kept on hand wines that were brought up from Bordeaux and the Rhone vineyards. The Count inherited that taste." He sighed heavily.

"Euclide," said Charron, "tomorrow it may be you or I; that is the way to look at death. Not all the wine in the Château, not all the wines in the great cellars of France, could warm the Count's blood now. Let us cheer our hearts a little while we can. Good wine was put into the grapes by our Lord, for friends to enjoy together."

When it was almost midnight, the visitor said he was too tired to go hunt a lodging, and would gladly avail himself of the invitation, often extended, but never before accepted, of spending the night here and sleeping on the sofa in the salon.

Cécile, in her upstairs bedroom, turned to slumber with the weight of doubt and loneliness melted away. Her last thoughts before she sank into forgetfulness were of a friend, devoted and fearless, here in the house with them, as if he were one of themselves. He had not a throne behind him, like the Count (it had been very far behind, indeed!), not the authority of a parchment and seal. But he had authority, and a power which came from knowledge of the country and its people; from knowledge, and from a kind of passion. His daring and his pride seemed to her even more splendid than Count Frontenac's.

Epilogue

O N the seventeenth day of August 1713, fifteen
years after the death of Count Frontenac, the
streets of Quebec and the headland overlooking the St.
Lawrence were thronged with people. By the waterside
the Governor General and Monsieur Vaudreuil, the Intendant, with all the clergy, regular and secular, the
magistrates, and the officers from the garrison, stood
waiting to receive a long-expected guest. Down the
river lay a ship from France, *La Manon*, unable to come
in against the wind. A small boat had been sent out to
bring in one of her passengers. As the little boat drew
near the shore, all the cannon on the fortifications, and
the guns on the vessels anchored in the roadstead, thundered a salute of welcome to Monseigneur de Saint-
Vallier, at last returning to his people after an absence of
thirteen years.

When the prelate put foot upon the shore of Quebec,
the church-bells began to ring, and continued to ring
while the Governor General, the Intendant, and the

Archidiacre made addresses of welcome. The Inden-
dant's carriage stood ready to convey the Bishop, but he
preferred, characteristically, to ascend on foot to the
Cathedral in the Upper Town, surrounded by the
clergy and preceded by drums and hautbois.

Euclide Auclair, the old apothecary, standing before
his door on Mountain Hill to watch the procession, was
shocked at the change in Monseigneur de Saint-Vallier.
When he sailed for France thirteen years ago, he was a
very young man of forty-seven; now he came back a very
old man of sixty. Every physical trait by which Auclair remembered the handsome and arrogant churchman had disappeared. He would never have recognized,
in this heavy, stooped, lame old man going up the hill,
the slender and rather dramatic figure he had so often
seen mounting the steps of the episcopal Palace across
the way. The narrow, restless shoulders were fat and
bent; the Bishop carried his head like a man broken to
the yoke.

Auclair watched the procession until the turn of the
way shut Monseigneur de Saint-Vallier from sight, then
went back to his shop and sat down, overcome. The
thirteen years which for him had passed quietly, happily, had been bitter ones for the wandering Bishop.
Nine years ago Saint-Vallier was on his way back to

Epilogue

Canada after one of his long absences, when his ship, *La Seine*, was captured by the English, taken into London, and sold at auction. The Bishop himself was declared a prisoner of state, and was sequestered in a small English town near Farnham until the French King should ransom him.

Politics intervened: King Louis had lately seized and imprisoned the Baron of Méan, Dean of the Cathedral of Liège. The German Emperor was much offended at this, and besought Queen Anne not to release the Bishop of Quebec under any other terms than as an exchange for the Baron of Méan. For five years Saint-Vallier remained a prisoner of state in England, until King Louis at last set the Baron of Méan at liberty and recalled the Bishop of Quebec to France. But this did not mean that he was free to return to Canada. During his captivity his enemies in Quebec and Montreal had been busy, had repeatedly written the Minister, Pontchartrain, that the affairs of the colony went better with the Bishop away; that the King would be assisting his Canadian subjects by keeping Saint-Vallier in France. This the King did. He kept him, indeed, almost as long as the Queen of England had done.

That period of detention in France had sobered and saddened the wilful Bishop. His captivity in England he could ascribe to the hostilities of nations; to himself and to others he was able to put a very good face on it. But he could not pretend that he was kept in France for any other reason than that he was not wanted in Quebec. He had to admit to the Minister that he had made mistakes; that he had not taken the wise course with the Canadian colonists. Only by unceasing importunities, and by working upon the sympathies of Madame de Maintenon, who had always befriended him, had he ever wrung from the King permission to sail back to his diocese.

On this day of his return, even his enemies were softened at seeing how the man was changed. In place of his former assurance he seemed to wear a leaden mantle of humility; he climbed heavily up the hill to the Cathedral as if he were treading down the mistakes of the past.

Auclair, the apothecary, on the other hand, had scarcely changed at all. His delicate complexion had grown a trifle sallow from staying indoors so much, but the years which had made the Bishop an old man had passed lightly over the apothecary. Even his shop was still the same; perhaps a trifle dustier than it used to be, and opposite his counter there was a new cabinet screwed fast to the wall, full of brilliant sea-shells, starfish and horseshoe crabs, dried seaweed and branches of coral. Everyone looked at this case on entering the shop, — there was something surprising and unexpected about such a collection. It suggested the South and blue seas far away.

On the third day after the Cathedral had welcomed its long absent shepherd, that prelate himself came to call upon the apothecary, arriving at the door on foot and unattended. He greeted Auclair with friendliness and took the proffered chair, admitting that he felt the summer heat in Quebec more than he used to do.

"But you yourself, Monsieur Auclair, are little altered. I rejoice to see that God has preserved you in excellent health."

Auclair hastened to bring out a glass of fortifying cordial, and the Bishop accepted it gratefully. While he drank it, Auclair regarded him. It was unfortunate that Saint-Vallier, of all men, should have grown heavy — it took away his fine carriage. His once luxuriant brown hair was thin and grey, his triangular cheeks had become full and soft, like an old woman's, and they were waxy white. Between them, the sharp chin had almost disappeared.

"I have been thinking how fortunate I shall be to have you for my neighbour once more, Monseigneur," said Auclair. "Every spring I have given some little advice to the workmen who were attending to your garden, and I have often wished you could see your shrubs coming into bloom."

The Bishop smiled faintly and shook his head.

"Ah, monsieur, I shall not live in the episcopal Palace again. Perhaps that was a mistake; I should have waited to understand the designs of Providence more perfectly."

"Not live in your own residence, Monseigneur? That will be a great disappointment to all of us. The building is in excellent condition."

The Bishop again shook his head. "I find myself too poor now to maintain such an establishment. I suppose you do not know anyone who would care to rent the Palace? The rental would be very helpful to me in my present undertakings. No, I shall reside at the Hôpital Général.* My good daughters there have arranged un petit appartement of two rooms which will meet my

---

*Some years before he sailed for France in 1700, Bishop de Saint-Vallier had founded the Hôpital Général, for the aged and incurable. The hospital still stands today, much enlarged; the wards which Saint-Vallier built and the two small rooms in which he lived until his death are unchanged.

needs very well. I shall reside with them for the remainder of my life, God willing. Their chaplain is old
and must soon retire, and I shall take his place. The
office of chaplain will be quite compatible with my
other duties."

Auclair was amazed. "In a hospital the duties of a
chaplain are considerable, are they not?"

"But very congenial to me — " (the old man folded his
hands over the kerchief he had taken out to wipe his
brow) — "to celebrate the morning mass for the sisters
and to hear their confessions; to administer the conso-
lations of the Church to the sick and the dying. As
chaplain I shall be in daily attendance upon the unfortunate, as is my wish."

Auclair sat silent for some moments, stroking his
short beard in perplexity. Evidently nothing in his former relations with Monseigneur de Saint-Vallier was a
guide for future intercourse. He changed the subject
and began to speak of happenings in Quebec during the
Bishop's absence, of common acquaintances who had
died in that time, among them old Monseigneur de
Laval.

Saint-Vallier sighed. "Would it had been permitted
me to return in time to thank him for the labours he
underwent for my flock during the years of my cap-

tivity, and to close his eyes at the last. I can never hope to be to this people all that my venerable predecessor became, through his devotion and his long residence among them. But I shall be with them now for as long as God spares me, and I hope to be deserving of their affection."

At this moment a countrywoman appeared at the door. She was about to withdraw when she saw what visitor the apothecary was entertaining, but the Bishop called her back and insisted that his host attend to her needs. He waited patiently in his chair while she bought foxglove water for her dropsical father-in-law, and liquorice for her baby's cough. While he was serving her, Auclair wondered how he could give a turn to the Bishop's talk and learn from him what was going on at home. When the farmer woman had gone, he took the liberty of questioning his visitor directly.

"You have been at Versailles lately, Monseigneur? And how are things there, pray tell me?"

"Very sad since the death of the young Duc and Duchesse de Bourgogne last year. The King will never recover from that double loss. In the Duc, his grandson, he foresaw a wise and happy reign for France; and the young Duchesse had been the idol of his heart ever since she first came to them from Savoie. She was the life of the Court, — as dear to Madame de Maintenon as to the King. The official mourning is over, but the Court mourns, nevertheless."

Auclair nodded. "And the King, I suppose, is an old man now."

"Yes, the King is old. He still comes down to supper to the music of twenty-four violins, still works indefatigably with his ministers; there is dancing and play and conversation in the Salle d'Apollon every evening. His Court remains the most brilliant in Europe, — but his heart is not in it. There is no one left who can charm away his years and his cares as the little Duchesse de Bourgogne did, and nothing can make him forget for one hour the death of the Duc de Bourgogne. All Christendom, monsieur, has suffered an incalculable loss in the death of that pious prince."

"They died within a few days of each other, we heard."

Saint-Vallier bowed his head. "They were buried in the same tomb, and their little son with them."

"There is still talk of poison?"

"Popular opinion accuses the Duc d'Orléans. Their second son, an infant in arms, showed the same symptoms of poisoning, but he survived."

"Ah," said Auclair, "a bad situation! The King is

seventy-seven, and the Dauphin a child in arms. That will mean a long regency. I suppose the young Duc de Berry will fill that office?"

"God grant it, monsieur, God spare him!" exclaimed the Bishop fervently. "If any mischance were to befall the Duc de Berry, then that arch-atheist and suspected poisoner the Duc d'Orléans would be regent of France!" Saint-Vallier's voice cracked at a high pitch.

Auclair crossed himself devoutly. "I should have liked to see my King once more. He has been a great King. Is he much altered in person?"

"He is old. I had a private interview with His Majesty last November, late in the afternoon, when he was taking his exercise in the Parc of Versailles. We had scarcely begun our conference when a wind arose, stripping the trees that were already half-bare. The King invited me to go indoors to his cabinet, remarking that it distressed him now to hear the autumn winds and to see the leaves fall. That seemed to me to indicate a change."

"Yes," said Auclair, "that tells a story."

"Monsieur," began the Bishop sadly, "we are in the beginning of a new century, but periods do not always correspond with centuries. At home the old age is dying, but the new is still hidden. I felt the same condition in England, during my long captivity there. There is now no figure in the world such as our King was thirty years ago. The changes in the nation are all those of the old growing older. You have done well to remain here where nothing changes. Here with you I find everything the same." He glanced about the shop and peered into the salon. "And the little daughter, whom I used to see running in and out?"

"She is married, to our old friend Pierre Charron of Ville-Marie. He has built a commodious house in the Upper Town, beyond the Ursuline convent. They are well established in the world."

"You live alone, then?"

"For part of the year. Perhaps you remember a little boy whom my daughter befriended, Jacques Gaux? His mother was a loose woman — she died in your Hôpital Général, some years ago. The boy is now a sailor, and when he is in Quebec, between voyages, he lives with me. He occupies my daughter's little chamber upstairs." Auclair pointed to the cabinet of shells and corals. "He brings me these things back from his voyages; he is in the West India trade. I should like to keep him here all the time; but his father was a sailor — it is natural."

"No," said the Bishop, "I do not recall him. But your daughter I remember with affection. Heaven has blessed her with children?"

The apothecary's eyes twinkled. "Four sons already, Monseigneur. She is bringing up four little boys, the Canadians of the future."

"Ah yes, the Canadians of the future, — the true Canadians."

There was something in Saint-Vallier's voice as he said this which touched Auclair's heart; a note humble and wistful, something sad and defeated. Sometimes a neighbour whom we have disliked a lifetime for his arrogance and conceit lets fall a single commonplace remark that shows us another side, another man, really; a man uncertain, and puzzled, and in the dark like ourselves. Had his visitor not been a bishop, Auclair would have reached out and grasped his hand and murmured: "Courage, mon bourgeois," as he did to down-hearted patients. The two men sat together in a warm and friendly silence until Saint-Vallier rose and said he must be going. "I shall have the pleasure of confirming your grandsons, I hope? They will live to see better times than ours."

Auclair accompanied him to the door and watched him tread his way up the hill and round the turn of the street. Then he went back to his desk with the feeling that old feuds were forgotten. He would have a great deal to tell Cécile when he went to supper there tonight. She would be quicker than anyone to sense the transformation in their old neighbour, who had built himself an episcopal residence approached by twenty-four stone steps, and who now proposed to spend the rest of his life in two small rooms in the hospital out on the river Charles. To be sure, the Bishop was a little theatrical in his humility, as he had been in his grandeur; but that was his way, Auclair reflected, and, after all, nobody can help his way. If a man admits his mistakes, that is a great deal, when he is a proud man and a Dauphinois — always a stiff-necked race.

While he was closing his shop and changing his coat to go up to his daughter's house, he thought over much that his visitor had told him, and he believed that he was indeed fortunate to spend his old age here where nothing changed; to watch his grandsons grow up in a country where the death of the King, the probable evils of a long regency, would never touch them.

Acknowledgments

T HE textual editing of *Shadows on the Rock* is the result of
contributions from many members of the Cather Edition staff, among whom we wish to acknowledge especially
Kari Ronning, Kathleen Danker, and Erin Marcus. The
graduate students who contributed to the textual work were
Kathryn A. Bellman, Heather Hiatt, Susan Moss, Kelly Olson, Michael Radelich, Megan Sedoris, and Heather Wood.

Consultations with several people were especially helpful
in the early stages of the preparation of the Cather Edition.
In *Willa Cather: A Bibliography* (Lincoln: U of Nebraska P,
1982), Joan Crane provided an authoritative starting place
for our identification and assembly of basic materials, then in
correspondence was unfailingly generous with her expertise.
The late Fredson Bowers (University of Virginia) advised us
about the steps necessary to organize the project. David J.
Nordloh (Indiana University) provided advice as we established policies and procedures and wrote our editorial manual. As editor of the Lewis and Clark journals, Gary Moulton
(University of Nebraska–Lincoln) generously provided expertise and encouragement. Conversations with Richard

Rust (University of North Carolina–Chapel Hill) were helpful in refining procedures concerning variants.

We are grateful to Professor Herbert H. Johnson (Roch-
ester Institute of Technology) for material assistance in the
interpretation of printing-house practices in the period.
Stella Partheniou of CDG Books Canada, Inc., was helpful in
our search for the Canadian issue of the novel. Donald Cook
(Indiana University) brought his expertise and keen eye to
his inspection of our materials on behalf of the Committee
on Scholarly Editions.

John J. Murphy and David Stouck were assisted in preparing the Historical Essay and Explanatory Notes with generous grants from, respectively, Brigham Young University
and Simon Fraser University. Murphy and Stouck also want
to thank the following individuals for their various contributions to the Historical Essay, Explanatory Notes, and illustrations: Ann Billesbach, Nebraska State Historical Society,
Lincoln; Betty Bohrer, Willa Cather Pioneer Memorial, Red
Cloud, Nebraska; Andrée Gendreau, Musée de l'Amérique
Française/Musée de la Civilisation, Quebec; Janet Giltrow,
University of British Columbia; Louise Godin, O.S.U.,
Monastère des Ursulines, Quebec; Richard C. Harris, Webb
Institute, New York; Daryl P. Lee, Brigham Young Univer-
sity; Martine Le Fèvre, Bibliothèque à l'Arsénal, Paris; Sister
Marie de la Trinité, Centre Catherine de Saint-Augustin,
Bayeux; Sally McMahon Murphy, Salt Lake City; Bishop
George H. Niederauer, Salt Lake City; Françoise Palleau-
Papin, Université François Rabelais, Tours; Nicole Perron,

A.M.J., Musée des Augustines de l'Hôtel-Dieu de Québec; Ann Romines, George Washington University; Kari Ronning, University of Nebraska–Lincoln; Susan J. Rosowski, University of Nebraska–Lincoln; Mireille Saint-Pierre, Musée de l'Amérique Française/Musée de la Civilisation, Quebec; Ben-Zion Shek, University of Toronto; Mary-Ann Stouck, Simon Fraser University; Hélène Tremblay, C.N.D., Centre Jeanne Le Ber, Westmount, Quebec.

We appreciate the assistance of Kay Walters, Mary Ellen Ducey, and Carmella Orosco, of Archives and Special Collections, University of Nebraska–Lincoln; Dr. Steven P. Ryan, former director of the Willa Cather Pioneer Memorial and Educational Foundation, Red Cloud; Ann Billesbach, first at the Cather Historical Center, Red Cloud, and later at the Nebraska State Historical Society, Lincoln. And we wish to acknowledge our indebtedness to the late Mildred R. Bennett, whose work as founder and president of the Willa Cather Pioneer Memorial and Educational Foundation ensured that Cather-related materials in Webster County would be preserved and whose knowledge guided us through those materials.

We are grateful to the staffs of Love Library, University of Nebraska–Lincoln, particularly those in Archives and Special Collections and in Interlibrary Loan; the Heritage Room, Bennett Martin Public Library, Lincoln; the Harry Ransom Humanities Research Center, University of Texas at Austin; the Houghton Library, Harvard University; and the Nebraska State Historical Society. We also wish to thank the

Department of Modern Languages and Literatures, University of Nebraska–Lincoln, especially Pamela LeZotte and Marshall Olds.

We wish to express our special gratitude to Mrs. Philip L. Southwick and Dr. James P. and Angela Southwick for their generous gifts of the typescript carbon of *Shadows on the Rock*, photographs, and for their assistance and encouragement throughout the project.

We thank the Public Archives of Canada and the National Library of Canada; Father Armand Gagné of the Archdiocese of Quebec; Sister Juliette Cloutier, A.M.J., of the Archives of Les Augustins de la Miséricorde de Jésus du Monastère de l'Hôpital Général, Quebec; Laval University Press, Quebec; Lucia Woods; the Lilly Library, Indiana University; the Church of the Ascension, New York; the Nebraska State Historical Society; the Archives and Special Collections of Love Library, University of Nebraska–Lincoln; the Musée national du Moyen Age-Thermes et Hôtel de Cluny; and *Time* magazine/Getty Images, for allowing us to use illustrations from their collections.

For their administrative support at the University of Nebraska–Lincoln we thank Gerry Meisels, John G. Peters, and Brian L. Foster, successively deans of the College of Arts and Sciences; Richard Hoffmann, dean of Arts and Sciences; John Yost, formerly vice-chancellor for research; and John R. Wunder, former director of the Center for Great Plains Studies. We are especially grateful to Stephen Hilliard and Linda Ray Pratt, who as chairs of the Department of English provided both departmental support and personal encouragement for the Cather Edition.

For funding during the initial year of the project we are grateful to the Woods Charitable Fund. For research grants during subsequent years we thank the Nebraska Council for the Humanities; and the Research Council, the College of Arts and Sciences, the Office of the Vice Chancellor for Research, the University of Nebraska Foundation, and the Department of English, University of Nebraska–Lincoln. We deeply appreciate the generous gift from the late Mr. and Mrs. William Campbell in support of the Cather Edition.

The preparation of this volume was made possible in part by a grant from the National Endowment for the Humanities, an independent federal agency.

Historical Apparatus

Historical Essay

JOHN J. MURPHY AND DAVID STOUCK

S HADOWS *on the Rock* has the shortest foreground in composition of any of Willa Cather's major works; Cather
first visited Quebec City in 1928 and published her novel
about it in 1931. However, Cather's previous experiences in
Canada no doubt prepared her for her creative response to
Quebec. E. K. Brown, her first biographer and a Canadian,
points out that even before she began *Shadows on the Rock*,
"Cather had been in Canada much more than most American writers" (204). In fact, she owned a house on Grand
Manan, a rocky island off the southern coast of New Brunswick that must have anticipated the rock of Quebec for her
and reminded her of Mesa Verde, Ácoma, and the other
sanctuaries she had written about.

Cather first learned of Grand Manan from a librarian at
the New York Public Library who told her the island fishing
village in the Bay of Fundy was "probably the quietest place
in the world" (Brown and Crone 5–6). She rented a cottage
on the island in 1922 and was so pleased with its tranquillity
and remoteness that she returned there with Edith Lewis

almost every summer for the next eighteen years. Grand
Manan was the one place in the world where she felt she
could work without interruption, and all of her books from *A
Lost Lady* to *Sapphira and the Slave Girl* were composed in
part on the island. In September 1926 she and Lewis bought
a piece of land in a spruce wood near Whale Cove and employed two carpenters to build a Cape Cod–style cottage,
which was completed for their arrival in the summer of 1928.
Above the living room was a large attic Cather chose for her
study and from the window of which she could look out over
the cliffs and the sea. To Cather, who had been forced out of
her Bank Street apartment in New York City the year before
and then suffered the loss of her father (soon followed by the
long illness of her mother and subsequent breakup of the
family home in Nebraska), Grand Manan "seemed the only
foothold left on earth" (Lewis 153), not just a retreat but a
refuge from an uncaring and rapidly changing world. On
that foggy rock in the Atlantic, writes E. K. Brown, she felt
"securely hemmed in from the world" (203) and at a considerable remove from all mundane things.

It was while Cather was on her way to the new cottage in
June 1928 that she discovered Quebec City. Lewis explains
that they decided to make their annual trip "by the round-
about way of Quebec, in order to try a new route and see
some new country" (153) and to plan brief stays in Montreal
and Quebec. But when Lewis came down with influenza on
the night of their arrival in Quebec, they extended their stay
at the Château Frontenac hotel for ten days. Cather was

immediately attracted to the city and its environs. Lewis describes the imaginative excitement Cather felt: "From the first moment that she looked down from the windows of the Frontenac on the pointed roofs and Norman outlines of the town of Quebec, Willa Cather was not merely stirred and charmed—she was overwhelmed by the flood of memory, recognition, surmise it called up; by the sense of its extraordinarily French character, isolated and kept intact through hundreds of years, as if by a miracle, on this great un-French continent" (153–54). She explored the city alone, visiting the Ursuline Convent, the Laval Seminary, the Church of Notre Dame des Victoires, and the marketplace, and when Lewis was well enough they made an excursion to the Île d'Orléans. All the while Cather was rereading Francis Parkman's great work on France and England in North America and introducing herself to other volumes of Canadian history in the hotel library.

Recognition and Reminiscences

Lewis's account of the epiphany Cather experienced on her first morning in Quebec emphasizes her memories of France. These memories were complemented, as *Shadows on the Rock* shaped itself in her imagination, by reminders of the Catholic Southwest that had absorbed her during the writing of *Death Comes for the Archbishop* and (in this period of parental loss and illness) by childhood memories of Nebraska and Virginia. Also, Cather's attitudes toward Canada, gained over the years from early reading and later visits, contributed

333

to the novel and were developed and somewhat transformed as its writing progressed.

Cather's enthusiasm for France and its culture was the main thrust behind *Shadows*. Lewis communicates the intensity of this enthusiasm in her use of "stirred and charmed" and "overwhelmed" in describing Cather's reaction to the discovery "on this great un-French continent" of what is described in the opening chapter of the novel as a "settlement [that] looked like something cut off from one of the ruder towns of Normandy or Brittany, and brought over" (10). Cather's first sight of that northern French coast, when she crossed from Newhaven to Dieppe in August 1902, had generated similar excitement: "I heard a babble of voices, in which I could only distinguish the word 'France' uttered over and over again with a fire and fervor that was in itself a panegyric. . . . The high chalk cliffs of Normandy were a pale purple in the dim light" (*World and Parish* 921). Cather experienced "the stillness and whiteness and vastness" as well as "the burning blue and crimson . . . rose windows" of Rouen's Norman Gothic cathedral (923) during her introduction to France, and anticipated her depiction of Quebec at the beginning of book 4 of *Shadows* in a view of Paris "bathed in violet light, with here and there white towers," below the "white gleam of Sacré-Coeur" that reminded her of "the city of St. John's vision" (924). But what most prepared Cather for Quebec was Avignon, "the fine old city of the popes" (936), where she would discover on Doms Rock, beetling above the Rhone, a twelfth-century Romanesque cathedral, the Palace of the Popes (who resided there from 1309 to 1377), and a garden offering views of the distant Alps to the east. Cather's description of this city in her travel sketches reads like her descriptions of Quebec in the beginning and throughout *Shadows*: "At the north end of the town there rises an enormous façade of smooth rock three hundred feet above the Rhone. This sheer precipice, accessible from the river side only by winding stone stairways, is crowned by the great palace of the popes. The palace is a huge, rambling Gothic pile, flanked by six square Italian towers, with a beautiful little cathedral in front. The palace faces toward the town, and behind it, overhanging the Rhone, are the popes' gardens" (*World and Parish* 936–37).

Cather made four additional trips to France, most of them lengthy stays, and after the publication of the *Archbishop* she planned another, which had to be canceled due to her father's declining health. In 1920, when working on *One of Ours*, she had spent four months in France, including seven weeks on Paris's Left Bank, because she wanted to imbue herself in medieval culture: "And we did live in the Middle Ages, so far as it was possible," Lewis recalls. "We spent nearly all our time in the section between the Seine and the Luxembourg gardens, and on the Île de la Cité and the Île-St. Louis" (119). They spent the late summer and fall in the south of France and "journeyed slowly back to Paris," for Cather "had to get the feeling of the whole of France to write about it" (120–21). In 1923, after she had completed *A Lost Lady*, Cather returned to France again for several months, sitting for a portrait by Leon Bakst commissioned by the Omaha Public Library and visiting Aix-les-Bains, where, Lewis speculates, Cather's next novel was conceived: "She did not work there, but it was perhaps in the peace and beauty of the Savoie countryside that the idea of *The Professor's House* took shape. She became very much attached to the little town itself, and resolved to go back there" (133). Lewis's summary of the creative effect of France on Cather explains her response to finding a piece of it on this side of the Atlantic: "French culture, coming to it as she did in her most impressionable years, and finding it so new, so challenging and awakening, spoke more directly to her imagination [than British culture], and more definitely influenced her writing" (56). In *Shadows*, Mme Auclair's boast as she instructs her daughter in housekeeping reflects Cather's own cultural bias: "At home, in France, we have learned to do all these things in the best way, and we are conscientious, and that is why we are considered the most civilized people in Europe and other nations envy us" (32).

Cather traveled again to France in the spring of 1930, this time concentrating on the Right Bank to acquaint herself with the Parisian settings of *Shadows*. She walked along the Quai des Célestins and about Frontenac's old quarter and the Village St. Paul, visited the church of Saint-Paul–Saint-Louis, and explored the Paris history collection at the Musée Carnavalet in the Marais district. With Jan and Isabelle (McClung) Hambourg she made a trip to Saint-Malo, the setting of the novel's she-ape story and home port of Jacques Cartier,

Canada's great "discoverer," before heading south to Provence and Aix-les-Bains (Lewis 158–59). Cather returned to America that fall on one of the Canadian Pacific Empress boats, sailing up the St. Lawrence "between woods on fire with October" (Lewis 160), following the route of those early colonists who had sailed from Normandy and Brittany to the little French capital perched on the rock above the river.

Her discovery of Quebec offered Cather the opportunity to live a bit longer in the world of *Death Comes for the Archbishop*. As Lewis puts it: "Cather's great pleasure in this Quebec visit came from finding here a sort of continuation, in a different key, of the Catholic theme which had absorbed her for two years, and which still lingered in her thoughts, after the completion of the *Archbishop*, like a tune that goes on in one's mind after the song is ended" (155). Both novels are devotional to a significant extent, especially with reference to the Virgin; both depict French missionaries laboring in the New World, and both concern bishops, church administration, and clerical feuding. However, the Catholicism of the Quebec novel is of an earlier vintage, close to that of the sixteenth-century Counter-Reformation, and thus more defensive and intense. There is greater emphasis on mysticism, relics, and the Real Presence of Christ in the Eucharist (as in the stories of Jeanne Le Ber, Noël Chabanel, and of Hector Saint-Cyr), a belief challenged by Protestant reformers. The landscapes of the novels are contrasting, yet both contain rock sanctuaries symbolic of the church: Ácoma in the *Arch-*

337

bishop and Quebec itself in the later novel. Indeed, Cather had become so accustomed to the similarities that she had absent-mindedly promoted her Quebec bishops to the rank of Arch-bishop Latour in her earlier novel, and expensive changes had to be made in the foundry proofs of *Shadows* (Lewis 161–62).

Memories of Charles Cather, her father, who had died that March, certainly occupied Cather when she encountered Quebec in June 1928. She had written to Dorothy Canfield Fisher on 3 April that her soul had been restored by her father, whose beautiful death made her rested and strong. Subsequently, as *Shadows* was shaping itself in her imagination that summer, she "sometimes spoke of her father" to Lewis, who speculates that "his gentle protection and kindness, the trusting relationship between them, in the old days in Virginia . . . entered into her conception of the apothecary Euclide Auclair and his little daughter" (155–56). During the following December, back in New York, Cather received word from California of her mother's stroke and immediately went to her. Virginia Cather's long illness had "a profound effect on Willa Cather," writes Lewis, "and I think on her work as well" (156). Such difficulties not only made *Shadows* a rock of refuge for Cather, as she told Fisher (1 May 1931), but infused a text based primarily on historical sources with purgatorial themes of pain, illness, mutilation, aging, and death. The loss of her parents also made Cather's text resonate with recollections of childhood, with those best years in Red Cloud, Nebraska, when all seven Cather children lived at home and Grandmother Boak read *The Pilgrim's Progress* to them.

The childhood perspectives of Cécile and Jacques, although criticized by some reviewers as escapist, define the religious dimension of *Shadows*. Cather transfigured her own childhood experiences and those of other family members in a manner reminiscent of St. Thérèse of the Child Jesus (Thérèse Martin, 1873–97), the French Carmelite of Lisieux whose *Story of a Soul* (1899) had become a spiritual classic translated into many languages in the early years of the twentieth century. Unlike Cécile, Thérèse had a religious vocation, but like Cécile, she had lost her mother at a very young age, was devoted to her father, delighted in wildflowers, and gave alms to the poor. The canonization of Thérèse in 1925 further popularized her "Way of Childhood," the so-called "little way" of spiritual growth based on passages from the Old and New Testaments. "[O]ften the Lord is pleased to grant wisdom to the little ones," writes Thérèse. "He blessed His Father for having hidden His secrets from the wise and prudent and for revealing them to the *little ones*" (209). It is in such a spirit that Cather wrote the childhood aspects of her novel (more than compensated for by Auclair's rationalism, Frontenac's worldliness, and Pierre Charron's secularism). The character of Jacques is a clear example of the religiously suggestive way Cather used family memories. She revealed to Fisher (June 1931) that the little boy had been based on her favorite nephew, Charles Cather, whom she used to pull in his sled and who, when he set up a crèche with her for her father's last Christmas, contributed a toy cow for "the Little Jesus" (Bennett 38–39), just as Jacques offers his toy beaver. Jacques

339

had also been suggested by Cather's youngest brother, Jack (John), the inspiration of her 1901 story "Jack-a-Boy," concerning scattered and rather joyless boarders made into a family through the life, death, and memory of a little boy, whom the narrator associates (as Bishop Laval associates Jacques) with "the greatest Revealer [who] drew men together" and to whom "Nicodemus . . . came . . . by night, and [whose feet] Mary, of Magdala, at the public feast, wiped . . . with her hair" (*Collected Short Fiction* 322). This was the little brother whose eyes, Cather told friends, "she would give anything just to look into . . . for ten minutes" (Bennett 38). Cather remembered and made holy her own silver baby mug in the scene where Cécile and Jacques drink chocolate and study the *Lives of the Saints*. The little boy takes "solemn satisfaction" (103) in Cécile's "silver cup with a handle; on the front was engraved a little wreath of roses, and inside that wreath . . . the name, 'Cécile,' cut in the silver." Cather had been given such a cup, with "Willa" engraved within a wreath of foliage, in Virginia by her grandfather William Cather (Bennett 234), a cup now displayed at the Cather Pioneer Memorial in Red Cloud.

The Canadian dimension of *Shadows on the Rock* can also be traced back to reminiscences of the Nebraska years and to Cather's tenure as a young book reviewer. In the Catherton precinct of Webster County, French Canadian settlers built a small frame Catholic church called St. Ann's, which became the center of the Wheatland, Nebraska, community Cather gives a vivid account of in *O Pioneers!* in the story of Amédée

Chevalier and the Sainte-Agnès church fair and confirmation service.[1] Although she refers to her settlers simply as "French," Cather leaves no doubt about their Canadian origins in the passage where Emil Bergson says teasingly to Amédée's wife that her baby looks like it might have had an Indian ancestor. Amédée's mother, we are told, "had been touched on a sore point, and she let out a stream of fiery *patois*" (216). Cather's awareness of Canada as a culture in process is evident in her early reviews, which exhibit some knowledge of Canadian literature and turn-of-the-century debates about Canadian identity. She cites Seth Low, then president of Columbia University, as having said there is no literature in Canada because there is no national life, but she refutes that statement in a discussion of Gilbert Parker's *The Seats of the Mighty: A Romance of Old Quebec* (1896), claiming that "a generation of young men . . . are making the most of Canada's literary possibilities" (*World and Parish* 355). Among these young men she would include poets Bliss Carman and Charles G. D. Roberts (and, mistakenly, American-born Richard Hovey), whose work she reviewed positively for their fresh treatment of nature as a literary theme. Roberts's verse, she wrote, is "rich in expression and redolent of wood life and field life, of Canadian forests and meadows" (*World and Parish* 886). Especially interesting in Cather's review of Parker's Quebec romance, as Merrill Skaggs has observed, is her citing of Low's remark that Canadian culture was like a plant whose roots drew nourishment from the other side of the Atlantic but lost most of it under the sea. As Skaggs puts it, we have formulated here a question — something like, "Where does such a transplant as Quebec find the nourishment that keeps it alive?" (127) — that would inform her Quebec novel more than thirty years later.

Cather first imagined Canada as a geographical setting when she wrote her debut novel, *Alexander's Bridge* (1912). Much of the action takes place along the wild rivers of Quebec, where the engineer hero, Bartley Alexander, has built a suspension bridge and is now constructing a cantilever bridge at a place named Moorlock. Near the site of the first project Alexander had met his wife, Winifred, a Canadian woman described as very proud and a little hard, and also took great pleasure in talking army and politics with Winifred's aunt. These are not sentimental portraits of women; rather they suggest Cather's view of British Canadians as shrewd, practical, and colonial in character. Cather based the novel's catastrophe on an actual event near Quebec City on 29 August 1907, when a bridge being built to span the St. Lawrence collapsed and more than eighty men were killed, including the chief engineer, who had gone out on the bridge just before it broke apart.[2]

As far as we know, Cather herself did not actually cross the actual border into Canada until after her close friend Isabelle McClung moved to Toronto with her husband, the violinist Jan Hambourg. Cather made at least two lengthy visits to the Hambourgs in Toronto: in 1919 she spent June and July in the city, and in 1921 she stayed nearly five months, from April until late August. Toronto served as a retreat from the attention of friends, businesspersons, and well-wishers. On both occasions Cather was absorbed with *One of Ours*, which she finished during her second visit. Perhaps she came to view Canada as an alternative to the American tradition.[3] Wallace Stegner reminds his readers in *Wolf Willow* that when Americans are aware of Canada at all, it is most often as a border, a margin, an end to things American (3). It is unusual that Cather, who was never a joiner and zealously guarded her privacy, belonged to the Grand Manan Historical Association (as indicated in the society's membership list printed in *The Grand Manan Historian* 5: 72). Early Grand Manan history focuses on the lives of United Empire Loyalists — New Englanders, chiefly, who had fought on the royalist side in the Revolutionary War and then left their American homes and took refuge in what remained of Britain's empire to the north. The Loyalists had sought to preserve an ideal of order and justice stemming from the British monarchy, and they saw Canada as providing a sanctuary. It is more than likely that the author of *One of Ours* and *The Professor's House*, profoundly disillusioned with the materialism of contemporary American life, came to regard English Canada as a boundary behind which lingered a pastoral alternative to America's increasingly urban, technology-driven culture.

Certainly by the late 1920s there is evidence in the fiction that Cather's political sympathies were conservative, and perhaps there was a strong attraction to living for part of the year within the British Empire. But when she came to know Quebec City, Cather crossed a border to the psychological heart of her artistic and spiritual being. In the preface to her *Borderlands/La Frontera*, Gloria Anzaldua writes that crossing borders brings one closer to "one's shifting and multiple identity and integrity," which is what Cather's discovery of Quebec involved. This is not to say that Cather came to identify herself as French Canadian or Catholic. On the contrary, in her letter about *Shadows* to Governor Wilbur Cross she says explicitly that she encountered in Quebec a "feeling about life and human fate that I could not accept, wholly" ("On *Shadows*" 387), something pious and resigned. She further marks her distance from French-Canadian life, perhaps regretfully, when she says of her novel, "It's very hard for an American to catch that rhythm — it's so unlike us" (388). But it was a feeling about life, persisting from another age, that she could not help but admire, and through her gift of sympathy she captured both the Canadian spirit of place and the integrated world of a Catholicism informed and regulated by spiritual rites.

In his argument for Cather as a "Canadian" writer, Benjamin George claims that "she came to hold a close affinity with Canadian ideals and attitudes, pointedly different from those of her own national ethos" (249). He develops his thesis by quoting Northrop Frye, who has characterized Canadians as hampered by a "garrison mentality," referring thereby to fear of the unknown, an inward-looking, negative aspect of colonial culture dedicated to holding the threatening wilderness at bay. Cather re-creates this beleaguered condition of early Canadian life in the opening chapter of her novel: outside of the settlement of two thousand, "[t]he forest was suffocation, annihilation; there European man was quickly swallowed up in silence, distance, mould, black mud, and the stinging swarms of insect life that bred in it" (11). (Incidentally, the prairie town of Red Cloud to which Cather came as a child of nine was of similar size and surrounded by vast prairies she described as being bare as sheet metal.) But Russell Brown has more recently suggested a positive aspect to this garrison consciousness, relating it to the human desire for sanctuary and safe borders (32). Here we recognize one of the strongest themes in *Shadows*: Canada is envisioned by the French apothecary as "a possible refuge, an escape from the evils one suffered at home" (39); in Quebec, even children are conscious of "the goodness of shelter" (79). When she is ill in bed, Cécile mentally roams about the town, always aware of "the never-ending, merciless forest beyond." The lives of her friends, the roofs and spires of the town, the crooked streets all "seemed to her like layers and layers of shelter, with this one flickering, shadowy room at the core" (183). There is no desire at the imaginative center of this text to repudiate or escape from the garrison, but rather to nurture and augment it, to keep alive and to shelter that bit of French culture on the rock.

In Cather's re-creation of it, seventeenth-century Quebec is a colony determined to preserve an old society within the new one instinctively generated as Cécile's Canadian identity matures and, with Pierre, she cooperates in the founding of a new race. As a regeneration rather than a repudiation of the

345

Old World, this new society represents an alternative that challenges the Puritan city upon a hill envisioned by John Winthrop, and in the background of Cather's novel (as throughout its Parkman sources) lurks ongoing conflict with the New Englanders to the south. In her letter to Wilbur Cross, who had written an appreciative review of *Shadows*, Cather chose words like "stronghold," "endurance," and "sacred fire" ("On *Shadows*" 387–88) to express the meaning Quebec had for her. She drew on religious and biblical imagery in her novel to overshadow the refuge aspect of the city and fashion it into a bastion of orthodox, almost medieval tradition. The "mountain rock" of Quebec, "cunningly built over with churches, convents, fortifications, gardens, following the natural irregularities of the headland," as described in the opening chapter of *Shadows*, resembles "nothing so much as one of those little artificial mountains . . . made in the churches [in France] to present the scene of the Nativity" (8–9). If in the first chapter Quebec is a new Bethlehem, by the beginning of the fourth book it becomes more emphatically the New Jerusalem, "gleaming above the [St. Lawrence] river like an altar with many candles, or like a holy city in an old legend, shriven, sinless, washed in gold" (195). In an earlier version of this passage,[4] Cather borrowed from Psalm 19:5 to describe the sun as the "bridegroom issuing from his chamber," or the Lord emerging from his heavenly tabernacle to light the world, and used Matthew 13:43 (depicting the children of heaven shining at judgment like the sun) to compare the colonial community to "the righteous in their Heavenly Father's house." The source of the entire passage in its final form is John's image of the transfigured city in Revelation 21, that of the tabernacle of the Lord adorned as a bride, generating its own light and descending to the righteous as their dwelling.

Sources and Composition

Cather's background reading was always a crucial component in the creation of her books. *O Pioneers!* would seem to be drawn solely from her Nebraska experiences, but she confided in a letter to H. L. Mencken that when writing that novel she probably had not yet overcome the enormous impact the Russian writers had on her, especially in their artistic treatment of prairie landscape. *Death Comes for the Archbishop* tapped Homer, Dante, and Bunyan, but it also combined reading in church and local history with holidays spent in the Southwest over a period of fifteen years. However, the element of reading preparation was probably most important in *Shadows on the Rock*, because Cather's own experience of place was confined to five brief visits to Quebec over a two-year period.

Edith Lewis tells us that during the first stay in Quebec City, Cather began reading the books on Canadian history she found in the Château Frontenac library and became especially absorbed in Parkman. Francis Parkman, with his strong feeling for narrative, had always been Cather's favorite American historian, and through his eyes she first came to see the life of Quebec in the seventeenth century. In telling her story she readily adopted his romantic portrait of Frontenac as an aristocratic professional soldier who, although he arrived in the New World past the age of fifty, proved nonetheless a resilient and invincible leader. Although she accepted Parkman's view of Frontenac as a man full of contradictions ("as gracious and winning on some occasions as he was unbearable on others" [2: 59]), she softened the egotistical and irascible side of his nature emphasized by other historians and conveyed great sympathy for him as an old man, disillusioned with his associates and king, alone in Quebec without family, who would die before he could return to France.[5] She found many other suggestive details in Parkman for her story, such as his view of French-Canadian woodsmen as both picturesque and dangerous, and to create Father Hector Saint-Cyr she borrowed Parkman's portrait of the Sulpician priest Dollier de Casson, who like Frontenac was a soldier and gentleman whose courage and physical strength filled the Native people with admiration. The closeness with which she worked with her sources is revealed in the repetition, in her opening chapter, of Parkman's whimsical notion that one could drop a stone from a terrace in the Upper Town directly to the narrow streets of the Lower Town below.

Central to Parkman's narrative is Frontenac's ongoing dispute with Bishop Laval and the Jesuits, who opposed Frontenac's policies toward Native peoples, particularly the trading of alcohol for fur. While Parkman himself approved of Frontenac's efforts to limit the authority of the church to spiritual matters and frequently portrayed the Jesuits as unreasonable and extreme in their behavior, Parkman's anticlerical views held little interest for Cather, and she turned instead to a new biography of Laval in the Makers of Canada series as the basis for a sympathetic portrait of the colony's spiritual leader. Edith Lewis tells us that Cather found this book in the hotel library during their first stay and arranged to visit its author, Abbé Henri Arthur Scott, the elderly vicar of nearby Sainte-Foy. According to E. K. Brown, Cather was so impressed by this sensitive and cultivated scholar that "she felt she could trust his judgment in his special subject," the history of the church in Canada, and adopted his sympathetic rendering of Laval and his policies (272–73). Laval is presented as an ecclesiastical analogue for Frontenac, an aristocrat by birth who had the resiliency and strength required for a leader of the church in the New World; like Frontenac, her Laval is in his last years, beset by physical ailments and political disappointments.

Cather's chief source for the missionary history of Quebec was the *Jesuit Relations and Allied Documents: Travels and Explorations of the Jesuit Missionaries in New France, 1610–1791*, edited by Reuben Gold Thwaites.[6] Lewis claims that Cather "read" the Relations (158), but as they number seventy-three volumes it is more likely that she would have restricted her reading to sections describing the century in which her story is set. (Also, selections made by Edna Kenton from the Gold Thwaites edition had been published in 1925.) Most important to her narrative in creating a legendary religious history

349

for Quebec are the martyrdoms of the Jesuit missionaries, including Fathers Brébeuf, Jogues, and Lalemant, whose tortures during the Iroquois raids of the 1640s are referred to in the novel. The massacre at St. Ignace was recorded by Paul Ragueneau in the Relation of 1649–50, and Cather took details of the story of Father Noël Chabanel, his difficulty with the Huron language, and his fastidious revulsion at Native customs from the same volume. Ragueneau's *La Vie de la Mère Catherine de Saint-Augustin*, written in 1671, would have been a likely source for Cather's story of the young Hospitaller who arrived in Quebec in 1648. The biographer was also Sister Catherine's confessor, and he gives an extended account of her physical infirmities and tormented visions, although as Gary Brienzo suggests, Cather muted the extremes to create a positive image of Catherine to fit the child-centered focus of the novel. In reading the letters of Marie of the Incarnation, founder of the Ursuline convent in Quebec, and Mother Juchereau's *Les annales de l'Hôtel-Dieu de Québec*, a valuable source of historical details, Cather gained a more intimate and feminine knowledge of religious life in seventeenth-century Quebec. Marie of the Incarnation's letters gave Cather her epigraph about the wildflowers of Quebec and also provided her (in Marie's separation from her son in France because of her religious vocation) with a powerful instance of an individual's sacrifice for God and of the remoteness of the French colony in North America. Mother Juchereau's book would have provided another version of Catherine de Saint-Augustin's life in the colony.

Edith Lewis tells us that Cather also read La Hontan's
Voyages while she was preparing herself to write the novel.
The Baron de La Hontan was a young soldier and explorer
(just seventeen when he arrived in Quebec) who wrote a
series of letters from the colony between 1683 and 1693.
Cather would have found in this book a vivid secular description of the world of her novel written just a few years before
her story takes place. La Hontan, for example, describes the
eel fishing and the dove slaughter that provided important
food sources for the colony, as well as the houses of stone and
wood, two stories high, with their vast fire-places and the
enormous quantities of wood consumed "by reason of the
prodigious Fires they make to guard themselves from the
Cold, which is beyond all measure" (38). The book is rich in
geography, ethnography, and natural history, all of it the record of personal knowledge. With his sharp eye for the rough
and licentious behavior around him, La Hontan provides
background for Cather's creation of Jacques's mother, 'Toinette, one of the "King's Girls" who regularly goes off with
the trappers and sailors, abandoning her child, and for Pierre
Charron out in the woods and squandering his earnings
on "drink and women and new guns" (199). "You would
be amaz'd if you saw how lewd these Pedlers [coureurs de
bois] are when they return; how they Feast and game, and
how prodigal they are, not only in their Cloaths, but upon
Women, . . . for they Lavish, Eat, Drink, and Play all away as
long as the Goods hold out; and when these are gone . . . they
are forc'd to go upon a new Voyage for Subsistence" (54).

Cather's description of Charron, who "shot up and down the swift rivers of Canada in his canoe" (197), owes much to her reading about the coureurs de bois in La Hontan. Cather probably responded, as did his enormous readership, to the baron's view of New France as a form of Arcady where the "free Frenchman of the great forests" (198) lived far from law courts and the pursuit of wealth and power that compromised the benefits of civilization.

The *Mémoires* of the Duc de Saint-Simon, who recorded firsthand the events and gossip of the court, is the major source of Cather's picture of the Old World under the extravagance and tyranny of Louis XIV. Saint-Simon's memoirs contain numerous instances of cruelty and injustice as well as accounts of disease, poison, and dying. Cather's stories of great ladies of France drinking viper broth, of poisonous bread made from human bones, of the fashions in bloodletting, and of a child's death at a carp pond all have suggestive analogues in these memoirs. Saint-Simon's view of humankind's base, self-seeking nature and essential depravity permeates *Shadows* in counterpoint to the miracles and piety generated by the church in Quebec. But the most memorable entries are portraits of members of the royal family — the king's son, known as Monsieur; his grandchildren, the Duc and Duchesse de Bourgogne — and the accounts of their deaths. Cather's references to these figures moving in the background of her story evoke Saint-Simon's lively sense of drama and her own awareness of profound historical ironies. Saint-Simon pictures the Duc de Bour-

352

gogne as a pious, compassionate man who believed his role as king would be to serve his people. Cather's poetic of things "not named," of touching and passing on, is no better exemplified than when Saint-Vallier tells Auclair near the end of the novel: "All Christendom, monsieur, has suffered an incalculable loss in the death of that pious prince" (317). Cather had in mind no less than the coming of the French Revolution.

The list of sources contributing to Cather's mastery of her subject must remain inconclusive and somewhat speculative. She depended, as during the writing of the *Archbishop*, on the *Catholic Encyclopedia* and on volumes in the Makers of Canada series, which includes A. Leblond De Brumath's *Life of Laval* and William Le Sueur's *Life of Frontenac*. *The Voyages of Champlain* and the 1744 *History and General Description of New France* by Pierre F. X. Charlevoix are likely sources. Directly or indirectly, readings from Thomas Aquinas and St. Augustine inform Cather's text, as do the saints' lives compiled by Butler and Baring-Gould. There is evidence of the inspiration of *Mont Saint Michel and Chartres*, by Cather's fellow countryman and medievalist Henry Adams, in her description of the "well-ordered universe" of the nuns of Quebec. Cather's plunge into this material — at least as wide in range as that assembled for the previous novel — was compulsive. In her June 1931 letter to Fisher she indicated not only that every little detail in the lives of the people in her novel had been taken from old books and letters but that searching out these details had helped her hold her life together during difficult times.

If the gathering of materials for the *Archbishop* lacked the therapeutic dimension of searching out materials for *Shadows*, the ways Cather shaped her material into fiction were similar. She developed episodes from brief incidents, expanding, for example, Laval's discovery of Jacques alone in the snow from a single sentence in Scott's biography, and she essentially reproduced episodes from her sources, at times almost verbatim, as the Noël Chabanel story from Ragueneau's Relation of 1649–50. Elsewhere she elaborated her sources, keeping an episode intact but adding details to make it concrete or give it a point — providing a Marian resolution to Captain Pondaven's Saint-Malo folktale, for example, to make it miraculous. Cather also clustered sources to achieve desired effects in portraying major historical figures — as in "The Dying Count," in which Parkman's account is complemented by details from Le Sueur, embellishments (like the carp-pond incident) from Saint-Simon, and Cather's own imagination (the Count's dream). As in the *Archbishop*, the rhetorical occasion underlying the composition of *Shadows* is that of travel writing. Cather came to write this book as a tourist; its substance was not mined from the material she referred to as her "cremated youth" but from her experiences as a reader of history and as a visitor to Quebec and France. She was writing her book chiefly for an American audience and, in accordance with the genre of travel writing, informed her readers about the history and nature of an ethnically different people in a remote North American location. Descriptions of landscape and ethnic practices, tales from local history, philosophical and religious meditations, and character portraits are all woven along a simple narrative line—a year in the life of the colony—that permits digression without risk to coherence.

In her letter to Wilbur Cross, Cather set forth something of her intention and method. She wrote that among the country people and the nuns in Quebec she had experienced the endurance of a culture from another age, something narrow but definite, a "feeling about life and human fate that I could not accept, wholly, but which I could not but admire" ("On Shadows" 387). Her problem was to render this feeling in language, which the elusive quality of the feeling made difficult; it was like an old song that was incomplete, or like "a series of pictures remembered rather than experienced" (388). She defined her method as "mainly anacoluthon" (387), a figure from classical rhetoric that signifies an incomplete syntactic structure, something unfinished and shifting within a sentence. Consider the passage where Cécile is anxious about their possible return to France: "On a foreign shore, in a foreign city (yes, for her a foreign shore), would not her heart break for just this? For this rock and this winter, this feeling of being in one's own place, for the soft content of pulling Jacques up Holy Family Hill into paler and paler levels of blue air, like a diver coming up from the deep sea" (123). In the parenthetical material of the first sentence there is an example of anacoluthon where the grammatical shift allows for two points of view simultaneously—the narrator's and the child's. The second sentence is actually a fragment consisting of a

355

series of appositive phrases that are cut adrift from their syntactic core and are grammatically incomplete and unnecessary but which poignantly evoke the child's feelings for her home in Quebec. The anacoluthon dimension of *Shadows* has been extended from syntax and style to narrative structure by Edward and Lillian Bloom, who write that Cather achieved "[t]he seeming disjunction implied by the term by initiating episodes and then disclosing their resolutions in subsequent appropriate phases of the novel" (198).[7] When Cather described her novel as more like an incomplete song than a legend she signaled something of the difference between *Shadows* and the *Archbishop*: the former is haunted and interrupted by the vicissitudes of history; the latter is timeless and complete, informed by one of the great metanarratives of Western civilization.

Cather also compared her method of composition to working on a tapestry and thus suggested something quite different from the monumental style of the *Archbishop*, which had its analogues in Holbein's *Dance of Death* and the allegorical panels of Puvis de Chavannes. Traveling back and forth across the country to see her mother meant that Cather had no quiet stretch of time for her novel, and she told Fisher in a letter (June 1931) that it was like working on a tapestry tent she could unfold in hotels and sanatoriums, picking it up and putting it down during her life in transit. Lewis tells us that while Cather was writing in the Grosvenor Hotel in New York she bought some full-size copies of the *Lady with the Unicorn* tapestries, which she had seen in the Cluny Museum in Paris, to hang on the blank wall facing her bed. Perhaps this explains why many of the historical and fictional figures Cather weaves into her narrative have the elusive presence of those Cécile detects in the tapestries on the walls of the Count's residence representing garden scenes: "one could study them for hours without seeing all the flowers and figures" (60). This metaphor suggests not only something of the rich design of the novel but also something of its theme. In the same letter to Fisher, Cather compared the novel to an old fur coat that keeps you warm in bitter weather, and in an earlier letter (1 May 1931) she compared it to a rock of refuge. Rather than having the expansive and open dimension of the *Archbishop*, the pictorial aspect of *Shadows* relates to enclosure, protection, and survival. The unicorn tapestries also have bearing on the self-denial theme of *Shadows*. Each of the first five tapestries is devoted, respectively, to sight, hearing, taste, smell, and touch; the sixth tapestry depicts a lady standing before a tent with a valance bearing the inscription *À Mon Seul Désir* (To My Only Desire), perhaps a reference to Christ, and depositing a necklace in a casket. A popular interpretation is that the worldly, sensual pleasures of the previous tapestries are being renounced.[8]

The contained world of refuge suggested by the tapestry metaphor has connections to Cather's use of Quebec's Notre Dame des Victoires church in *Shadows* and her proximity to New York's Episcopal Church of the Ascension during the writing of the novel. When Cécile and Jacques view Notre Dame's castle-like altar, it is "taken . . . for granted that the

357

Kingdom of Heaven looked exactly like this from the outside[,] . . . was surrounded by just such walls" (77), and (like the altar) was populated with the saints and members of the Holy Family. Back in New York, Cather herself could escape from her desk in the Grosvenor by crossing Fifth Avenue to her "favourite church in New York," according to Lewis. Cather "loved the beautiful altar, with John La Farge's great fresco above [of Christ encircled by angels while rising over the Apostles] and for years went regularly to the vesper services" (151). Such refuges of faith prompted and sustained the well-ordered universe that Cather bestowed on the nuns of Quebec: "[T]his all-important earth, created by God for a great purpose, the sun which He made to light it by day, the moon which He made to light it by night, — and the stars, made to beautify the vault of heaven like frescoes, and to be a clock and compass for man. And in this safe, lovingly arranged and ordered universe (not too vast, though nobly spacious), in this congenial universe, the drama of man went on . . . " (115).

Controversial Reception

The publication of *Shadows on the Rock* (1 August 1931) attracted attention due to Cather's status as a major American novelist (Cather made the cover of *Time* on 3 August) and to the large sales that its selection by Book-of-the-Month Club ensured (167,679 copies from ten printings were distributed by the end of 1931 [Woodress 433]). Because the appearance of another "Catholic" historical novel proved that *Death*

Comes for the Archbishop marked a turn of direction for Cather rather than a mere career pause, reviewers felt obligated to assess that career and applaud or condemn its perceived course. The sides taken were sometimes heated and anticipate the significant political differences that would divide the literary establishment and reading public later in the century.

The positive reviews focused on Cather's artistry and sympathetic evocation of French-Canadian history and culture. Wilbur Cross's commentary in the *Saturday Review of Literature* pleased Cather enough to generate a grateful response, which was printed in that publication two months later (17 October 1931). Cross detected the experimental nature of *Shadows* and its distinction in method from the *Archbishop*: the new novel "is no study of character in detail" but rather the maintenance of a "tone . . . subdued to a poetic atmosphere" and is composed of "sketches . . . like the pastels of [Maurice Quentin de] Latour and Watteau." Cross noted the action as intentionally minimized, and he grasped the structural principle: that "scenes and characters separate and coalesce," as in Sterne's *A Sentimental Journey*. He was perhaps most perceptive on Cather's stance toward character: well aware of the essential mystery of each individual, she hesitates to "tell the world what is going on in the mind" ("as Virginia Woolf and others profess to do"), allowing readers "to determine whether she ever gets behind the shadows." In the *Virginia Quarterly Review*, Walter L. Myers continued the attempt to pin down the elusive text of *Shadows*, using it to define a new form of novel dedicated to the ineffable, in

359

which ordinary stratagems of fiction are sacrificed, language is fashioned to carry the reality of what is depicted directly to consciousness, and the creative reader is offered possibilities — a point made by Cross relative to characterization. Such a novel "will be at its best when it treats the familiar and commonplace, not enhancing it greatly or concealing it or transforming it detail by detail but in fine [and here he touched the mystical theme of *Shadows*] effecting a miraculous transubstantiation" (Myers 417).

In an earlier review in the same journal, James Southall Wilson addressed technical achievements, among them Cather's successful combining of opposites: "The method seems episodic but the effect does not seem episodic"; its "tenderest compassion . . . springs from no soft sentimentality but [is] the flower of something hard and bitter." While acknowledging the contribution of tone to unity, Wilson noted the skillful use of the "cut-back" into earlier lives and the interweaving of memory, legends, matters of faith, politics, and affairs of the heart into "one stuff" (587). The book "does not generalize," he added, but achieves "circumference" (588) through things: Cécile's cup, Jacques's beaver and shoes, the glass fruit, the sprigs of parsley. These make it a more intimate if smaller novel than the *Archbishop*, but in it "old Quebec comes alive . . . through its people. We do not feel that we are reading an historical romance" (586). Fanny Butcher offered support in the *Chicago Daily Tribune* and anticipated Myers in attributing to the novel's syntax its "intensely beautiful" effect on her; the "eternal rhythm" of life, "the burthen" of the novel, has been put "in some magic way . . . into her prose, superbly."

More general issues were taken up by William Lyon Phelps in *Scribner's* and Kenneth C. Kaufman in *Southwest Review*. Phelps felt that *Shadows* "surpassed" the *Archbishop* in depicting and interpreting the simple and devout people of a Catholic community, but he classified both works as "social history written with impeccable art." He noted that Cather, "writing deliberately outside of the typical American manner," had produced "a book of healing." The sympathy and tenderness in this work he "would not have suspected in the author of *A Lost Lady*." Kaufman saw in *Shadows* a clash of racial and national ideas during a time when Old World limitations were yielding to the limitless New World and a new order was being established. Such a theme made Cather a world novelist, even though we view such a "gigantic stage where Titans play their destined roles" through the eyes of a twelve-year-old "as through a peep hole" (xi). Kaufman distinguished *Shadows* from the *Archbishop* in its compression of life into thirteen months and in the secondary status of its protagonist: "Here is a huge canvas with the major figures merely outlined and with the high lights playing upon the minor ones" (xiii).

The skeptical and negative reviewers of *Shadows* were chiefly concerned (like critical theorists later in the century) with Cather's relation to contemporary life. Carl Van Doren was among those who expressed major reservations about the new novel and felt compelled to assess the stages of Cath-

er's career. "Her successive books . . . have come from successive layers in her own actual or imagined experience," he
wrote in the *New York Herald Tribune Books*. The layers of the
Nebraska pioneer and the Indian Southwest have failed to
sustain her art: "Nebraska was too new and raw" and had
little to offer after nature was mastered. "The cliff villages
were too old and dead." Cather subsequently embraced Catholicism, an inherited discipline able "to support and to
renew" her in the *Archbishop*, but in turning to Catholic Quebec, Van Doren observed, Cather was forsaking familiar material for less abundant stores of observation. This has led
her to reduce the drama of the time and place to a child's
perspective; "[h]er epic is consequently domesticated," its
heroism secondhand. Like Wilson, he detected dependence
on objects to give the chronicle body: seasonal landscapes;
churches and markets; domestic interiors with food, costume, a parrot and a cup. Enthusiastic for "ordered, fruitful,
comely societies" from the start, Van Doren concluded, Miss
Cather has now played Miss Jewett to Quebec.

In the *North American Review*, Herschel Brickell appreci-
ated the "lovely prose" of the novel and its resemblance to a
"historical tapestry wrought with all possible artistry, Puvis
de Chavannes frescoes in words." Yet he, like Van Doren,
was disappointed in the direction Cather was taking: "Is she
abandoning the contemporary scene altogether for this sort
of tapestry-weaving?" Helen MacAfee took up the implica-
tions of Cather's title in the *Yale Review*. The shadows are cast
by old men's reveries, she suggested, by the religious faith of

those who have renounced the world, and by the wonder of children: "delicate wavering images . . . on the enduring background of nature that . . . is always unmindful of the brief frailty of man." To enforce the insubstantial impression, Cather relied on description and "little everyday events," although she failed to achieve "the cumulative effect ["of mounting emotion"] that a novel . . . should communicate to the reader." Yet MacAfee conceded that this major flaw is somewhat compensated for "in the weight of reflection that the book gathers . . . on what [French] values are worth saving from an old world." *New York Evening Post* reviewer William Soskin compared *Shadows* to "a historical fresco based upon . . . very real history" but dismissed it as a "legitimate novel." He also found fault with Cather's character portraits, specifically those of Pierre Charron and Bishop Saint-Vallier, judging them as "lamentable" and Cécile as a "rather unreal daughter." These failures made him wonder if Cather's "method of composition by atmospheric detail and by omission of concrete character development is dictated by necessity."

These critics' reservations, however, were nothing compared to what Cather was forced to swallow from emphatically negative reviewers, whose major complaint was her choice of subject. On the cover of the *New York Times Book Review* for 2 August 1931, John Chamberlain placed *Shadows* far down on his merit graph of Cather fiction. Although beautifully written, the novel lacks any "memorable incident," has a "shrinking" heroine (whose distaste for country life symbolizes the author's retreat from the "salt," "sweat," "riot," and "rigor of pioneering"), is plotless, without conflict, and has "precious little of actuality." Cather "colloquialize[s] Parkman," he continued, reduces to "anecdote" what Parkman "tells as history." Instead of following the coureurs de bois into the forest, "she sticks to . . . the rock" and "the transplanted amenities of Catholic civilization." Rather than leaving out the best in Parkman, she should have developed a "live body with poetic eyes" such as Diony Hall, Elizabeth Madox Roberts's heroine in *The Great Meadow*, a vital eyewitness and participant in dramatic pioneer history. Chamberlain speculated that Cather had used up the limited experiences refracted even in the Nebraska novels and was offering "pearly" panels of a "world of the mind" as substitutes. These were inadequate, however: "the two-dimensional life of the fresco [is] beautiful, pale and rightly alien to the novel form." Perceived lack of experience also concerned Newton Arvin in the *New Republic*. In "judiciously" evading the "real life of her time, . . . mass production and technological unemployment and cyclical depressions," Cather has chosen escapist material she does not believe in and has little experience with. The result, Arvin insisted, is a novel "born dead" and with "no center and forward drive." While a few of her books have "genuine largeness of contour [and] . . . density of implication," many of them are "weak" and this last "so disappointing." Arvin identified the culprit as Emersonian individualism defining itself against rather than within the social group. Cather's concept of individualism, like

that of other writers of her period, "has had its day, and now
... betrays its incurable sterility."

In order to set up *Shadows on the Rock* for total dismissal,
Louis Kronenberger, in a lengthy piece in the *Bookman*, divided Cather's books into periods of affirmation (*O Pioneers!*
and *My Ántonia*), unrest (*One of Ours* to *My Mortal Enemy*),
and tranquillity (the *Archbishop* and *Shadows*). In the first period, according to Kronenberger, Cather treated Homeric
material from a Virgilian perspective; in the second she
touched contemporary life, however inadequately; in the
third she retreated into legend (the *Archbishop*) and fairy tale
(*Shadows*). These last novels lack the reality of the Nebraska
fiction tapped from Cather's childhood experiences, and in
them the idyllic has replaced the real. Cather, he insisted, is
moving in the wrong direction — backwards — using history
to distance rather than to deal with life. In *Shadows*, potentially dramatic historical material (the kind from which Sig-
rid Undset fashioned "true and important chronicles of human experience" [140]) has been stylized into a minuet.
Cather "adds nothing to her reputation with *Shadows on the
Rock*," Kronenberger concluded; it is "not quite perfect
enough of its kind to survive in its own genre" (139–40).
Frances Lamont Robbins, in *Outlook*, similarly disparaged
the miniscule nature of the book: compared to the *Archbishop*, "a bell ringing between heaven and earth," *Shadows*
resembles "a pure, thin tinkle in a sanctuary"; its characters
are "lovely ghosts, but ghosts," its "shadows have no souls."

In the *Nation*, Dorothy Van Doren admired the fine writing and the celebration of simple virtue; however, she felt that Cather's work was becoming increasingly disparate and episodic and that the "blood has gone out of [her characters and] into the color of the Quebec sky, into the red of Cécile's curtains." Because "Miss Cather is still at the height of her middle years," Van Doren concluded, it is "not time for her to become reminiscent or resigned" as she is here. Cather's apparent retreat was also the subject of Granville Hicks's review in the *Forum*, which begins with an approving nod to *Shadows* as a convincing re-creation ("made . . . glamorous by the magic of her pen") of colonists "poised between the vast uncertainties of frontier isolation and the . . . consoling certainties of their faith." However, Hicks proceeded to dismiss the novel as picturesque local color without a central theme, reduce Cather to minor status, and then condemn her for "abandon[ing] herself to her softness." He defines softness as "failure of the will. Even [her] style . . . suggests a kind of passivity." Hicks concluded that Cather lacked the "disciplined resolution that must guide the imagination of a great writer."

Hicks was benign compared to Horace Gregory, who demolished Cather in the *Symposium* for "refusing to express a moral issue in terms of adult experience" (551). *Shadows* contains an "anatomy of virtue" in which "physical dirt is a symbol of evil" and Cécile's "conversion" of Jacques "is a matter of continually washing his hands and face" (552). Gregory detected "opposing ideologies" in the children, who were "perfect examples of Rousseau's natural man-the-child whose instincts lead quite naturally toward the Good Life" yet also "embodiments of a consciousness of guilt and a sense of the original sin" (553). He claimed that Cather's highly selective use of her sources produced "an ingeniously contrived distortion of pioneer life." Unlike her successful Nebraska novels treating pioneer stock from the cultural mainstream, *Shadows* and the *Archbishop* represent a Catholic devotion to the Old World running counter to the North American Puritan traditions. Appreciation of such novels requires "a sophisticated, urban, if not downright decadent imagination" (554).

Approval of Cather's attention to Catholic cultural history came from what Gregory would have considered an organ of decadence, the Catholic press. Here, not surprisingly, the reviews were favorable and also insightful in terms of Cather's art and imagination. *Commonweal*'s Michael Williams claimed that *Shadows* possessed "a quality similar to that of the best folklore, in which a story that is almost naïve is yet so deeply rooted in the ultimate mystery of human life." The portrait of Jeanne Le Ber "expresses the quintessence of that spirit of ascetic mysticism which in all ages exists in the Church." Williams argued that Cather's understanding of the past, "in the spirit of modernity, . . . looks backward; and looks forward as well," capturing humanity with its sins, sorrow, and virtues, "humanity conscious of its source and its end in divinity." Without a "trace of artificial arrangement," he continued, Cather has woven together episodes and characters "with the seeming haphazardness of everyday life" and thus illuminated old Quebec "as volumes of history could not do." Camille McCole argued in the *Catholic World* that because Cather refused to subscribe to the more "meretricious phases" of her period, she has become "a most enduring part of it." Through a "perfect fusion of style and subject," wrote McCole, she has achieved in *Shadows* an "undertone of feeling" that will outlast the historical background in the memory of the reader. No other living novelist "seems to possess the comprehensive sympathies so necessary in the handling of such material . . . [of] our [Catholic] heritage." Like other reviewers, *America's* Francis Talbot used the publication of *Shadows* as an excuse to evaluate Cather's contribution to the national literature. Her fiction, he observed, manages to be "old-fashioned without being dull. . . . She has mastered . . . the fine art of sobriety in word . . . in an age . . . preposterously loud and bizarre." Yet she is not afraid of life's unpleasantries and handles them with "restraint . . . characteristic of her style." After commenting on "things Catholic" in *The Professor's House* and *My Mortal Enemy*, Talbot praised *Shadows* as "superb . . . artistic writing . . . as wholly and as sincerely Catholic . . . as a well-educated Catholic could make it." Let it be placed, he concluded, "among the best Catholic books of our times." The Protestant *Christian Century* bestowed its "undenominational" praise in a review by Arthur Dygert Bates, who felt Cather's handling of Jeanne Le Ber and her miracle beautifully wrought, and her stories of missionaries, particularly Noël Chabanel's, "moving." Bates disparaged the treatment given *Shadows* by professional critics, particularly condemning John Chamberlain's representation of such "a thing of beauty" as "a decline . . . on a graph depicting the business cycle."

Among reviewers in the secular press who praised the sacred dimension of *Shadows* was the *Boston Evening Transcript*'s William E. Harris, who saw the novel as the expression of an aging writer's natural interest in religious mysticism. Having depicted the pioneers' struggle with nature, Cather had now taken up the relationship of devout souls with God. Harris detected Cather's aesthetic commitment to writing history in terms of fiction as her interest shifted from individuals to times and places, and he connected mysticism to her movement from realism and "terse, rugged emotions" to "a very high order of romance . . . dealing in sentiment." In *McCall's*, Alexander Woollcott tried to define the novel's "serene art . . . no other American writer can match" by recalling a soldier in the Great War who was able to read William Morris in the midst of battle: in depicting the carrying of "the Word into the parched wilderness" and the French colony that "held the fort and kept the faith," Cather has proven herself unperturbed at Armageddon and too strong to be decivilized by the collapse of the world around her. The preservation of the flame of French life in the storm was epitomized for Woollcott in the dinner given for Captain Pondaven of *Le Faucon*, as it had been in the *Archbishop* in Father Vaillant's first Christmas dinner in Santa Fe.

A sampling of the Canadian and British reviews indicates positive response to *Shadows*. Because these reviewers had fewer preconceptions about the kind of books American novelists should be turning out, they had fewer reservations about the appearance of a novel not in the mainstream. To the reviewer in the *Toronto Globe*, *Shadows* "restores for us so perfectly the atmosphere of the beautiful old city and of that picturesque age" and re-creates "so faithfully and so vitally" the French exiles. Cather's particular genius and restricted experience with the Canadian material had been "turned to advantage," claimed the *Globe*, by her replacing an action-blurred panorama with a domestic "reconstruction" representative of what Quebec truly was — "the bosom of Mother Church" — for the missionaries, soldiers, and woodsmen of the time. In the *Canadian Bookman*, John Murray emphasized Cather's domestic intent and castigated those critics who "cruelly" ignored it to complain that *Shadows* is not an action novel. But those who read the book "in tune with the spirit of its author," he continued, will be satisfied "consummately." Murray pointed out how this novel might promote brotherhood by making bigoted non-Catholics aware of the role of Catholicism in early Canadian history.

The reviewer in the *Canadian Magazine* delighted in Cather's ability to "come closer to . . . the peculiar genius of the French-Canadian people than most of our native writers." Others have followed their history "with more meticulous exactness, but few if any have caught so well that unswerving spirit of those priests and pioneers that made that stubborn French colony . . . the germ of a nation." However, it bothered the *Toronto Daily Star* reviewer that Cather's reasons "for deliberately discarding ["the struggle . . . over the

370

sale of firewater to the Iroquois"] to write continually of its effects are only dimly apparent when her book is finished." The *Montreal Gazette* noted that *Shadows* "is having a great appeal," even among those who know Quebec "as well as the proverbial 'palm of [one's] hand,'" and suggested that copies of the novel be sent across the border to "help make Canada and Quebec better known and maybe secure more visitors."

In the *Canadian Forum*, Margaret Fairley noted Cather's recent tendency to lead her readers to the exterior of the casket and trace the mosaics and jewels there while only occasionally suggesting the less beautiful things within. In *Shadows* Cather has produced "an exquisite and fragrant work of art, delighting all the senses, and as satisfying as a Chaucerian tale." Fairley reminded her readers that artists are under no obligation to be professional historians or psychologists and that Cather has chosen to concentrate on the externals and manners of ordinary daily life to give them "almost sacramental significance. . . . The ordinances of the church, the daily ritual of the good housewife . . . give protection and ballast to life as Cécile knows it." The British reviewer in *Punch* applauded Cather for using the missionary exploits of the first French apostles of Canada (material this reviewer felt was oddly neglected by novelists) as a "fiery shuttle" threading through the quiet lives of Euclide and Cécile Auclair, Blinker, and Jacques. The book's "enchanting unity of impression, grace of detail and graciousness of handling" make it "far more than a companion-piece to *Death Comes for the Archbishop*." An equally enthusiastic British notice in the *New Statesman and Nation* classified *Shadows* as a "religious" tale of "eagle-eyed faith" and distinguished its "sense of spiritual space" as rare in modern fiction. This reviewer also praised "its imaginative truth, its eager, unflagging desire to escape, its soaring, undaunted spirit" as extraordinary achievements. In London's *Times Literary Supplement*, Cather was applauded for breathing life into old Quebec society, for peopling it with interesting and believable characters, and for highlighting the seasonal sailings between Europe and the New World.

Two essays appeared in 1932 to cap the controversy created at home over Cather's Quebec novel. In the *Nation*, Clifton Fadiman felt compelled to repeat the division of Cather's career into pioneer sagas, novels of manners, and dream histories, but then he attached his own list of her career limitations. Morality in Cather is in harmony with convention rather than in conflict with the social order, he asserted, and Cather's concept of passion leaves out sex — *Shadows* being a clear case in point. Her Virgilian outlook is least suited to portraying contemporary life. Unlike Proust's, her preoccupation with the past is a retreat into her own childhood and youth, he contended. Her world of the mind is shrinking and fastened with shutters, as indicated by the "precious, over-calculated" (565) effects of the *Archbishop* and *Shadows*. Essentially detached and out of step, she thus lacks influence and disciples. Fadiman concluded by reducing Cather from major to minor writer status. However, Archer Winsten addressed such charges as these in a "De-

fense" of Cather in the *Bookman*. He accused dissenting
critics of misreading Cather's "return to childhood" statement relative to writing the *Archbishop* (635) and dismissed as
matters of taste those complaints that the characters in *Shadows* are unreal, countering them with responses by Catholic
reviewers claiming otherwise; then he traced the development of Cather's theory of simplification of character, "of
doing away with expedients and wholesale invention" (636).
The *Archbishop* and *Shadows* are the triumphs of her art and
"reminiscent of musical tone-poems," he concluded. "They
have to do with . . . values, with ways of living, with the
peace . . . that a man makes with his god before he dies"
(637). Are such basic ideas, he asked, "divorced from reality
now that we have big cities, 'mass production,' 'technological
unemployment,' and critics in whom the knife must be
turned twice in the wound before it is felt?"

Coda: Toward Avignon

Despite a majority of positive or respectfully uncertain responses, *Shadows on the Rock* did receive, as Woodress puts it,
"a good many unfavorable reviews" (433), some bordering
on nastiness. Much to the relief of some detractors, the direction of Cather's career now seemed to shift away from the
Catholic historical past of *Shadows* and the *Archbishop* to familiar Nebraska materials in the three stories in *Obscure Destinies*. Because these stories were either completed prior to
Shadows ("Neighbour Rosicky" was finished in 1928) or near
completion at the novel's publication (Cather sent "Old Mrs.

373

Harris" and "Two Friends" to her publisher by the end of the summer of 1931 [Woodress 441]), this return to Nebraska cannot be construed as a response to negative reviews. Such reviews might have stalled Cather's taking up the French Catholic material employed in the *Archbishop* and developed in *Shadows*, but a closer look at "Neighbour Rosicky" and "Old Mrs. Harris" reveals a continuation of the religious and family nostalgia themes at the heart of *Shadows*, although washed of Catholicism and Francophilia. "Two Friends" opens with a regretful narrator using the same sanctuary metaphor Cather does in *Shadows* when Father Hector observes a group of exiled Frenchmen enjoying dinner with Captain Pondaven, that of seagulls returning "at certain seasons . . . to something they have known before" (*Obscure Destinies* 161). If Cather's thematic direction swerves somewhat in *Lucy Gayheart* (1935), it is redirected, if Protestantized, in both her last completed novel, *Sapphira and the Slave Girl* (1940), and her last short story, "The Best Years" (1948).

On 2 February 1933, a year and a half after the publication of *Shadows on the Rock*, Cather was awarded the first annual Prix Femina Américain by a committee organized by the Prix Femina of France that included, among others, Mary Austin, Dorothy Canfield Fisher, Ellen Glasgow, Edna St. Vincent Millay, Harriet Monroe, and Elizabeth Shepley Sergeant. *Shadows* had been selected from a final list of three novels (the others being *1919* by John Dos Passos and *State Fair* by Phil Stong) as the best "original literary work by an American . . . which will increase in France the understanding of American

374

life" ("Miss Cather Wins" 15). Millay presented the illuminated parchment and a message from Ambassador Paul Claudel, who had been instrumental in establishing the prize. This honor provided for translation of *Shadows* into French and publication in Paris, and later that year the novel was brought out by Librairie Hachette as *Les Ombres sur le Rocher* in a translation by Maurice Rémon. A preface by Lucie Delarue-Mardrus singles out Cather from the frigid Anglo-Saxon tradition for the Latin warmth of her prose and appreciates her uniqueness in being a deeply rooted American able to glorify France. "Willa Cather has shown these seventeenth-century French people to be in many ways similar to those of our contemporary countryside," wrote Delarue-Mardrus. "Minus *le bovarysme*, [the novel] recalls the same life as that of our current small villages" (9). The book's charm, she added, lies in "traditions, nobility, good cuisine, fine dressings, simple life, and homesickness . . . the autumn ships departing for France, leaving behind them an emptiness — herein lies the charm of this book, the most anti-machine, anti-Americanization novel we could read."

Four years after the publication of *Shadows*, Cather returned to France for the last time and eventually decided to uproot her fiction from North American soil and make Avignon the locale of a story set during the exile of the popes, when the Roman church was actually French. Edith Lewis provided George Kates with an account of the proposed plot, involving two boys, Pierre and André, mutilated for thievery and blasphemy, respectively. The misery of their plight was

375

to be heightened against the splendor of the papal court, and the central scene would involve an elderly blind priest comforting the blasphemer. A major theme was to be an analysis of the betrayal of the sacred in the sinner, and the priest would succeed in transforming André's disability into a challenge involving Pierre (Kates 482–84). As to style, Lewis told Kates that it was to be "completely *démeublé*" and the length of a long *nouvelle* (490), that is, like *My Mortal Enemy*. Thus Avignon, which Cather had first visited in 1902, serves as a frame for forty-five years of fiction writing, anticipating *Death Comes for the Archbishop* and *Shadows on the Rock* as well as its own unfinished story, the one Lewis compared to the young guide's song she and Cather heard on their last visit to the papal palace: "It echoed down the corridors and under the arched ceilings like a great bell sounding . . . from some remote past; its vibrations seemed laden, weighted down with the passions of another age — cruelties, splendours, lost and unimaginable to us in our time" (190).

Notes

1. In "The Influence of Willa Cather's French-Canadian neighbors in Nebraska in *Death Comes for the Archbishop* and *Shadows on the Rock*," *Great Plains Quarterly* 20 (2000): 35–54, Kathleen Danker provides local background for Cather's early memories of French religious and domestic culture in the towns of Wheatland and Campbell, Nebraska; Danker speculates on the contributions of these communities to characterization and history in the two novels and in *O Pioneers!*

2. In "The Real Alexander's Bridge," *American Literature* 21

(1950): 473–76, John P. Hinz explores the genesis of the *Alexander's Bridge* catastrophe in accounts of the 1907 disaster.

3. For a fuller treatment of Cather's feelings about Canada and the various dimensions of borders and boundaries, see David Stouck, "Willa Cather's Canada: The Border as Fiction," *Cather Studies 4: Willa Cather's Canadian and Old World Connections*, ed. Robert Thacker and Michael A. Peterman (Lincoln: U of Nebraska P, 1999), 7–27.

4. A facsimile of this typescript of the opening of book 4 with Cather's corrections appears as the frontispiece in the Autograph Edition of *Shadows on the Rock*, vol. 10, and as illustration 4 in this edition.

5. Gary Brienzo treats Cather's "imaginative softening" of Parkman's Frontenac into "a spiritual parent, with nurturing characteristics" (60–63).

6. The Relations and other sources mentioned but not quoted in this essay are listed under Works Consulted at the end of the Explanatory Notes.

7. John J. Murphy has applied this extension of anacoluthon to the narrative structure of each of the novel's six books in "The Art of *Shadows on the Rock*," *Prairie Schooner* 50 (spring 1976): 37–51.

8. Information and reproductions of the Cluny Museum tapestries are available in Adolfo Salvatore Cavallo, *The Unicorn Tapestries at the Metropolitan Museum of Art* (New York: Abrams, 1998), 93–100. The 1996 Michelin Green Guide to Paris offers the traditional interpretation of the sixth tapestry (172).

Works Cited

Anzaldua, Gloria. *Borderlands/La Frontera: The New Mestiza*. San Francisco: Spinster/Aunt Lute, 1987.

Arvin, Newton. Rev. of *Shadows on the Rock*. *New Republic* 12 Aug. 1931: 345–46.

Bates, Arthur D. Rev. of *Shadows on the Rock*. *Christian Century* 9 Sept. 1931: 1118–19.

Bennett, Mildred R. *The World of Willa Cather*. New edition. Lincoln: U of Nebraska P, 1961.

Bloom, Edward A., and Lillian D. Bloom. *Willa Cather's Gift of Sympathy*. Carbondale: Southern Illinois UP, 1964.

Brickell, Herschel. Rev. of *Shadows on the Rock*. *North American Review* 232 (1931): 380.

Brienzo, Gary. *Willa Cather's Transforming Vision: New France and the American Northeast*. Selinsgrove, Penn.: Susquehanna UP, 1994.

Brown, E. K. *Willa Cather: A Critical Biography*. Completed by Leon Edel. New York: Knopf, 1953.

Brown, Marion M., and Ruth Crone. *Only One Point on the Compass: Willa Cather in the Northeast*. Danbury, Conn.: Archer Editions, 1980.

Brown, Russell. "The Road Home: Meditation on a Theme." *Context North America: Canadian/U.S. Literary Relations*. Ed. Camille R. LaBossière. Ottawa: U of Ottawa P, 1994. 23–48.

Butcher, Fanny. Rev. of *Shadows on the Rock*. *Chicago Daily Tribune* 15 Aug. 1931: 10.

Cather, Willa. *Collected Short Fiction, 1892–1912*. Ed. Virginia Faulkner. Lincoln: U of Nebraska P, 1970.

——. Letter to H. L. Mencken. 6 Feb. 1922. Enoch Pratt Library, Baltimore.

——. Letters to Dorothy Canfield Fisher. 3 Apr. 1928, 1 May 1931, June 1931. U of Vermont Library, Burlington.

——. *Obscure Destinies*. 1932. Willa Cather Scholarly Edition. Ed. Kari A. Ronning et al. Lincoln: U of Nebraska P, 1998.

———. "On *Shadows on the Rock*." Pp. 387–89 of this edition.

———. *O Pioneers!* 1913. Willa Cather Scholarly Edition. Ed. Susan J. Rosowski et al. Lincoln: U of Nebraska P, 1992.

———. *The World and the Parish: Willa Cather's Articles and Reviews, 1893–1902*. Ed. William M. Curtin. 2 vols. Lincoln: U of Nebraska P, 1970.

Chamberlain, John. Rev. of *Shadows on the Rock*. *New York Times Book Review* 2 Aug. 1931: 1.

Cross, Wilbur. Rev. of *Shadows on the Rock*. *Saturday Review of Literature* 22 Aug. 1931: 67–68.

Delarue-Mardrus, Lucie. Preface. *Les Ombres sur le Rocher*. By Willa Cather. Trans. Maurice Rémon. Paris: Librairie Hachette, 1933. 5–9. (Preface translated into English for this essay by Natalie Critchfield and P. J. Woolston.)

Fadiman, Clifton. "Willa Cather: The Past Recaptured." *Nation* 7 Dec. 1932: 563–65.

Fairley, Margaret. Rev. of *Shadows on the Rock*. *Canadian Forum* Nov. 1931: 64.

George, Benjamin. "The French-Canadian Connection: Willa Cather as a Canadian Writer." *Western American Literature* 11 (1976): 249–61.

Gregory, Horace. Rev. of *Shadows on the Rock*. *Symposium* Oct. 1931: 551–55.

Harris, William E. Rev. of *Shadows on the Rock*. *Boston Evening Transcript* 1 Aug. 1931: 8.

Hicks, Granville. Rev. of *Shadows on the Rock*. *Forum* Sept. 1931: vi, viii.

Kates, George N. "Willa Cather's Unfinished Avignon Story." 1956. *Willa Cather Collected Stories*. New York: Vintage, 1992. 464–93.

Kaufman, Kenneth C. Rev. of *Shadows on the Rock. Southwest Review* 16 (summer 1931): xi–xiii.

Kronenberger, Louis. "Willa Cather." *Bookman* Oct. 1931: 134–40.

La Hontan, Baron de. *New Voyages to North America.* Ed. Reuben Gold Thwaites. Chicago, 1905. Reprinted from the English edition of 1703.

Lewis, Edith. *Willa Cather Living: A Personal Record.* New York: Knopf, 1953.

MacAfee, Helen. Rev. of *Shadows on the Rock. Yale Review* 21 (autumn 1931): xi.

McCole, Camille. Rev. of *Shadows on the Rock. Catholic World* Sept. 1931: 752–53.

"Miss Cather Wins French Book Prize." *New York Times* 3 Feb. 1933: 15.

Murray, John. Rev. of *Shadows on the Rock. Canadian Bookman* Aug. 1931: 167–68.

Myers, Walter L. "The Novel Dedicate." *Virginia Quarterly Review* 8 (1932): 410–18.

Parkman, Francis. *France and England in North America.* 1851–92. 2 vols. New York: Library of America, 1983.

Phelps, William L. Rev. of *Shadows on the Rock. Scribner's* Oct. 1931: 444.

Rev. of *Shadows on the Rock. Canadian Magazine* Jan. 1932: 31.

Rev. of *Shadows on the Rock. Montreal Gazette* 29 Aug. 1931: 22.

Rev. of *Shadows on the Rock. New Statesman and Nation* 16 Apr. 1932: 498.

Rev. of *Shadows on the Rock. Punch* 20 Jan. 1932: 83.

Rev. of *Shadows on the Rock. Times Literary Supplement* 21 Jan. 1932: 42.

Rev. of *Shadows on the Rock*. *Toronto Daily Star* 8 Aug. 1931: 4.

Rev. of *Shadows on the Rock*. *Toronto Globe* 8 Aug. 1931: 20.

Robbins, Frances L. Rev. of *Shadows on the Rock*. *Outlook* 5 Aug. 1931: 441.

Skaggs, Merrill M. *After the World Broke in Two: The Later Novels of Willa Cather*. Charlottesville: UP of Virginia, 1990.

Soskin, William. Rev. of *Shadows on the Rock*. *New York Evening Post* 1 Aug. 1931: 10.

Stegner, Wallace. *Wolf Willow: A History, a Story, and a Memory of the Last Plains Frontier*. 1955. Lincoln: U of Nebraska P, 1980.

Talbot, Francis, S.J. Rev. of *Shadows on the Rock*. *America* 22 Aug. 1931: 476–77.

Thérèse of Lisieux, St. *Story of a Soul: The Autobiography of Saint Thérèse of Lisieux*. 1899. 3rd ed. Trans. John Clarke. Washington, D.C.: ICS Publications, 1996.

Van Doren, Carl. Rev. of *Shadows on the Rock*. *New York Herald Tribune Books* 2 Aug. 1931: 1–2.

Van Doren, Dorothy. Rev. of *Shadows on the Rock*. *Nation* 12 Aug. 1931: 160.

Williams, Michael. Rev. of *Shadows on the Rock*. *Commonweal* 30 Sept. 1931: 528.

Wilson, James S. Rev. of *Shadows on the Rock*. *Virginia Quarterly Review* 7 (1931): 585–90.

Winsten, Archer. "A Defense of Willa Cather." *Bookman* Mar. 1932: 634–40.

Woodress, James. *Willa Cather: A Literary Life*. Lincoln: U of Nebraska P, 1987.

Woollcott, Alexander. Rev. of *Shadows on the Rock*. *McCall's* Nov. 1931: 20, 101.

Cécile

Some words in this surviving but unused fragment of Cather's manuscript of *Shadows on the Rock* were almost indecipherable; they are indicated in this transcript by bracketed notes. Questionable resolutions are followed by bracketed question marks. One word and a period have been supplied in brackets. Cather's spelling has been preserved, including the errors "especialy" and "It's." Interpolated words and phrases are included but not marked as such, and Cather's deletions appear in angle brackets. The reader is referred to the facsimile (illustration 33) for the physical form of the text.

"WHAT is there for your daughter here?" the Count had said, and Auclair had echoed him. That question through the years since her mother died had been answered by the reply "she will return to her mother's sister." But now there seemed to be no answer. She seemed a girl without a fortune-unprovided for. He knew well his own failing; that he was weak in decision, that he evaded when he should confront and let chance determine for him. He reproached himself with failing in parental forethought. He loved his daughter and he had made no provision for her. She trusted him absolutely in everything, and he had poorly repaid her confidence. One day she must realize the fact that he had arranged no portion for her.

That she was making a portion for herself, neither he nor the Count could understand⟨. Even⟩; they were exiles, she was not. Ever since she was big enough to run about the hilly streets of Quebec she had had a life of her own, a kind of vocation of her own-one of the loveliest and happiest of all vocations, and especialy beautiful in a girl. Her life, like that of her teachers at the Ursulines, was made up of love — but a different kind of love. She had for her town ⟨the⟩a feeling her elders could never know; for its streets & lanes, its people, its history, its [*one word indecipherable*] and legends. It's weather, which her father thought abominable, was for Cecile a long story of adventure like the Chansons de Gestes of the middle ages. When she walked about she did not see what her father saw a number of shapely [?] buildings and churches surrounded by houses or lying in patches of raw untamed ground, without relation to each other, without harmony or composition. Cecile saw a beautiful town built in rising tiers on a splendid lonely rock, watered by a great river, shadowed by everlasting and interminable forests. And the people who came and went up and down that rocky headland, priests and bishops, indians and trappers, merchants and artisans, were for her the only real people in the world. Some she loved and some she feared, but ⟨she⟩all were [*one word indecipherable*] to her. Since she had known anything at all she had never known a dull day there⟨.She⟩, had never been lonely. She had the kind of patriotism that is a form of piety, that is a spiritual life. Whenever her father talked to her about their future in France, she felt something within her cling tighter and tighter to [the] chair in which she sat; her heart seemed to take fright and burrow down into something, as she had seen the little wood animals do when they were pursued.

To be everyday about in her town, to feel the well worn stones under her feet, to have happy chance encounters with its people, to see Mme Le — passing in her *carrosse*, to observe that [white space] to watch the ever-changing weather drift about her — that was life, that was reality and security. Anything else was merely separation from one's good.

People who have not been limited and held fast by their love of one spot on the rolling earth know nothing about it-cannot imagine it. It is ⟨the mark of⟩ a loyalty that has the force and blindness of a passion[.] Perhaps it is some biological survival a feeling left over from some very remote past.

On Shadows on the Rock

[This letter appeared in the *Saturday Review of Literature* on 17 October 1931.]

D EAR Governor Cross: —
  I want to thank you most heartily for the most understanding review I have seen of my new book. You seem to have seen what a different kind of method I tried to use from that which I used in the *Archbishop*. I tried, as you say, to state the mood and the viewpoint in the title. To me the rock of Quebec is not only a stronghold on which many strange figures have for a little time cast a shadow in the sun; it is the curious endurance of another kind of culture, narrow but definite. There another age persists. There, among the country people and the nuns, I caught something new to me; a kind of feeling about life and human fate that I could not accept, wholly, but which I could not but admire. It is hard to state that feeling in language; it was more like an old song, incomplete but uncorrupted, than like a legend. The text was mainly anacoluthon, so to speak, but the meaning was clear. I

took the incomplete air and tried to give it what would correspond to a sympathetic musical setting; tried to develop it
into a prose composition not too conclusive, not too definite:
a series of pictures remembered rather than experienced; a
kind of thinking, a mental complexion inherited, left over
from the past, lacking in robustness and full of pious resignation.

Now, it seemed to me that the mood of the misfits among
the early settlers (and there were a good many) must have
been just that. An orderly little French household that went
on trying to live decently, just as ants begin to rebuild when
you kick their house down, interests me more than Indian
raids or the wild life in the forests. And, as you seem to
recognize, once having adopted a tone so definite, once having taken your seat in the close air by the apothecary's fire,
you can't explode into military glory, any more than you can
pour champagne into a salad dressing. (I don't believe much
in rules, but Stevenson laid down a good one when he said:
You can't mix kinds.) And really, a new society begins with the
salad dressing more than with the destruction of Indian villages. Those people brought a kind of French culture there
and somehow kept it alive on that rock, sheltered it and
tended it and on occasion died for it, as if it really were a
sacred fire — and all this temperately and shrewdly, with
emotion always tempered by good sense.

It's very hard for an American to catch that rhythm — it's
so unlike us. But I made an honest try, and I got a great deal
of pleasure out of it, if nobody else does! And surely you'll

388

agree with me that our writers experiment too little, and produce their own special brand too readily.

With deep appreciation of the compliment you pay me in taking the time to review the book, and my friendliest regards always,

Faithfully,
Willa Cather

1. Willa Cather in the Luxembourg Gardens. During her 1920 visit to France, Cather expressed her preference for medieval Paris and confined her seven-week visit to the Left Bank area between the Seine and the Luxembourg Gardens. Philip L. and Helen Cather Southwick Collection, University of Nebraska–Lincoln Libraries, Archives and Special Collections.

2. Château Frontenac, Quebec City, from the deck of a Canadian Pacific steamship, c. 1930. Cather stayed at the Frontenac during her discovery of France on this continent, and on subsequent visits. Photographer unknown. Canadian Pacific Archives, L. 1003.

Book IV – Pierre Charron

I

It was
~~The~~ first day of June, ~~golden, glorious.~~ Before dawn a wild
calling and twittering of birds in the bushes on the cliff-side
~~behind~~ *over* the apothecary's ~~shop~~ *back door,* announced ~~the~~ *clear* weather. *when* The sun came
up over he Île d'Orleans ~~like a bridegroom issuing from his chamber~~
the rock of Kebec stood gleaming above the river like an altar
with many candles, *or* ~~like a~~ *holy city* ~~kxxxxxings~~ in an old legend, shriven,
sinless, washed in gold. ~~shining like the reighteous in their~~
~~Heavenly Father's house.~~ That quickening of all life and hope
early
which had come to France in May, had reached the far north at
last. Now it was spring. ~~As they~~ drank their chocolate, all the
doors and windows open, ~~both the Auclairs felt that something~~
~~delightful would happen today.~~
Euclide
Auclaire was at his desk, making up little packets of saffron
flowers to flavor fish soups, when a slender man with a quick
swinging step crossed the threshold and embraced him before he
had time to rise. He was not a big *fellow* ~~man,~~ this Pierre Charron,

3. The sundial in the Quebec Seminary courtyard
with its inscription *Dies nostri quast umbra*, "Our
days as if a shadow" (Chronicles 29:15), which the
title *Shadows on the Rock* echoes. Photograph by John
J. Murphy.

4. Facsimile of a page of the original typescript
of *Shadows on the Rock* with Cather's corrections.
Philip L. and Helen Cather Southwick Collection,
University of Nebraska–Lincoln Libraries, Archives
and Special Collections.

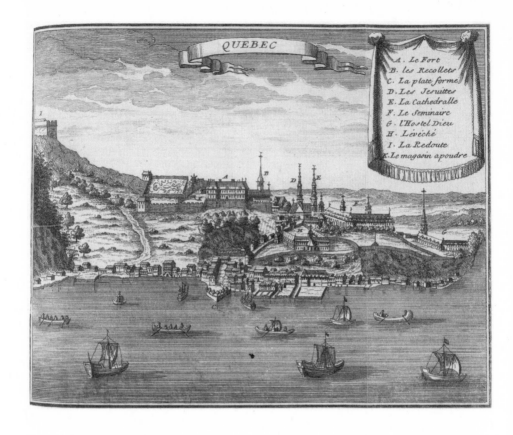

QUEBEC

A. Le Fort
B. les Recollets
C. La plate forme
D. Les Jesuittes
E. La Cathedralle
F. Le Seminaire
G. L'Hostel Dieu
H. L'éveché
I. La Redoute
K. Le magasin apoudre

5. View of Quebec c. 1700, from Claude-
Charles Bacqueville de La Potherie, *Histoire
de l'Amérique septentrionale*, vol. 1, *Contenat le
Voyade du Fort de Nelson* (Paris: Jean-Luc Nion
and François Didot, 1722; FC305 B326), 232.
National Library of Canada's website Early
Images of Canada: Illustrations from Rare
Books.

6. Map of the city of Quebec toward the end of the French regime with details of Cather's setting. (1) Fort and Château Saint-Louis; (2) Cathedral of Quebec; (3) Notre Dame des Victoires church and the marketplace; (4) Quebec Seminary; (5) Ursuline Convent and school; (6) Hospital Hôtel-Dieu; (7) Jesuit College and monastery; (8) Récollet monastery and chapel; (9) the Bishop's Palace; (10) Mountain Hill (Côte de la Montagne); (11) Holy Family Street (rue de la Sainte-Famille); (12) Redoubt of Cape Diamond (Cap aux Diamants). From Marcel Trudel, *Atlas historique de la Nouvelle-France/An Atlas of New France* (Quebec: Les Presses de l'Université Laval, 1968), 200.

7. Charles Cather, Willa's father. Philip L. and Helen Cather Southwick Collection, University of Nebraska–Lincoln Libraries, Archives and Special Collections.

8. Willa Cather with a boy's haircut, at about thirteen, the age of Cécile Auclair in the novel. Edith Lewis believed that the relationship between Willa and her father contributed to the "conception of the apothecary and his little daughter." Philip L. and Helen Cather Southwick Collection, University of Nebraska–Lincoln Libraries, Archives and Special Collections.

9. Louis de Buade, Count de Frontenac and governor of New France. Detail of a full-length statue in Quebec by Phillipe Hébert. From Francis Parkman's *Count Frontenac and New France under Louis XIV*, vol. 2 (1897).

10. Louis XIV of France c. 1706, attributed to Antoine Benoist. Versailles-National Museums of France; Art Resources.

11. François Xavier de Laval,
bishop of Quebec. Engraving
by Claude Duflos (1665–1727).
Courtesy of the Archives of the
Archdiocese of Quebec.

12. Jean Baptiste de la Croix
Chevrières de Saint-Vallier, bishop
of Quebec. Courtesy of the Archives
des Augustines du Monastère de
l'Hôpital Général de Québec.

CANADA

AND ADJACENT COUNTRIES

towards the close

OF THE

17ᵀᴴ CENTURY.

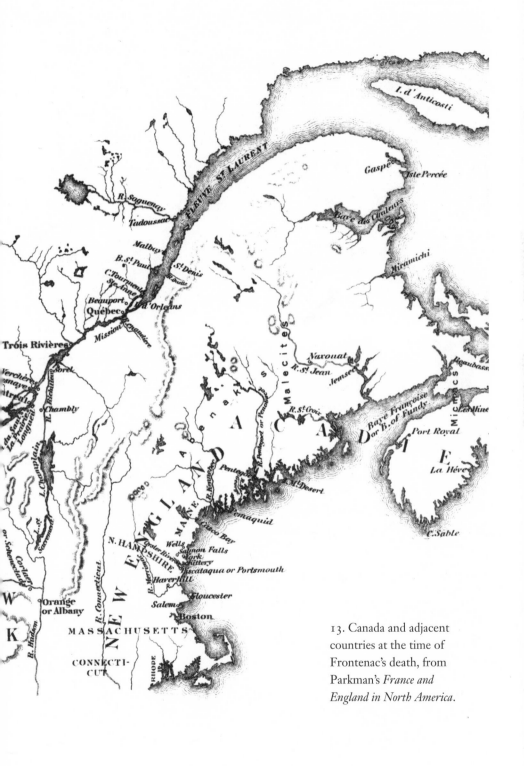

13. Canada and adjacent countries at the time of Frontenac's death, from Parkman's *France and England in North America*.

14. *The Jesuit Martyrs.* A 1664
engraving by Gregoire Huret with
victims identified by number: Isaac
Jogues (2), Jean de Brébeuf (6),
Gabriel Lalemant (7); Noël Chabanel
(9) appears stretched out on the
hillside above Lalemant's head. From
Parkman, *The Jesuits in North America
in the 17th Century.*

15. A passageway in Quebec Seminary,
founded by Bishop Laval in 1663.
Photograph courtesy of Lucia Woods.

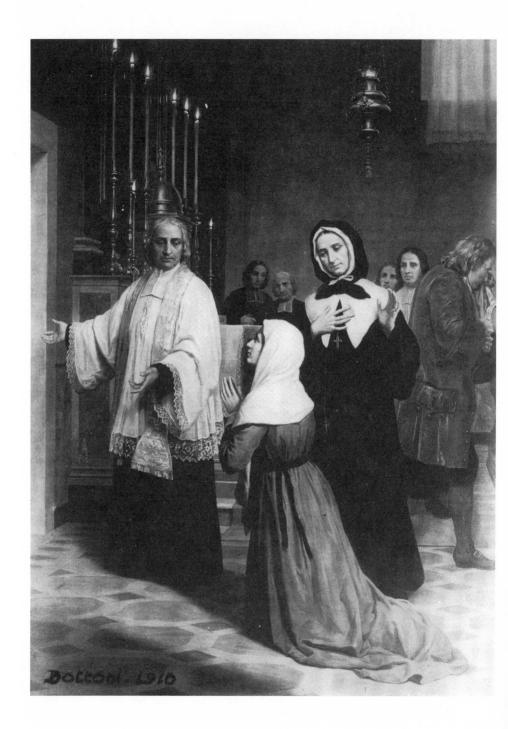

16. A 1910 painting by Enrico Bottoni (after an engraving by Millin in Faillon's *Vie de la Soeur Bourgeoys*) depicts Jeanne Le Ber entering her cell in the Chapel of the Congregation de Notre-Dame, Montreal, 1695. On either side of her are Dollier de Casson and Marguerite Bourgeoys; Jacques Le Ber is to the right, overcome by emotion. Courtesy of Hélène Tremblay, C.N.D., Director, Centre Jeanne Le Ber, Westmount, Quebec.

17. Marie-Catherine de Simon Longpré, Sister Catherine de Saint-Augustin of the Hospitalièrs de Saint-Augustin of Quebec's Hôtel-Dieu. Courtesy of Nicole Perron, A.M.J., the Musée des Augustines de L'Hôtel-Dieu de Québec.

18. Jeanne-Françoise Juchereau de la Ferté, Mother Juchereau of Quebec's Hôtel-Dieu. Courtesy of Nicole Perron, A.M.J., the Musée des Augustines de L'Hôtel-Dieu de Québec.

19. Saint-Malo, the birthplace and home port of Jacques Cartier, discoverer of Canada, was the port of embarkation for many Canadian colonists. Cather visited Saint-Malo in 1930 and used it as the setting for the ape story in chapter 3 of book 5 of *Shadows on the Rock*. This view by Jules Noel (from M. J. Janin's *La Bretagne*, Paris, 1844) depicts the walled city as seen from the English Channel; Île du Grand Bé is on the right. Courtesy of John J. Murphy.

20. The Marais district of Paris (the original home of the Auclairs), showing (1) the Quai de Celestins; (2) the Convent of the Célestins; (3) the Arsenal; (4) the developed Île Saint-Louis with the Pont-Marie; and (5) the village Saint-Paul. From the Turgot map, c. 1739. Courtesy Lilly Library, Indiana University, Bloomington.

21. Early-seventeenth-century engraving of Paris by Leonard Gaultier, showing Notre Dame in the center, the unjoined islands that would become the Île Saint-Louis to the right, and above them the Village Saint-Paul area and the Bastille; on the far left is the Louvre with Montmartre towering above it.

f. 15

Cet Icy vn

depûte du boutg de gannachiou
avé pouessles inuites au jeu les
Messieurs de qandaouyeatza.
Ils tiennent que le serpent est
le dieu du peuple linuoquent
le tenant en main en dansant
et chantant

22. Indian of the Iroquois tribe, from *Les Raretés des Indes: Codex Canadiensis* by Louis Nicolas.

23. French Canadian *gentilhomme* with snowshoes, from Bacqueville de la Potherie's *Histoire de l'Amérique Septentrionale*. National Library of Canada.

24. The last of the six *La Dame à la Licorne* tapestries,
showing the lady depositing a necklace in a casket
and renouncing the worldly pleasures depicted in
the previous tapestries. Cather hung full-size copies
of *The Lady with the Unicorn* at the foot of her bed
while working on *Shadows on the Rock* when she lived
at the Grosvenor Hotel on Fifth Avenue, New York.
In a June 1931 letter to Dorothy Canfield Fisher she
compares the writing of her novel during a period of
family loss to the shelter of a tapestry tent. Courtesy
of the Musée national du Moyen Age-Thermes et
hôtel de Cluny, Paris.

WILLA CATHER

LES OMBRES SUR LE ROCHER

(SHADOWS ON THE ROCK)

Traduit par Maurice RÉMON

(PRIX FEMINA AMÉRICAIN)

HACHETTE

LES OMBRES SUR LE ROCHER

Vous me demandez des graines de fleurs de ce pays. Nous en faisons venir de France pour notre jardin, n'y en ayant pas ici de fort rares ni de fort belles. Tout y est sauvage, les fleurs aussi bien que les hommes.

MARIE DE L'INCARNATION.
(Lettre à une de ses sœurs.)

Québec, le 12 août 1653.

LIVRE PREMIER

L'APOTHICAIRE

1

Un après-midi, vers la fin d'octobre 1697, Euclide Auclair, l'apothicaire-philosophe de Québec, debout au sommet du cap Diamant, contemplait le large fleuve qui s'étendait, vide, bien au-dessous de lui : vide parce qu'une heure plus tôt la tache brillante des voiles qui le descendaient avait disparu derrière l'île verte qui partage le cours du Saint-Laurent au-dessous de Québec, et le dernier des navires, venus de France l'été, était parti pour son long voyage de retour.

Tant que *La Bonne Espérance* avait été en vue, beaucoup des amis et voisins d'Auclair lui avaient tenu compagnie sur la falaise, mais quand le dernier point blanc fut caché par la courbe du rivage, ils regagnèrent leurs boutiques ou leurs cuisines pour affronter les sévères réalités de la vie. Pendant huit mois désormais, la colonie française établie sur ce rocher du Nord serait absolument séparée de l'Europe, du monde. On était en

---

25. The Church of the Ascension (Episcopal), Fifth Avenue at Tenth Street, with its John La Farge fresco and Augustus Saint Gaudens angels, was Cather's favorite church in New York. Cather went regularly to vespers there, and while writing *Shadows on the Rock* she lived across from this church. Its influence can be detected in the lovingly arranged, fresco-like universe described in chapter 6 of book 2. Whitney Cox photograph, courtesy of the Church of the Ascension, New York.

26. The main altar of Notre Dame des Victoires. Although this altar was built by David Ouellet in 1878, Cather places it in the church in the seventeenth century and has Cécile Auclair imagine that "the Kingdom of Heaven looked exactly like this from the outside." Photograph by John J. Murphy.

27. Title page of the 1933 French edition of *Shadows on the Rock*.

28. First page of chapter 1, book 1, of the French edition of *Shadows on the Rock*.

29. Cather in the woods at Grand Manan Island, New Brunswick, Canada, 1931. Photograph courtesy of Helen Cather Southwick.

30. Cather's cottage on Grand Manan Island. It was during a journey to this island that Cather "discovered" Quebec in 1928. Philip L. and Helen Cather Southwick Collection, University of Nebraska–Lincoln Libraries, Archives and Special Collections.

31. Early-twentieth-century photograph of Avignon, France, as Cather saw it in 1902 and on subsequent visits, from Cather's 1902 scrapbook. Parc Rocher des Doms, Notre Dame des Doms Cathedral, and the Papal Palace (which, according to Edith Lewis, "stirred" Cather "as no building in the world had ever done") dominate the city. Set in rock and walled like Quebec, Avignon is the locale of the novel Cather left unfinished at her death in 1947. Courtesy of the Philip L. and Helen Cather Southwick Collection, University of Nebraska–Lincoln Libraries, Archives and Special Collections.

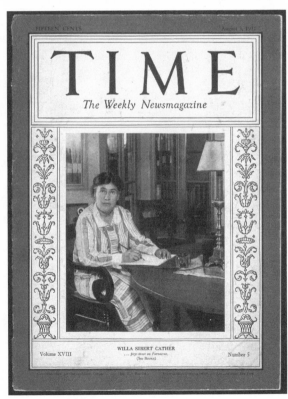

32. Cather on the cover of *Time* magazine, 3 August 1931. Getty Images.

... of WILLA CATHER

Cécile

33. One page of a four-page fragment not used in the novel, in Cather's hand.
Transcript on pp. 383–85. Courtesy of the Drew University Library.

Explanatory Notes on
Shadows on the Rock

JOHN J. MURPHY AND DAVID STOUCK

S HADOWS *on the Rock*, although a slightly shorter novel than *Death Comes for the Archbishop* and focused on a single year in the history of colonial Quebec, resembles the earlier novel in being the product of a wealth of sources tapped to shape its narrative and give it the perspective of a larger world. In a June 1931 letter to her friend and fellow novelist Dorothy Canfield Fisher, Willa Cather admitted that every detail in the lives of her characters in this novel had been taken from old books and letters. Although it is impossible to identify everything Cather read that contributed to her text, we have tried in the process of composing these notes to draw on Cather's sources as well as tap additional early and more recent authorities. As in the *Archbishop*, Cather's creative method involved combining, altering, and adding fictional components to historical materials.

Cather drew heavily on Francis Parkman's histories of France and England in North America, at times even approximating descriptive passages. However, she was aware of Anglo-American bias in Parkman and judiciously supplemented his works with those by twentieth-century Canadian historians and biographers as well as with seventeenth-century sources. Among the former are the volumes of the *Makers of Canada* series, particularly Abbé Henri Arthur Scott's biography of Bishop Laval. Cather's seventeenth-century sources include the letters of Marie of the Incarnation, the *Jesuit Relations*, Mother Juchereau's history of Quebec's Hôtel Dieu, and the Baron de La Hontan's *Voyages*. Cather's picture of France during the time of her novel's setting is informed to a significant degree by the *Mémoires* of the Duc de Saint-Simon.

The notes that follow are intended to complement Cather's text by making explicit items Cather left unnamed, by noting compositional strategies revealed in the course of exploring her sources, and by identifying historical figures and events, geographical locales, domestic and religious objects, flora and fauna, and so forth. As in the Scholarly Edition of the *Archbishop*, the cyclical and repetitive structure of this novel necessitates multiple cross-references in the notes. Major explanations are linked to pages where subjects are emphasized in Cather's text; where the text merely mentions a subject or deals with a minor detail, a brief note will direct the reader to the full note. At the end of the notes, sources for them and for Cather's narrative are listed.

Title: The Latin words *Dies Nostri Quast Umbra* (the *i* in *Quasi* altered to *t* to avoid elision) are inscribed over a wall sundial in the courtyard of the Laval Seminary, Quebec City. They translate "Our days as if a shadow." The source of this inscription is a line from 1 Chronicles 29:15, which in the King James Version reads "Our days on the earth are as a shadow." In fact, the whole verse has resonance in relation to Cather's novel: "for we are strangers before thee, and sojourners, as were all our fathers; our days on the earth are as a shadow, and there is none abiding."

Vous me demandez ... 1653: "You ask me for seeds of the flowers of this country. We have those for our garden, brought from France, there being none here that are very rare or very beautiful. Everything is savage here, the flowers as well as the men. Marie of the Incarnation (letter to one of her sisters [a sibling]), Quebec, 12 August 1653." See note for 113 on "Marie de l'Incarnation."

Book 1

Euclide ... philosopher apothecary: Beginning in the Middle Ages, 7 the term *apothecary* was used to identify those who prepared and sold drugs. Cather amplifies her description of Auclair with the term *philosopher* to suggest someone who read widely and thought about the moral and historical significance of his trade. Euclid of Megara (c. 450–c. 375 BC), his namesake, combined Socratic teaching on the virtue of knowledge with pre-Socratic notions of unchanging reality variously named wisdom, mind, God, etc. E. K. Brown speculates that Auclair may have been suggested to Cather by the historical person of Michel Sarrazin, who arrived in Quebec

393

in 1685 as a barber-surgeon to the troops (285). He treated civilians as well as soldiers, was held in high esteem by the sisters of the Hôtel Dieu in Quebec and in Montreal, and prepared specimens of nearly all the flora in the vicinity of Quebec for the Jardin du Roi (later the Jardin des Plantes) in Paris (see Parkman 1: 1358). It is of note as well that the first permanent settler in Quebec, Louis Hébert, who arrived with his family in 1617, was a Parisian apothecary (Le Sueur 16). Edith Lewis writes that the conception of the apothecary and his daughter likely owes something to Cather's affectionate relationship with her father (156). Charles Cather died shortly before the book was begun and was much on the author's mind at that time.

7   Quebec: The capital of New France, founded in 1608 by Samuel de Champlain on the northern shore of the St. Lawrence about 450 miles upriver at the location of the Indian village Stadacona, which Jacques Cartier visited in 1535–36. See notes below on "St. Lawrence" and "Kebec," for 8 on "little capital," for 13 on "Champlain," and for 215 on "Jacques Cartier."

7   Cap Diamant: See note for 8 on "Cap Diamant."

7   the green island: See notes for 10 on "Île d'Orléans" and for 129 on "north channel."

7   St. Lawrence: The largest river in Canada, flowing northeast from the Great Lakes to the Atlantic, and the major water entrance into the heart of the North American continent. It derived its name from that of the Gulf of St. Lawrence, which explorer Cartier entered in 1535 on or about the August 10 feast day of the third-century Roman martyr saint. Subsequent French explorers and traders used the St. Lawrence to establish a colonial empire stretch-

ing as far south as Louisiana, and the river became the focus of settlement for much of the province of Quebec.

La Bonne Espérance: *The Good Hope*. Martin Desgreves's *Navires de*   7
Saint-Malo (34) lists a corsair by this name weighing eight tons and carrying a crew of eighteen men. It went into service in 1696, a year prior to the opening of the novel. (A *corsaire* is defined as a privateering vessel sanctioned by the country of its owner for pirate activities against hostile nations, especially the capture of merchant shipping.)

King Louis: Louis XIV (1638–1715), known as the Sun King for   8
the magnificence of his court at Versailles, came to the throne at the age of five and ruled France for seventy-two years. During his mother's regency the French nobility tried unsuccessfully to take power away from the crown in a civil war known as the Fronde (1648–53); as a result Louis devoted his energies to centering power in the figure of the king, and his reign exhibited the strengths and the weaknesses of absolute monarchy. He used his enormous powers to expand France's borders both in Europe and abroad and to develop French arts to a pinnacle of achievement, but his appetite for glory was excessive and increasingly put him out of touch with his subjects. He lived for seventeen years beyond the 1697–98 time period of Cather's novel.

the Minister: See note for 273 on "Pontchartrain."   8

English ships . . . Fort Orange: Fort Orange was established in 1624   8
by the Dutch West India Company at the present site of Albany on the Hudson River for political protection and trade. By the time of the novel's setting, the English had taken control of what is now New York State, renamed this settlement in honor of James, the

Duke of York and Albany, and replaced Fort Orange with Fort Frederick. In winter, when the St. Lawrence River was frozen, this settlement was an important link to Europe because British ships continued to sail in and out of New York.

8   Montreal: Montreal was established in 1642 by Paul de Chomedey, Sieur de Maisonneuve, as an Indian mission on a mountain island in the Hochelaga Archipelago, some 150 miles upriver from Quebec, at the confluence of the St. Lawrence and Ottawa rivers. Cartier had visited a Mohawk village there (Hochelaga) in 1525 and named the place Mont Royal. The French settlement developing around the mission soon became the fur-trading center from which the coureurs de bois and explorers set out, and also a base for the long-standing war between the French and the Iroquois. (See notes for 195 on "coureurs de bois" and for 295 on "English and Dutch traders.") Since fur trading did not provide employment in the city, Montreal had barely a thousand inhabitants at the time period of Cather's novel. See note for 152 on "Ville-Marie de Montreal."

8   Cap Diamant: Cape Diamond, the highest point (330 feet) of the city of Quebec, is located west of the city center and adjacent to the Plains of Abraham. The name refers to the minerals discovered there by Champlain, which he thought were diamonds but proved to be quartz crystals. Defense works have been located there since the beginning of European settlement, and Quebec accordingly became famous as a bulwark: the city's motto is "*natura fortis*," and Charles Dickens distinguished Quebec as the "Gibralter of North America."

8   "Kebec": In this spelling Cather alludes to the origin of the city's name in an Algonquin word *Kebec* or *Kepac*, which refers to the narrowing of the river.

two rivers: Quebec is located at the confluence of the St. Charles 8
and St. Lawrence rivers.

little capital . . . fantastic dreams: From its founding in 1608, Cham- 8
plain envisioned Quebec as an outpost for discovering a route to
the Indies and as a mission center for the conversion of Native
peoples to Catholicism. Cardinal Richelieu (1585–1642), chief
minister of King Louis XIII, attempted to stifle French Protestant
(Huguenot) interference in the colony by increasing immigration
and restricting it to Catholics. By Frontenac's arrival in 1672, Quebec seemed destined by the French court to become the capital of a
vast empire from the Gulf of the St. Lawrence to the Gulf of Mexico (see note for 012 on "Governor . . . Frontenac"). If great in
potential, however, the capital was small in population. As Cather
notes in chapter 2, "Quebec had fewer than two thousand inhabitants."

theatric scene of the Nativity: Tradition locates Christ's birth in a 9
cave, or grotto, on the eastern hill of Bethlehem. By the sixteenth
century Nativity settings throughout Catholic Europe had become
fanciful scenic landscapes containing groves, waterfalls, villages,
and numerous elaborate figures complementing those of Jesus,
Mary, Joseph, and the shepherds. A famous French crèche dating
from 1604–8 was displayed until 1796 in the church of Notre-
Dame-des-Marais in Nogent-le-Rotrou, a Norman town southwest of Paris. See notes for 125 and 126 on "crèche" and "two
terraces."

mountain rock . . . streets below: Parkman (1: 1270–71) gives a 9–10
similar if less exquisite catalog of the city's buildings, the obvious
source of Cather's, including the imagined tossing of a stone from
Upper Town to Lower (see note for 10 on "Lower Town . . . Upper
Town").

9   Château Saint-Louis: The governor's residence was built in 1620
by Samuel de Champlain on the edge of the Upper Town overlooking the St. Lawrence, when Quebec had no more than fifty persons.
By the end of the century it was in total disrepair, and Count Frontenac had it rebuilt from the foundation. The Château Frontenac
Hotel now stands near the site.

9   convent and church of the Récollet friars: This order of reformed
Franciscans, who developed houses of "recollection" in France late
in the sixteenth century, was the first to undertake the Quebec
missions, arriving in 1615 and eventually administering parishes
and schools in the larger settlements between Quebec and Montreal. The first priests located temporarily in the Lower Town and
then at Notre Dame des Anges on the St. Charles River (see note
for 128 on "*cabine*"), where the Jesuits (see note below on "foundation of the Jesuits"), who subsequently took charge of the missions,
joined them in 1625. Both orders were expelled when the English
occupied Quebec in 1629. Upon their return in 1670 the Récollets
angered Bishop Laval (see note for 82 on "old Bishop Laval") by
interfering in the dispute over trading liquor with the Indians, and
as a result he tried unsuccessfully to stop the construction of a
convent and church on land they were granted in 1681, near the
Jesuit and Ursuline complexes in the area of the cathedral. The
English Cathedral of the Holy Trinity has occupied the site since
1804.

9   Convent of the Ursulines: The residential component of this religious order's complex, which included the school and chapel mentioned later in the text (see notes for 72 on "Ursuline school" and
for 111 on "Ursuline chapel"). The Ursulines (the oldest Catholic
community of teaching women), founded in Italy in 1525 as a so-

398

ciety of virgins dedicated to Christian education but living in their own homes, achieved status as a religious institute in 1612, after which convents were established. Under the patronage of Mme de la Peltrie, a wealthy Norman widow, three Ursulines from Tours arrived in Quebec in 1639 to teach Indian and French girls. One of them, Marie de l'Incarnation (see note for 113 on "Marie de l'Incarnation") emerged as leader of the enterprise and one of Canada's great missionaries. The building Auclair views, parts of it still extant, was constructed after 1686.

foundation of the Jesuits: The "massive" complex (the adjective is Parkman's [1: 1271]) of this preeminent missionary order in New France included a college and monastery (see notes for 42 on "Jesuits' college" and "the monastery"). The Society of Jesus (Jesuits), founded in Paris by Ignatius Loyola and approved by Pope Paul III in 1540, became a major force of the Counter Reformation (Catholic Reform) to restore the church after the Protestant Reformation and to preach the gospel in non-Christian lands. Colleges were established in Europe to respond to the first purpose, and missionary enterprises developed in Asia, Africa, and the Americas in response to the second. Jesuits first came to Canada in 1611, to a temporary settlement at Port Royal (Nova Scotia); they landed at Quebec in 1625 to begin their major missionary effort. Loyola based the society on spiritual "exercises" designed to amend life and imitate Christ.

the Cathedral: In the 1690s, the Cathedral of Our Lady of Quebec was an enlarged and renovated 1650 stone church in the form of a Roman cross. Parkman distinguishes it and the Jesuit complex as "marvels of size and solidity in view of the poverty and weakness of the colony" (1: 1271). Major renovation continued through 1749, but ten years later the structure was destroyed in the British conquest. After reconstruction, architects of the Baillairgé family contributed the ornate south belfry, interior, facade, and porch gates. The cathedral received the papal designation of basilica in 1874. After a devastating 1922 fire, the structure was restored according to old plans and illustrations to recall Bishop Laval's church.

9 Bishop Laval's Seminary: This institution (affiliated with the Seminary of Foreign Missions in Paris) was founded in 1663 by Canada's first Catholic bishop (see note for 82 on "old Bishop Laval") and by 1681 was housed in what is now the Procure wing (containing a sundial with an inscription that probably suggested Cather's title — see note on "Title"), one of three sections presently arranged around a courtyard. Laval stated the mission of his enterprise: "There shall be educated and trained such young clerics as may appear fit for the service of God" (Drummond 421). In 1668 he opened the Petit Séminaire for the religious and liturgical training of boys contemplating ecclesiastical life. Laval conceived the Séminaire de Québec as a base from which his movable secular (diocesan) priests would be sent out and to which they would return (see note for 140 on "Saint-Vallier . . . Laval's system"). In 1852 the seminary established a university (Laval University), Canada's first francophone institution of higher learning.

10 new Bishop's new Palace: See notes for 27 on Saint-Vallier's "new episcopal Palace" and for 137 on "Monseigneur de Saint-Vallier."

10 Lower Town . . . Upper Town: When Champlain established Quebec, the first buildings were located on the narrow shore of the St. Lawrence at the foot of Mountain Hill. When the city spread up the mountain, this area by the river became known as Lower Town (Basse Ville). The streets of the Lower Town were the colony's

economic crossroads, where furs were traded, merchants established their businesses and residences, and off which ships docked. The buildings in the Upper Town (Haute Ville) constituted the settlement's government and religious centers.

Norman Gothic: A type of Gothic developing out of Norman Romanesque abbey architecture (characterized by pure lines, bold proportions, sober decoration, and planklike stonework) and the lighter Gothic style of quadripartite vaulting and pointed arches originating in Île-de-France. The application of this combination to Quebec architecture is somewhat hyperbolic but tempered by emphasis on "effect" and the adjective "roughly." 10

Normandy . . . Dieppe: Normandy and Brittany are regions and former historic provinces of northwestern France from which the greatest number of French settlers to Quebec emigrated. When Cather uses the term "ruder" she may be indicating a contrast with the more temperate provinces of central and southern France. The northern regions endure a cold, windy, and damp climate, and buildings are accordingly built of stouter materials and are more weathered in appearance. For several centuries, Normandy and Brittany were scenes of warfare with the English, and their towns were surrounded by protective stone battlements. Saint-Malo, a fortified Breton city near the border of the two provinces, was the embarkation port for many colonists. Rouen is located in central Normandy, eighty-four miles northwest of Paris; Dieppe is on Normandy's north coast. 10

Laurentian mountains: The south-facing escarpments of the Canadian Shield when viewed from the St. Lawrence River give the appearance of low, rounded mountains but are in fact scarps marking the southern edge of a plateau encircling most of Hudson Bay 10

and stretching for more than one hundred miles north of Quebec
City.

10   Cap Tourmente: Cape Torment (or Stormy Cape) juts out into the
St. Lawrence some thirty miles northeast of Quebec City at a
height of nearly two thousand feet above the river on its northern
shore. Champlain gave it this name because the waters below are
frequently turbulent.

10   Île d'Orléans: This fertile island, twenty miles long and five miles
wide, situated downstream from Quebec in the St. Lawrence River,
is divided into six parishes dating from the late seventeenth to early
eighteenth centuries. Jacques Cartier originally called it the "Île de
Bacchus" because of the abundance of vines growing there, but the
island was soon renamed in honor of the Duc d'Orléans, son of
King Francis I. French settlers arrived there in 1651 and began
dairy and fruit and vegetable farming to supply fresh produce for
Quebec City.

11   the forest . . . a slow agony: This passage is clearly indebted to
Parkman's description of the northern forest: "dim and silent as a
cavern, columned with innumerable trunks, . . . nightmares of
strange distortion, gnarled and knotted . . . ; roots intertwined
beneath like serpents petrified in an agony of contorted strife" (1:
1322).

11–12   frail man . . . blue eyes: The details in this passage match Woodress's description of Charles Cather, Willa's father (19–20).

12   Quai des Célestins: A Parisian street fronting the Right Bank of the
Seine (see note for 198 on "the Seine") from rue des Nonnains
d'Hyères to Boulevard Henri IV and named for the convent of the
Célestins (Benedictine nuns) established there in 1352. The convent

was exceptionally large and surrounded by gardens that stretched north to what would become the Bastille and west to the rue du Petit-Musc; the royal family took pleasure in walking these gardens. In 1541 a church was added that was considered one of the finest buildings of Renaissance Paris.

Governor . . . Count de Frontenac: Louis de Buade, Comte de Pal-   12
luau et de Frontenac, was born in 1622 (according to Parkman) at Saint-Germain-en-Laye into a distinguished military family and was named godson to Louis XIII. He entered the army at fifteen and by twenty-four had risen in the ranks to brigadier general. Frontenac was a man of great personal charm and influence but at the same time egotistical and extravagant, accumulating huge personal debts and making numerous enemies. In 1669, after being dismissed by the Venetian forces in their war with the Turks on Crete, Frontenac retired to his family estate near Blois; however, in 1672, at the age of fifty, he was appointed governor general of New France, escaped his debts, and began the career for which he is known in history. Although Frontenac is credited with extending the French North American empire as far west as Winnipeg and south to the Gulf of Mexico, his motives were more financial than patriotic. He was actively involved in the fur trade, which both the French court and the Canadian clergy opposed — the court favoring a diverse economy, the clergy opposing the use of brandy in trading with the Indians. Because of his wrangling with the bishop and Jesuits and usurping the functions of the colony's civil authorities, Frontenac was recalled to France in 1682. But seven years later he was reappointed to organize an attack on New York, which materialized in a series of minor raids and guerrilla warfare with the Iroquois (see note for 22 on "Iroquois" and for 273 on "King had sent him").

Frontenac led his final campaign against the Iroquois in July 1696, when he was seventy-four. He died at Quebec in November 1698, after years of unsuccessful petitions to return to France. Cather's portrait of Frontenac leans heavily on Parkman's romantic account, which extols strength of leadership and minimizes the count's irascibility and self-aggrandizing qualities.

13   Mountain Hill: Côte de la Montagne (literally, side of the mountain) remains the only street directly connecting the Upper and Lower Town in Quebec City.

13   Champlain: Samuel de Champlain, born at Brouage, France, c. 1570, established a "Habitation" with stockades at Quebec on July 3, 1608, and is honored as the city's founder. As explorer, Champlain opened up the French route to the West, while as geographer and cartographer he contributed valuable maps of New France and what would become New England. Although Quebec initially served as a base for his Indian expeditions and searches for mines and a route to China, Champlain subsequently directed his efforts to developing the colony's population and diversifying its economy from dependence on the fur trade. Increasingly envisioning Quebec as a mission center, in 1615 he persuaded the Récollets to come to Canada, and they in turn encouraged the Jesuits to join them. At the height of his career Champlain became lieutenant and representative in Canada of Cardinal Richelieu, the king's chief minister. Although Champlain is considered the first great colonizer of New France and functioned as colonial governor, he never received a governor's commission. He died at Quebec on Christmas Day, 1635.

13   to plant the French lilies: Champlain records having "planted" in 1613 "a cross . . . with the arms of France" on the island of St. Croix

"as I had done in other places" (*Voyages* 242). The watercourse is described in Parkman: "from this strand, by a rough passage gullied downward from the place where Prescott Gate [Mountain Hill] now guards the way, one might climb the height to the broken plateau above" (1: 245). The flag of the King of France carried the design of the lily flower (fleur-de-lis), a symbol of the purity of the Virgin Mary (to whom France had been dedicated) often seen in representations of the Annunciation.

house . . . in the earliest Quebec manner: La Hontan remarks on   14
two-story wooden houses with vast fireplaces that consumed enormous quantities of wood "by reason of the prodigious fires they make to guard themselves from the cold, which is there beyond all measure, from the month of December to that of April" (38). Wilson explains that the first settlers from Normandy built wooden frame houses with stone in-filling (akin to half-timber) and then sheathed exterior walls in wood to protect vulnerable lime-mortar from freezing rain, thus giving the appearance of wooden dwellings (11–12). Wooden houses existed but were discouraged, especially in towns, due to the risk of fire. See note for 55 on "dormers."

sailor's jersey: A circular, upper-body garment knitted in plain stitch.   14

hair shingled . . . like a boy's: A short haircut popular in the 1920s.   14
Cécile's shingled hairstyle reflects Cather's at the same age and supports Edith Lewis's speculation that the Auclair father-daughter relationship is an idealization of Cather's with her recently deceased father. Woodress notes that Cather "before she was thirteen . . . had cut her hair shorter than most boys" (55). As if to remind us of this link, Cather has Pierre call attention to Cécile's hair in the novel's final book (see note for 304 on "*Petite tête*").

14 *"Pas de clients?"* . . . *"Mais, oui! Beaucoup de clients"*: "No customers?"
. . . "But, yes! Lots of customers."

15 daughter's eyes . . . very dark blue: The autobiographical dimension
Lewis detects in the Auclair father-daughter relationship (see note
for 7 on "Euclide") is supported by the color of Cécile's eyes. Both
Lewis and Elizabeth Sergeant, biographers who knew Cather, describe her eyes as similar in color to Cécile's. Lewis notes that "one
noticed particularly . . . her eyes. They were dark blue eyes" (xi);
Sergeant describes Cather's eyes as "sailor-blue" (33).

15 made the ménage: Making the ménage, or keeping house, develops
into a major theme climaxing at the end of book 4, where it is
equated with making life.

16 La Rochelle: The location of La Rochelle on the west coast of
France in the former province of Aunis made it a major port of
embarkation for emigrants bound for Quebec from other parts of
France, and its vitality as a commercial center gave it a key role in
trade between France and Canada. Because La Rochelle was also
the stronghold of Calvinism in France, settlers from there (Hugue-
nots, or Protestants), often in contention with Quebec officials and
missionaries, were unwelcome. Those from the northwestern
provinces of France were preferred.

16 Gulf: The Gulf of the St. Lawrence River.

16 Percé: The town of Percé is located 450 miles northeast of Quebec
City on the Gaspé shore of the Gulf of St. Lawrence. It is named for
a spectacular monolith offshore, Percé Rock, which has been
eroded (pierced) by the sea to form an archway large enough for
boats to pass through in full sail. Jacques Cartier arrived there in
1534, and European fishermen used the bay as a landmark and

haven in the sixteenth and seventeenth centuries. See note for 258 on "certain naked islands."

bien sérieuse: Very serious.   17

prepared for confirmation: Preparation would involve instruction   17
in church doctrine and in the responsibilities of belonging to the
Christian community. Originally part of the baptismal rite, confirmation became a separate sacrament in the Roman church and was
customarily restricted to those reaching "the age of discretion,"
usually seven years.

wild strawberries: See note for 218 on "wild strawberries."   18

gooseberries: *Ribes hirtellum* is the native variety. Before the small,   18
prickly fruits are fully ripened they have a fresh, sharp taste and are
very flavorful.

"*En France nous avons tous les légumes, jusqu'aux dattes*": "In France   18
we have all the different vegetables, even dates."

day-school at the Ursulines: About half of the estimated fifty to   18
sixty students at the Ursuline school were day students. In 1668
Marie de l'Incarnation claimed that "all the girls both of Upper and
of Lower Town" were "day pupils" (Gosselin 353). See note for 72
on "Ursuline school."

to post his ledger: To enter the day's transactions in a book contain-   19
ing debits and credits.

refuse . . . into the river: Parkman notes that early city regulations   20
required inhabitants "to remove refuse and throw it into the river"
(1: 1369).

20 "Merci, ma'm'selle, merci beaucoup": "Thank you, Miss, thank you very much."

21 "Bon soir, ma'm'selle": "Good evening, Miss."

22 crooked thoughts . . . crooked eyes: The medieval theory of physiognomy identified inward spiritual states as manifest in outward physical features. This has remained a folklore commonplace in the twentieth century.

22 unserviceable men . . . in the woods: Cather is here describing some of the men who became known as coureurs de bois, or runners of the woods. See note for 195 on "coureurs de bois."

22 fear of Indians . . . Iroquois: The Iroquois nation or confederacy, occupying territory now embraced by New York, consisted of (in geographical order from east to west) Mohawks, Oneidas, Onondagas, Cayugas, and Senecas. Iroquois hostility toward the French dated from Champlain's ill-advised 1609 promise to the Algonquins and Hurons to assist them in their feud with the Iroquois. In July of that year the French killed a band of Iroquois on the shores of what is now known as Lake Champlain, and hostilities followed for the rest of the seventeenth century. The Iroquois became notorious for their audacity and atrocities against the missionaries. Blinker would be particularly conscious of them because Frontenac had participated in a campaign against them a little more than a year prior to this time. See notes for 27 on "Count . . . last campaign" and for 175 on "Iroquois raid."

22 traffic in beaver skins: The fur trade was central to exploration and establishment of forts in New France. Especially prized was the fur of the beaver (see notes for 131 on "beaver" and for 295 on "English and Dutch traders"), whose coarse outer coat guards a dense,

soft underfur. In Europe, felt hats made from beaver underfur were symbols of prestige and very costly.

Cataraqui: Where the Cataraqui River enters Lake Ontario (the site of present-day Kingston, Ontario). See note for 67 on "Fort Frontenac." 22

goûter: snack. 22

the fables of La Fontaine: Jean de La Fontaine (1621–95) wrote numerous narrative poems based on Aesop's fables to illustrate moral truths. They rank among the masterpieces of French literature. 23

Plutarch: The Greek biographer and moralist (c. 46 to c. 120) is best known for his *Parallel Lives*, a series of paired biographies of Greek and Roman soldiers, legislators, and statesmen intended to provide model patterns of behavior and encourage mutual respect between Greeks and Romans. See note for 151 on "Plutarch . . . Alexander the Great." 23

Spanish snuff: A preparation of ground tobacco inhaled through a nostril or chewed. Snuff had been used since pre-Columbian times in the Spanish territories of Central and South America; its adoption in Europe was encouraged by its supposed medical benefits. 23

old shop . . . town house: Frontenac's father owned a house on the Quai des Célestins (see notes for 12 on "Quai des Célestins" and for 26 on "Quarter"), and while residing there the future governor met his wife, Anne de La Grange-Trianon, whose widower father lived in the same neighborhood. See note for 36 on "unfortunate marriage." 23

24   porte-cochère: A passageway through a building or wall allowing vehicles access to an interior courtyard.

24   swallows: See note for 191 on "swallow."

25   equerries: Officers in a noble house charged with the care of horses, or footmen in personal attendance on members of the noble household.

25   Fontainebleau: See note for 276–77 on "Fontainebleau."

26   Quarter: This would be the Village Saint-Paul in the Marais district on the Right Bank of Paris, which is partly fronted along the Seine by the Quai des Célestins, where the Auclairs lived. This area took its name from the Saint-Paul church. See note for 35 on "parish of Saint-Paul."

26   old Bishop Laval: See note for 82 on "old Bishop Laval."

26   feud . . . Frontenac and . . . Laval: Cather refers here to the disagreement over the use of brandy in fur trading with the Indians. Frontenac insisted that trading brandy was necessary to compete with the English, while Laval and the Jesuits argued that brandy debauched the Indians and defeated the efforts of the missionaries. Laval declared the trading of brandy to the Indians a mortal sin. See note for 294 on "worldly ends . . . brandy traffic."

26   Monseigneur de Saint-Vallier: See note for 137 on "Monseigneur de Saint-Vallier."

26   Count . . . quarrelling with [Saint-Vallier]: Frontenac's most celebrated quarrel with the new bishop concerned a proposed performance of *Tartuffe*, Molière's satire on religious hypocrisy, at the governor's château in 1694. Saint-Vallier paid to have the play can-

celed. There seems to have been no specific incident of contention after the bishop's return to Quebec in 1697, although Saint-Vallier took up Laval's campaign against liquor traffic with the Indians. The text perhaps refers to mutual dislike: Parkman writes: "Saint-Vallier . . . loved power as much as Frontenac himself, and thought that as the deputy of Christ it was his duty to exercise it to the utmost. The governor watched him with a jealous eye" (2: 233–34).

quarrel between the two Bishops: Saint-Vallier opposed Laval's sys-   26
tem of a movable rather than resident clergy. See notes for 9 on "Bishop Laval's Seminary" and for 140 on "Saint-Vallier . . . Laval's system."

diocese: An ecclesiastical district created by the pope and admin-   26
istered by a bishop. New France was elevated to diocesan status with its seat at Quebec in 1674, having previously been under the jurisdiction of the archbishop of Rouen.

Count . . . last campaign: In the summer of 1696, Frontenac, age   27
seventy-four, organized a campaign against the Onondagas, who were backed by the English and considered the most hostile and powerful of the Iroquois confederacy. But when the governor and his 2200 troops reached the targeted villages south of Lake Ontario, they found them in smoking ruins and the villagers gone. The troops destroyed the Onondagas' maize fields and food caches and then returned to Quebec. Frontenac sent a triumphant report of this expedition to the king, who in turn rewarded him with the Cross of the Military Order of St. Louis, but Frontenac felt this was not adequate, as several of his inferiors in the colony were already in receipt of this honor for lesser achievements.

27   new episcopal Palace: Scott explains that Saint-Vallier, refusing to
       reside at the seminary with his predecessor, purchased property in
       1688 to exchange for a "magnificent" site on rue Desjardins where
       he built a "vast episcopal palace . . . he was to occupy but seldom,
       and his successors still less, and which Providence destined to be
       the first parliament house of Quebec. He gave [it] . . . such large
       proportions because he intended to take the seminarists with him
       and to withdraw them from the guidance of the seminary priests"
       (318–19).

27   King . . . fifteen thousand francs: Before his return to Quebec in
       1688, the new bishop had successfully tapped the munificence of
       Louis XIV, securing funds for retired seminary priests and fifteen
       thousand francs for his own ambitious palace (De Brumath 211).

27   not fond of children, as the old Bishop was: Saint-Vallier, in fact,
       shared Laval's deep commitment to the needs of both the girls and
       boys of the colony, establishing schools and seeing to the adequate
       preparation of teachers (Gosselin 330–56).

28   redoubt: Defense works, fortifications. See note for 8 on "Cap Dia-
       mant."

28   Canadian-born Seminarians . . . Church Fathers: Parkman writes
       that Laval established the Quebec seminary "to provide priests for
       Canada, drawn from the Canadian population" (1: 1218), the "true
       school" of which was "the forest, lake, and river" (1380). Latin, the
       official language of the Roman church, would have been a difficulty
       for these young men, and the saintly writers of early Christianity a
       significant challenge. These writers, divided into Latin fathers (in-
       cluding Ambrose, Augustine, Benedict, Jerome, and Tertullian)
       and Greek fathers (including Basil the Great, Cyril of Jerusalem,

John Chrysostom, and Justin Martyr), are recognized as special witnesses of Christian faith; their texts are distinguished by "[a]ntiquity, orthodoxy, sanctity, and approval" (Hardon 208). See note for 9 on "Bishop Laval's Seminary."

Auclair had come over . . . eight years ago: See note for 41 on "again appointed him Governor General." 29

specifics . . . carboys: Auclair's catalog includes remedies for specific diseases or ailments; bowl-like vessels (mortars), in which substances are pounded or ground with a pestle; long-tubed containers (retorts), in which substances are distilled by heat; and glass bottles enclosed in wicker or wood (carboys) to hold corrosive liquids. 29

stuffed baby alligator . . . West Indies: See note for 319 on "West India trade." 30

carpet, made at Lyon . . . china shepherd boy: These domestic objects judiciously reflect the efforts of Louis XIV and his finance minister, Jean Baptiste Colbert, to develop French industrial arts (textiles, ceramics, furniture) and make French products touchstones for the rest of Europe. The floor carpet would have been made in the Paris region or at Aubusson (central France), however, since Lyon had been developed as a silk-weaving center. Walnut was a common wood for Louis XIV furniture, and red velveteen reflects popular French imitations of colorful fabrics from India, *indiennes*. The china figurine, probably a French soft-paste porcelain (an Asian import is unlikely in this context), would be of eighteenth-century manufacture — a decorative container or dish would better represent the novel's historical period. 30

(she died of her lungs): Mme Auclair died of tuberculosis. 30

413

32 poor savages: Cather evokes here the etymology of the English word in the French word *sauvage*, meaning simply wild, uncultivated, as opposed to ferocious and cruel.

32 most civilized people in Europe: Besides expressing traditional French notions of cultural superiority, Mme Auclair is reflecting Cather's lifelong glorification of French art, architecture, domestic arrangements, cookery, and language. Woodress quotes from Cather's 1902 paean on her arrival in France to suggest these prejudices: "Above the roar of the wind and thrash of the water I heard a babble of voices, in which I could only distinguish the word 'France' uttered over and over again with a fire and fervour that was in itself a panegyric" (160).

32 Canadian blueberries: Such blueberries are dark blue (see note for 15 on "daughter's eyes"). Found in rocky or sandy soil from Newfoundland to Saskatchewan, *Vaccinium angustifolium* produces small berries highly prized for pies and preserves. In 1639 Jesuit Paul Le Jeune wrote: "Some of [the Native people] imagine a Paradise abounding in blueberries; these are little blue fruits, the berries of which are as large as the largest grapes. I have not seen any of them in France" (Kenton 62 n. 1). Other early travelers report the Native people making a feast of dog's flesh boiled with blueberries.

32 "*Oui, elle a beaucoup de loyauté*": "Yes, she has a lot of loyalty."

33 Laval . . . varicose legs: De Brumath notes that Laval's infirmities "especially affected his limbs, which he was obliged to bandage tightly every morning, and which could scarcely bear the weight of his body" (249). Scott adds that every morning during the last five years of his life, Laval "bandaged without help his legs swollen with varicose veins" (315).

calomel pills: A medicinal compound used as a purgative.   33

denied himself: De Brumath states cryptically of Laval: "Few saints   33
carried mortification and renunciation of terrestrial goods as far as
he" (253). Scott details Laval's austerities (314–16) as proofs of
saintliness; however, Parkman sees "playing at beggar, sleeping in
beds full of fleas, or performing prodigies of gratuitous dirtiness in
hospitals" as of little avail against the bishop's imperious and un-
yielding nature (1: 1180).

four-post bed . . . child's bed: What is described is the high bed and   34
truckle bed (also called trundle or wheelbed) combination popular
in the seventeenth century. The truckle was stored under the high
bed during the day and wheeled out at night on its wooden castors
to sleep personal servants or children.

"*Qu'est-ce que tu fais, petite?*" . . . "*Papa, j'ai peur pour le persil*":   34
"What are you doing, little one?" . . . "Papa, I'm afraid for the
parsley."

Jesuits on the rue Saint-Antoine: See note below on "parish of   34–35
Saint-Paul."

Île Savary . . . near Blois: Frontenac's estate, Château Île Savary,   35
located near Clion about fifty miles south of Blois in the château
country of the Loire, was built in the fifteenth century and reputed
to be beautiful and well furnished. Mlle de Montpensier, Mme
Frontenac's intimate friend, gives this account: "It is a pretty enough
place for a man like him. The house is well furnished, and he gave me
excellent entertainment. He showed me all the plans he had for
improving it, and making gardens, fountains, and ponds. It would
need the riches of a superintendent of finance to execute his schemes,
and how anybody else should venture to think of them I cannot

comprehend" (Parkman 2: 18). Improving the château is thought to have been the chief reason for Frontenac's financial ruin.

35   parish of Saint-Paul: The Gothic church of Saint-Paul (or Saint-Paul-des-Champs) served a parish in the Marais district of Paris from 1107 until the late eighteenth century. During the thirteenth and fourteenth centuries most of the royal infants were baptized in this church. After the building fell into disrepair and was demolished, parishioners went to worship at the nearby seventeenth-century Romanesque church of Saint-Louis (King Louis IX) on rue Saint-Antoine, which then became the parish church of Saint-Paul-Saint-Louis. Saint-Louis had been part of a Jesuit complex that included a school.

35   few friends . . . got on . . . with inferiors: Cather would have read in Parkman of the violent prejudices, irritability, jealous vanity, and passion for having his own way that made it difficult for Frontenac to tolerate an equal; however, in recounting Frontenac's death, Parkman admits, "He was greatly beloved by the humbler classes" (2: 308).

35   Italy and the Low Countries: Frontenac was sent to Holland in 1635, at fifteen, to serve under the Prince of Orange in the Thirty Years' War. Later, in 1646, while commanding the Normandy regiment at the siege of Orbetello, Italy, Frontenac was wounded and permanently crippled in the right arm. "Low Countries" was the collective political, historical, and geographical term for Belgium, Holland, and Luxembourg.

36   unfortunate marriage . . . Madame de la Grange-Frontenac: The wife of Count Frontenac, Anne de la Grange-Trianon, daughter of La Grange-Trianon, Sieur de Neuville, was born in 1632. She and her father lived near the Quai des Célestins, and while visiting his

own father there, Frontenac fell in love with her. Although she was only sixteen, Anne was considered one of the most beautiful women in Paris. They were married in 1648, but according to Parkman their happiness was short lived, whether because of rumors connecting Frontenac with Mme de Montespan (see note for 274 on "Madame de Montespan") or the incompatibility of their headstrong and imperious temperaments (2: 16, 20). Anne was not of a tender nature, Parkman adds, and she abandoned the care of their only son to a professional nurse near Île Savary, preferring instead pleasures of the court and high society. (See note for 284 on "son . . . killed.") Parkman claims that she and Frontenac lived apart permanently, but recent scholarship has found no evidence for this story beyond the notoriously unreliable memoirs of Mlle de Montpensier. Eccles points out that the Frontenacs remained married, exchanged letters regularly, and that Mme Frontenac was of great value in advancing her husband's cause at court (28–30). Nonetheless, it was reported in Canada after Frontenac's death that she refused to accept his heart when it was sent to France, saying that she had not possessed it while he lived and did not want it when he was dead (Parkman 2: 309). Cather followed Parkman's pessimistic view of the Frontenac marriage. Mme Frontenac died in 1707 and was buried at Saint-Paul's in the Marais district of Paris.

Arsenal building: L'Arsenal, built in the sixteenth century on land 36 appropriated from the Célestins by King Louis XII, was the chief repository for military arms in Paris; there also was a foundry at the Arsenal where royal cannon were forged. At the beginning of the seventeenth century, additions were made for living quarters, public receptions, even for ballet and comedy performances. By 1664, because of the adjacent convent gardens and good air, the Arsenal

had become a *lieu d'asile*, a retreat where the arts and society flourished. Mme de Sévigné, who chronicled the era in her letters, came
to visit friends here, as did King Louis XIV himself. Saint-Simon
writes that Frontenac's wife lived most of her life in an Arsenal
apartment with her friend Mlle d'Outrelaize and that for their
beauty, refinement, and superior attitudes the pair became known
as *les Divines* (1: 609).

36   Venetians . . . Turks: In 1669 Count Frontenac accepted an appointment to command Venetian troops in an unsuccessful defense
of Crete against Ottoman Turks making one of their last attempts
to push westward. Eccles contradicts Cather's and Parkman's estimate of this campaign as enhancing Frontenac's reputation, indicating instead that the count was dismissed by the Venetians for
quarreling with other senior officers (Parkman 2: 19; Eccles 25–
27).

36   appointed . . . Governor General of Canada: Frontenac was appointed governor general in 1672 and served until 1682, then reappointed in 1689, serving until his death in 1698. In the colonial
period, Canadian governors general represented imperial govern-
ments and were responsible to colonial ministers, first in France
and then in England.

37   reign of Louis XIV . . . low period in medicine: Saint-Simon, whose
Mémoires is one of Cather's principal sources, insists that Louis XIV
surrounded himself with second-rate doctors who were more concerned with their position at court than with the health of their
patients. See note for 8 on "King Louis."

37   time of Ambroise Paré . . . golden ages in medicine: Paré (1510–
90), one of the most notable surgeons of the northern Renaissance

and regarded by most medical historians as the father of modern surgery, devised new treatments for gunshot wounds, advocated the tying of arteries during amputations, and encouraged the use of artificial limbs and eyes. But three centuries earlier in Italy an important revival of medical knowledge from ancient and Arabian sources led to new procedures in dissection and surgery and to Mondino de' Luzzi's description of the human body, published in 1316, the first practical manual of anatomy.

Fagon: Gui Crescent Fagon (1638–1718) was a distinguished bota- 37
nist and physician who in 1680 became a doctor in King Louis XIV's court. Cather probably adopted a negative view of Fagon from reading Saint-Simon, who seldom misses the opportunity to ridicule Fagon as a biased and incompetent fool.

tisanes . . . poultices: Tisanes are infusions, generally of herbs, used 37
as beverages for medicinal purposes; poultices are heated medicated substances spread on cloth for application to swellings or lesions.

blood-letting . . . from the feet: Glasscheib explains that bloodlet- 37
ting, rooted in an ancient theory of body juices, was practiced as a way of ridding the body of poisonous fluids (154–62). There were competing theories in the seventeenth century about whether blood should be drained from the ailing region or from the furthest distance possible. Usually a vein in the inner elbow was opened, but bleeding from the feet was done to relieve pains or congestion in the upper body. A small cut was made with a surgeon's knife, and the patient's blood gathered in a cup or bowl. Bloodletting was the height of fashion at the French court, along with purges and enemas, and doctors assured their patients that they acquired a fresher, healthier complexion from these practices. Within a six-

month period, Louis XIII was subjected to 47 bleedings, 215 purgings, and 312 enemas.

37   barber-surgeons: In the Middle Ages and early Renaissance, surgery was not practiced by physicians; rather, barbers wielded the knife, hence the term "barber-surgeons." It was not until the late eighteenth century that surgery was finally established in the medical curriculum. Ambroise Paré (see note above) was a barber-surgeon.

38   Versailles: Established as a country residence by Louis XIII on the southwestern outskirts of Paris near a medieval castle and village, Versailles was developed by Louis XIV (convinced by civil disturbances during his childhood that Paris was a dangerous place for him to live — see note for 8 on "King Louis") and served as the government headquarters and political center of France from 1682 to 1789. During a massive operation involving landscape gardeners, architects, sculptors, carvers, painters, and interior decorators, forests were transplanted, lakes created, and a vast palace constructed. In 1684, two years after the king moved to Versailles from the Louvre in Paris, twenty-two thousand workers were employed at the various sites of the new estate, which lodged three thousand courtiers and attendants. See note for 317 on "Salle d'Apollon."

38   Count's difficulties . . . recall by the King: In his quarrels with Laval and the clergy, Frontenac received no support from Jacques Duchesneau, the intendant (civil authority) of New France from 1675 to 1682. When Duchesneau backed Laval in his fight against the sale of alcohol to the Native peoples, Frontenac accused him of being a pawn of the church (see note for 26 on "feud . . . Frontenac and . . . Laval"). Duchesneau denounced the illegal trafficking of many of the coureurs de bois and accused Frontenac of permitting this practice for personal gain. In 1682 Louis XIV recalled the two antagonists to France. Frontenac did not return until 1689.

the Innocents: The cemetery of the Holy Innocents, named for an   39
adjacent church on the Right Bank, was the most important burial
place in Paris until 1785. It included several ossuaries, and when it
was closed the bones were taken to the Catacombs. The area subsequently became a marketplace (Les Halles), and a fountain now
marks the location of the cemetery. See note for 148 on "Henry of
Navarre."

the churchyard of Saint-Paul: See note for 35 on "parish of Saint-   39
Paul."

Robert Cavelier de La Salle: See note for 98 on "Robert Cavelier de   39
La Salle."

poverty and hunger . . . fantastic extravagance: Contemporary re-   40
ports by Archbishop Fénelon, Mme de Sévigné, and Jean de La
Bruyère complain of poverty, crime, and uprisings among the lower
classes due to the heavy taxes necessary to sustain the extravagance
at Versailles. Maurois quotes from a prayer to Louis XIV that made
the rounds: "Our Father who art in Versailles, thy name is no
longer hallowed; thy kingdom is diminished; thy will is no longer
done on earth or on the waves. Give us our bread, which is lacking
to us." In 1690, continues Maurois, "the destitution of the realm
was so great that in order to replenish the treasury the King himself
had to have his silver furnishings, his gold plate and even his throne
melted into bullion" (226).

mill at the Châtelet: Originally a fort on the Right Bank of the   40
Seine guarding the northern approach to the Île de la Cité, the
Grand Châtelet became a court of law in the twelfth century and
eventually the seat of justice for all of France. In the seventeenth
century, Louis XIV established it as headquarters for a security

officer responsible for public order in Paris, and the building was remodeled to accommodate prisoners awaiting trial for common law violations (state prisoners were held in the Bastille) and for those condemned to die. The jurisdiction of the Châtelet was abolished at the time of the Revolution. Cather's reference to the grinding of the mill at the Châtelet seems an ironic echo of Henry Wadsworth Longfellow's translation of Friedrich von Logau's aphorism on justice: "Though the mills of God grind slowly, yet they grind exceeding small."

41   again appointed him Governor General: This would have been in 1689; see note for 36 on "appointed . . . Governor General."

42   Hôtel Dieu: A Quebec hospital taking its name, like all hospitals administered by the Hospitallers, from the Augustinian rule that when serving the sick, one serves Jesus Christ, hence the house in which this service is rendered becomes the House of God (Hôtel Dieu). The Quebec Hospitallers began operating this institution at 32 rue Charlevoix in a wooden structure in the Upper Town in 1644. Among the first nursing sisters was Mother Marie-Françoise Giffard (Marie de Saint-Ignace), the aunt and religious namesake of Mother Juchereau de Saint-Ignace (see note for 45 on "Jeanne Franc Juchereau de la Ferté"). The building was enlarged in 1695, and the hospital has since undergone significant expansion. The original structures are now part of the convent.

42   Reverend Mother: The form of address for the superior of a religious community of women.

42   Jesuits' college: The College of Quebec, financed by a generous grant from the Marquis of Gamache, whose son was a Jesuit, commenced operation in 1635 to instruct French and Indian boys.

Latin, French, and Indian language lessons were in place by 1637, and catalogs for 1655 indicate professors of grammar, humanities, rhetoric, and philosophy; a theology course was added in the 1660s. When Bishop Laval opened the Little Seminary in 1668, he arranged that seminarians take classes at the college. The student population by the end of the seventeenth century (the time of Cather's novel) numbered from 130 to 140, including day students and boarders. By this time the college was housed in the 1666 complex (an earlier building had burned to the ground in 1640) viewed by Auclair at the opening of the novel (see note for 9 on "foundation of the Jesuits"). The college closed after the fall of Quebec to the English in 1759 and became a barracks for the British garrison. The College of Quebec was a small-scale reproduction of Jesuit colleges in France, and Gosselin compares its curriculum favorably with that of La Flèche (see note for 266 on "La Flèche"), concluding that the celebrated pedagogy of La Flèche "was adopted almost in its entirety by the Jesuits of Canada" (367).

the Fathers: The Jesuit priests. See note for 9 on "foundation of the Jesuits."   42

the monastery: The residence of the Jesuit priests, and part of the complex that included their chapel and college.   42

river St. Charles: The St. Charles is a small, shallow river that can be forded near its mouth at low tide. It divides the old city on the rock from the Beauport flats to the east. Parkman contends that this is the river Cartier named the St. Croix in 1535 (1: 157).   43

Mother Juchereau de Saint-Ignace: See note for 45 on "Jeanne Franc Juchereau de la Ferté."   43

43   novices: Those formally admitted to religious communities to prepare for eventual profession of vows. At least one year of novitiate is
required to enable superiors to evaluate the suitability of candi-
dates. Novices receive religious garb (habits), which in women's
communities includes a white veil. The girls Mother Juchereau is
directing would be at least fifteen years of age.

44   Indians . . . deer thongs: Although archivists at Quebec's Musée de
la Civilisation could find no record of this treatment for sprains,
they were advised of its probability by Denys Delâge of Laval University.

44   artificial flowers: "The nuns of the Hotel-Dieu made artificial flowers for altars and shrines, under the direction of Mother Juchereau," notes Parkman (1: 1311–12). Gosselin explains that convent
boarding school instruction for girls during the French regime included "various arts and accomplishments such as embroidering on
silk, gold [leaf] or bark, and occasionally drawing and painting"
(360). Making paper and silk flowers would be one of these "arts."

44   Beauport: The area directly east of Quebec City, which today is
part of metropolitan Quebec.

45   Sister Marie Domenica: A series of sisters served as hospital pharmacists; however, this one is not mentioned in Mother Juchereau's
history of the Hôtel Dieu and is presumably a fictional character.

45   Jeanne Franc Juchereau de la Ferté: Jeanne-Françoise Juchereau de
la Ferté (1650–1723) — Cather abbreviated the middle name to that
of her own Aunt Franc (Frances A. Smith Cather) — received her
calling early, boarding with the Augustinian Hospitallers of Quebec
at the Hôtel Dieu before of age to take the veil as novice. She was
named to positions of responsibility in her religious community

from age twenty, becoming its first Canadian-born superior at thirty-three. Her labors during the 1688 epidemics in Quebec drew praise from the governor, and she developed a reputation for kindness and charity. However, as a protective and orthodox leader, she had a chaplain removed for his Jansenist sympathies and resisted Saint-Vallier's efforts to have her community staff the Hôpital Général at the former complex of the Récollets at Notre-Dame-des-Anges (see notes for 128 on "*cabine*" and for 314 on "Hôpital Général"). In 1716 she began dictating her *History of the Hôtel-Dieu of Quebec*, a valuable source of historical details.

scolded him for teaching . . . Latin: As the language of the Catholic priesthood, Latin usually would be reserved for males. In detailing the basic curriculum (reading, writing, and arithmetic) for elementary schools Gosselin adds, "To these were sometimes added the elements of grammar, and, to boys, the elements of Latin" (360).   45

Mother Catherine de Saint-Augustin: See note for 50 on "Catherine de Saint-Augustin."   46

at Bayeux . . . a *pécheresse* named Marie: Bayeux, the Normandy town most famous for its eleventh-century tapestry depicting William the Conqueror and the Battle of Hastings, is the location of the convent of the Augustinian Hospitallers that Catherine de Saint-Augustin entered as a novice in 1644. The story of Marie the *pécheresse* (sinner) was included in Paul Ragueneau's biography of Catherine (1671) and subsequently in St. Alphonsus de Liguori's popular defense of Marian devotions, *Les Gloires de Marie* (1750), as an example of Mary's intercession. March locates in the Ligouri text the sinner's thanks to Catherine that Cather essentially repeats: "I thank thee, Catherine; behold, I go to Paradise, to sing the mercies of my God, and to pray for thee" (March 465). See note for 50 on "Catherine de Saint-Augustin."   46

425

47   pray for the souls . . . from purgatory: See note for 111 on "All Souls' Day."

48   saved, thanks to . . . *Queen of Heaven*: Although the sinner's appeal to the Virgin Mary is part of Ragueneau's account (March 465), Cather's rendering of it doubtlessly owes to numerous similar episodes in Dante's *Divine Comedy*. Mary's role as maternal intercessor applying Christ's redemptive grace to human beings is a traditional Catholic belief (Hardon 344–45).

48   masses . . . required: The mass, the Eucharistic offering and central act of worship of the Catholic Church, can be (and usually is) celebrated for a particular intention, for some person living or dead. In the case of the latter, it would be to shorten the waiting period of the soul of the deceased to enter heaven. See note for 111 on "All Souls' Day."

49   *"N'expliquez pas, chère Mère, je vous en supplie!"*: "Don't explain, dear Mother, I beg you."

49   vocation: In this context the term refers to a call from God to achieve holiness through a distinctive state of life, usually the priesthood or the religious life of a nun or lay brother.

49   Hospitalières: Augustinian nursing sisters, or Hospitallers (hospital nuns), maintain many hospitals in Europe; they trace their origin to St. Augustine (354–430), although their first house was founded in Venice in 1177. Responding to a call from the Jesuits, the Hospitallers of Dieppe sent three nuns to Canada in 1639 to found the Hôtel Dieu at Quebec. See note for 42 on "Hôtel Dieu."

49–50   Cécile read . . . for the priesthood: Mother Juchereau believes that Cécile's home schooling is too intellectual for a girl. "In communities of women," writes Gosselin, "children were taught different kinds of work suited to their sex. . . . Strictly speaking, the instruction given to girls under the French regime was neither extensive, nor profound, nor varied; on the other hand, . . . the early religious communities succeeded in disseminating among the people . . . affability . . . [and] gentle and polished manners" (360).

Catherine de Saint-Augustin: Marie-Catherine de Simon de Long-pré, a descendant of Thomas à Becket, was born into an aristocratic Norman family at Saint Sauveur-le-Vicomte (near Cherbourg) in 1632. She was reared by devout maternal grandparents who had dedicated their lives to charity. Marie-Catherine, though a sickly child, was similarly determined to devote her life to God and relieving the suffering of others. In 1644, at age twelve, she entered the convent of Bayeux, where she became a novice in 1646 and took the name of Catherine de Saint-Augustin. Her father was deeply reluctant but finally gave consent for her to go to Quebec, where she served with the Hospitallers at the Hôtel Dieu from 1648 until her death twenty years later. Cather almost certainly would have read the account of her life written in 1671 by her confessor and the superior of the Canadian missions, Paul Rageuneau. Brienzo identifies differences between Cather's story and the seventeenth-century biography, focusing chiefly on Cather's making the much-admired nun a "powerful symbol of a life lived unstintingly for and with others" (46) and muting the biographer's extended account of Catherine's physical infirmities, nervous instability, tormented visions (see note for 52 on "spirit of Father Brébeuf"), and temptations to sin. He concludes that Cather "selected details to create the most realistically positive images possible of Mother Catherine" (49) in keeping with the child-centered focus of her novel.

50

50 *Relations* of the Jesuit missionaries: Detailed reports of the activities of Jesuit missionaries in New France addressed to their superior were published annually in Paris from 1632 to 1673 as *Relations de ce qui s'est passé en la Nouvelle France*. Reuben Gold Thwaites credits the photographic realism of the series with an "accurate picture of the . . . aborigine" and as illuminating the French regime in America "as [f]ew periods of history are . . . illuminated" (Kenton l–li). He also speculates that Frontenac had the series discontinued because of his disdain for the Jesuits.

51 *Je mourrai au Canada* . . . That table: "I will die in Canada / Sister Saint Augustin." The table where Catherine signed papers committing herself to the Canadian mission is kept in the Musée Catherine de Saint-Augustin in Bayeux, but the story of her cutting her finger while peeling vegetables and writing her vow in blood on the table is not part of the account of Catherine's novitiate there. According to the *Jesuit Relations*, Catherine would have signed her vow in blood if the mistress of novices had not stopped her as she was pricking her finger (March 135).

51 Père Vimont . . . at Bayeux: Father Barthélemy Vimont, a Jesuit who had first come out to Canada in the 1620s and again in 1639 (on the ship with the first Ursulines and Hospital nuns) to assume duties as superior-general of the missions of New France, visited the Bayeux convent in 1648 to encourage volunteers for Canada. Catherine committed herself at this time and traveled to Nantes, where she made her solemn vows "in the hands of Father Vimond [*sic*]" (Charlevoix 3: 114). Vimont said the first mass at Montreal in 1642, participated in peace negotiations with the Iroquois at Three Rivers in 1645, and for a time administered the College of Quebec (Jesuits' college). He prepared six volumes of the *Relations* for publication and returned to France in 1659.

428

Queen Mother, Anne of Austria: Married to King Louis XIII at age   51
fourteen, Anne was queen consort from 1615 to 1643 and with her
first minister, Cardinal Jules Mazarin, a powerful regent during the
opening years of the reign of her son Louis XIV. She was naturally
inclined to religious interests and was a benefactor of the Hospitallers at Bayeux, which is why Catherine de Saint-Augustin's petition was brought to her attention. She was also instrumental in
appointing Laval to his post in New France. Historians have speculated that she might have been secretly married to Mazarin, a lay
cardinal (prior to 1918 cardinals need not have been priests), although she was known for her high moral standards, which was
why her son refrained from publicly acknowledging his adulterous
relationships during her lifetime. She died in 1666.

kissed the earth: This ritualistic gesture of thanksgiving upon ar-   51
rival at the destination of one's mission also honors the place. As
Parkman writes of the arrival at Quebec of the Ursulines and Hospitallers, "All the nuns fell prostrate, and kissed the sacred soil of
Canada" (1: 527). The ritual has added significance in Cather's text
as it anticipates Cécile's desire to perform the same gesture when
she arrives at Quebec from the Isle of Orleans near the end of the
novel's book 4.

spirit of Father Brébeuf: According to Ragueneau, Catherine had   52
visions of the martyr Father Brébeuf (see note for 120 on "martyrdoms") helping her ward off surprise attacks from the demons that
hounded her, but in Cather's story his spirit simply appears to tell
her of the glories of heaven and to help her select Jeanne Franc
Juchereau de la Ferté as her successor. In fact, Mother Juchereau
was not chosen superior until fifteen years after Catherine's death,
and Catherine never served as superior.

Book 2

55   Notre Dame de la Victoire: See note for 59 on "Notre Dame de la Victoire."

55   market square: Cather would have read the following in Parkman: "On Tuesdays and Fridays there was a market in the public square [in the Lower Town], whither the neighboring *habitants*, male and female, brought their produce for sale. . . . Smoking in the street was forbidden, as a precaution against fire" (1: 1369).

55   Lower Town . . . fire: The Lower Town burned to the ground in 1682 and was subsequently rebuilt; however, as Parkman notes, even then, while masonry gables were required, many houses had wooden fronts and all had roofs covered with cedar shingles (1: 1369).

55   dormers: The style of architecture in Quebec emphasized dormers, windows for upper-story bedrooms set in gables. See note for 14 on "house."

56   very ugly statue of King Louis: According to March (443–44), when Jean Bochart de Champigny arrived in Quebec in July 1686 to be intendant of the colony (see note for 67 on "Intendant"), he brought a bronze bust of Louis XIV cast from Bernini's marble original in Versailles, installed it in the Lower Town market square, and gave the square the name Place Royale. However, the statue was removed because it impeded traffic and was then lost. In 1931 another casting of the original, presented by the French government, took its place.

56   maple sugar: The sap of the sugar maple (*Acer saccharum*) was known and valued as a sweetener by the Native peoples of eastern North

America long before the arrival of Europeans. Although Douville and Casanova claim that maple sugar did not come into fashion until the English administration (58), French settlers learned from the Indians how to tap trees to obtain sap, reduce the sap by boiling it to a sweet syrup, and crystallize it into loaves of sugar. Extensive maple forests provide Quebec with two festive times of the year: "sugaring off" in the early spring and *"le rougissement"* in the fall, when the trees assume their brilliant autumn colors.

spruce beer: Known as *sapinette* in Quebec, spruce beer is made by   56
boiling the young branches and cones of the native spruce (*Picea*), then adding hops, yeast, and molasses or maple sugar to the liquid when it is put into casks to ferment. Spruce beer was renowned as a cure for scurvy.

Indian meal: Ground corn (maize) was an Indian staple. Father Le   56
Jeune explains in the Relation of 1634 that Hurons traveling with him hid cornmeal along the route for their return trip and that at daybreak a bowlful mixed with water enabled them to "ply their paddles all day, and at night they [ate] as they did at break of day" (Kenton 86).

native tobacco: Tobacco grown in Canada, as by the Tobacco na-   56
tion (see note for 175 on "mission of Saint Jean") in southeastern Ontario; most likely *Nicotiana rustica* (the species raised in Virginia), a mild-flavored, fast-burning tobacco cultivated for ceremonial purposes by the Indians of eastern North America. Tobacco was grown by the colonists with promising results but was banned by French authorities to prevent competition with tobacco (*N. tabacum*) from the French West Indies.

431

56   "beaver dams": The beaver dams the flow of water in rivers and lakes in order to build its lodgings. (See notes for 131 on "beaver" and for 197 on "big beaver towns.") Parkman notes that Quebec law required inhabitants to construct gutters along the middle of the streets in front of their houses (1: 1369).

56   black frosts: Black frost refers to autumn temperatures cold enough to freeze and subsequently darken the vegetation.

57   carrots . . . even salads: Agriculture flourished from the beginning of the colony. Champlain speaks of fine wheat cut in Quebec in 1616; Father Le Jeune writes in 1636 of good crops of barley, rye, oats, and all kinds of vegetables; in 1663 Pierre Boucher specifies peas, beans, sunflowers, turnips, beets, carrots, parsnips, and all types of cabbage but cauliflower (Chapais 512–13).

57   great vaulted cellars . . . cold-frames: neither the Jesuits nor the Récollets would have had such gardens, for the monastery architecture did not allow for sufficient light. However, the Château St. Louis had such greenhouses as Cather describes. Cold-frames are unheated glass-covered enclosures for starting seedlings and protecting plants against frost.

57   wood doves . . . in melted lard: Cather likely means the passenger pigeon (*Ectopistes migratorius*), a large wild pigeon once native to forested zones like Quebec. La Hontan writes that they were so abundant that the trees had more pigeons than leaves and a thousand men in a field could feed on them for three weeks without exertion (109–10). In *The Pioneers*, James Fenimore Cooper laments the destruction of these birds, which were hunted to extinction by 1914.

Renaude-le-lièvre: Mme Renaude's name is linked with the hare (*le*   58
lièvre) because she suffers the deformity of a cleft, or split upper lip,
and probably a related speech defect — "She spoke very loud."

firkins: Small wooden tubs, usually equivalent to a quarter barrel, or   58
about eight U.S. gallons.

Three-Rivers: Trois-Rivières is an industrial city located midway   59
between Quebec and Montreal, where the St. Maurice River joins
the St. Lawrence on the north shore. Its name derives not from the
confluence of three rivers but from the three-armed delta formed
by islands at the river's mouth. Champlain established a fur-trading
post there in 1634, thus the community is the second oldest in New
France after Quebec City.

Here grease is meat: Dependence on grease was learned from the   59
Natives, who, according to Father Le Jeune, skimmed it from
cooking meat to use as a drink or ate it hardened "as we would bite
into an apple"; Father Marquette recalls being offered bear grease
with white plums as a delicacy (Kenton 63, 160). Antoine Frichette
and Father Hector consume cold grease in the novel's book 3.

Notre Dame de la Victoire: This church was built in 1688 on the   59
site of Champlain's "Habitation" (see note for 13 on "Champlain")
in the Lower Town on land granted by Louis XIV after Bishop
Laval wrote to explain that in harsh winter weather old people,
children, and the infirm could not make the climb to the Upper
Town to attend mass. It was first dedicated to the Infant Jesus, but
two years later, after the defeat of the English under Sir William
Phips (see note below on "bombardment"), the name was changed
to Notre Dame de la Victoire (Our Lady of the Victory). When a
second English fleet was defeated in 1711 (considered a miracle

433

occasioned by the recluse Jeanne Le Ber—see note for 152 on
"Jeanne Le Ber"), the name became Notre Dame des Victoires.
The church burned during the siege of 1759 but was rebuilt on the
same walls and foundation in 1765.

59   bombardment: When England declared war on France in 1689,
war broke out between English and French colonies as well. Frontenac made a raid to the south and destroyed three New England
villages, after which the governor of Massachusetts, Sir William
Phips, organized a party of thirty-two warships with more than two
thousand men that attacked Quebec City in October 1690. But the
shore batteries successfully defended Quebec, and after five days
Phips and his troops retreated, leaving the city scarcely damaged.

60   Stations of the Cross: A series of fourteen representations of Christ's
suffering and death, beginning with the condemnation of Christ and
ending with the entombment. Stations are usually affixed to the
interior walls of a church and used for group or individual meditation at each stop. Indulgences (remission of punishment for sin) are
gained from making the Way of the Cross (*Via crucis*). See note for
64 on "felt a need of expiation."

60   figure of a salt-shaker: Cather has a cone-shaped container in mind
and is perhaps suggesting this child's role as "the salt of the earth"
(Matthew 5:13) and an inspiration of charity in others: "Salt is
good. . . . Have salt in yourselves" (Mark 9:50).

60–61   King's Girls" . . . regiment of Carignan-Salières: "King's Girls" was
the name given to the 150 women who sailed from France in 1668
as wives for the French regulars sent to Quebec three years earlier
to drive back the Iroquois and protect the colony from Indian attacks. When the soldiers were concluding their tour, Intendant

Jean Talon arranged with the king to offer land and money to induce them to stay, enhancing his offer with these women. Talon requested women from strong, healthy peasant families, but those who came were more often girls from charitable institutions and poor urban families overburdened with children. In spite of these inducements, however, only sixty of about a thousand soldiers decided to stay.

La Gironde: A 600-ton French storeship with forty-two cannons 61
built at Rochfort in 1695 and launched into service in 1696. Although the ship was sailing to Quebec during the time of the novel (Mother Juchereau de Saint-Ignace tells of Saint-Vallier's 1697 arrival on *La Gironde*), it would not yet have been built when Jacques's father is said to have come to Quebec. The storeship was sunk in 1702 to avoid capture by the English.

sailors' lodging-house: See note for 74 on "behind the King's ware- 61
houses."

unfortunate child, Jacques: A fictional character perhaps suggested 62
by the waif-child befriended by Laval (see note for 86 on "Bishop Laval . . . saw a little boy") but drawing on Cather's nephew Charles Cather (Madigan 49; Bennett 38–39) and her youngest brother, John (Jack) Cather, who inspired the early story "Jack-a-Boy."

felt a need of expiation: Auclair surmises that Jacques is attempting 64
to compensate for his mother's sins by performing this devotion (see note for 60 on "Stations of the Cross") to gain indulgences that will mitigate her punishment in purgatory.

Count . . . kind to children: Cather would have read in Parkman's 65
biography of Frontenac's "adoption" of eight Indian children, four girls and four boys: "He took two of the boys into his own house-

435

hold . . . and he supported the other two, who were younger, out of his own slender resources, placed them in respectable French families, and required them to go daily to school. The girls were given to the charge of the Ursulines" (2: 28).

66   Picard: March associates Picard with a man by the name of Du-Chouquet (581), whom he designates as Frontenac's valet, but no one with that name is mentioned by any of Frontenac's biographers.

66   Haute-Savoie: The northern part of the former independent Duchy of Savoy, an Alpine region adjacent to Switzerland on the east and Italy on the southeast.

66   Alpine horn: See note for 129 on "Alpine horn."

66   the native militia: This was the army made up of habitants (Canadian colonists) so efficient in guerrilla-type Indian warfare that Intendant de Champigny (see note below) grew concerned about their being sacrificed for the regular troops from France, and he introduced reforms to increase the effective use of the latter.

67   Intendant, de Champigny . . . formal rather than cordial: Cather read in Parkman that relations between Frontenac and Intendant Jean Bochard de Champigny, who served from 1686 to 1702, "were commonly smooth enough on the surface" because the intendant, who had been "warned by the court not to offend" the governor, "treated him with studied deference, and was usually treated in return with urbane condescension" (2: 231). Beneath this surface, however, lurked disagreements over defense and the fur trade. Although as civil administrator an intendant had little authority over military strategy, de Champigny disapproved of Frontenac's policy of scattered raids rather than concentrated attacks against the Brit-

ish and Iroquois. Conflicts over the fur trade reached a crisis when Frontenac rejected the king's injunction forbidding the transport of brandy to Indian villages and supported a monopoly in the West by the successors of La Salle (see note for 98 on "Robert Cavalier de La Salle"). Prior to Frontenac's death, the king's chief minister, Pontchartrain (see notes for 273 on "Pontchartrain" and for 275–76 on "unpopular . . . geography of New France"), had taken the intendant's side against Frontenac.

Madame de Champigny: See note for 302 on "Madame de Champigny."   67

carrosse: A closed carriage or state-coach.   67

Dollier de Casson: See note for 154 on "Dollier de Casson."   67

Sulpician Seminary: See note for 154 on "Sulpician Seminary at Montreal."   67

Jacques le Ber: See note for 152 on "Jacques Le Ber."   67

Daniel du Lhut: Daniel Greysolon Dulhut (born at Saint-Germain-Laval, France, c. 1639; died at Montreal in 1710) was a coureur de bois (see note for 195 on "coureurs de bois") and explorer who extended the French fur-trading empire around the upper Great Lakes while La Salle was establishing a commercial empire to the south. Because of his military service in France, Dulhut was put in command of Fort Frontenac (see note below) during the Iroquois war campaign of 1696. The city of Duluth, Minnesota, bears his name.   67

Fort Frontenac: Count Frontenac personally supervised the building of this military fort and fur-trading post in 1673 at the place where the Cataraqui River enters Lake Ontario, a strategic location   67 for military operations against the Iroquois and British to the south and for further explorations along the Great Lakes to the west. The fort was lost to the Iroquois in 1689, but Frontenac rebuilt it in 1695 against the orders of the court. It remained a seat of military operations until 1758, when it was destroyed by the British.

67   Henri de Tonti: Born at Gaeta, Italy, in 1650, Tonti joined the French army in 1668 and during a campaign in Sicily nine years later had his right hand blown away by a grenade. He was nicknamed *bras de fer* (iron hand) as much for his courageous spirit as for his hook-shaped forearm. In 1678 he traveled to New France as La Salle's lieutenant and supervised the construction of forts along the Illinois and Mississippi rivers. He accompanied La Salle when he reached the Gulf of Mexico in 1686 and claimed the territory for France. Tonti served with La Salle until the latter's assassination in 1687. After trading in the Northwest with Frontenac's blessing to upgrade the quality of furs, Tonti returned to the Mississippi in 1698, helping to establish French presence to the south. He died of yellow fever at Fort St. Louis on Mobile Bay, Alabama, in 1705.

68   cardamon seeds: Spelled cardamom, *Elettaria cardamomum* is a herbaceous perennial of the ginger family. The seeds have a pungent, warm, highly aromatic flavor and are used as a condiment and in cooking.

68   Turkish wars: See note for 36 on "Venetians . . . Turks."

68   hardest Indian campaigns: See note for 27 on "Count . . . last campaign."

69   took great care of his person: Parkman quotes from the memoirs of Mlle de Montpensier, granddaughter of Henry IV and sometime companion of Frontenac's wife, that Frontenac "praised everything

that belonged to himself," paraded in new clothes "like a child," and displayed them for her on her dressing table: "His Royal Highness came into the room and must have thought it odd to see breeches and doublets in such a place" (2: 18).

lavender-water: Toilet water made from the aromatic oil of the   69
blue-gray flowers of the lavender plant (*Lavandula stoechas*).

women . . . work, — in Holland: This observation would again owe   70
to Frontenac's experiences as a young soldier in the Low Countries.
See note for 35 on "Italy and the Low Countries."

fruits of coloured glass . . . Saracens: Glassblowing was the inven-   71
tion of Syrian craftsmen in the first century and was practiced in
Asia Minor for many centuries. The term "Saracen" was used generally by Christians in the Middle Ages to indicate Muslim enemies, both Arab and Turkish.

dark citron: *Citron* is the French word for lemon; however, the   71
adjective "dark" suggests *Citrullus citroides*, a small, dark-green fruit
of the watermelon family used in pickles and preserves; Cather
mentions it in chapter 4 of book 1 of *O Pioneers!*

the South: The term defines and generates Mediterranean and   71
tropical associations in Cather, as in *Death Comes for the Archbishop*,
where it is used to describe the cathedral; in Quebec's cold climate,
such associations tend to the exotic and become life-supporting.
The term "South" embraces subsequent items like the swallow and
the parrot, shells and corals, and even the apothecary's stuffed alligator.

tapestries . . . garden scenes: The text here describes tapestries of   72
the *mille-fleurs* ("thousand flowers") design Cather would have seen

439

at the Musée de Cluny in Paris, which houses a series of fifteenth-
and sixteenth-century Dutch tapestries depicting love of nature
through arrangements of human and animal figures among flowers.

72 borax de Venise . . . asafoetida: Borax is a soft, colorless, crystalline
substance used as a solvent and cleansing agent, a disinfectant, a
water softener, and a preservative. Asafoetida is the fetid gum resin
of various plants of the carrot family formerly used in folk medicine
as a general protective against disease; it is also used as an anti-
spasmodic.

72 Ursuline school: Founded in 1639 by Mme de la Peltrie and Marie
de l'Incarnation and still in operation, this is the oldest school for
girls in North America. From the beginning the Ursulines in Canada devoted themselves to educating young Indian women, although their principal work was destined to be with French girls. In
1642 a boarding school was opened, which prospered in spite of
devastating fires in 1650 and 1686. From 1639 to 1740 twelve hundred boarders studied at the school, which would be much less than
half the total of boarders and day pupils. The basic course of study
included catechism, reading, writing, and simple arithmetic; beyond these, elements of grammar, and (because young women were
involved) deportment, correctness of speech, elocution, embroidery, drawing, and painting (Gosselin 360). Parkman adds "horror
of the other sex" as a component of this curriculum (1: 529). See
notes for 9 on "Convent of the Ursulines" and for 18 on "day-
school at the Ursulines."

72 Sister Anne de Sainte-Rose: While there is no record of a Sister
Anne de Sainte-Rose or of any niece of the bishop of Tours in the
Quebec Ursulines' list of professed nuns, her life recalls that of the
foundress of the Quebec Ursulines (see note for 113 on "Marie de

l'Incarnation"), and of their financial foundress, Mme de la Peltrie, who had lost both husband and child prior to her Canadian venture. The miracle plays Cather attributes to Sister Anne are historical, however, and were performed at the school on certain feasts, "*et surtout au temps de Noel*" (537), as the first volume of the 1878 edition of the Ursulines' history records.

miracle plays: Miracle plays proper developed out of the annual   73
cycle of the Roman Catholic liturgy during the Middle Ages and depicted miraculous events attributed to Our Lady in the lives of the saints; however, the term also identifies the more numerous mystery plays devoted to sacred history (the Creation, Fall, Nativity, Crucifixion, etc.). As the form developed, vernacular languages replaced Latin, dialogue and dramatic action were added, and performances moved from the church to the churchyard and marketplace.

pensionnaires: Boarding students at the Ursuline school; Marie de   73
l'Incarnation estimated their number in 1668 as "ordinarily from twenty to thirty" (Gosselin 353).

Sister Agatha, porteress: March speculates on a possible prototype   73
in Sister Sainte-Agathe (Marie Madeleine Gaultier de Comporte), born at Quebec in 1674, who joined the Ursulines after the death of both parents in 1687. Sister Agatha died at Quebec in 1703 during an epidemic.

flèche of the Récollet chapel: The spire and bell of this chapel were   73
controversial, resented by Bishop Laval (in dispute with the Récollets over the liquor trade), taken down by royal order, and later rebuilt (Scott 302–3). See note for 9 on "convent and church of the Récollet friars."

74 behind the King's warehouses . . . the slum of Quebec: This description seems to locate the slum along what is now Boulevard Champlain, although a more likely location would have been along rue
Sous-le-Cap, beside the foot of the rock and, at the time of the
novel's setting, behind the wharves and warehouses of the old port
on the banks of the St. Charles. The area has since been widened by
fill.

75 a few benches: Notre Dame des Victoires at present has stationary
pews; however, prior to the sixteenth century, when movable, back-
less benches began to be common for congregational seating,
church naves were open spaces, and benches (usually placed against
the walls) were available only for the aged and infirm.

76 Saint Anthony of Padua: Born at Lisbon of a noble family in 1195,
Anthony first joined the Augustinians but in 1220 became a Franciscan and briefly did missionary work among the Moors in Africa.
He participated with Francis of Assisi in the 1221 general chapter
of the Franciscan order and subsequently lectured in theology at
Bologna, Montpellier, and Toulouse. Anthony retired from teaching to preach in Padua, where he died in 1231. He is petitioned for
the recovery of lost articles (due to the supposed miraculous return
of a lost Psalter) and to inspire charitable work among the poor, to
whom he was devoted.

76 sheaf of lilies . . . Holy Child: St. Anthony is represented with a lily
and a book upon which the Infant Jesus is seated. The book represents the saint's knowledge and the lily his purity. The inclusion of
the Holy Child recalls an incident when one of Anthony's hosts,
glancing toward a window, saw the saint holding the Infant Christ
in his arms.

*The charm . . . 1929: This is one of Cather's rare footnotes; others   76
sketch the history of Quebec's General Hospital in the epilogue,
direct the pronunciation of Ántonia's name in *My Ántonia*, and
explain the adjustment of historical time in the Pecos chapter in the
Archbishop. The complaint relates to the novel's title (see note on
"Title") and the attempt here to reduce the physical to shadows and
glimpse spiritual reality with Cécile's and Jacques's candles.

Sir William Phips's besieging fleet . . . Church of the Infant Jesus: 76
See notes for 59 on "Notre Dame de la Victoire" and "bombardment."

Two paintings . . . of Sainte Geneviève: The first described is by   76
Théophile Hamel and is dated 1865; the second is identified as by
" 'Van Loo' (1705–65)." While generally accurate, these descriptions freely mix aspects of both paintings. In the Van Loo, angels
hover above the saint's head, which is illuminated by a heavenly ray
as she reads beneath a tree. In the Hamel, a tree is in the distance
(and thus smaller and of less significance) and a dog lies at the saint's
feet, but there are no angels. The distaff, held by the saint in the
Hamel, lies at her feet in the Van Loo. In both, a city, presumably
Paris, is evident in the background. What Cather refers to as "the
Lady Chapel" was added to the left of the principal nave of Notre
Dame des Victoires in 1724. See note for 120 on "devotion of
Sainte Geneviève."

high altar . . . feudal castle: The magnificent main or central altar of   77
this church (built by David Ouellet in 1878) fits Cather's description, although angels with banners rather than statues of saints
occupy the lesser towers. The altar, like the paintings of St. Geneviève, would not have existed at the time of the novel's setting.

443

77 arched gateway . . . Host: This "gateway" between the tallest towers
    of the outer wall of the castle-like altar contains the door of the
    tabernacle, a boxlike receptacle for the consecrated bread (round
    wafers) of the Blessed Sacrament, which, according to Catholic
    belief, embodies Christ. Because the Sacrament is adored as well as
    consumed in Communion, the tabernacle is the heart of the church
    building. The curtains hung before its locked door are changed to
    reflect feasts and cycles of the liturgical year. "Host" refers simulta-
    neously to the Eucharistic Bread and the sacrificial victim, Christ,
    embodied in it. See notes for 153 on "a rich lamp" and for 165 on
    "Blessed Sacrament."

77 the Holy Family: See note for 120 on "the Holy Family."

78 Sainte Anne: The mother of the Blessed Virgin Mary, Anne is
    mentioned by name in the second-century apocryphal gospel of
    James (Gospel of the Infancy) but is without biblical source (see
    note for 119 on "Saint Joachim"). Her cult was especially popular
    in Brittany and became so in Canada, where a major shrine, Ste-
    Anne-de-Beaupré, located twenty-seven miles northeast of Que-
    bec, has existed since 1658. Cather's description recalls the shrine's
    venerated "miraculous" statue of Anne, her face creased with age
    (according to tradition she gave birth to Mary late in life), with the
    young Virgin seated on her arm.

78 sorrows of her own family: The reference links Anne to the be-
    trayal, suffering, and death of her grandson, Jesus, to atone for
    humanity's sin; however, it would include her daughter Mary's sor-
    rows (dolors), traditionally seven: the prophecy of Simeon (Luke
    2:34–35), the flight into Egypt (Matthew 2:13–21), Mary's three-
    day separation from the twelve-year-old Jesus in Jerusalem (Luke
    2:41–50), and events related to Christ's suffering and death.

444

Blessed Mother and Child: The statue of the Virgin Mary holding 78
young Jesus in a gesture of presentation to those below is accurately
described. On each side of this statue, wall frescoes celebrate Quebec's survival in 1690 and the defeat of an attacking English fleet in
1711. See note for 59 on "Notre Dame de la Victoire."

votive candle-stand: A structure holding candles for burning before 79
statues and shrines of Our Lord, Our Lady, and the saints, to honor,
petition, and thank the personages depicted. "The word 'votive'
goes back to the ancient custom of lighting candles in fulfillment of
some private vow (*votum*)" (Hardon 565).

light a candle . . . money: The money referred to is the offering (a 79
suggested amount — in this case ten sous, or pennies) customarily
requested to light a votive candle.

"And . . . I'd die in sin": Cécile suspects that owing for a candle 80
offering might be sinful and compounds her misconstruction by
conceiving of a sin mortal enough to condemn her to hell, even
though she fully intends to pay her debt. See notes for 83 on "old
man . . . amused" and for 150 on "which angels."

Breton sailor: The sailor from Brittany who joins the West India 81
trade and whose gift to Jacques becomes a Christmas offering. See
note for 131 on "beaver."

La Garonne: A freighter of seventy tons and four guns built by the 81
English in 1668 and named *The Fortune*. In 1690 it was purchased
by the French, renamed *La Garonne* (a major river in southwestern
France), and sailed between France and the New World. Although
in the novel it arrives in Quebec in 1698, it actually had been taken
out of service and broken up in 1692 (Demerliac 77).

445

82   shovel hat . . . skull-cap: The clerical hat is shallow-crowned and with a wide brim curved up on the sides. The skullcap, or zucchetto, is a small, round cap worn by prelates; Laval's would be purple, the color for bishops.

82   old Bishop Laval: François Xavier de Laval, born at Montigny-sur-Avre (near Chartres) in 1623, was descended from a branch of the Montmorencys, one of the oldest and noblest of French families. The finances of his nuclear family were precarious, however, and after the deaths of his father and two brothers, Laval was pressured by his mother to leave the ecclesiastical life he had begun preparing for at an early age. The influence of the Jesuits at the colleges he attended at La Flèche and later at Paris prevailed, and Laval was ordained a priest in 1647. Ascetically inclined, he joined a group from La Flèche (the Bons Amis) dedicated to piety and spiritual improvement, and later he became a disciple of lay mystic Jean de Bernières de Louvigny at the Hermitage in Caen. (See notes for 89 on "Bernières's Hermitage" and for 266 on "La Flèche.") Knowing of Laval's attraction to the foreign missions (he was considered briefly for an assignment in Indochina), the Jesuits advanced his candidacy as bishop of Quebec in order to preserve their ecclesiastical autonomy there. In spite of jurisdictional protests from the bishop of Rouen, Laval was consecrated bishop in 1658 with the support of Louis XIV and his mother, Anne of Austria, and sailed to Canada the following year. Although Quebec did not achieve the status of diocese until 1674, Laval secured the king's backing to share power with the governor, to preserve the illegality of liquor trade with the Indians, and in 1663 to establish a seminary supported by tithing to administer the clergy in the parishes. One of the bishop's great trials was his successor Saint-Vallier's separation

of the seminary from parish administration. Laval retired in 1688, but from 1700 until his death in 1708 he administered affairs in the absence of Saint-Vallier. See notes for 26 on "feud . . . Frontenac and . . . Laval" and on "quarrel between the two Bishops."

Monseigneur l'Ancien: Laval's title in retirement, literally, "My   82
Lord Old One," but in English more like "My Venerable Lord."

large, drooping nose . . . bitter mouth: Scott notes that Laval's "long   82
drooping nose would have marred features even more delicately delineated than his, . . . while his thin lips . . . and his large forehead evinced firmness of will and high intelligence" (82). De Brumath writes that Laval's "thin lips and prominent chin showed a tenacious will" (29).

old man . . . amused: Bishop Laval is responding to Cécile's childish   83
scrupulosity of conscience. See note for 80 on "And . . . I'd die in sin."

Bishop Laval . . . saw a little boy: Cather develops this incident from   86
the following passage in Abbé Scott's biography of Laval: "Once he met on the street in winter time a poor child half-naked and shivering with cold; he led him to the priest-house, washed and kissed his feet, gave him shoes, stockings, a complete suit of clothes and sent him home as content as himself" (316).

episcopal mitre: Originally a kind of pope's crown, this folding   86
liturgical headdress of ornamented silk or linen worn by a bishop, originating in the metal forehead plate of the Jewish high priest, assumed a truncated version of its present form by the tenth century and its extensive peaked height by the sixteenth. It is described as "the helmet of protection and salvation" when placed on a bishop at his consecration (De Ligney 182).

447

86   valet . . . *donné* . . . Houssart: Hubert Houssart arrived from France in 1688 and became a *donné* at Laval's seminary; that is, according to Scott, "a man who engaged himself to serve the seminary without wages" (314). He assumed the role of personal servant to the retired bishop, remaining with him until his death. In a letter to the foreign mission seminary in Paris he detailed the bishop's final years.

87   Priests' House . . . of his Seminary: Quebec's first rectory, or clerical residence, was constructed as part of the seminary under the direction of the first superior, Henri de Bernières. Laval moved in upon completion of the structure in 1663 and made it his residence until 1701, when it burned down.

87   given away . . . vast grants: To assure support for his seminary, Laval took advantage of the French seigneurial system introduced to Canada by Cardinal Richelieu. Under this system, feudal seigneurs received dues and annual rents for land used within their territorial grants. Laval acquired the vast seigneury of Beaupré on the north shore of the St. Lawrence below (northeast of) Quebec, as well as grants for land above (southwest of) Quebec near Sillery, in Montreal, and along the Ottawa River. He secured the union of his Quebec diocese with the Benedictine Abbey of Maubec in the diocese of Bourges, France, which possessed rich farms and vineyards, but he was less successful in attempting union with the Cistercian abbey named Lestries near his hometown in Normandy. "Before leaving Paris [to return to Canada], in 1680," writes Scott, "[Laval] made a deed conferring on his seminary, for the education of Canadian youth, all that he possessed" (294).

87   He lived in naked poverty: Scott details the austerities of Laval's life: the mattress on hard boards, lack of sheets, room without a fire, meager diet, etc. (314–16). See note for 33 on "denied himself."

very large old man: In describing Laval, Scott emphasizes "his tall   87
and well-built frame" (82).

rang the bell for early mass: Scott paraphrases the following from   88
Houssart's letter on Laval: "After long prayers, he went, at four
o'clock, lantern in hand, to open the church door, rang the bell for
the mass he said at half-past four to suit the workmen" (314). See
note for 124 on "It was his custom."

reminder of his Infant Saviour: De Brumath commemorates Laval's   89
ability to see the poor, the orphan, and the unfortunate as "the
suffering members of the Saviour, . . . the image of Jesus Christ
himself" (258).

that house . . . a thorn in his flesh: See note for 27 on "new episcopal   89
Palace."

Bernières's Hermitage at Caen: In the 1640s, Jean de Bernières de   89
Louvigny, royal treasurer at Caen, Normandy, renounced the affairs of the world and built a retreat which became known as the
Hermitage. De Brumath writes simply that Bernières, a layman,
lived there with some of his friends for the purpose of aiding each
other in the practice of the highest piety and charity (24–25). Parkman, on the other hand, describes them as zealots who continually
disturbed the peace with their determination to expunge all signs of
Jansenism (Calvinistic teachings on predestination) in the area (1:
1167–72). During his more than three years at the Hermitage,
from 1654 to 1658, Laval led a life of prayer, meditation, and extreme mortification of the flesh.

His life . . . fell into two even periods: Cather's arithmetic is almost   90
accurate. Laval's departure for Canada as bishop in 1659, at thirty-
six, ended the contemplative spirituality of time spent with the

Bons Amis and at the Hermitage (see notes for 82 on "old Bishop Laval" and above on "Bernières's Hermitage"); at this time in the novel, fall 1697, Laval would have been administering the church in Canada for thirty-eight years. Since he would assume administrative duties from 1700 to 1708 in the absence of his successor, Laval would never be given the opportunity to "return to that rapt and mystical devotion of his earlier life."

91   *Les ourses et les louves protègent leurs petits*: The bears and the wolves protect their young. This line echoes act 2, scene iii, lines 185–89 of Shakespeare's *The Winter's Tale*: "Come on, poor babe. / Some powerful spirit instruct the kites and ravens / To be thy nurses! Wolves and bears, they say, / Casting their savageness aside, have done / Like offices of pity."

91   Sisters of the Congregation . . . in Montreal: The Congregation of Notre Dame, a teaching order founded by Marguerite Bourgeoys, who began a school for both girls and boys in Montreal in 1653, was officially recognized as a religious community in 1671. Bishop Laval supported the efforts of these sisters, praised the quality of the education they made available to children, and encouraged their development of several schools outside Montreal, including one at Sainte-Famille on the Île d'Orléans and another at Château-Richer, between Quebec and Sainte-Anne-de-Beaupré. See note for 202 on "Marguerite Bourgeoys."

91   A rich man . . . a girl over from France: Parkman provides the basis of this incident in a 1659 letter of Vicomte d'Argenson (governor general, 1658-61) complaining of Laval's arbitrary conduct: "A few days ago he carried off a servant girl . . . and placed her . . . in the Ursuline convent on the sole pretext that he wanted to have her instructed, thus depriving her master of her services, though he had

450

been at great expense in bringing her from France" (1: 1184). Argenson explains that he was forced to permit the master to seize the girl "wherever he should find her."

bonne: Maidservant.   91

Holy Family Hill: Rue Sainte-Famille on Holy Family Hill (see   92
note for 120 on "the Holy Family") extended at the time from the
seminary bakery (adjacent to the cathedral) to the ramparts above
the port area. According to March, by 1716 "[s]even families, forty-
five people in seven houses, lived on the hill" (361).

chirurgien Gervais Beaudoin: Surgeon Gervais Beaudoin was born   95
near Chartres in 1645 and died in Quebec in 1700. He was a physician of good reputation who administered to the Ursulines and
Laval's seminary (March 50).

"*Tirez, tirez*": "Pull, pull."   96

slippers, embroidered in gold and purple: Actually episcopal san-   96
dals, one of the vestments worn (with liturgical silk stockings) during solemn masses by those having the rank of bishop. Probably
derived from the footwear of ancient senators, such sandals were
worn by persons of rank and subsequently by the high clergy when
celebrating the liturgy. The sole is of leather, as Cather describes it,
and the upper part usually of velvet or silk and ornamented with
embroidery. The liturgical color of the day determines the color of
both sandals and stockings.

Montmorency . . . noble blood: Laval traced his ancestry to the   97
younger branch of the Montmorencys, one of the noblest families
of France, through the marriage of Emme de Laval, daughter of
Earl Guy de Laval, to Mathieu de Montmorency (d. 1230), Lord

High Constable of France. Their son took his mother's name, becoming Guy de Laval, and Bishop Laval was descended from him. The Montmorencys gave to the church and kingdom several other constables as well as cardinals, marshals, admirals, and generals. Though Laval's mother, Michelle de Péricard, could not boast such illustrious ancestry, she also belonged to the nobility, and two of her brothers were bishops. Scott makes Laval's genealogy available in some detail (9–11).

97   wooden lasts: A last is a form shaped like the human foot, over which a shoe is shaped or repaired.

98   "R.CAV.": See next note.

98   Robert Cavelier de La Salle: René-Robert Cavelier de La Salle, fur trader and first European explorer of the Mississippi delta, was born at Rouen, France, in 1643. At fifteen he began his novitiate with the Jesuits, but inability to conform to the disciplines required resulted in his release from vows nine years later. He traveled to New France in 1667 and through the influence of his brother, a Sulpician priest at Montreal (see note below), received a seigneury on the island of Montreal. Falsely claiming knowledge of Iroquois, he joined Sulpician Dollier de Casson (see note for 154 on "Dollier de Casson") two years later in an abortive attempt to explore the Ohio River and discover a route to China. In 1673, subsequent to mysterious travels claimed by some to have led to the discovery of the Ohio and Mississippi rivers, he attached himself to Governor Frontenac and helped build Fort Frontenac. Through this connection, La Salle obtained a commission to develop trading posts in the Midwest. He descended the Mississippi to its mouth with Henri de Tonti in 1682, then by falsifying geography won the king's support to establish a fort at the mouth of the Rio Grande from which to

452

launch the conquest of New Spain (Mexico). In 1687, after mis-
management of troops and personnel, loss of food and munitions,
confusion over where they had landed, and Indian attacks, La Salle
was killed by some of his own men during an expedition to the
Mississippi. Nineteenth-century historians view him as a betrayed
romantic hero (a view Cather seems to share), but later historians
consider him a victim of his own ambition, delusions, and incompe-
tence.

Abbé Cavelier: Jean Cavelier, born at Rouen in 1636, was the older   99
brother of explorer Robert Cavelier de La Salle. He entered the
Sulpician seminary in Paris in 1658, was ordained in 1662, arrived
in Canada in 1666 with Dollier de Casson, and encouraged his
brother to follow and seek his fortune there. In 1684 he joined La
Salle's ill-fated expedition to found a settlement in what is now
Louisiana. There was no love between the brothers (the abbé
seemed bent on exploiting his brother financially, and the explorer
on making his brother the butt of erratic impulses); however, there
is no evidence that Jean Cavelier was involved in his brother's murder. March notes that Robert complained of "treachery" relative to
Jean's foiling his plans and finances; perhaps this complaint is the
basis of this speculation on intrigue. The abbé did conceal news
about the murder so he could collect his brother's furs and money in
Canada, revealing it sometime after his return to France in 1688.
Parkman adds in a note that "the prudent abbé died rich and very
old [in 1722], at the house of a relative, having inherited a large
estate after his return from America" (1: 33).

All Saints' Day: A November 1 feast of required mass attendance   99
honoring the innumerable throng of the elect in St. John's vision in
Revelation 7:2–12. Unable to institute feasts for (or even identify)

every saint in glory, the church groups them for solemn commemoration and for the consolation of the faithful, who may contemplate the eventual inclusion of their loved ones and themselves among these unidentified saints.

100 boiling pine tops . . . a cough syrup: The Indians of eastern North America made a bitter, turpentine-tasting cough syrup from the boiled mixture of the bark, catkins, and new shoots (*bourgeons*) of the white pine (*Pinus strobus*). It was very rich in both vitamins A and C, and Europeans quickly adopted this herbal remedy for their own use.

100 *Lives of the Saints*: The title identifies any collection of biographies of canonized saints intended to inspire readers to emulate the subjects. *The Lives of the Fathers, Martyrs, and Principal Saints* compiled by Father Alban Butler (1710–73) is the most popular English-language collection and the basis of revised and enlarged twentieth-century editions, but there are many such compendiums of stories in English and other languages.

100 Saint Edmond . . . Archbishop of Cantorbéry: Edmund Rich of Abingdon (c. 1175–1240) studied at Paris and taught mathematics at Oxford until his deceased mother admonished him in a dream to return to Paris to pursue theology. After ordination he became a pioneer of Scholasticism and a biblical scholar at Oxford, preached a crusade against the Saracens for Pope Gregory IX, and (subsequent to three years of annulled elections) was appointed archbishop of Canterbury in 1233. As the result of disputes among the papal legate, King Henry III, and his barons (Edmund's mediations in 1234–36 are credited with preventing civil war), and also resentment of his reforms by his own monks, Edmund sought refuge during his final years in the Cistercian abbey (see note for 145 on

"La Trappe") in Pontigny (Burgundy), where his remains are kept. Details of his childhood vision of Jesus (even to the tracing of the name on the brow) can be found in Baring-Gould's *Lives of the Saints* (13: 349–50).

"*Edmond . . . de même*'": "Edmond was throughout his childhood a model of virtue, thanks to his pious mother's tender care. One only saw him either at school or at church, dividing his days between prayer and study, and depriving himself of the most innocent pleasures in order to converse with Jesus and his divine Mother, to whom he had made a vow of special devotion. One day when he had fled his playmates in order to meditate in private, the Infant Jesus appeared to him, radiant with beauty, and looked at him with love while he said: 'I greet you, my beloved.' Edmond, completely overwhelmed, did not dare to reply and the Saviour continued: 'Don't you recognize me then? — No, admitted the child, I have not had the honor, and I think you must not recognize me either but mistake me for someone else. — Why, continued the little Jesus, don't you recognize me, I who am always at your side and accompany you everywhere? Look at me; I am Jesus, engrave my name on your heart and print it on your brow for always and I will preserve you from sudden death like all those who will do the same.'" 101

apparition: A psychic experience in which a person or object not accessible to normal human perception is seen and sometimes heard. While acknowledging the divine origin of apparitions from biblical times to the present, the church requires proof to distinguish apparitions from illusions and hallucinations. See note for 160 on "miracles." 101

floating . . . as visions are wont: In depictions of visions or apparitions, celestial beings (saints, angels, divine personages) are tradi- 102 tionally suspended in the atmosphere or supported by cloud formations.

102   recluse in Montreal: See notes for 149 on "miracle at Montreal" and for 152 on "Jeanne Le Ber."

102   *moi . . . partout*: This repeats part of the penultimate sentence of the Saint Edmond story above.

103   silver cup with . . . the name, "*Cécile*": Cather herself owned such a cup with "Willa" engraved on it inside a wreath of foliage; it was given to her when she was a baby in Virginia by her paternal grandfather, William Cather, and is displayed at the Willa Cather Pioneer Memorial in Red Cloud, Nebraska. Bennett quotes from a letter of Cather's sister Elsie identifying the origin of the cup (234).

105   "Je suis mère, vous savez!": "I am the mother, you know!"

105   those poor creatures: See note for 60–61 on "King's Girls."

107   Frontenac heard mass every morning: See note for 284–85 on "In spiritual matters."

107   knife-grinder . . . wheel: A rotating wheel (in this case portable) of sandstone, or clay composition containing abrasives, against which objects are held for sharpening.

108   rue du Figuier: A short street on the Right Bank of the Seine off the Quai des Célestins, connecting rue de Fauconnier and rue Charlemagne. Its principal residence of note is the fifteenth-century Hôtel du Sens, one of the few surviving medieval private residences in Paris.

108   Fontainebleau: See note for 276–77 on "Fontainebleau."

456

Châtelet: See note for 40 on "mill at the Châtelet."   109

strappado: A machine for punishment or torture by which a victim   110
is hoisted into the air by a rope and then allowed to fall the length of
the rope.

Nobody is tortured here, except by the Indians: Cécile's comment   110
is naive, since Parkman's summary of punishments for breaking
civil or religious laws in Quebec includes the pillory and stake,
dragging, branding, mutilation, etc. "In case of heinous charges,
torture of the accused . . . permitted under French law . . . was
sometimes practised in Canada. Condemned murderers and felons
were occasionally tortured before being strangled; and the dead
body, enclosed in a kind of iron cage, was left hanging for months at
the top of Cape Diamond, a terror to children and a warning to
evil-doers. Yet, on the whole, Canadian justice, tried by the standard of the time, was neither vindictive nor cruel" (1: 1299–1301).

the King . . . the Law: The "absolutism" of the king in matters of   110
justice (considered his first function) was compromised by regional
law courts, or *parlements*, defining themselves as independent of the
royal will, and by the general concept that the law was divine and
incapable of alteration. The sixteenth-century political philosopher
Jean Bodin, although himself an advocate of absolute royal sov-
ereignty, "put divine law, natural law, and the fundamental laws of
the state beyond the king's reach" (Lossky 297–98).

thief on the cross: In Luke 23:39–43, when one of the two thieves   110
crucified with Jesus silences his companion's ridicule of Jesus, admits his own guilt, proclaims Jesus innocent, and asks to be remembered in the Kingdom, Jesus forgives him and grants him salvation:
"Today shalt thou be with me in paradise."

111   All Souls' Day: This November 2 feast day originated in the tenth century to commemorate the faithful departed, or holy souls in purgatory, those who died in grace but in need of purification to enable them to enter heaven. On this day, the faithful on earth are reminded of their ongoing responsibility to pray for the dead and are urged to have masses said and to seek the intercession of the saints to lessen or shorten the suffering of these souls.

111   Ursuline chapel: The present chapel of the Ursuline complex, like many of the other components (see notes for 9 on "Convent of the Ursulines" and for 72 on "Ursuline school"), is of post-eighteenth-century construction, although it contains statuary, paintings, and decorations from the seventeenth and eighteenth centuries. The chapel Cather visited in 1928–29 was completed in 1902 in the eclectic style of the time and contains the tomb of Marie de l'Incarnation.

111   Hôtel Dieu: See note for 42 on "Hôtel Dieu."

112   "*Priez . . . tré-pas-sés!*": "Pray for the Dead, / You who rest, / Pray for the departed!"

112–13   shades of . . . glorious company of martyrs . . . heroes: The term "shades" at once suggests ghosts or spirits and the "shadows" of the novel's title (see note on "Title"), that is, both the celestial reality of these personages and memories of their earthly lives. The passage also owes to the ancient Christian hymn of praise and thanksgiving *Te Deum laudamus*, popular at the time of the novel's setting, which catalogs the "glorious choir of the Apostles," the "admirable company of Prophets," and "the white-robed army of Martyrs." Cather has collapsed three into one to honor the Jesuit martyrs. See note for 120 on "martyrdoms of . . . Brébeuf."

Jesuits' . . . solid walls: See note for 9 on "foundation of the Jesuits."   112

Marie de l'Incarnation: Marie Guyart, founder of the Ursuline   113
order in Canada, was born in Tours, France, in 1599. She yearned
from an early age to enter a convent, but her parents arranged that
she marry Claude Martin, a silk merchant. After Martin died, leaving her with a six-month-old son and a bankrupt business, Marie
withdrew into secluded meditation and prayer and in 1620 experienced a mystical and highly emotional conversion. However, she
continued to work in the secular world, helping her sister and
brother-in-law in their shipping business. In 1632 she entered the
Ursuline cloister at Tours, and after reading the *Jesuit Relations* and
being prompted by visions, she decided her vocation was in Canada. Arriving in Quebec in 1639, she worked zealously at educating
French and Indian girls, wrote numerous spiritual treatises, and
compiled an Iroquois catechism as well as Algonquian and Iroquois
dictionaries. She died at Quebec in 1672. Her letters to the Ursuline cloister at Tours and to her son, Claude, a Benedictine priest,
have been published in both French and English.

Phips's bombardment: See note for 59 on "bombardment."   113

a shell had fallen: This episode is developed from a passage in   113
Parkman based on an account in *Les Ursulines de Quebec*: "The
cellars of the Ursuline convent were filled with women and children. . . . At the convent of the Ursulines, the corner of a nun's
apron was carried off by a cannon-shot as she passed through her
chamber" (2: 204–5). The nun is not identified in either Parkman
or his source.

they brought . . . the heavenly host: This also borrows from the *Te*   114
Deum (see note above on "shades of . . . glorious company"); in the
original hymn the Apostles make up a "glorious choir."

114–15   Dieppe or Tours: The choice of these towns is significant. In 1639 the first Ursulines and Hospitallers sailed to Canada from Dieppe, Normandy, where the Hospitallers ran a hospital. Among the passengers was Marie de l'Incarnation from the Ursuline convent at Tours, a city on the Loire in the old province of Touraine, southwest of Paris. Tours was a center of Christian learning in the early Middle Ages. See note for 10 on "Normandy . . . Dieppe."

115   well-ordered universe: This passage (and, indeed, the entire worldview of Cather's novel) reflects the universal order Henry Adams praises Thomas Aquinas for bequeathing to the late Middle Ages: "Saint Thomas and his God placed Man in the center of the universe, and made the sun and the stars for his uses" (354).

115   nuns . . . cloistered and those . . . about the town: Cather distinguishes between nuns confined within convent walls, such as the Ursulines and Augustinian Hospitallers, and those who were free to leave their convents, such as the Sisters of the Congregation.

115   veiled grille: A screen or divider used to delineate the residential enclosure of cloistered religious women; it is usually of metal and with small openings for communication with visitors.

115   the exquisite French of Tours: During the sixteenth and seventeenth centuries the speech of Touraine province in the Loire valley, the "Garden of France," commanded high prestige. A distinction in this French was the pronunciation of the lowercase "o" in words like *nostre*, *vostre*, and *dos* as *nustra*, *vustra*, and *dus*. Upperclass Parisians commonly preferred forms associated with Touraine in order to distinguish their speech from the vernacular dialects spoken by lower-class social groups in the capital (Lodge 166–71).

(*Inferretque deos Latio*): And he brings his gods to Latium. Book 1,   116
line 6 of the *Aeneid*. At the opening of Virgil's epic narrative we are
told that Aeneas flees Troy with his household gods and takes them
to Latium, where he establishes the Roman people.

St. Nicholas' Day: December 6 is the feast of Nicholas, a fourth-   116
century bishop of Myra in Asia Minor, whose patronage of children
(resulting in his popularization as Santa Claus) is appropriate for
the novel's emphasis on childhood. Of interest also is his patronage
of unmarried girls (to three of whom he is reputed to have given
gold for dowries to save them from prostitution), sailors, and
apothecaries.

hill named for the Holy Family: See notes for 92 on "Holy Family   117
Hill" and for 120 on "veneration . . . the Holy Family."

squares of maple sugar: These would have been sliced from sugar   119
loaves. See note for 56 on "maple sugar."

Saint Joseph: Joseph appears or is mentioned as the foster father of   119
Christ and husband of the Blessed Virgin in Matthew 1–2 and
13:55, and in Luke 1–2 and 4:22. Although poor and a carpenter,
Joseph came from the royal line of David. In the seventeenth century, to complement the dedication of France to Mary, St. Joseph
became the patron saint of Canada. Joseph is also the patron saint
of the church, of fathers of families, of carpenters, and of a happy
death.

Saint Joachim: According to the second-century apocryphal gospel   119
of James (Gospel of the Infancy), Joachim was the father of the
Virgin Mary and husband of St. Anne. Neither Joachim nor Anne is
biblical, but their cults were popular in Canada due to the popularity there of devotion to the Holy Family. A village named for St.

Joachim is located on the north shore of the St. Lawrence about ten miles northeast of Ste-Anne-de-Beaupré. See note for 78 on "Sainte Anne."

120   veneration . . . Holy Family . . . in Kebec: Jesus, Mary, and Joseph constitute the Holy Family, although Mme Pommier includes Anne and Joachim (Mary's parents) as well. When Leo XIII encouraged devotion to the Holy Family at the end of the nineteenth century, he credited Bishop Laval and Sister Marguerite Bourgeoys (see note for 202 on "Marguerite Bourgeoys") with establishing this devotion. De Brumath attributes promotion of the cult to Jesuit missionary Joseph Marie Chaumonot, whom Laval brought to Quebec as superior for the Holy Family Brotherhood (86–87).

120   martyrdoms of . . . Brébeuf . . . Lalemant . . . Jogues: Isaac Jogues and Jean de Brébeuf are the best known of this group of martyrs canonized in 1930 and identified as "North American Martyrs" (see note for 112–13 on "shades of . . . glorious company"). Charles Garnier, Antoine Daniel, Gabriel Lalemant, and Noël Chabanel were, like Jogues and Brébeuf, Jesuit missionary priests. René Goupil and Jean de la Lande worked with them as lay missionaries. Their missions among the Hurons extended from the St. Lawrence to the Great Lakes region, and their executioners (in all but Chabanel's case) were the Iroquois. Goupil, an aide to Jogues during his first captivity and imprisonment in an Iroquois village west of Fort Orange (Albany, New York), was the first to die, in 1642. La Lande was killed with Jogues after returning to this village four years later. Daniel died in an Iroquois raid on the Huron mission of St. Joseph in 1648. The others were killed in the Iroquois raids of 1649 (see note for 175 on "Iroquois raid of '49"). Brébeuf and Lalemant were

cannibalized at the mission of St. Ignace, Garnier was killed at St. Jean mission, and Chabanel was killed by an apostate Huron after the raid on St. Jean (see note for 174 on "Noël Chabanel"). The tortures suffered by these missionaries have become legendary and include braining with hatchets, scourging, burning with hot coals, piercing with arrows, and mutilation of the hands to prevent the priests from celebrating mass. Details on the lives and deaths of the eight are available in accounts for 1647–50 in the *Jesuit Relations* and in Jogues's undated life of Goupil in the same source (see Kenton 189–243).

thrown into the Rhone or the Moselle: The Rhone reference is to 120 the martyrs of Lyon and Vienne (Bishop Pothinus, Blandina, Attatus, Maturus, and companions), who were put to death and cast into the river after a variety of tortures (they were fried, scourged, thrown to animals) during the persecution under Marcus Aurelius in 177. The Moselle reference is to a third-century massacre of Christians at Trèves (Trier, Germany), where their bodies were thrown into that river. Nancy Gauthier cites a version of the so-called Passion of Saints Fuscianus, Gentianus, and Victoricus as a source of this legend (68–69); the Lyon martyrs are treated at length by Eusebius in the fifth chapter of his fourth-century *History of the Church*. Both groups are intended as counterparts of the Jesuit martyrs of North America.

devotion of Sainte Geneviève or Sainte Philomène: Geneviève, a 120 fifth-century saint honored as patroness of Paris, was born at Nanterre (north of Paris) and took the veil as a teenager. Legend credits her efforts to obtain provisions with saving Paris during a siege by the Franks; also, her encouragement of prayers and fasting was believed to have miraculously changed the route of Attila and his

Huns during their march toward the city. Cather was aware of this saint as the subject of the Puvis de Chavannes murals in the Pantheon (Geneviève's burial site) and claimed them as the structural inspiration for *Death Comes for the Archbishop*. Geneviève's exemplary childhood is depicted in paintings in Notre-Dame-des-Victoires (see note for 76 on "Two Paintings . . . of Sainte Geneviève"). Philomène is a less fortunate example because the cult of the more popular saint of that name (identified as a martyr subsequent to the discovery of the bones of an adolescent girl in the catacomb of Priscilla in Rome in the early nineteenth century) was officially suppressed by the Vatican in 1960. The body of the other Philomène was discovered in the ruins of an Italian altar in 1527 and identified as a sixth-century saint by a scrap of parchment attached to her neck supposedly written in the eighth century but in sixteenth-century style (Baring-Gould 7: 128–29).

121 *La Licorne*: See note for 238 on "*La Licorne.*"

121 crèche: See note for 125 on "crèche from France."

121 Christmas Eve . . . midnight mass: Mass at midnight, the first of three masses celebrated on December 25, the Feast of the Nativity, can be traced back to the fourth century. The dominant theme of this mass is the birth of Christ in time on earth; the object of the mass at dawn is the coming of the light of Christ to human souls, and that of the daytime mass is the eternal birth of the Son in the bosom of the Father.

122 Madame de Champigny . . . sent her *carrosse*: This is one of two charitable acts attributed to the intendant's wife. See note for 302 on "Madame de Champigny got a mirror."

122 second afterglow: See note for 267 on "afterglow."

464

the evening star: A bright planet, usually Venus, appearing after 123
sunset in the western sky and linked here to the star appearing at
Christ's birth in Matthew 2.

holy water: Water blessed by a priest to symbolize spiritual cleans- 124
ing is commonly available in fonts in church vestibules for wor-
shipers to dip their fingers in when making the sign of the cross
upon entering. See note for 189 on "sign of the cross."

It was his custom . . . to keep it from freezing: Laval's servant, 124
Houssart, recalled that his master "exercised particular care in
seeing every day whether the vessels of the church were supplied
with [holy water] . . . and during the winter . . . used to bring them
himself every evening and place them by our stove, and take them
back at four o'clock in the morning" (De Brumath 252–53).

consecrated oils: Symbols of spiritual nourishment and grace used in 124
baptism, confirmation, and anointing the sick; holy oils (oil of cate-
chumens, holy chrism, and oil of the sick) are blessed annually by a
bishop in a cathedral and stored in locked boxes in local churches.

forms: The rituals (actions, words, and symbols) relative to private 124
as well as public devotions and administration of the sacraments.

Jesuits' wood: Most likely their fief at Notre Dame des Anges (see 125
note for 128 on "*cabine*").

crèche from France: The word *crèche* means crib or manger when 125
applied to representations of human, angelic, and divine figures, as
well as animals, traditionally associated with the Christmas story.
Although representations of the Nativity have existed since the
early church, the crèche tradition was popularized by St. Francis of
Assisi, who arranged a crèche with living animals in the mountain

town of Grecchio, Italy, in 1223. See note for 127 on "the ox and the ass."

126   two terraces . . . as . . . at home: The two-story arrangement of the crèche duplicates the Upper and Lower Towns of Quebec and echoes the initial comparison of the city to the Nativity display (see note for 9 on "theatric scene of the Nativity").

126   "Regardez, ma'm'selle . . . mouton!": "Look, Miss, a beautiful little donkey!" . . . "There, the beautiful sheep!"

127   Blessed Virgin . . . country girl . . . Saint Joseph, a grave old man: The second-century apocryphal gospel of James (Gospel of the Infancy) makes Joseph an old man at his betrothal to Mary, but the duties implied in his protection of the Holy Family and upbringing of Christ make this unlikely. See note for 119 on "Saint Joseph."

127   the ox and the ass before the manger: These traditional animals and the sheep (*mouton*) associated with the Christmas story and placed in crèches are not biblical; their presence at the birth of Christ is merely implied by Luke's use of the word "manger" (2:7, 12, 16), a hay trough for horses or cattle, and by the angel interrupting shepherds "keeping watch over their flock" (Luke 2:8).

127   angels . . . over Him": In Luke 2:9–15 the "angel of the Lord" appears to shepherds and informs them of the birth of Christ. This angel is then accompanied by a heavenly host singing the first "Gloria." Luke subsequently refers to the departure of "angels . . . into heaven." The two angels on guard over the Holy Child are traditional, not biblical.

128   *cabine* . . . Notre Dame des Anges: The Récollets (Franciscans) were the first missionaries to celebrate mass at this site on the St. Charles

River just beyond Quebec (c. 1615), but early masses at other locales are recorded as taking place under pine bough shelters (March
includes an account of one at Tadoussac in 1617 [538]). In 1626,
Notre Dame des Anges became the first of the Jesuit seigneuries
(feudal grants), and the first Jesuit residence was constructed there.
"Here was nourished the germ of a vast enterprise," writes Parkman, "and this was the cradle of the great mission of New France"
(1: 405).

camels . . . without water: The camels associated with the Nativity   128
story are of the one-humped Arabian variety (*Camelus dromedarius*).
The introduction of camels is based on Isaiah 60:6: "camels shall
cover thee, and dromedaries of Midian and Ephah." The New
Testament mentions camels only in figures of speech (McKenzie
116).

three Kings . . . gold and frankincense and myrrh: The kings re-   128
ferred to are the wise men, or Magi (priests) or astrologers (Matthew 2:1–12), who follow the star to Bethlehem to find the Infant
Christ. Biblical scholars classify this text as a theological compila-
tion of Old Testament ones, including Psalm 60:6, which mentions
gifts of gold and frankincense (incense). Popular devotion has
added nonbiblical details: the number three, the transformation of
wise men into kings, the names of the kings (Caspar, Melchoir, and
Balthasar), and their connection to certain regions (McKenzie
534). The gifts have been traditionally interpreted as symbolic:
gold represents Christ's royalty; incense, his divinity; myrrh (a spice
derived from gum resin), his suffering and death. The adoration of
these wise-men-turned-kings fulfills messianic prophecies (e.g.,
Isaiah 49:23) of the homage paid by other nations to the God of
Israel. See note for 132 on "Epiphany."

128   the Shepherds: The appearance of shepherds in Luke's account of
the Nativity (12:8–20) involves complex symbolism: Christ, the
Good Shepherd and leader of shepherds (the disciples), is the son
(descendant) of David, the king who was a shepherd; also, he is born
in a sheepfold and is first manifested to a group of poor shepherds
— an intended contrast to the leaders of Judaism.

128   the story: The most detailed account of the birth of Christ, events
leading to it and those immediately subsequent, is available in Luke
1:26–79, 2:1–39. Matthew 2:1–17 recounts the coming of Magi,
the Holy Family's flight into Egypt, and Herod's slaughter of the
Innocents.

129   Montmorency: A village on the north shore of the St. Lawrence at
its confluence with the Montmorency and across from the Île d'Orléans. Named for Henri, Duc de Montmorency and Viceroy of
New France (1620–24), it is the site of Montmorency Falls.

129   north channel: Chenal de l'Île d'Orléans, the north branch of the
Saint Lawrence; the south channel, the main route for shipping,
keeps the river's name.

129   paroisse: His own parish church.

129   réveillon: In this case a Christmas Eve dinner and party; the term
also applies to New Year's Eve celebrations.

129   blood sausages and pickled pigs' feet: Blood sausage, or black pud-
ding, a concoction of oatmeal, suet, and hog's blood, is a local
specialty in both Brittany and Normandy, especially in Mortagne-
au-Perche, a Norman town west of Chartres associated with the
colonizing of Quebec. There are several French recipes for pigs'
feet, an offal meat that may be stewed in wine, grilled, or broiled;

pickling pigs' feet (popular in northern Germany) involves boiling and simmering them in vinegar and spices.

Alpine horn: The alphorn, a shepherd's instrument used tradition-   129
ally for intermontane communications and at musical festivals, is remarkable for its length, measuring in some instances as much as twelve feet, and for its upcurved bell at the end, although some horns are shorter and more trumpet-shaped. It is carved from wood and bound with birch bark and produces the natural harmonics of the tube.

cloves and bay-leaves: Cloves are the small, dried flower bud of the   129
tropical evergreen tree *Syzygium aromaticum*, which grows in the Moluccas (Spice Islands) of Indonesia. They have a hot, pungent taste and are used to preserve, flavor, and garnish food. Oil of cloves was a traditional anesthetic for toothaches. See note for 241–42 on "bay-leaves."

for the little Jesus . . . my . . . beaver: Jacques's offering, according to   131
Bennett (38–39), is based on Cather's nephew Charles Cather's gift of a toy cow to the "little Jesus" when setting up a crèche with Willa in Red Cloud in 1927. See note for 62 on "unfortunate child, Jacques."

Our Lord died for Canada as well: Mme Pommier's universal ap-   131
plication of Christian redemption at once joins the Nativity and the Crucifixion, explains the sometimes fanatical missionary outreach in New France, and responds to the restrictions on redemption imposed by Calvinists (including those in neighboring New England) and the Jansenists permeating the French Catholic church during this period.

131 beaver: *Castor canadensis* is a large, thick-set rodent weighing up to sixty pounds that inhabits the lakes and rivers of Canada and the northern United States. (*Castor fiber* is the Eurasian species.) The beaver was trapped almost to extinction in the seventeenth and eighteenth centuries, but its populations have recovered and it is now the national symbol of Canada. See notes for 22 on "traffic in beaver skins" and for 197 on "big beaver towns."

132 Epiphany: This January 6 feast commemorates Christ's manifestation to the Gentiles in the persons of the three kings, or Magi; at this time figures of the Magi and their camels are introduced to crèches in churches. (See note for 128 on "three Kings.") In some countries the Epiphany is known as Twelfth Night and is an occasion for special celebrations. Christmas decorations are usually kept in the home through this feast, which explains Cécile's question about the beaver. The manifestation of divinity is a theme Cather sustains by mentioning the Epiphany relative to the Le Ber miracle (see note for 149 on "night after Epiphany") and the Frichette episode with Father Saint-Cyr in the woods.

132 "Non, . . . toujours": "No, it's for always."

132 "C'est . . . ça": "That's so, Ma'am, that's so."

133 aube: The English word is alb, which denotes a full-length, long-sleeved, white linen vestment gathered at the waist with a cord or sash and worn under a chasuble (a mantle bearing the image of a cross) by a priest at mass.

133 Madame de Maintenon: See note for 143 on "Madame de Maintenon."

Saint-Sulpice, in Paris: This grand Parisian church in the Quartier 133
Saint-Sulpice on the Left Bank replaced a parish church for peasants living within the domain of Saint-Germain-des-Prés abbey.
The rebuilding began in 1646 and represents the work of six architects over a period of 134 years. This church serves as headquarters
for the Sulpician priests (see note for 154 on "Sulpician Seminary").
Here Saint-Vallier was consecrated Quebec's second bishop on January 25, 1688.

Laval . . . kept himself . . . poor: "A lover of poverty for himself," 133
Scott writes, Laval "loved the beauty of God's temple and the magnificence of the Church ceremonies. . . . [T]he offices of the Quebec
cathedral were celebrated . . . with real splendour" (317).

Book 3

Monseigneur de Saint-Vallier: The aristocrat Jean-Baptiste de la 137
Croix de Chevrières de Saint-Vallier, born at Grenoble, France, in
1653, succeeded Laval as bishop of Quebec in 1688. He was reared
in the château of Saint-Vallier on the Rhone in Dauphiné country,
educated at the Jesuit college in Grenoble, and entered Saint-
Sulpice seminary in Paris, where he was ordained a priest in 1681.
He was serving as almoner at the French court when Laval offered
him Quebec, the most wretched of missionary dioceses, but during
his tour of Canada in 1685–86, prior to his consecration, Saint-
Vallier antagonized the superiors of the Quebec seminary, and
Laval unsuccessfully tried to get him to withdraw. However, he was
consecrated bishop in Paris two years later and returned to Canada
to begin sixteen years of contention with his predecessor (see note
for 140 on "Saint-Vallier . . . Laval's system"). After receiving the
king's permission in 1691 to reorganize the seminary, Saint-Vallier

feuded with Frontenac (see note for 26 on "Count . . . quarrelling"), officials at Montreal, the Récollets, the Jesuits (who later accused him of Jansenism and other heresies), and the communities of nuns. He was recalled to France in 1694 and kept there until 1697, during which time the king failed to persuade him to resign. He returned to France again in 1700 and on his home voyage four years later was captured by the British (see note for 311 on "Bishop . . . prisoner of state"). When he finally did reach Quebec in 1713 he was in many ways a changed man, although still contentious, and he gave up his palace (see note for 27 on "new episcopal palace") for a barren room in his charity hospital (see note for 314 on "Hôpital Général"). He is characterized in Cather's sources as "rigid, austere, and contentious" (Parkman 2: 233) and as possessing a "violent and imperious temper" (Scott 320). Perhaps Cather's negative portrait owes much to Scott's comment that Saint-Vallier's letters do him "little honour . . . when he says [to the seminary priests] that he would not be contented until he deprived them of their last mouthful of bread! He moreover appropriated many things that did not properly belong to him. But peace to his ashes!" (320). Scott concludes by referring to Saint-Vallier as "[t]he troublesome bishop" (321).

137   black cassock with violet piping: A long, close-fitting, robe-like ecclesiastical vestment common to all clerics, it is usually black and sometimes belted. Cardinals may wear red and bishops violet cassocks, or black cassocks with red or violet piping; the pope's cassock is always white.

138–39   ulcer . . . cauterization: In cauterization a hot iron is used to sear diseased tissue; however, in this case it is used to draw disease from one limb by searing another. See note for 33 on "Laval . . . varicose legs."

Père La Chaise: François de La Chaise d'Aix, a Jesuit priest, be- 139
came confessor (spiritual adviser) to Louis XIV in 1675 and remained so for life. He supported Saint-Vallier's attempt to reorganize Laval's seminary, but to protect the Jesuits in Canada he kept
neutral when Louis pressured Saint-Vallier to resign. La Chaise
arranged the king's marriage to Mme de Maintenon (see note for
143 on "Madame de Maintenon") and acquired for the Jesuits land
in Paris that in the nineteenth century became the famous cemetery
bearing his name. Saint-Simon writes that, late in his life, the
priest's legs broke open, and he suggests that they were already
rotting before his death (3: 340).

medicine . . . of the last century better: Auclair holds sixteenth- 139
century advances in medicine in higher esteem than those practices
in his own time emanating from the court of Louis XIV. See notes
for 37 on "reign of Louis XIV," "time of Ambroise Paré," and
"Fagon."

Saint-Vallier . . . Laval's system: The king hardly needed to be 140
"induced" to reverse Laval's system of movable clergy. Parkman
clarifies that the system, "by which the bishop like a military chief
could compel each member of his clerical army to come and go at
his bidding, was from the first repugnant to Louis XIV," who
viewed Laval's request for a successor as an opportunity to change it
(1: 1338). But even prior to his consecration as bishop, Saint-Vallier
had made so many changes and caused such resentment that the
king was having second thoughts. "The Canadian priests . . . met
the innovations of Saint-Vallier with an opposition which seemed
only to confirm his purpose," writes Parkman (1339). "Laval . . .
was driven almost to despair. The seminary . . . he beheld . . .
battered and breached before his eyes." See note for 9 on "Bishop
Laval's Seminary."

473

141   books and furniture: In 1685, prior to his first visit to Canada,
      Saint-Vallier presented the Quebec seminary with a deed for
      42,000 francs for the missions and "bequeathed . . . all the furniture,
      books, etc., which he should possess at his death" (De Brumath
      202). Upon his arrival at Quebec "he placed in the seminary a
      magnificent collection of books which he had brought with him,
      and deposited in the coffers of the house several thousand francs in
      money" (203). However, in 1692, after receiving the king's approval
      to reorganize the seminary, he reversed his munificence, taking
      back the library he had given the seminary and directing that "the
      institution could lay no claim on sacred [vessels] given to the mis-
      sions or on the furniture placed in the priest-houses" (Scott 319).

142   almond-shaped eyes . . . eccentric Florentine nobles: The portrait
      of Saint-Vallier (specified as after "an original painting") in the final
      chapter of Scott's biography of Laval both resembles those of Flor-
      entine nobles by Botticelli and Raphael and matches Cather's de-
      scription: eyes, hair, eyebrows, long nose, diminishing face, large
      mouth, and dimpled chin. However, since the mouth is closed,
      teeth are not visible.

142   Bishop . . . twelve years . . . seven . . . in France: Saint-Vallier was
      consecrated bishop of Quebec in January 1688, ten rather than
      twelve years earlier. Up to this time, he had spent four, not seven,
      years in France — 1691–92 and 1694–97 — since his consecration.

142   Seminary . . . debt: In 1685, before his consecration as bishop,
      Saint-Vallier began an exhaustive eighteen-month tour of Cana-
      dian parishes from Acadia to Montreal as Laval's vicar general.
      While his braving of the extremes of Canadian weather won him
      admiration among the clergy, his lavish charity as the king's al-
      moner (see note below) caused alarm and left the seminary in sig-

nificant debt. Laval tried to caution his vicar in a letter: "My particular admiration has been aroused by . . . so great a reliance on the lovable Providence of God . . . for the support of all the works which it has suggested to you, but . . . it is certain He demands from us the observance of rules of prudence" (in De Brumath 206–7).

King's almoner: A court official, usually a priest, who distributes   143
alms or offers charity on behalf of the king. Because of his family's connections, Saint-Vallier was appointed almoner in 1676, five years prior to his ordination, and served at the court in this capacity for ten years. He became noted, writes Scott, "for his piety, his zeal, and his irreproachable conduct" (309).

Madame de Maintenon: Françoise d'Aubigné was the second wife   143
(and untitled "queen") of Louis XIV. Born in 1635 into an impoverished literary family (her grandfather was the Huguenot poet and soldier Agrippa d'Aubigné), she spent part of her childhood on the island of Martinique in the West Indies, returned to France at age sixteen, and then married the middle-aged and crippled writer Paul Scarron, whom she dutifully looked after until his death nine years later. She became governess to Louis XIV's illegitimate children by her friend Mme de Montespan (see note for 274 on "Madame de Montespan") and gradually rose in the king's favor until either in 1683, after the death of Queen Marie-Thérèse, or 1697 (historians debate this matter) she became his secret wife in a morganatic marriage (one between a royal and a commoner in which the latter's rank remains unchanged). There is no question that she had enormous influence on the king. Cather may owe her vignette of Mme de Maintenon as a "grave and far-seeing woman" to Saint-Simon's description of her in Parkman: "She rarely spoke, except when the king asked her opinion, which he often did; and then she answered

with great deliberation and gravity. She never or very rarely showed
a partiality for any measure, still less for any person; but she had an
understanding with the minister [see note for 273 on 'Pontchartrain'], who never dared do otherwise than she wished" (1: 1303). In
old age, piety and works of charity were her steady preoccupations.
She died in 1719 (four years after the king) at Saint-Cyr, an institution she founded for the education of impoverished daughters of
the nobility.

143   band-box: A round box usually made of cheap materials, cardboard
or thin wood, and used to carry light articles of clothing. The detail
indicates that Cather adopted Saint-Simon's colorful view of Mme
de Maintenon as a penniless adventurer from "the American Isles"
(5: 540), when in actuality she was born in France into a well-
educated, if impoverished, family.

143   Dauphiné: An old province north of Provence in the southeast of
France; its ruler was known as the Dauphin, which became the
name for the eldest son of the reigning King of France (parallel to
the Prince of Wales in England).

143–44   Comte de Saint-Vallier . . . found them ridiculous: Henri-Bernard
de la Croix de Chevières was the bishop's senior by nine years, a
counselor of Louis XIV, and colonel of the Guards of the Door.
Through his influence Saint-Vallier was appointed almoner to the
king, yet the count resented his brother's manner at court, especially his wearing a cassock. March quotes a passage from Helena
O'Reilly's 1882 biography of the bishop containing the contents of
Cather's version: "On returning to the palace [after the bell-ringing
incident] the brother, with a military frankness, told him that since
he continued to insult the family by his bigotry, he would do better
to close himself in La Trappe [see note below] so that no one would
hear him spoken of" (March 660).

Aumônier ordinaire: See note for 143 on "King's almoner"; the term   144
ordinaire (ordinary) refers to a cleric with ordinary jurisdiction or
authority limited by office rather than unlimited, in this case to
distribute alms at court in the name of the king.

Archbishop of Paris disliked him: François Harley de Champval-   144
lon, archbishop of Paris from 1671 to 1695, sided with Saint-Vallier
in his dispute with Laval over reorganizing the Quebec seminary;
however, he later sided with the king in trying to prevent the young
bishop's return to Quebec.

black gown . . . at Versailles: Rather than assuming court dress as   144
the king's almoner, Saint-Vallier wore his cassock at court (see note
for 137 on "black cassock").

ringing a little hand-bell: When carrying Holy Communion to the   144
sick a priest is customarily accompanied by a person ringing a hand-
bell to announce the presence of Christ in the Sacrament. Since
Saint-Vallier was appointed almoner prior to his ordination, he was
perhaps accompanying a priest on a sick call.

La Trappe: An abbey located in La Trappe Forest north of the   145
Norman town of Mortagne-au-Perche. It was founded in 1140 by
Cistercians (monks following an austere form of Benedictinism)
and reformed by Abbé Armand de Rance in the seventeenth century, when it was absorbed into the Cistercians of the Strict Observance, later known as Trappists. Reformed Cistercian life is contemplative and emphasizes penance, silence, manual labor, and
ascetic diet.

refused . . . Tours: Drummond reports that prior to being offered   145
Quebec, Saint-Vallier "had already refused more than one French
mitre" (422); he also notes that in 1687, in an effort to get Saint-

Vallier to withdraw subsequent to his initial tour of Canada, "the king offered a French bishopric to Saint-Vallier, [and] he peremptorily refused" (425). Similar offers were undoubtedly made when the king pressured the bishop to resign upon his recall to France in 1694.

145 King . . . could detain: There was even a limit on the king's authority to detain bishops, since canon (church) law forbade a bishop's being kept away from his diocese. Saint-Vallier's capture and imprisonment by the English in 1704 amounted to a convenience for the king (see notes for 311 on "Bishop . . . prisoner" and "his enemies").

145 ordain . . . consecrate: The duties listed are customarily reserved for bishops.

146 horehound . . . laudanum: European horehound (*Marrubium vulgare*) is an aromatic member of the mint family used in the manufacture of cough remedies and candy. The apothecary must have imported his supply of horehound from France, because the North American variety has no scent. Laudanum is an alcoholic tincture of opium with sedative properties and can lead to addiction when used too frequently; it is still used in medicines for the treatment of diarrhea.

146 English sailor . . . Brébeuf's skull: Mother Juchereau de Saint-Ignace tells this story in her history of the Hôtel-Dieu (148), but Cather would also have read Parkman's recounting of the story (1: 1232). One small detail differs: in the historical accounts the converted man was a Huguenot, whereas Cather makes him English.

147 He became a Christian: To the pious Catholic mentality of the time, the Protestant sailor (whether English or Huguenot) would have been considered not only heretical but outside Christendom.

sacred relics . . . work miracles: Such relics include body parts and   147
clothing of those canonized or beatified and objects used or touched
by them and authenticated for veneration. First-class relics are restricted to body parts (those of martyrs are placed in altar stones),
and when touched to other objects (usually cloth) they produce
third-class relics, the kind worn around the neck. Parkman notes
that in the early 1660s the church of Quebec received from Rome
two first-class relics, the bones of St. Flavian and St. Félicité (1:
1232). The term "miracles" would apply (unofficially at least) to
effects surpassing the powers of nature that have been worked
through the medium of relics as witnesses to some truth or to the
sanctity of the persons whose relics are involved. The English sail-
or's case would be labeled a "miracle of grace," a sudden and unexpected conversion from ignorance to faith, doubt to certainty, sin-
fulness to holiness, not due to ordinary causes but to grace, to divine
intervention. See note for 160 on "miracles."

pulverized human skulls: An extract of ground human skull was   147
believed to be effective in allaying convulsions (Glasscheib 162). It
was especially popular in England in the seventeenth century and
was given to King Charles II when he was dying.

Henry of Navarre . . . cemetery of the Innocents: Henry de Bourbon-   148
Navarre (1553–1610), son and heir of the Queen of Navarre (a
Basque province in Spain), came to power during the height of the
religious civil wars in France. His sympathies were Protestant, and
when he succeeded to the throne of France as Henry IV he had to do
battle for several years with the Catholic League in order to take
control of the kingdom. He laid siege to Paris in the spring of 1590,
and a terrible famine ensued, during which the citizens of the capital
resorted to eating horses, dogs, cats, and even human flesh. On the

recommendation of the Duchesse Montpensier, human bones were taken from Paris cemeteries, including the Innocents (see note for 39 on "the Innocents"), and ground into flour for bread. Those who ate the bread died. In spite of the mass starvation, the resistance of the capital was successful, for in 1593 Henry abjured his Calvinism and was crowned King of France the following year. However, in 1598 he signed the famous Edict of Nantes, which proclaimed freedom of conscience and granted places of refuge and worship for Protestants.

148   those of St. Peter: This reference concerns the bones reputedly entombed beneath St. Peter's Basilica in Rome, where Peter was crucified (c. 64). All four Gospels, Acts, and two of the Epistles establish Peter's leadership role among the Apostles. Peter's authority as bishop of Rome and first pope is traditional, although based on the biblical evidence that Jesus changed Simon's name to Peter, or "Rock," promised to build the church upon him, and gave him the keys of the kingdom, the power to bind and loose (Matthew 16:16–18). Auclair emphasizes Peter's distinction in eschewing even *his* bones as medicine.

149   miracle at Montreal: Cather would have read in Parkman that recluse Le Ber (see note for 152 on "Jeanne Le Ber") "herself declared that once when she had broken her spinning-wheel, an angel came and mended it for her" (1: 1353). March includes the exact words attributed to Le Ber when one of the sisters apologized for forgetting to get a repairman for the broken spinning wheel: "The matter is attended to: I prayed to the Holy Angels to help me and they repaired the spinning wheel. Oh! when I am in need, they come to my aid. Do as I; have confidence in them, and you will receive everything" (426).

night after Epiphany: The association of the "miracle" with this   149
feast develops the theme of divine manifestation. See note for 132
on "Epiphany."

which angels . . . Saint Joseph: Since Catholic teaching emphat-   150
ically defines divine, angelic, and human natures as distinct, speculating that Joseph might have been an angel indicates theological
naïveté (like Cécile's earlier scruples about owing money for a candle). See notes for 80 on "And . . . I'd die in sin" and for 119 on
"Saint Joseph."

light shining from the room overhead: See note for 156 on "The cell."   150

Plutarch . . . Alexander the Great: Plutarch's account in *Lives* (see   151
note for 23 on "Plutarch"), which traces the career of the Macedo-
nian king and general from his mysterious birth in 356 BC (the
Delphic oracle hinted he was sired by Zeus) to his death in Babylon,
perhaps by poison, in 323, functions as a foil for Jeanne Le Ber's
piety and self-abnegation. The most interesting aspect of the Plutarch story relative to Cather's text is its opening paragraph, which
Cather echoes in a letter to Wilbur Cross on her strategy in *Shadows*. Committed to communicating in language a "feeling about life
and human fate . . . full of pious resignation," she observes, "you
can't explode into military glory" (15–16). Plutarch writes: "it is my
task to dwell upon those actions which illuminate the workings of
the soul. . . . I leave the story of [Alexander's] greatest struggles and
achievements to be told by others" (252).

Jeanne Le Ber: "The venerated recluse of Montreal," as Parkman   152
distinguishes her (1: 1350), was born to wealthy merchant Jacques
Le Ber (see note below) and Jeanne Le Moyne at Montreal in 1662,
boarded at the Ursuline school in Quebec from 1674–77, and upon

her return to Montreal was influenced by Marguerite Bourgeoys (see note for 202 on "Marguerite Bourgeoys") and later by her Sulpician confessor Dollier de Casson (see note for 154 on "Dollier de Casson"). In 1679, moved by the death of a local nun (and obviously unaffected by her position as the most eligible girl in New France), Jeanne retreated to a cell in the parish church. Although she had not yet formalized her vows of seclusion, she refused to leave her cell to attend her dying mother in 1682. Subsequently she formalized her vows but, as befitted her social rank and responsibilities as an heiress, retained an attendant and conducted business matters. In 1695, after having special rooms constructed behind the altar of the new church of the Sisters of the Congregation, which she generously endowed, Jeanne took solemn and final (perpetual) vows. She spent the rest of her life in these rooms, making finely embroidered vestments and altar cloths for the churches. (See notes for 174 on "a vow . . . irrevocable" and for 178 on "vow of.") She popularized the practice of perpetual adoration of the Sacrament, a devotion begun in France earlier in the seventeenth century, prostrating herself before the altar each night after the sisters had retired. She became famous throughout Canada during her lifetime, and many miracles were attributed to her. She died in 1714, leaving her fortune to the Congregation.

152   Jacques Le Ber: Born near Rouen, France, c. 1633, Le Ber sailed to Montreal in 1657 and the following year wed Jeanne Le Moyne, becoming partners in a mercantile business with her brother Charles. As the business flourished the two men became influential in colonial affairs, although they clashed with Frontenac when he transferred their lease on the fur trade at Fort Frontenac to La Salle. Le Ber's ambitions extended to the cod fisheries, West India trade,

and lumbering; in 1696 he purchased a letter of nobility from a financially strapped Louis XIV. He held his recluse daughter in great affection and received permission to visit her twice a year and be buried near her cell in the church of the Congregation. He died in 1706; eight years later his daughter was buried at his side.

Ville-Marie de Montreal: The name given the Catholic utopian 152 colony founded in 1642 by the Société Notre-Dame de Montreal to bring Christianity to the Indians. In 1663 it was taken over by the Seminary of Saint Sulpice in Paris. Situated in a key region for the development of agriculture and the fur trade, the mission of Ville-Marie was gradually eroded by commercial interests and became known for its fashionable society. Today it is the heart of the city of Montreal, which in the mid-seventeenth century was often referred to as Ville-Marie. See note for 8 on "Montreal."

haircloth shirt: A garment of coarse cloth or goat's hair worn next to 153 the skin to put to death (mortify) sinful tendencies, strengthen the will through penance, and develop the wearer in the likeness of Christ.

parish church of Montreal: Montreal's new parish church on rue 153 Notre Dame was completed in 1678 under the supervision of Dollier de Casson (see note for 154 on "Dollier de Casson"), who served there as curé (pastor) and had the Sulpician seminary moved to an adjacent site (Flenley 22–23). The church served the parish of Montreal until 1829, when it was replaced by the massive neo-Gothic Notre Dame Basilica. Although rue Notre Dame runs one block parallel to rue St-Paul, where the Le Bers resided, the light the recluse watched during her vigils was in the chapel of the Hôtel Dieu (also on rue St-Paul), which had served as the parish church.

483

153   a rich lamp . . . "*I will be that lamp*": The gift is obviously a lavish receptacle for a sanctuary lamp (as identified a few lines below), a wax candle, generally in a red glass container, kept burning before a tabernacle in which the Blessed Sacrament is reserved (see note for 77 on "arched gateway"). The lamp "is an emblem of Christ's abiding love [and presence in the Sacrament] and a reminder to the faithful to respond with loving adoration" (Hardon 488). Jeanne Le Ber's stated intention is to embody this response. See note for 157 on "inches from the Blessed Sacrament."

153   fifty thousand gold écus: Cather's figure is historically accurate. The écu, an old French coin depicting a shield (*écu*) or escutcheon, varied in value during the seventeenth and eighteenth centuries; in 1794 it was replaced by the five-franc piece. At this rate the Le Ber dowry would amount to 250,000 francs, or about $50,000.

154   Pierre Charron: See note for 195 on "Pierre Charron."

154   *beau monde* of Ville-Marie: The fashionable society of Ville-Marie.

154   Dollier de Casson: The soldier-priest François Dollier de Casson was born in Brittany in 1636 and served as a cavalry officer there in his youth. While still in his twenties he entered the Sulpician seminary in Paris (see note below) and in 1666 was sent to Canada as a military chaplain. In 1669 he started out with La Salle toward the Mississippi but got separated and confined his exploration to the Great Lakes region. He returned to Montreal, became superior of the Sulpician seminary there in 1695, and worked to establish a conciliatory climate between the colony's civil and religious authorities. The range of his activities was remarkable, including laying out a street plan for Montreal, building Notre Dame parish church, and attempting to construct a canal at Lachine. In 1695 he presided

at the service when recluse Jeanne Le Ber entered her cell. He was respected by the Indians for both his firmness and fairness, a respect expressed in their accolade "There is a man!" (*Dictionary of Canadian Biography* 2: 196). See notes for 162 on "Father Hector Saint-Cyr" and for 171 on "He took a high hand." Dollier de Casson died in Montreal in 1701.

Sulpician Seminary: Compagnie des Prêtres de Saint-Sulpice is the official title of the Sulpicians, a society of diocesan priests established in 1642 by Abbé Olier to prepare men for the priesthood. The name is derived from the society's headquarters at the church of Saint-Sulpice in Paris. In 1657 Olier sent four of his priests to Montreal, and by 1663 the society had inherited the ownership and administration of the Ville-Marie colony. Eleven Sulpicians were laboring in Montreal in 1668, teaching boys, serving the inhabitants, and doing missionary work among the Indians. 154

domestic retreat of Sainte Catherine of Siena: The famous Dominican nun and visionary (1347–80), who actively worked with the poor, nursed the sick, led disciples on campaigns for reform and renewal, and politically intervened in conflicts between the Florentines and Pope Gregory XI (whom she petitioned to return the papacy to Rome from Avignon), consecrated herself as a child to a life of prayer and attempted to sustain such a life at home, despite her parents' efforts to discourage her pious inclinations and see her married. 154

solitariness of . . . Sainte Marie l'Égyptienne: A legendary third-century desert ascetic often confused with Mary Magdalene (reputed to have concluded her life as a hermit in the Alps), Mary of Egypt lived as a prostitute in Alexandria prior to her conversion and escape to the wilderness, where she subsisted on dates and berries. 154

A year before her death she took the Sacrament from a pious monk, who subsequently found her dead body, which a tame lion helped him bury. Her story appears in Jacobus de Voragine's *The Golden Legend*, where the monk is identified as Zozimus.

154   **desert of the Thebais:** Saint Mary of Egypt's story in *The Golden Legend* merely identifies the desert as across the Jordan; however, Cather locates it far up the Nile, in the area of ancient Thebes, near modern Luxor.

155   **high mass . . . feast days:** A mass in which the liturgy is sung or chanted by a priest and choir rather than read. Major church feasts (Christmas, Ascension Thursday, All Saints' Day, etc.) would be celebrated with high masses.

156   *dot* **. . . to build a chapel:** Actually, the church was planned independently by the Sisters of the Congregation, and Jeanne Le Ber provided the capital funds for building and decorating from her dowry (*dot*) subsequent to negotiations with the sisters about constructing her cell there. See note for 91 on "Sisters of the Congregation."

156–57   **The cell . . . her atelier:** This description of the cell is historically accurate. The recluse had access to the convent garden as well as the church through the lowest cubicle, and in the cubicle above the bedchamber, her studio or workroom (atelier), she fashioned the liturgical embroidery that became famous throughout the colony.

157   **grille:** See note for 115 on "veiled grille."

157   **inches from the Blessed Sacrament:** Parkman writes, "Her bed . . . was so placed that her head could touch the partition, that alone separated it from the Host on the altar" (1: 1352). Jeanne Le Ber's attempt to live as a spouse or bride of Christ, a way of life shared by

women who vow their chastity to God to be more spiritually intimate with Christ, becomes so strongly literal that she attempts to share Christ's pillow. See note for 153 on "a rich lamp."

cloister garden: A garden usually situated in the center of a covered 158
quadrangular walk and restricted to the residents of the convent or
monastery enclosing it. Jeanne Le Ber had access to such a space
through her basement cubicle.

Ah, mon père . . . de l'univers: "Oh, my father, my room is my earthly 158
paradise; it is my center; it is my element. There is no place more
delightful, nor more salutary for me; no Louvre, no palace, would
be more agreeable to me. I prefer my cell to all the rest of the
world." March locates the source of this passage in Faillon's biography of Jeanne Le Ber but finds no source for Jeanne's other statements (427).

miracles . . . flowering of desire: This definition echoes the end of 160
book 1 of *Death Comes for the Archbishop*, where Bishop Latour
explains miracles as finer perceptions. In both passages, humanity's
desires and perceptions, rather than direct divine intervention,
seem to generate effects surpassing the powers of nature. See note
for 147 on "sacred relics . . . work miracles."

bearskin coat and cap: Bearskin pelts used for clothing, blankets, 160
etc. were similar in value to beaver pelts (the trading standard).
These would be from the so-called black bear (*Ursus americanus*),
plentiful in eastern Canada and the Great Lakes region. They
range in color from black to light brown and even gray and nearly
white in northern regions. Father Le Jeune records that the Indians
trapped bears in spring and in winter felled trees where they hibernated (Kenton 68). Bears were also prized as meat and were a major
source of grease.

161   Sault Saint-Louis: Also known as Long or Grand Sault (river rapids) and later (c. 1669) named Lachine (China) in dubious acknowledgment of Robert Cavelier de La Salle's extravagant ambition, the area became an outpost of Montreal, a few miles north. A missionary reported to his superior in France that "the waters of this great river [the St. Lawrence] fall here with a loud roar, and roll over many cascades, which frighten one to look at. The water foams as you see it do under a mill-wheel" (Kenton 291). See note for 164 on "Sault mission."

161   down from Montreal: Although Montreal is southwest of Quebec, it is upriver, because the St. Lawrence flows north.

161   woodsman: There is a significant difference between a woodsman and a coureur de bois (see note for 195 on "coureurs de bois"). The latter lived all year in the forests, trapping and trading with the Indians, while the woodsman was a logger, working out of a camp. Most so-called woodsmen were farmers or craftsmen who went logging to make extra money during the winter months when they were not needed on their farms or when they could not work at trades such as building and carpentering.

162   cordial . . . healing herbs: A medicinal drink (not a liqueur) concocted to stimulate the heart, invigorate, and revive a patient.

162   "*C'est jolie, la couleur*": "The color is pretty."

162   buckskin shirt and breeches: Buckskin garments would have been of deerskin rather than sheepskin leather; popular among the Indians, they were adopted by woodsmen and coureurs de bois. Deerskin was a staple of the fur trade and used for blankets and carpets as well as clothing; it was also cut into thongs for lacing, straps, etc.

488

"C'est . . . toujours": "It is peaceful here at your place, as always."   162

Father Hector Saint-Cyr: March suggests (652) the Sulpician   162
soldier-priest François Dollier de Casson (see note for 154 on "Dollier de Casson") as the prototype of this fictional missionary. Like
Saint-Cyr, Dollier de Casson was strong and fearless (Parkman 1:
1241), high-handed with, but respected by, the Indians (see note for
171 on "He took a high hand"), carried his portable chapel on his
back to dying men in the wilderness (1246–47), and was a man in a
thousand: "The soldier and the gentleman still lived under the
cassock of the priest" (1247).

Nipissing country . . . Nipissings: An Algonquian-speaking people   163
closely related to the Ottawas and Algonquins, the Nipissings in-
habited the area around Lake Nipissing, west of Ottawa. In his
account of Champlain's explorations, Parkman writes that the
Nipissings were "a race so beset with spirits, infested by demons,
and abounding in magicians, that the Jesuits afterwards stigmatized
them as 'the Sorcerers'" (1: 289).

trade for skins: See note for 295 on "colony exists . . . fur trade."   163

punk wood: Wood so decayed as to be dry and crumbly, useful for   164
tinder, and in this case as an absorbent bandage.

boiled pine chips . . . turpentine: A solvent distilled from pine wood,   164
turpentine is used here as an antiseptic.

time to get a priest: Antoine Frichette is following the prescription   164
in James 5:14–15 to get a priest for those sick and in danger of
death. The rite of anointing the sick, traditionally one of the sacraments of the church, may be combined with confession of sins and
receiving the Eucharist, referred to in this context as "viaticum,"
meaning provision for the journey to God.

164   Sault mission: In 1676 the Jesuit mission of St. Francis Xavier was moved to Sault Saint-Louis (see note for 161 on "Sault Saint-Louis") from Laprairie, a few miles north opposite Montreal. As a community of converted Mohawks (one of the five Iroquois tribes), the mission was considered a guarantee against Iroquois attack. It was to this community that the so-called "Lily of the Mohawks," Kateri Tekakwitha (1656–80), since beatified by Rome, fled from her home in central New York. In 1689 the mission was brutally attacked and burned by about fifteen hundred Iroquois, who massacred the residents. Caughnawaga, the settlement that developed around the mission, is today a Mohawk reservation.

164   snowshoes: The snowshoe, a foot-extender for easier travel over snow, originated in Asia about 4000 BC, was introduced to the Americas through the Bering Strait area, and was perfected by the Algonquins along the St. Lawrence river valley before the coming of the Europeans. The French were the first white people to make extensive use of the snowshoe, and their forest heroes (see note for 198 on "free Frenchman of the great forests") were experienced snowshoers.

164   flint rock . . . white pine: Frichette is traveling from Nipissing country to the Sault mission through a Canadian Shield area (see note for 10 on "Laurentian mountains") of gneiss rock and pine forests. The eastern white pine (*Pinus strobus*), a valuable source of soft lumber, is the tallest conifer in eastern Canada; gneiss, a granitic rock, is a source of flint for sparking fires.

165   Blessed Sacrament on his back: Father Hector is literally carrying Christ on his back, since, according to Roman Catholic belief, the Eucharist is a permanent sacrament (rather than merely a rite) in which Christ is present under the appearance of bread and wine (in

this case bread alone). This explains his comment to Antoine to "never fear," that "while we carry that, Someone is watching over us." See notes for 77 on "arched gateway" and for 167 on "little box."

smoked eels: Eel is the common name of various snakelike fish of the order Anguilliformes, both marine and freshwater species. The reference here is to *Anguilla rostrata*, the freshwater eel of eastern North America, plentiful throughout the colony, including the environs of Quebec City (see note for 212 on "great eel-fishings"). Father Le Jeune notes the importance of the eel in the Indian diet, detailing not only how it is netted and harpooned (Kenton 64, 68–69) but also how it is prepared: "[T]he French salt it, the Savages smoke it, both make provision thereof for the Winter" (161). Smoked eels became not only a French staple in the forest in winter but an ingredient in *pièce tourtière*, a fashionable habitant pie-dish (Douville and Casanova 56). 165

cold grease: See note for 59 on "Here grease is meat." In the following paragraph of Frichette's story the grease is identified as lard, or pork grease. 165

Ave Maria: The Latin title of the Hail Mary, the most familiar of all prayers addressed to the Virgin. It contains the salutation of the angel Gabriel to Mary at the Annunciation and Elizabeth's greeting to Mary at the Visitation (Luke 1:28 and 42); it concludes with a medieval petition to pray for sinners. 166

Latin poem . . . learned at school: March suggests (421) that Cather had in mind Virgil's *Aeneid*, quoted earlier in her text (see note for 116 on "*Inferretque deos Latio*") to celebrate the transplanting of a people and their culture in a new country. 166

167   little box: Pyx is the name given to any metal box or vessel used to carry or store the Blessed Sacrament. The term more aptly applies to the round metal case (usually gold-plated) used to take consecrated hosts to the sick. See notes for 77 on "arched gateway" and for 165 on "Blessed Sacrament."

168   mercy of God . . . kind Indian: This meeting recalls the appearance of the mysterious stranger episodes from chapter 4 of Francisco Palou's 1787 biography of Padre Junípero Serra that Cather used for Jean Latour's recollection of missionary legends in chapter 4 of the final book of *Death Comes for the Archbishop*. The appearance of the kind Indian with the hares is an Epiphany manifestation like the angelic repair of Jeanne Le Ber's spinning wheel, which occurred two days before. See note for 149 on "miracle at Montreal."

168   Christian burial: Usually refers to interment accompanied by the church's funeral rites in consecrated ground reserved for those who have died in grace. In Michel Proulx's case, Father Hector would have blessed the grave before the burial.

169   a support: A truss or belt fashioned to sustain an injured area of the body and relieve pain.

169   canoes over portages: Light birchbark canoes were the major means of transportation for Canadian explorers and fur traders. Portages (from the French *porter*, to carry) referred to places where canoes had to be carried between rivers or where rivers were not navigable.

169   "*Courage, mon bourgeois*": "Take heart, my good fellow" (as in fellow citizen).

492

Aix-en-Provence: Founded by the Romans in 123 BC near mineral springs, Aix became the capital of the kingdom of Provence and then seat of the province (see note for 258 on "Provence"); it flourished during the Middle Ages as a university site and center for the arts, especially music.   170–171

savages . . . believed that a man . . . what he looked: The practice of reading character from bodily characteristics, especially facial, is universal and can be traced to primitive tribes as well as to Plato and Aristotle.   171

He took a high hand: Cather would have read in Parkman how Dollier de Casson, when interrupted in his prayers by an "insolent savage . . . , knocked the intruder flat by a blow of his fist, and the other Indians . . . were filled with admiration" (1: 1247). See notes for 154 on "Dollier de Casson" and for 162 on "Father Hector Saint-Cyr."   171

wild rice: *Zizania aquatica*, also known as Canada rice, Indian rice, or wild oats, is a broad-bladed grass growing in shallow water in the Great Lakes region; its seeds supplied the basic grain for certain Native tribes.   171

Burgundy: *Bourgogne* (in French) identifies white and red wines from this former province of eastern France, famous since Roman times as a wine-producing area. Major grape varieties include pinot noir and gamay for red wines and chardonnay for whites. As Cécile's dinner includes fish soup and fowl, Auclair is probably serving a chardonnay.   171

nepotism of the popes: Ecclesiastical preferment based on blood or family relationships, especially in the conferral of church offices. Nepotism (derived from *nepos*, "nephew" in Latin) plagued the   173

493

hierarchy for centuries, led to the legislation of clerical celibacy, and became a major impetus for the Reformation. In 1692, Innocent XII decreed that "in the future no pope should be permitted to bestow the cardinalate on more than one of his kinsmen" (*Catholic Encyclopedia* 8: 22).

174   a vow . . . irrevocable: While Hector Saint-Cyr's promise would bind him under pain of sin, its purpose would be both positive and liberating. From a religious perspective, writes Hardon, such vows "unite the soul to God in a new bond of religion, and so the acts included under the vow become . . . more meritorious. By taking a vow, a person surrenders to God the moral freedom of acting otherwise. . . . [V]ows forestall human weakness, since they do not leave matters to the indecision or caprice of the moment. Their very purpose is to invoke divine grace to sustain one's resolution" (566). This explains how Father Hector has "vanquished" his temptation to return to France. His vow is "irrevocable" because it is a perpetual vow; see note for 178 on "vow of."

174   Noël Chabanel: One of the Jesuit martyrs (see note for 120 on "martyrdoms"), Father Chabanel (b. 1613) entered the novitiate of the Jesuit College at Toulouse in 1630, joined the Canadian mission in 1643, spent a year in Quebec, and then went on to the Huron country (present-day Simcoe County, Ontario). Although a brilliant teacher of rhetoric in France, he could not master the Huron language, "no little mortification to a man who burned with desire for the conversion of the Savages," writes Paul Ragueneau in the Relation of 1649–50 (Kenton 239). During the Iroquois raids in 1649, Chabanel was martyred on the way to Ste. Marie (actually Ste. Marie II, a mission relocated on Christian [St. Joseph] Island in Georgian Bay) by an apostate Huron. Cather took the details for Chabanel's story from Ragueneau.

Brébeuf or Jogues or Lalement: See note for 120 on "martyrdoms."   174

Iroquois raid of '49: As the Iroquois nation or confederacy (see note   175
for 22 on "Iroquois") grew dependent on European trade goods in
the seventeenth century, it embarked on successful campaigns to
subjugate or disperse neighboring groups in order to have total
control of the fur trade with the Europeans. In March 1649 the
Iroquois attacked and destroyed the Huron villages of St. Ignace
and St. Louis, where the Jesuits had established missions.

Toulouse: Known as *la Ville Rose* because of its pink brick buildings,   175
this Garonne River city in the former province of Languedoc in the
Midi (southern France) was a leading artistic and literary center of
medieval Europe (see note for 198 on "Languedoc"). Its famous
university dates from the thirteenth century, and its eleventh-
century brick Basilica of St. Sernin is France's largest Romanesque
church; as famous is the thirteenth-century brick Gothic Church of
the Jacobins, the mother church of the Dominican order and tomb
of St. Thomas Aquinas.

Huron language: In the broad classification of indigenous North   175
American languages, Huron belongs with the Iroquoian group;
there are only dialectal differences between the languages of the
Hurons and the Iroquois confederacy, their traditional enemies.

mission of Saint Jean in the Tobacco nation: Founded in 1646 by   175
Father Charles Garnier (see note below) in the hill country southeast of Georgian Bay, mission St. Jean became a refuge for the
Hurons after the Iroquois attack of March 1649. The Tobacco
nation (Petun, or Tionontati), which derived its popular name from
growing and trading tobacco, was an Iroquoian tribe outside the
Iroquois confederation and with kinship to the Hurons and the

Neutrals (Atiwandaronks), who also provided sanctuary for the Hurons. In December 1649 the Iroquois destroyed the mission and exterminated the tribe.

175 Father Charles Garnier: One of the Jesuit martyrs (see note for 120 on "martyrdoms"), Garnier was born at Paris c. 1605 and ordained there in 1635, arriving at Quebec a year later to begin his missionary work among the Hurons and the Tobacco nation. Ragueneau reports in the Relation of 1649–50 that Garnier "had mastered the language of the [Hurons] so thoroughly that they themselves were astonished at him" (Kenton 233). He was killed at mission St. Jean on December 7, 1649.

175 savages . . . repulsive: Ragueneau indicates that "in consequence" of not being able to make himself understood by the Hurons, "the temper of [Chabanel's] mind was so opposed to the ways and manners of the Savages, that he saw in them scarce anything that pleased him" (Kenton 237).

176 flesh of dogs: Among eastern tribes, only the Huron appear to have eaten dogs regularly. Dog feasts were prepared to celebrate marriages, when entertaining visitors, during dances, and to cure the sick. The Iroquois ate dogs only at ceremonial feasts or as subsistence fare when other provisions were scarce (Schwartz 82). According to a chronicler in the *Jesuit Relations*, dogs were raised for consumption "like sheep" (7: 223).

176 Huron converts . . . brutal: In Ragueneau's account Chabanel is tormented by "the temper of his mind" and sense of abandonment by God rather than by the Hurons.

177 eaten . . . Iroquois: Cannibalism was practiced among the Hurons and Iroquois in the context of war. The consumption of an enemy's

body was believed to increase the feaster's ardor for war and pass along the enemy's strength. Parkman quotes a 1687 letter by Governor Denonville describing how his troops witnessed Indians after a battle "cut[ting] the dead bodies into quarters, like butcher meat, to put into their kettles" (2: 116).

withdrawal of God . . . temptation: Ragueneau defines such tempta- 177
tion as a "test" of fidelity that left Chabanel "prey to sorrow, to disgusts, and repugnances of Nature" (Kenton 240) and thus motivated his vow to remain with the Hurons.

Corpus Christi day . . . Blessed Sacrament exposed: The Feast of 177–78
the Blessed Sacrament (Body of Christ) was solemnly celebrated at this time on the Thursday after Trinity Sunday (ninth Sunday of Easter) with exposition of the Sacrament and a procession of the Sacrament through the streets. Cather's primary source, Ragueneau's Relation of 1649–50, dates the vow as "on the feast of Corpus Christi, in the year 1647," and contains the language of the vow relative to the Sacrament: "I, Noël Chabanel, — being in the presence of the most holy Sacrament of your Body and your precious Blood, which is the tabernacle of God among men, — make a vow of perpetual stability" (Kenton 241). Parkman quotes a version of this passage (1: 686); however, neither source contains the word "exposed." Exposition involves removing the Host from the tabernacle and displaying it in a monstrance, or merely opening the door of the tabernacle and moving the vessel of consecrated bread forward (see note for 77 on "arched gateway").

mission of Saint Matthias: This seventeenth-century Jesuit mission 178
was located near Ste. Marie in one of the valleys near present-day Collingwood, Ontario. The historical Chabanel actually made his vow of stability at the first (mainland) Ste. Marie mission (March

656), although he is said to have spent the night at St. Matthias just before he was killed.

178 vow of . . . (*perpetuam stabilitatem*): Vows of stability were taken under the sixth-century Rule of St. Benedict (the standard for Roman Catholic monasticism) for monks to commit themselves to the particular monastery of their profession and thus ensure the continuity of religious communities. Perpetual (final) vows, mainly of poverty, chastity, and obedience (although others may be added), bind subjects (male and female) for life. Chabanel (like Saint Cyr at a later date) committed himself to the mission of the Hurons until death. His vow concludes: "I conjure you, . . . O my Savior, to be pleased to receive me as a perpetual servant of this Mission, and to make me worthy of so lofty a ministry" (Kenton 241). See note for 174 on "a vow."

180 precious ointment . . . the disciples: In both Matthew (26:6–13) and Mark (14:3–9) the anointing of Jesus is set at the house of Simon the Leper in Bethany and there are multiple complainers — in Matthew the disciples as a group and in Mark some who were present. However, in John (12:3–8), where the incident is set at the house of Lazarus in Bethany, and where his sister Mary (often confused with Mary Magdalene), does the anointing, Judas Iscariot, the betrayer of Jesus, is cast as the sole protester. Judas argues that the ointment might have been sold to benefit the poor, but Christ justifies Mary's gesture because his days on earth are numbered, while "the poor always ye have with you." This incident seems to motivate the betrayal.

181 wild cherry bushes: The reference may be to the pigeon cherry (*Prunus pennsylvanica*) or, possibly, to the choke cherry (*P. nana*), both of which can grow as bushes on rocky slopes and hilltops and

produce small, astringent, red to nearly black fruits that can be used for making jelly. In the Relation of 1634, Father Paul Le Jeune describes native cherries "of which the flesh and pit together are not larger than the pit of the Bigarreau cherry in France" (Kenton 62).

knotty little Canadian willows: Perhaps the peach-leafed (or black)   181 willow (*Salix amygdaloides*), a small, scaly-barked tree that grows along rivers in Quebec.

hot mustard bath: The seed of the mustard plant (*Sinapis*) has long   181 been recognized for its medicinal properties. Mustard concoctions and plasters are used to relieve lung congestion, and baths of hot mustard are considered relaxing.

sassafras . . . Sir Walter Raleigh: Pioneers prepared a tonic from the   182 fragrant root bark of the sassafras tree (*Sassafras albidum*), which grows in sandy soils from Ontario south to Florida but is not native to Quebec. Father Le Jeune writes with reference to sassafras in the Relation of 1656–57 that "the most common and most wonderful plant in those countries [of the Iroquois] is that which we call the universal plant, because its leaves, when pounded, heal in a short time wounds of all kinds" (43: 259). Sassafras was popularized in England as a remedy for malaria and syphilis by Sir Walter Raleigh (1554–1618), an English adventurer and sponsor of the ill-fated settlement on Roanoke Island (in present North Carolina) in 1585.

Virginia colony: By the historical period of Cather's novel the name   182 *Virginia* (honoring Elizabeth I as Virgin Queen) referred to the agricultural settlements along the James River; the name previously designated all of North America not held by Spain or France.

182 *"Mais non, nous sommes plus tranquilles comme ça"*: "But no, we are more peaceful this way."

185 *"Sale service, . . . sale métier!"* "Dirty work, . . . a dirty trade!"

186 Not long afterwards . . . decomposition: See note for 22 on "crooked thoughts."

187 Le Havre: Like Saint-Malo, this seaport on the Normandy coast, 134 miles northwest of Paris, was an important center for transatlantic trade in the seventeenth century.

187 *mousse*: Ship's boy.

188 Suffering teaches us compassion: The mystery of suffering has basis in both the Old and New Testaments: for example, Job dramatizes the compassionate effects of suffering, and Jesus as "Man of Sorrows" is sensitive to every human suffering (Matthew 9:36, 14:14, 15:32). The "good chance" of Blinker's sickness is the Christian opportunity to suffer and "be crucified with Christ" (Galatians 2:20). The citing of Virgil rather than the Bible as the authority here (see note for 189–90 on "Queen Dido") seems intended to reflect secular and rationalistic strains in the apothecary's character.

188 confessor . . . Father Sébastian, at the Récollets': Most likely a fictional character, but the Récollet designation indicates Cather's awareness, perhaps through Parkman (1: 1349), of the commitment of these Franciscans to pastoral work and their popularity among the colonists. See note for 9 on "convent and church of the Récollet friars."

189 stone faces . . . of the Last Judgment: Sculptural depictions of Christ's judgment of the human race at the end of time, his separation of the blessed from the cursed (Matthew 25:31–46), are com-

mon in tympanums over cathedral doorways: in the south portal of
Chartres, the north of Rouen, and over the central (west) doorways
of Amiens and Paris. Auclair would be familiar with the latter's
Weighing of Souls, in which the damned are led to hell by demons.

sign of the cross: The most popular profession of Christian faith in   189
action form, this sign is usually made on the forehead, breast, and
shoulders while saying the names of the Father, Son, and Holy
Spirit aloud or silently. The sign can be made over the heart, as
Auclair makes it, and over other parts of the body and sacramental
objects during various rites. See note for 124 on "holy water."

galleys in France: The term refers to ships propelled chiefly by oars.   189
By the seventeenth century ships were powered by sail, but galleys
continued to function as convict ships to which criminals were
sentenced to labor.

Queen Dido . . . *miserable*: In Virgil's rendering of the Roman   189–90
legend, Queen Dido, the founder of Carthage, welcomes the exiled
Aeneas to her city with the words "*Non ignara mali miseris succurrere
disco*" (I, 630 *Aeneid*), a reference to her suffering in Tyre, where her
husband was slain by her brother. Her words have the power of
foreshadowing as well, for Dido falls in love with Aeneas, and when
he leaves her at Jupiter's command she constructs a funeral pyre on
which she stabs herself. Aeneas sees her once again during his journey through the underworld.

swallow . . . in the South: Probably the cliff swallow (*Petrochelidon*   190–91
pyrrhonota) that ranges from coast to coast and migrates as far north
as northern Canada and as far south as tropical Mexico. Cliff swallows return to ancestral breeding sites every year. Their song is a
series of squeaking and grating notes. See note for 71 on "the
South."

191 where . . . La Salle was murdered: Louisiana/Texas; see note for 98 on "Robert Cavelier de La Salle."

192 orange-trees growing under glass: Auclair is referring here to the orangeries, greenhouses heated by stoves in winter, which had become so fashionable in France. In northern Europe, orangeries became the most elaborate architectural feature of the great gardens of the seventeenth and eighteenth centuries. The most famous one was at Versailles, where fruiting orange trees were brought out in summer to line the promenades.

192 Laval . . . weather record: It seems unlikely that Laval himself kept such a record; however, such information was noted in the Quebec seminary's *Journal du Seminaire*, MS 34.1 to 34.17.

Book 4

195 When the sun . . . a holy city: This description compresses several biblical passages and suggests Quebec as the transfigured church on its rock. In her original typescript Cather borrowed from Psalm 19:5 to compare the sun to the "bridegroom issuing from his chamber," or the Lord emerging from his heavenly tabernacle to light the world. Cather's original sentence also compared the city to "the righteous in their Heavenly Father's house," a line from Matthew's depiction (13:43) of the children of heaven shining at judgment like the sun. The image of the holy city reflects the image of the transfigured Jerusalem in Revelation 21, that of the tabernacle of the Lord adorned as a bride, generating its own light and descending to the righteous as their dwelling.

195 saffron flowers: The dried stigmas of the purple-flowered crocus (*Crocus sativus*) are used for orange-yellow dyes as well as to give an

502

aromatic flavoring to foods. Culpeper lists a variety of medicinal uses for saffron in the seventeenth century.

Pierre Charron: This fictional character shares the name of a sixteenth-century French Catholic theologian who (influenced by Montaigne) attempted to negotiate skepticism and religious faith. Richard Harris sees Cather's Charron as "the perfect example of the . . . ideal natural man" (73) in the historical Charron's *A Treatise on Wisdom* and evaluates Jeanne Le Ber against its philosopher's dictum on living life within rather than separate from the world.   195

fur trade: See note for 295 on "colony exists."   195

coureurs de bois: Coureurs de bois, or runners of the woods, were, according to Le Sueur (88–89), of two kinds: on the one hand, men who merely traded in the woods with the Indians, and on the other, those who attached themselves to different Indian bands and lived the common life of the Native peoples. Because this "reversion to savagery," as it was termed by contemporary writers, had a great fascination for many Canadian youths, it was opposed by colonial authorities (Intendant Duchesneau primarily — see note for 38 on "Count's difficulties"). Cather would have read contradictory reports in Parkman, who presented the coureur de bois as a figure "picturesque . . . to animate the scenery" yet confessed he had "a dark and ugly side" (1: 1321–22). See notes for 161 on "woodsman" and for 198 on "free Frenchman of the great forests."   195

quick as an otter: This association with the North American river otter (*Lutra canadensis*) suggests swiftness of movement and perhaps friendly intelligence. The otter, a semi-aquatic member of the weasel family, was an important commodity in the fur trade during the seventeenth century. The coat of the northern otter was especially prized for its gloss and durability.   195

503

196   *"Je me porte bien, comme toujours"*: "I am doing well, as always."

196   Michilimackinac: Refers to St. Ignace mission, established by Jesuit Jacques Marquette (c. 1668) on the Straits of Mackinac, between Lake Huron and Lake Michigan. The site became the center of the beaver trade and, much to the chagrin of the missionaries, the scene of "a riotous invasion of *coureurs de bois*" (Parkman 1: 1326).

196   tablier: Apron or pinafore.

197   great falls . . . Niagara: The falls of the Niagara River, which flows from Lake Erie to the lower elevation of Lake Ontario and acts as drainage for the upper Great Lakes, are among North America's scenic wonders. Niagara Falls are 162 feet in height and divide into the Horseshoe Falls on the Canadian bank, 2,600 feet wide, and the American Falls, 1,000 feet wide.

197   big beaver towns: Beavers build extensive lodgings (three feet high and five feet wide) in colonies (towns) as well as burrows in banks with underwater entrances. Each lodging houses a large family (parents and two litters of two to eight offspring). Father Le Jeune notes that the beaver's "Cabin" is "two stories high and round" and contains "great numbers under one roof"; it is constructed of "wood and mud so well joined" that "no musket ball can pierce it." After the "Savages" have broken the upper story with hatchets and the animals seek cover under the ice, he continues, the ice is cut open and the beavers clubbed to death (Kenton 66–67). See notes for 56 on "beaver dams" and for 131 on "beaver."

197   Niagara . . . Lake Superior: The French had established a chain of fur-trading forts all along the Great Lakes. Sault Sainte Marie, the rapids of the Saint Mary's River between Lake Huron and Lake Superior, took its name from the Jesuit mission established there in 1668.

free Frenchman of the great forests: A cognomen reflecting posi-   198
tive views of the coureurs de bois based largely on the lives of earlier
adventurers and traders, among whom Parkman lists Jean Nicollet,
Jacques Hertel, François Marguerie, and Nicolas Marsolet as "the
most conspicuous." Their "home was the forest, and their companions savages." Freed from clerical vassalage "yet, for the most part,
they were good Catholics. . . . Some of the best families in Canada
claimed descent from this vigorous and hardy stock" (1: 515–16).
Douville and Casanova contend that "it is not possible completely
to separate one group from the next [according to social status], so
closely did their ways of life coincide" (146).

the Seine: One of France's most navigable rivers, the Seine rises in   198
the Langres Plateau south of Troyes and meanders northwest for
some 480 miles before emptying into the English Channel between
Honfleur and Le Havre. The Seine divides Paris into Right and
Left Banks and flows through Rouen.

Languedoc: A historic province of southern France, it derived its   198
name from the language (*langue*) of those who say *oc* rather than *oui*
to mean "yes." In the early Middle Ages, Languedoc, with its government at Toulouse, was politically independent, had a language
much closer to Latin than northern French, and had a literature
written in the *langue d'oc*. Through a series of political marriages, it
became a province of France in the late thirteenth century and after
the Revolution was divided into *départements*.

Saint Paul street . . . Le Ber: See note for 153 on "parish church of   198
Montreal."

Lombardy . . . quince-tree: The trees and shrubs mentioned in this   201
passage — Lombardy poplars (*Populus nigra italica*), lilac (*Syringa*),

and quince (*Cydonia*) — are not native to North America and would have been brought from France. The Lombardy poplar is especially interesting in this context because there were native poplars known commonly as balsam and Gilead poplars, but the tall, columnar form of the Lombardy variety, widely planted in Quebec, was prized above the rest for its aesthetic value and familiar recall of the French landscape.

202   Marguerite Bourgeoys: The founder of the Congregation of Notre Dame (see note for 91 on "Sisters of the Congregation"), born in Troyes in 1620, experienced conversion in 1640, joined a religious association (not yet a religious order) directed by the sister of Maisonneuve (see note for 8 on "Montreal"), and sailed to Canada at his invitation to instruct colonial and Indian children in Ville-Marie. In 1658 Marguerite organized an association similar to the one she had joined in France and opened a school in a stable on rue St-Paul, which the future recluse Jeanne Le Ber attended prior to her education with the Ursulines in Quebec. By 1681, after two recruiting voyages to France by the association and the granting of a civil charter from the king, eighteen sisters (seven Canadian) were staffing several schools. Marguerite resigned as superior in 1693 due to age but joined the other sisters in taking religious vows in 1698, becoming Sister Marguerite of the Blessed Sacrament. She died in 1700 and was canonized a saint in 1982.

203   fiery Bordeaux: Wine from the wine-producing region (considered the world's greatest) around the Atlantic port of Bordeaux on the Garonne in southwestern France. The fame of Bordeaux wines dates back to Roman times and, although the region produces red and white as well as dry and sweet varieties, rests on the dry red wine known in England as claret. See note for 307 on "gold-coloured wine."

the Count's last Indian campaign: See note for 27 on "Count . . . last   204
campaign."

Gaillac: Highly reputed wines (white, red, and rosé) from the Tarn   204
region of Languedoc and named for the town northeast of Toulouse which most of the vineyards encircle. Much of the production
goes into the slightly sweet sparkling wines known as Gaillac
Mousseux.

I hid myself . . . stone face: Pierre's invasion of Jeanne Le Ber's   209–10
privacy is fiction, but Cather would have read Parkman's vicarious
one: "We will permit ourselves to cast a stolen glance at her through
the narrow opening. . . . Her bed, a pile of straw. . . . Here she lay
wrapped in a garment of coarse gray serge. . . . She remained in this
voluntary prison . . . in a state of profound depression, and what her
biographer calls 'complete spiritual aridity' " (1: 1352).

resignation and despair: According to her confessor, Jeanne Le Ber   210
"did not find complete consolation in her self-abnegation and her
religious exercises were always burdensome" (*Dictionary of Canadian Biography* 2: 377).

great eel-fishings: Parkman notes that eel fishing was one of the   212
trades engaged in by the Jesuits to support themselves; he records
that "[i]n 1646, their eel-pots at Sillery [mission site near Quebec
City] are said to have yielded no less than forty thousand eels, some
of which they sold at the modest price of thirty sous a hundred" (1:
1333). La Hontan describes in detail the method of catching eels
with hurdles and baskets at Sillery (49–50).

Beaupré: The north coast of the St. Lawrence from Montmorency   214
Falls (see note for 129 on "Montmorency") to Cap Tourmente (see
note for 10 on "Cap Tourmente"). The name of the region is at-

tributed to Cartier (see note below), who supposedly exclaimed, "*Quel beau pré!*" ("What a fine meadow!") when he sailed past it. Ste-Anne-de-Beaupré is the coast's most famous town (see note for 78 on "Sainte Anne").

215 Jacques Cartier: One of the great Renaissance navigators, Cartier (born at Saint-Malo in 1491) was the first to explore the St. Lawrence, which became the axis of French power in North America; he is usually credited with discovering Canada. He led three voyages to the New World between 1534 and 1542. On his first he reached as far as the Baie de Gaspé, where he made contact with a group of Iroquois and raised a cross bearing the arms of France. It was on his second expedition in 1535–36 that he reached Stadacona (Quebec City) and named the Île d'Orléans, where wild grapes were growing, the Île de Bacchus. Cartier died at Saint-Malo, his home port, in 1557.

216 *à la campagnarde*: Country style.

216 dogs boiled with blueberries: See notes for 32 on "Canadian blueberries" and for 176 on "flesh of dogs."

216 *tripe de roche*: Rock tripe (*Umbilicaria*) is the common name for lichens that are boiled and eaten as emergency food in the northern woods. Although high in nutritional value, lichens are acidic and can cause stomach and intestinal irritations. Father Jean-Claude Allouez is quoted in the Relation of 1666–67 as being "forced . . . to eat a certain moss growing upon the rocks. It is a sort of shell-shaped leaf which is always covered with caterpillars and spiders; and which, on being boiled, furnishes an insipid soup, black and viscous, that rather serves to ward off death than to impart life" (Kenton 318).

Lac la Mort: A lake by this name does not appear on maps of   216
Quebec, nor is it mentioned in the *Jesuit Relations* or other seventeenth-century exploration narratives. March speculates (412) that
Cather might have intended Lac la Motte near Val d'Or in southwest Abitibi County, about 180 miles northwest of Quebec City.

Sainte-Pétronille: This western tip of the Île de Orléans was known   217
as Bout-de-l'Île or Beaulieu, after the seigneurs. In the 1650s a
chapel was constructed at the site for French and Huron use. The
present church, named for Petronilla, an early Roman martyr reputed to be a daughter of St. Peter (Saint-Pierre is the adjoining
parish on the island), dates from 1871.

south channel: See note for 129 on "north channel."   217

wild strawberries: The fruits of *Fragaria virginiana* are smaller,   218
sometimes sweeter versions of domestic strawberries and grow
plentifully on the Île d'Orléans because of its relatively mild, marine climate.

daisies . . . buttercups . . . blue and purple iris: Cather follows   218
Parkman's lead in presenting habitant rustics among wildflowers: in
Parkman, "purple and yellow" fringe the clearing where "wild-
looking women, with sunburnt faces and neglected hair," appear
with lethargic men and "bare-footed . . . half-clad" children (1:
1341). In Cather's text, since the common white daisy (*Chrysanthe-
mum leucanthemum*) is a European import, the native daisy fleabane
(*Erigeron ramosus*) would most likely be the daisy on the island.
Among native irises of Quebec is Hooker's blue-flag (*Iris hookeri*),
which grows along river shores; moist soil buttercups native to Quebec include Allen's buttercup (*Ranunculus alleni*), although it blooms
later in summer, and the marsh buttercup (*R. septentrionalis*).

509

219   pale eyes and hay-coloured hair: These features reflect the Breton and Norman origins of the colonists, who were drawn primarily from northwestern French provinces. Historiographer Louis Hamilton attributed the resilience of French Canadians to the fact that they "were not principally Frenchmen, but rather Germans and Celts" (Choquette 28).

219   mosquitos . . . herbs: At least seventy-four species of mosquito (order *Diptera*, family *Cullicidae*) occur in Canada. In northern boreal forests mosquitoes are serious insect pests because the bite of the female, seeking blood for egg production, causes considerable irritation and can transmit diseases such as equine encephalitis. The prevalence of mosquitoes during the warm months has hindered northern development by reducing the hours spent outdoors for industrial and recreational purposes. The first edition read "eucalyptus balls"; the leaves of the eucalyptus, or gum tree, produce an aromatic oil, the bark a pungent resin, and the burning of eucalyptus balls is a common method of fending off mosquitoes. But March points out (250) that its mention was anachronistic, since the genus *Eucalyptus*, native to Australia, New Zealand, and Tasmania, was not introduced to Europe until the early nineteenth century.

222   sagamite: Porridge of boiled cornmeal. See note for 56 on "Indian meal."

222   harp-shaped elm: Both elms native to Quebec fit Cather's setting and description: the white or American elm (*Ulmus americana*), one of the largest trees of eastern North America, and the red elm (*U. pubescens*), also known as the moose or slippery elm. Both prefer rocky hillsides and riverbanks, and when isolated in a field they divide into large limbs (the red elm closer to the ground) that curve gracefully outward and into a rounded or flat top.

510

grasshoppers: Cather mentions grasshoppers in several works, in- 222
cluding the giant grasshoppers in *My Ántonia* (identified in the
Scholarly Edition as lubber grasshoppers) and the locusts (from the
Latin word for grasshopper) in *O Pioneers!* While there are many
species of the order Orthoptera (including crickets and katydids)
throughout Quebec and Nebraska, of those particularly associated
with the Canadian province, the gladiator katydid (*Orchelimum
gladiator*), a green insect with tan or brown markings whose habitat
is tall grass, seems likely in this context.

grape-vine swing: As Pierre Charron makes clear earlier in this 223
chapter, grapevines would be plentiful on the island. See note for 10
on "Île d'Orléans."

remembered . . . Catherine de Saint-Augustin: See note for 51 on 225
"kissed the earth."

"*tous les deux!*": "Both of us!" 226

Book 5

Tadoussac: Tadoussac, a village located at the confluence of the 231
Saguenay and St. Lawrence rivers, was already an important trading center when the Europeans arrived and was the scene of the first
treaty made between Europeans and Native peoples (negotiated by
Samuel de Champlain in 1603).

La Garonne . . . sailor: See notes for 81 on "Breton sailor" and "*La* 233
Garonne."

salt meat and ship's bread: Meat cured or corned with salt or brine, 234
and unleavened, saltless biscuit made of flour and water, sometimes
called hardtack.

234   holiday costume . . . native town: Cather is most likely referring to the traditional costumes of Brittany, home to many of these colonists and their sailor customers. Distinctive aprons and headpieces, ranging from starched cylinders to lace hairnets, identified the local origin of women; men's costumes included embroidered waistcoats and felt hats with ribbons.

234   *pays*: Country, but here Cather means region.

237   *Les Deux Frères*: The first vessel by this name (*The Two Brothers*) listed by Martin Desgreves was an eighty-ton, twelve-man boat launched for cod fishing (likely off Newfoundland) in 1725. March finds no vessel with that name sailing in the time period of the novel (210).

237   *Le Profond*: Le Sueur (347) lists the *Profond* (*The Deep*) as one of five warships sent from France in 1697 to do battle with the English. March describes it as a thirty-gun ship of 400 tons (599).

237   ordnance . . . redoubt: Cannon sounded from the fortifications.

237   Monsieur le Dauphin: Louis de France, Louis XIV's only legitimate son (1661–1711), held the title of "Dauphin" used to designate the heir apparent (see note for 143 on "Dauphiné"). Fat, apathetic, and with little political will or imagination, Louis de France was mainly interested in the hunt and womanizing. There is historical irony in the reference to the Dauphin's "good health," for he died suddenly of smallpox in 1711 before he came to the throne.

237   Duc de Bourgogne: Oldest grandson of Louis XIV and for one year the Dauphin and heir apparent to the throne of France, Louis, Duc de Bourgogne, born in 1682, was exemplary for his learning, candor, and selflessness. He had a reputation for self-discipline, virtue,

and piety and was the hope of the court until his sudden death in 1712. Louis was a complex individual: he was reputed to be bisexual, according to Saint-Simon (4: 413), though he loved his wife passionately; he was humpbacked but never acknowledged his deformity. He believed strongly that kings were made for their people; if he had lived, French history might have taken a different course. See note for 316 on "death of the young Duc and Duchesse."

Princess of Savoie: Marie-Adelaide of Savoie (1685–1712) was 237–38 brought to the French court when she was eleven and married the Duc de Bourgogne a year later. Saint-Simon writes that when she arrived "everyone was surprised by her graciousness, her spirited conversation, and her easy, yet respectful manner, and that the king was charmed from the first" (1: 339). Louis XIV and Mme de Maintenon, he continues, "made a pet of her, because her flattering, coaxing ways and good manners pleased them vastly" (341). She was the life of the court and beloved by the whole royal family, although it was said after her death that she had been passing state secrets to her father, Victor Amédée, Duc de Savoie, which was then an independent duchy. See note for 316 on "death of the young Duc and Duchesse."

mais bien sage: But very wise (i.e., mature, grown up). Saint-Simon 238 describes the Princess of Savoie as "incomparably more intelligent and agreeable than is usual at her age" (1: 341).

The war was at a standstill: See note for 275 on "peace of Rijswijk." 238

La Reine du Nord: Martin Desgreves lists a vessel with this name 238 (*The Queen of the North*), but it was not launched until 1789.

238   *La Licorne*: March describes *La Licorne* (*The Unicorn*) as an eight-gun storeship of 300 tons captured from the Dutch at Dunkerque (430). Martin Desgreves describes a 200-ton ship of this name with eighteen cannons in service in 1691. His entry, however, records that, while returning from Quebec to France with a cargo of twenty-two thousand cod, it was shipwrecked at Belle Isle and its crew rescued by *L'Amitié*.

238   *Le Faucon*: *The Falcon*, a 450-ton French ship built in 1673 at Rochefort (March 260).

239   Newfoundland . . . Belle Île: The roughly triangular island of Newfoundland, separated from mainland Labrador by the Strait of Belle Isle, thrusts into the Atlantic as the most easterly portion of the North American continent. From the beginning of the sixteenth century the waters immediately south of the island, off the Grand Banks, have been known as one of the world's richest fishing grounds. The island and mainland Labrador were politically joined and became the Canadian province of Newfoundland in 1949.

240   sailors . . . went to confession: Parkman marvels at the "air of conventional [priest-governed] decorum" in early Quebec, when "[g]odless soldiers . . . whipped themselves in penance for their sins" (1: 328); however, he notes as an exception that during the annual arrival of the ships from France, "the rock swarmed with godless sailors" (507).

241   salts, gums, blue crystals: The salts are most likely laxatives; gums, dried plant exudates for pill making; and blue crystals refer to copper sulfate in blue vitriol or bluestone form, used to induce vomiting.

bay-leaves . . . mustard: The leaves of the sweet bay (*Laurus nobilis*),   241–42
which grows wild in the Mediterranean region, are used chiefly for
flavoring food, especially stews. Culpeper lists medicinal properties
for the bark and berries but not for the leaves. The flowers of the
linden tree (*Tilia*), also known as the lime, were infused to make a
tea. According to Culpeper, lime tea was thought to be good for
apoplexy, epilepsy, vertigo, and palpitations of the heart (216). Camomile (*Anthemis nobilis*) was thought in the seventeenth century to
cure almost all human ailments. A tea from its flowers was especially
popular as a tonic. The leaves of the senna (*Colutea cruenta*) were
used as a purgative and to purify the blood. Hyssop (*Hyssopus of-
ficinalis*), part of the mint family, is boiled with honey and taken as a
cough remedy; according to Culpeper, in the seventeenth century it
was thought to help relieve a wide variety of ailments, including
worms, jaundice, and various inflammations. Culpeper provides a
long list of the medicinal "virtues" found in mustard (*Sinapis*), including treatments for rheumatism, gout, worms in children, and
the making of poultices for fevers.

lemon rind, and crystalized ginger: These candied items are more   242
than confections (sweetmeats): lemon (*Citrus limon*) and candied
ginger (*Zingiber officinale*) relieve throat ailments and coughing;
ginger also possesses anti-clotting properties and has been used
since ancient Greek and Roman times as a digestive aid.

"*Bitumen — oleum terrae*" . . . borax: The Latin phrase Cather   242
quotes and explains in some detail identifies mineral pitch, oil of the
earth from the island of Barbados in the Caribbean. It was used to
relieve rheumatism and skin diseases. See note for 72 on "borax de
Venise."

242 snow-blindness: Inflammation of the eyes caused by exposure to ultraviolet rays reflected from the snow.

242 physician in Montreal . . . goose grease and lard: According to researchers at Quebec's Musée de la Civilisation/Musée de l'Amérique Français, no proof of such an experiment is available, although they consider the Montreal physician's attempt a very plausible one.

243 medicinal oil . . . codfish: Cod-liver oil was prescribed as a medicinal ointment in the fifteenth century; in 1730 it was discovered as a tonic for curing rickets, and in the nineteenth century it became a treatment for malnutrition. Cather links it to Breton fishermen because they had been fishing in the cod-rich waters off Newfoundland since the early sixteenth century (March 90, 162).

243 viper broth: March credits Moyse Charas's *Nouvelle expériences sur la vipère* (1669) with this craze over the benefits (tempering of the blood, general good health, rejuvenation) of bouillon made from skinned venomous snakes, speculating that secretions from adrenal glands beneath the viper skins may have strengthened those who tried the remedy (798–99).

244 epilepsy . . . unicorn's horn: Probably powdered horn from the African rhinoceros (*Diceros bicornis* or *D. simus*), whose double horn is actually a fibrous protein material like hair. Part of the lore of the mythological unicorn, a small horselike animal with a single horn on its forehead, was that those who drank from the horn were protected against epilepsy and stomach trouble.

244 Arabian spices: Spices (in this case medicinal) brought from southern Asia and the Spice Islands (Moluccas) by Arabian traders, who had a monopoly on the spice trade.

coral beads: These would be of Mediterranean coral, the precious   245
red *Coralium* brought to the American Southwest by Spanish explorers for barter.

Maître Pondaven: While there is no identifiable source for Master   245
(of the ship) Pondaven (March labels him "fictional" [589]), his life
typifies Saint-Malo (see note for 249 on "Saint-Malo") as a "nur-
sery of hardy mariners" (Parkman 1: 154).

tête de veau: Calf's head, an offal meat that, after being boned,   246
cleaned, and soaked in vinegar, becomes a French delicacy when
stewed with vegetables and herbs, sautéed in brown butter, frittered
and fried, or served cold with sauces.

parrot . . . Count's glass fruit: See note for 71 on "the South."   246–47

talking bird . . . cut out the bird's tongue: Cather combines univer-   247
sal folktale motifs in this passage: the speaking bird, bird adviser,
bird of truth, imprisoned heroine, and mutilation punishment. She
would have been familiar with Chaucer's "Manciple's Tale," which
(like its primary source in Ovid's *Metamorphoses*) combines these
motifs, including the silencing of the bird of truth (by defeather-
ing). Tongue removal as a punishment appears in European and
Asian tales and is of interest here because of Cather's intention to
use it as a subject in her Avignon story (Kates 483–86).

Magpies . . . speak: Any of various long-tailed species of the family   247
Corvidae (crows and jays), magpies are conversational birds capable
of a variety of sounds, from guttural chuckling to soft whistling, and
when kept in captivity can be trained to reproduce human speech.

beaver hat: See note for 22 on "traffic in beaver skins."   248

248   Dinan . . . Breton pancakes: A medieval castle town on the Rance River in northeastern Brittany, some fifteen miles south of Saint-Malo, Dinan is famous for its creperies and as the site of one of several tombs of legendary French hero Bertrand du Guesclin, who drove the English out of France in 1357.

249   Breton holiday suit . . . hat with a shallow crown: See note for 234 on "holiday costume."

249   Saint-Malo: This walled English Channel port in Brittany is important in the history of Quebec; Jacques Cartier (see note for 215 on "Jacques Cartier") sailed from Saint-Malo, and a number of settlers from Normandy embarked there for New France in the seventeenth century. Also, it was chiefly traders and merchants from Saint-Malo who formed the Company of New France (sometimes known as the Company of One Hundred Associates), established by Cardinal Richelieu in 1627 to conduct the fur trade in North America and to control lands stretching from Quebec to Florida.

249   Jamaica rum: Fermented from the molasses and foam rising to the top of boiled sugarcane, rum produced in Cuba, Trinidad, Puerto Rico, and Jamaica became a staple in the West Indies trade (see note for 319 on "West India trade"). Rum is naturally colorless, but Jamaica rum is dark and heavy-bodied due to the addition of caramel and storage in casks.

250   the Channel: The English Channel, upon the south coast of which Le Havre and Saint-Malo are located.

251   Madagascar: A large island off the eastern coast of Africa important in the slave trade. It was a French colony in the nineteenth century.

leek soup: Actually a leek and potato purée common in every French 251
household as a base for other ingredients or as a soup in itself. The
leek (*Alium porrum*), related to but sweeter than the onion, is a staple
of French cookery; in book 1, chapter 3 of *Death Comes for the
Archbishop*, Father Vaillant refers to the leek as "that king of vegetables."

parrot . . . Coco: Captain Pondaven's parrot was probably suggested 251–52
by the blasphemous one owned by Father Anton Docher of Isleta,
New Mexico, identified by March (391) as the prototype for Padre
Jesús de Baca in *Death Comes for the Archbishop*. Docher served the
pueblo from 1891–1926, during the time of Cather's visits to New
Mexico. See note for 255 on "live to be a hundred . . . African
parrot."

King's peace: See note for 275 on "peace of Rijswijk." 252

English had captured . . . *Le Saint-Antoine* . . . relics: A French boat of 252–53
this name with twenty-four guns and a capacity of 270 tons was
launched at Saint-Malo in 1684 (March 651). See note for 147 on
"sacred relics . . . work miracles."

"*Sales cochons anglais, sales cochons!*": "Dirty English pigs, dirty pigs!" 253

"*Vive . . . le Roi!*": "Long live the King!" 254

live to be a hundred . . . African parrot: The gray parrot (*Psittacus* 255
erithacus) of Africa, which fits Cather's description of Coco, is the
most skilled in reproducing human speech. These birds average
thirteen inches in length and are light gray in color except for red
tail feathers. Individual African grays are known to live to eighty
years.

255   *"Bon petit Coco . . . ici!"*: "Good little Coco, good little Coco. Here, here!"

255   *A Saint-Malo . . . sont arrivés*: "At Saint-Malo, beautiful seaport, / Three great ships have arrived." This medieval French folk song was collected in Canada in 1865, although the publisher, Ernest Gagnon, did not identify its origins. A rhythmic work, or canoe song, it tells of three ships arriving laden with oats and wheat and of three ladies in the market who come to bargain for grain. Its popularity in nineteenth-century Quebec perhaps reflected French Canadian nationalism at that time; Marius Barbeau speculates that "the name of Saint-Malo, well known to historians and politicians, may have sounded like a patriotic catchword, no matter what the contents of the song" (128). Cather is likely to have heard it when visiting Quebec in the late 1920s.

256   "Has Coco a soul . . . ?": According to the Scholastic speculation still popular at this time, plants as well as animals are said to possess souls, although Thomas Aquinas distinguishes them from human souls in his "Treatise on Man" (75 iii) in the *Summa Theologica*: souls of animals and plants are "material" in their dependence upon bodily organisms, whereas human souls, because endowed with intellects and wills, are only extrinsically dependent upon bodies and can exist and operate separately. The topic is an appropriate introduction to Pondaven's ape story.

256   a great she-ape . . . Our Lady: In the city museum of Saint-Malo there is a small granite sculpture (titled "La Moune") of an ape cradling a human baby which, before the bombing in World War II, was affixed to a house overlooking the fish market. It was carved and placed there to commemorate the story that Cather uses here. In the local account the she-ape is discovered near the eaves feeding

the baby rubbish from her perch and then is persuaded to return the
child to safety by imitating the behavior of a human mother who
places her baby in its bed (Harvut 51–52). Cather would have seen
the celebrated Virgin of the Grand Gate in its alcove in the city wall
nearby and included it in her version. Another matter of artistic
license concerns the dating: the actual incident took place in Saint-
Malo in 1774, almost eighty years after the time of the novel.

Friday the beaver . . . a fish: Pierre is referring to the ecclesiastical   257
law mandating abstinence from mammal meat on Fridays as a vir-
tuous practice or penance to commemorate Christ's passion and
death. Where or when adequate food substitutes (fish was the customary substitute) were unavailable, a dispensation would permit
the consumption of meat. During the papal residence at Avignon
(1309–78) the beaver's tail was exempt as meat because "it was
believed that it never left the water and . . . qualified as fish" (Wheaton 12), a line of medieval reasoning operating in New France,
where beaver and muskrat were allowed to be eaten on Fridays
because they were amphibious (Douville and Casanova 61). Manda-
tory Friday abstinence (except during Lent) was abolished in 1966.

put into the stocks: See note for 110 on "Nobody is tortured here."   257

when a child is naughty: During Cather's time children in Saint-   257
Malo were still being told the she-ape story to coerce them to
behave.

Provence: A historic French province on the Mediterranean and   258
adjacent to Italy, Provence has a distinctive culture, language, and
literature. Cather first visited this region in 1902 and felt a special
love for it; when she made her first trip to the American Southwest
ten years later, she wrote Elizabeth Sergeant that it reminded her

of Provence (Sergeant 81). See note for 170–71 on "Aix-en-Provence."

258   certain naked islands: The reference is either to the Mingan Archipelago off the north coast of the Gulf of St. Lawrence near Anticosti Island, where the Atlantic puffin (*Fratercula arctica*), or sea parrot, breeds, or to Île Bonaventure near Percé Rock to the south, nesting ground for North America's largest colony of gannets (*Morus bassanus*). See note for 16 on "Percé."

259   gum Arabic: A water-soluble gum obtained from acacias, especially *Acacia senegal*, and used in the manufacture of adhesives and pharmaceutical products.

260   milkweed . . . *le contonnier*: The cotton plant. The reference is to common milkweed (*Asclepias syriaca*), which produces pods containing silky tufted seeds and is native to North America. Marc Lescarbot wrote in 1606 that "of this cotton, or whatsoever it be, good beds may be made, more excellent a thousand times than of feathers, and softer than common cotton. We have sowed of the said seed, or grain, in divers places of Paris, but it did not prove" (296–97).

260   gentians: The roots of the gentian (*Gentiana*) are used to make a tonic which in Culpeper's time (seventeenth century) was thought to aid digestion.

261   *Le Duc de Bretagne*: Martin Desgreves lists a vessel of this name (55), although it was not in service until 1704. That ship was probably named after Louis XIV's first great-grandson, the Duc de Bretagne, who was born in 1704 and who, if he had lived, would have become King of France.

Le Soleil d'Afrique: A French frigate built in 1680 and, according to Le Sueur (309), famous as a very rapid sailer. Demerliac lists a freighter of the same name (*The African Sun*) chartered for service to Quebec in 1688 and with a capacity of 300 tons (201). 261

transmutation of autumn . . . never seen in France: Autumnal coloring of foliage in Quebec is generally called *le rougissement* (reddening) of autumn; see note for 56 on "maple sugar." This *rougissement* set piece introduces a variety of native Quebec trees and shrubs. Reds are represented by the pigeon cherry (see note for 181 on "wild cherry bushes"), a fast-growing reforester providing food for birds; the staghorn or smooth sumac (*Rhus hirta* or *R. glabra*), favoring hillsides as a tree or bush; and the northern blackberry (*Rubus canadenses*), a bristly branched shrub (rather than a vine) thriving in rocky wooded areas. The yellow (or gray) birch (*Betula lutea*), its curling silvery or golden gray bark a striking feature in northern forests, and balsam poplar (*Populus balsamifera*), a river-bordering tree, are included to anticipate the darker golden colors. In a group by itself is the American (or small-fruited) mountain ash (*Sorbus americana*), a slender flowering tree (often a shrub) said to be "one of the most beautiful trees of our northern forests," especially in autumn when "its bunches of red [not orange] berries" make it "even a more beautiful object" (Hough 239). Tarnished gold is provided by the native elm, most likely the red elm (*Ulmus pubescens*) prevalent on hillsides and with autumn leaves varied enough to suggest the hues Cather mentions, even to the bluish purple of amethyst. For contrast in gold, the birch is placed against the peach-leaved willow (see note for 181 on "knotty little Canadian willows"), favoring river shores. The concluding coppery entry is 262 the American beech (*Fagus grandifolia*), a large nut-bearing tree of the Canadian uplands.

263   behind . . . Saint Anthony: Since this saint is petitioned for the recovery of what has been lost (see note for 76 on "Saint Anthony"), Cécile weeps behind his image "for all that she had lost, and . . . must lose so soon."

263   "*O ma mère . . . comme toi!*": "Oh my mother, I am weak! I don't have a courageous spirit like you!"

266   Brothers' school in Montreal: In 1694 the Hospital Brothers of St. Joseph of the Cross, under the leadership of François Charon, began admitting orphan children into their almshouse to teach them crafts and give them an education.

266   "Schools are . . . without happiness": This aphorism (apparently Cather's) is generic and intended to reflect the austere realism of Laval's devotion to and philosophy of education; it echoes numerous terse statements of this kind in Montaigne, which draw on Cicero, Plato, Plutarch, and the Bible. A boy must be "broken in to . . . pain," Montaigne argues in "Of the Education of Children" (113), and in the "Man's knowledge cannot make him happy" section of *Apology for Raymond Sebond*, he equates knowledge with suffering (359–60), quoting Ecclesiastes 1:18, that "in much wisdom is much grief: and he that increaseth knowledge increaseth sorrow" (366). An anonymous entry collected by Forman is very similar to Cather's: "The most important purpose of education is not so much to prepare a person to succeed in the world as to enable him to sustain failure" (201).

266   "La Flèche . . . a severe school": Founded in 1604 by Henry IV in the château town of La Flèche on the river Loire (some twenty-five

miles upstream from Angers) and administered by Jesuits, this royal college reached a peak of twelve hundred students by the mid-seventeenth century. Laval attended from 1631 to 1641 (René Descartes was an earlier alumnus), studying philosophy and theology under Father Jean Bagot, a controversial theologian who taught at various French colleges before becoming the theologian of the order's superior-general. Laval continued his studies at the College of Clermont in Paris.

"... *domus ... Domine*": These Latin words, "... habitation ... O   266 Lord," seem to be from a prayer probably learned at school and derived from a psalm. A likely candidate is Psalm 84, which expresses longing for God's dwelling place as a refuge for the vulnerable: "How amiable are thy tabernacles, O Lord of hosts! My soul longeth, yea, even fainteth for the courts of the Lord: my heart and my flesh crieth out for the living God. Yea, the sparrow hath found an house, and the swallow a nest for herself, where she may lay her young, even thine altars, O Lord of hosts, my king, my God" (1–3).

afterglow ... peculiar to Quebec ... rainbow: Afterglow refers to   267–68 the arch of radiance caused by atmospheric particles scattering white light components in the western sky after sunset. The term embraces the purple and bright phases of twilight: the purple generated by particles in the red-rich middle atmosphere and the blue-rich upper atmosphere, and the brightness following the increasing depression of the sun preceding darkness. The duration of twilight phenomena depends on the angle of the sun's rays, thus is shortest at the equator and prolonged in higher latitudes like Quebec's. Cécile's subsequent reflection on the rainbow has its source in Genesis 9:8–17, where God sets his bow in the cloud as a sign of the covenant he establishes with Noah and his seed.

Book 6

273 *The Dying Count*: This title evokes sequences in the *Mémoires* of
Saint-Simon presenting lives and chapters of history from the perspectives of dying personages and titled "The Death of . . ."; Saint-
Simon placed these "titles" in the margins of his manuscript, which
is not formally divided into chapters.

273 Pontchartrain: Louis Phélypeaux, Comte de Pontchartrain (1643–
1727), a relative of Frontenac, was one of Louis XIV's most capable
ministers and his secretary of state at the novel's time period.

273 disappointment . . . release from office: Frontenac had repeatedly
requested transfers through Pontchartrain. Parkman quotes from a
1691 Frontenac letter asking consideration for a position closer to
the king and "a little more secure and tranquil than the government
of Canada"; the following year Frontenac begged additional funds
due to the expense of living in Canada, and in 1693 he appealed for
"some permanent and honorable place attended with the marks of
distinction" (2: 230–31). Frontenac received funds but his requests
for a position in France were ignored.

273 King had sent him . . . to save Canada: When, according to Parkman, Frontenac arrived at Quebec in October 1689 to succeed Bri-
say de Denonville as governor, the fur trade had been damaged by
Iroquois raids, Fort Niagara had been abandoned and demolished,
and in the Montreal area colonists had been massacred and homes
destroyed by an estimated fifteen hundred Iroquois. Cather also
follows Parkman in making Denonville's botched handling of the
Iroquois the cause both of these disasters and of Frontenac's reappointment. "Canada lay bewildered and benumbed under the shock
of this calamity," Parkman writes. "The Iroquois alone had brought

the colony to the brink of ruin; and now they would be supported by the neighboring British colonies" (2: 136). In fact, both the abandonment of the fort and the massacre occurred months after Frontenac's reappointment. However, the new governor was expected to save Canada by launching an attack on New York with the same number of troops Denonville had begged to have increased. The proposed invasion materialized as a series of minor raids and guerrilla warfare with the Iroquois.

Cross of St. Louis: Cross of the Military Order of St. Louis; see 274 note for 27 on "Count . . . last campaign."

Madame de Montespan: Françoise-Anthénaïs Rochechouart (1641– 274 1707), daughter of the Marquis de Mortemart and wife of the Marquis de Montespan, by whom she had two children, was a remarkably beautiful woman and gifted conversationalist who became lady-in-waiting to Queen Marie-Thérèse in 1664 and the king's mistress in 1667. Parkman reports that rumors linked Frontenac and Mme de Montespan before she became the king's mistress and that the king appointed Frontenac governor of Canada to be rid of a rival (2: 20). He quotes a scurrilous song of the day circulated secretly among the courtiers, which translates: "I am delighted that the king, our sire, loves La Montespan; I, Frontenac, am bursting with laughter, knowing what hangs on him; And I will say, without being one of the more stupid, you have only my leavings, King, you have only my leavings." Mme de Montespan lived at the court in this capacity for twenty-four years and bore the king seven children, four of whom survived into adulthood and were legitimized. She was eventually replaced in the king's affections by Mme de Maintenon (see note for 143 on "Madame de Maintenon") and in 1691 withdrew to the convent of Saint-Joseph and a life of charity and penance.

274   *La Vengeance*: Martin Desgreves does not list a vessel of this name until 1756. Cather's selection of the name may bear on the Mme de Montespan rivalry between Frontenac and the king.

275   peace of Rijswijk: The treaties ending the War of the Grand Alliance (1689–97), with France on one side and England, the Netherlands, Spain, and the Holy Roman Empire (central Europe) on the other, were signed at Rijswijk (Ryswick), a village near The Hague, the capital of the Netherlands, in September and October 1697. These treaties largely restored the conditions that had existed before the war, including prewar status quo in French and British colonies, which meant the return of Acadia (later Nova Scotia) to France.

275   the courtier's address: Frontenac was too proud for the fawning required for advancement at court and, Le Sueur notes, "tried to make his way by dint of self-assertion, but his success was only moderate. The enemies whom he thrust aside . . . could whisper at opportune moments, and . . . secure gratifications for themselves decidedly worth having" (354).

275–76   unpopular . . . geography of New France: Frontenac tried to convince Louis XIV of the need to occupy forts in the western territories to protect Indian allies, contain the English, and increase trade; however, the king listened to the advice of Intendant Champigny (see note for 67 on "Intendant, de Champigny") and the Jesuits, who recommended the abandonment of the forts and a general pulling back to the settled limits of the colony. "In vain Frontenac represented that to abandon the forest posts would be to resign to the English . . . the country itself," writes Parkman. "The royal ear was open to his opponents. . . . The king . . . wished to govern Canada as he governed a province of France; and this could be done only by keeping the population within prescribed bounds" (2: 301).

"After my reappointment . . .": These audiences would have taken   276
place in spring 1689, the year of Frontenac's reappointment.

Fontainebleau . . . carp basins: The royal hunting seat at Fon-   276–77
tainebleau Forest, some seventy-five miles southeast of Paris, dates
from the twelfth century and its earliest extant buildings from the
sixteenth, when Francis I had the medieval buildings pulled down
and imported Italian artists and artisans to create a "New Rome."
Henry II and IV and Louis XIV, XV, and XVI continued the expansion of the palace, adjacent to which is an extensive carp pond with a
pavilion Louis XIV had renovated.

carp tore her to pieces: In describing the pleasure Louis XIV took   277
in his various carp ponds and how he singled out particular fish for
comment, Saint-Simon includes a scene at the Marly Palace suggesting ingredients of Cather's Fontainebleau scene. The king is
interrupted at the pond by news that the Duchess of Bourgogne
(see note for 237–38 on "Princess of Savoie") has miscarried. He
flies into a rage as his gardeners look on but then announces he is
glad because he dislikes being inconvenienced by the duchess's
pregnancies (3:112–14). In actuality, carp (*Cyrinus carpio*), an edible
freshwater fish introduced to Europe from Asia and frequently
bred for ponds and lakes, are incapable of consuming anything
larger than a very small mammal (March 123). Carp can grow to
three feet in length and weigh twenty-five pounds; they usually eat
insects and aquatic plants.

the Cardinal: The rusty carp is probably named for Jules Mazarin   277
(1602–61), a lay cardinal who served as first minister to Anne of
Austria during Louis XIV's childhood (see note for 51 on "Queen
Mother"), but it could refer to Armand Jean du Plessis, Duc de
Richelieu (1585–1642), French cardinal and Louis XIII's first min-
ister, who appointed Mazarin to the council of state.

279   Pont-Neuf: The oldest of surviving Paris bridges, the Pont-Neuf connects the Right and Left Banks of the Seine (see note for 198 on "the Seine") to the western tip of Île de la Cité, the Seine's largest island and cradle of Paris. Built in halves between 1578 and 1604, the bridge has a broken axis and twelve rounded arches; it was once crowded with stalls.

280–83   curious dream . . . Noémi: Le Sueur laments the lack of biographical information on Frontenac prior to his governorship of Canada (61), and both Parkman and Eccles begin their biographies with this 1672 appointment after prefatory treatments of Frontenac's marriage and early military career. The childhood details in the novel as well as the nurse Noémi are probably fictional and based on the common practice of nobles placing their young children in the care of servants. The rearing of Frontenac's own young son by a nurse in the village of Clion near Château Île Savary (Parkman 2: 16) may have suggested to Cather the conditions of his father's childhood. Pontoise is a town northwest of Paris. See notes for 36 on "unfortunate marriage" and for 284 on "son . . . killed."

283–84   Madame de la Grange Frontenac . . . long letter: In spite of their estrangement (see note for 36 on "unfortunate marriage"), Frontenac and his wife regularly corresponded. Parkman quotes the following excerpts from a 1691 letter from Frontenac to Pontchartrain requesting a transfer and attempting to correct rumors (see note for 273 on "disappointment"): "Please permit my wife . . . to refresh your memory now and then [that New France has been made 'a little more secure' under his leadership]. . . . I have been informed by my wife that charges have been made to you against my conduct since my return to this country" (2: 231–32).

son . . . killed: In May 1651 the Frontenacs had a son, François-   284
Louis, who as a child was left in the care of servants, as was customary in noble families during this time. François-Louis had a career
in the army and became colonel of the Munster regiment (Eccles
29). According to Parkman he was killed in service in Germany (2:
325).

In spiritual matters: Cather's estimate of Frontenac's ambiguous   284
relationship with the church has its source in Parkman's biography:
"However heterodox in doctrine, [Frontenac] was still wedded to
the observances of the Church, and practised them, under the Récollets, with an assiduity that made full amends to his conscience
for the vivacity with which he opposed the rest of the clergy" (2:
313).

Baron de La Hontan: Louis-Armand de Lom d'Arce (1666–c.   285
1716), French soldier, explorer, and writer, spent ten years in New
France (1683–93), explored the Mississippi, fought the Iroquois,
and in 1690 helped defend Quebec against the English. His wit and
cynical scorn of ecclesiastical authority found a sympathetic ear in
Frontenac, who gave him lodgings at the Château Saint-Louis and
engaged him as an adviser and traveling companion. La Hontan's
fame rests on the 1703 publication of his colorful travel memoirs,
known in English as *New Voyages to North America*, and on a series of
fictional dialogues with an Indian chief describing the values of
primitive life over civilization. The latter contributed to the eighteenth-century vogue of the "noble savage" and influenced the
writings of Montesquieu, Voltaire, and Swift.

brown Holland: A cotton or linen fabric heavily starched for use in   286
bookbinding, window shades, and clothing; unbleached holland is
referred to as "brown."

531

287   Saint-Nicholas-des-Champs: A fifteenth-century parish church on
the Right Bank of the Seine with major additions from the sixteenth
and seventeenth centuries combining Flamboyant Gothic and Renaissance styles. The church contains some twenty-eight chapels,
and it would have been in one of these that Frontenac's heart was
buried. (Parkman tells the story of Frontenac's wife refusing to
receive her husband's heart [2: 309].) During the Revolution the
church became the Temple of Marriage and Fidelity, its artworks
were scattered, and the graves of the nobility were destroyed. See
note for 298 on "Montmort chapel."

288   river not the St. Lawrence: A reference to the Seine; see note for
198 on "the Seine."

288   Pont-Marie: A bridge first built in 1635 by Jean-Christophe Marie,
developer of Île Saint-Louis, at his own expense and named for
him. Pont-Marie connects Île Saint-Louis to the Quai des Célestins. See notes below on "bells" and "Île Saint-Louis."

288   Port-au-Foin: A port on the Right Bank of the Seine west of Pont-
Neuf (see note for 279 on "Pont-Neuf") opened in the sixteenth
century for handling hay.

288   bells . . . Célestins' and . . . Saint-Paul: See notes for 12 on "Quai des
Célestins" and for 35 on "parish of Saint-Paul."

288   Île Saint-Louis . . . were joined: This Parisian island in the Seine,
connected by a pedestrian bridge to Île de la Cité (the cradle of
Paris and site of its cathedral), was developed into lots for expensive
residences by Jean-Christophe Marie during a project begun in
1627 and lasting more than thirty-five years. Marie joined two islets
(Île aux Vaches and Île Notre-Dame) of swampy pasture separated
in the fourteenth century by a defense canal and connected the

restored island to the Quai des Célestins on the Right Bank and the Tournelle Castle area on the Left by bridges. The fashionable area that resulted was named Île Saint-Louis in 1726 when its parish church, Saint-Louis-en-l'Île, was completed and consecrated.

A Saint-Malo . . . chargés de bléd: At Saint-Malo, beautiful seaport, /   289
Laden with oats, laden with wheat. Cather uses an archaic spelling of wheat ("bléd") to suggest the medieval origin of this song. See notes for 249 on "Saint-Malo" and for 255 on "*A Saint-Malo.*"

poêle: Stove.   290

messieurs les clients: Gentlemen customers.   290

mixture of rhubarb and senna: According to Culpeper, both rhu-   291
barb (*Rheum rhubarbum*) and senna (see note for 241–42 on "bay leaves") were used as purgatives, but among other uses of rhubarb he lists relief for aches and pains and sciatica, which would relate to Mme Pommier's rheumatism.

"*Et préféreriez-vous . . . Et votre père?*": "And will you prefer the pills   291
or the liquid, Mr. Noel?" "The pills, please, Miss. And [where is] your father?"

worldly ends . . . brandy traffic: During both his terms as governor,   294
Frontenac not only ignored clerical demands to stop and royal efforts to limit supplying the Indians with brandy but actually augmented its use. During the guerrilla warfare against the Iroquois in the 1690s, Frontenac sent annual shipments of brandy and trade goods, ostensibly as defense supplies, to expand the fur trade westward into Sioux and Assiniboin countries (Eccles 276).

Septentrional France: Northern or Boreal France (Quebec).   294

295   English and Dutch traders: By the middle of the seventeenth century, French dominance of the fur trade had been challenged by the
Dutch, who supplied the Iroquois with firearms in an effort to
divert trade from Montreal to Fort Orange (Parkman 1: 548). By
the 1680s the English in New York were increasing the competition from the south and threatening French control to the north
and west through the Hudson's Bay Company. Auclair's argument
for brandy was one "frequently advanced by Frontenac's coterie"
but, according to Eccles, "will not bear too close an examination"
(66). For one thing, English authorities fined or whipped traders
caught supplying liquor to the Indians, and the Iroquois themselves
petitioned the New York governor to prohibit rum sales "since our
soldiers cannot be kept within bounds when they are drunk" (qtd.
in Eccles 64). See note below.

295   colony exists by the fur trade: By the end of the sixteenth century,
furs (beaver particularly) had replaced fish as the economic impetus
of French exploration, but with the establishment of Quebec as a
missionary and trading headquarters, the French court attempted
to contain territorial expansion and develop the colony agricultur-
ally to make it less dependent on the Indians. But the depletion of
furs in eastern areas pushed the trade westward, and an ongoing
conflict arose as to whether colonizing or fur trading was primary.
Frontenac continually ignored royal efforts to restrain this trade as
well as clerical efforts to stop the use of brandy to help it flourish. In
the final years of his life Frontenac struggled with the king's order
to close trading posts on the frontier because the glut of Canadian
beaver was collapsing the French fur market. "Frontenac was extremely bitter at this turn of events," writes Eccles (288). See notes
above on "worldly ends" and "English and Dutch traders."

Father Joseph . . . take the casket: Cather further identifies this   298
Récollet as the priest who attended Frontenac at death and administered last rites. According to Parkman and Le Sueur this was
Father Oliver Goyer, a friend and confessor, who also delivered the
funeral oration, which Parkman includes in his biography (Parkman 2: 308–13; Le Sueur 359). Eccles's more recent scholarship
reveals Bishop Saint-Vallier as administering to his old enemy on
his deathbed (324–25).

Montmort chapel: A chapel in Saint-Nicholas-des-Champs built by   298
Henri-Louis Habert, seigneur de Montmort, counselor of the king,
a founder of the French Academy, and husband of Frontenac's favorite sister, Marie-Henriette de Buade (who had already been buried
there). Frontenac was always welcome at his sister and brother-in-
law's house and met eminent personages of the day there (March
503). See note for 287 on "Saint-Nicholas-des-Champs."

de Champigny: See note for 67 on "Intendant, de Champigny."   300

Count . . . received the Sacrament . . . last word: Both Parkman and Le   301–02
Sueur emphasize Frontenac's full possession of faculties and compo-
sure at death. Le Sueur adds that the clerical party expected a final
statement of contrition from Frontenac for his ongoing opposition to
church policies but that "in this they were disappointed" (356).

Madame de Champigny: See note for 302 on "Madame de Cham-   301
pigny."

Hector de Callières: Louis Hector de Callières (1648–1703), of   301
Norman nobility, made his career in the army, came to Canada as
governor of Montreal in 1684, and was an able commander in the
wars with the Iroquois and the English. He was made governor of
Canada after Frontenac's death and held that office until his own

535

death in 1703. His most significant achievement as governor was negotiating a peace with the Iroquois in 1701.

302   Madame de Champigny got a mirror: This is the second charitable act (see note for 122 on "Madame de Champigny . . . sent her *carrosse*") attributed to the intendant's wife, Marie-Madeleine de Chaspoux, who in 1686, while pregnant, accompanied her husband to Canada, where she subsequently gave birth to a daughter. She is chiefly remembered as the beneficiary, along with her husband, of what Parkman refers to as Frontenac's deathbed "mark of kind feeling" (2: 309): she received Frontenac's personal reliquary, "filled with the most rare and precious relics that could be found" (Eccles 325), and Frontenac asked her husband to accept a treasured crucifix given him by his sister. See note for 147 on "sacred relics . . . work miracles."

303   Latin poets: March suggests (800) that Auclair is recalling Book I, lines 94–95, of Virgil's *Aeneid*, wherein Aeneas, in the midst of a heavy storm at sea, raises his hand to heaven and cries: "O thrice and four times blessed those whose lot it was to die before the faces of their fathers beneath the lofty walls of Troy."

304   "*Petite tête de garçon!*": Literally, "Little head of a boy," referring to the shingle cut of Cécile's hair. See note for 14 on "hair shingled."

306   "*je n'ai pas de chance*": "I am not lucky" or, more colloquially, "I'm out of luck."

307   gold-coloured wine from the South: The wine described is white — although both the Bordeaux and southern Rhone regions are more famous for red vintages (see note for 203 on "fiery Bordeaux") — and is most likely one of the rich sweet wines from the townships of the Sauternes district about twenty-five miles southeast of Bor-

deaux, where a beneficial mold causes the ripened grapes to shrivel, leaving a sugar-laden fruit that contributes a honeyed aroma and flavor.

Epilogue

Governor General and Monsieur Vaudreuil, the Intendant: Philippe de Rigaud de Vaudreuil (c. 1643–1725) arrived in Canada in 1687 as commander of troops to fight the Iroquois. He enjoyed the confidence of Count Frontenac and in 1703 became governor general, remaining in that office until his death. There is some confusion on Cather's part here because the Marquis de Vaudreuil never held the office of intendant. 309

La Manon: Demerliac (245) lists a vessel with this name in service in 1683. 309

Saint-Vallier . . . returning . . . a very old man: Cather's description of the altered bishop and the crowd is historically accurate. Alfred Rambaud reports from contemporary sources that the "whole town was there . . . [and] found him aged, tired, changed in appearance. He was no longer the slender, brisk, haughty young bishop of the early years of his episcopate, but a melancholy old man with heavy, drooping shoulders and thick, flabby jowls" (*Dictionary of Canadian Biography* 2: 333). Rambaud adds that during the following winter the bishop almost died and that for the rest of his life (he died in 1727) Saint-Vallier struggled with poor health as well as unpopularity. 309–10

Archidiacre: Archdeacon, an official delegated by a bishop to administer part of a diocese. The office today would be filled by an auxiliary bishop or a vicar general. March identifies this archdeacon 310 as Joseph de la Colombière (27), who became Bishop Saint-Vallier's vicar general in 1698, the same year he received the title of archidiacre.

311   *La Seine*, was captured: Demerliac lists this storeship built in Rochefort as having forty-four to forty-six cannons and a tonnage of 640; it was put into service in 1698 (81). Mother Juchereau de Saint-Ignace mentions Saint-Vallier's departure for France on this ship in October 1700 (297), and March provides an account of its capture four years later: "The boat was escorting several merchant vessels to Quebec carrying an extremely rich cargo, many ecclesiastics, and several of the richest Canadian settlers. On July 26, 1704, the commander, M. Le Chevalier de Maupeaux, seeing what appeared to be English barks and giving chase, suddenly found himself in the middle of the Virginia Fleet. Maupeaux could not fight well because he refused to throw overboard the baggage that blocked his guns, and *La Seine* was captured and taken to Plymouth and then to London, where it was sold for 300,000 pounds. Bishop Saint-Vallier was among the prisoners taken" (688).

311   Bishop . . . prisoner of state: Saint-Vallier was roughly treated at the capture of *La Seine*, "even insulted by a sailor who seized him by the throat to take his pectoral cross" (*Dictionary of Canadian Biography* 2: 232). He and sixteen other ecclesiastics in his company were carried to England as prisoners, the bishop remaining in captivity in towns on the outskirts of London for five years. England's Queen Anne used Saint-Vallier as a pawn to force the release of the Baron de Mean, senior canon of the Belgian city of Liège, who had been seized by Louis XIV for exchanging dangerous correspondence with the enemies of France. Louis refused to consent to the exchange until 1709, partly because he feared intrigue and partly

538

because enemies of the bishop wanted his captivity prolonged to force his resignation.

town near Farnham: Farnham is a market town in Surrey about 311 forty miles southwest of London; it was at this time the residence of the bishops of Winchester.

his enemies . . . period of detention: Immediately upon his libera- 311 tion from England and arrival in France in 1709, Saint-Vallier requested to return to Canada (Laval had died the previous year, and Quebec was without a bishop). However, the king kept him waiting in France. Drummond explains that "Louis XIV . . . got his minister, de Pontchartrain [see note for 273 on "Pontchartrain"], to bombard the bishop with all sorts of reasons for resigning his diocese, and, finally, seeing that he could not bend that iron will, allowed him to return" (429). Although Saint-Vallier was aware of his unpopularity, he repeatedly wrote the king of the grievous consequences of preventing a bishop's return to his flock. In the summer of 1713, Louis capitulated and Saint-Vallier sailed for Quebec from La Rochelle.

sympathies of Madame de Maintenon: See note for 143 on "Ma- 312 dame de Maintenon."

leaden mantle of humility: In *Inferno*, canto 22, two hypocritical 312 friars guilty of inciting strife explain to Dante how they can barely creak along under heavily leaded gilt cloaks; in *Purgatorio*, canto 12, the proud make their way around the mountain doubled under slabs of rock that press down according to the degree of their sin. Cather combines both punishments in her portrait of the repentant Saint-Vallier.

314 Hôpital Général: Like most of Bishop Saint-Vallier's projects, this one was fraught with controversy. When planning the hospital, Saint-Vallier initially involved the Sisters of the Congregation, but when they stepped aside in 1692 to establish schools, he prevailed upon the Hospitallers to staff it. The Hôtel-Dieu nuns at first resisted (see note for 45 on "Jeanne Franc Juchereau") but subsequently administered the hospital until 1965, when it was taken over by the government. Drummond explains that to finance this project the bishop transferred funds from (and thus annihilated) Quebec's very efficient Bureau des Pauvres and had to take charge of the poor himself. Nevertheless, he concludes, Saint-Vallier "succeeded in founding a hospital in which the poor have been tenderly provided for . . . for the past two hundred years" (427). Located at Notre-Dame-des-Anges (see note for 128 on "*cabine*") on the south bank of the St. Charles, the General Hospital houses a museum and displays the altar, bed, and ossuary of its founder.

314 My good daughters: The Augustinian Hospitallers, the nuns of the Hôtel Dieu. See note for 49 on "Hospitalières."

315 remainder of my life . . . chaplain: Rambaud comments on the severity of the living conditions and regimen of the bishop during his last years: daily mass for the nuns, sharing of his single meal with the poor, administering to the sick and dying, and accompanying the dead to the hospital cemetery. "This austerity was accompanied by untiring activity to assure . . . orthodoxy and morality in his immense American diocese . . . creating parishes, building churches, condemning Jansenism . . . [and] pursuing . . . libertines, drunkards, traffickers in spirits, and tavern-keepers" (*Dictionary of Canadian Biography* 2: 333).

foxglove water: The foxglove plant (*Digitalis purpurea*) is best 316
known medicinally for the production of heart-stimulating drugs
(dropsy is characteristic of congestive heart failure), but Culpeper
also notes its importance as a topical salve and as a purgative for the
liver and spleen.

liquorice for ... cough: Culpeper writes that when boiled in water, 316
the licorice plant (*Glycyrrhiza glabra*) makes a good drink for those
who have a dry cough or hoarseness, or wheezing and shortness of
breath.

death of the young Duc and Duchesse: See notes for 237–38 on 316
"Duc de Bourgogne" and "Princess of Savoie." The great pleasure
that Louis XIV took in his grandson and his grandson's wife was cut
short when the young couple and their older surviving son died
within a few days of each other in the winter of 1712. The king was
especially devastated to lose the company of the princess, and
Saint-Simon writes that "[w]ith her death all joy vanished, all forms
of pleasure, entertainment, and delight. Darkness covered the face
of the Court. She was its light and life; she was everywhere at once;
she was its centre; her presence permeated its inner life. And if,
after her death, the Court continued, it merely lingered on. No
princess was ever more worth regretting" (4: 408).

Salle d'Apollon: The Apollo Salon was the throne room of Louis 317
XIV and the last and sixth in the suite known as the Grand Apartment of the Palace of Versailles (see note for 38 on "Versailles").
The ceiling contains a fresco by Charles de La Fosse (1636–1716),
Apollo in a Sun Chariot, which identifies the room as appropriate for
the "Sun King." Dances and concerts were held here and ambas-
sadors received.

317 poison . . . Duc d'Orléans: Although doctors were fairly certain that the Duc and Duchess de Bourgogne and their son had died as the result of either measles or scarlet fever, there were rumors of poisoning. The chief suspect in these rumors was Philippe, Duc d'Orléans (1674–1723), the son of King Louis XIV's brother (Philippe d'Orléans) and regent during the minority of Louis XV, because he was close in the line of succession to the throne. Saint-Simon also believed the royal family had been poisoned, but he was certain that the king's illegitimate son by Mme de Montespan, Louis-Auguste, Duc du Maine, was responsible. The latter was also agitating to be king someday, and by an edict in July 1714 he was admitted to the succession of the crown with his full brother and their male descendants if no prince of royal blood was available.

318 the Dauphin: Louis, the third and only surviving son of the Duc de Bourgogne, was born at Versailles in 1710 and became Louis XV of France five years later.

318 Duc de Berry . . . mischance: The youngest brother of the Duc de Bourgogne, the Duc de Berry (1686–1714), died in a hunting accident before the king himself died, thus the Duc d'Orléans did serve as regent until his own death in 1723.

318–19 new century . . . nothing changes: Saint-Vallier's comments are both prophetic and, ironically, blind: he anticipates the social and political upheavals of the revolution of 1789, but he is shortsighted regarding the changes that will occur in Quebec when it falls to the English in 1759.

319 West India trade: The Spanish were the first Europeans to colonize on the archipelago (1496), but by the middle of the seventeenth century the French, English, and Dutch had established settle-

ments and were competing for the trade generated by sugarcane plantations. These islands became part of the scheme of Louis XIV and his finance minister, Jean Baptiste Colbert, to strengthen the French economy (see note for 30 on "carpet"). Jean Talon, intendant of New France (1665–72), cooperated in the resulting triangular trade: fish, peas, and lumber from Canada were exchanged for sugar, molasses, and rum from the islands, and these exchanged for French manufactured goods for Canada (Parkman 1: 1252–53). For adventurous young Canadian males, joining the crews in the West India trade began to vie in popularity with life in the woods as coureurs de bois.

"Courage, mon bourgeois": "Take heart, my friend" or, literally, "Take courage, my fellow citizen."   320

hospital out on the river Charles: Actually, the river St. Charles; see note for 314 on "Hôpital Général."   321

a Dauphinois: Bishop Saint-Vallier came from Dauphiné. See notes for 137 on "Monseigneur de Saint-Vallier" and for 143 on "Dauphiné."   321

Works Consulted

Adams, Henry. *Mont Saint Michel and Chartres.* 1904. New York: Viking Penguin, 1986.

Aquinas, Thomas. "Treatise on Man" (Question 75, Third Article). *Summa Theologica.* Trans. English Dominicans. 5 vols. Westminster, Md.: Glencoe, 1981. 1: 365–66.

Barbeau, Marius. *Jongleur Songs of Old Quebec.* New Brunswick, N.J.: Rutgers, 1962.

Baring-Gould, S. *The Lives of the Saints.* Rev. ed. 16 vols. Edinburgh: Grant, 1914.

Bennett, Mildred R. *The World of Willa Cather*. New edition. Lincoln: U of Nebraska P, 1961.

Boone, Marylou. *Terre et Feu: Four Centuries of French Ceramics from the Boone Collection*. Seattle: U of Washington P, 1998.

Brienzo, Gary. *Willa Cather's Transforming Vision: New France and the American Northeast*. Selinsgrove, Pa.: Susquehanna UP, 1994.

Britton, Nathaniel, and Addison Brown. *An Illustrated Flora of the Northern United States and Canada*. 1913. 3 vols. New York: Dover, 1970.

Brown, E. K., and Leon Edel. *Willa Cather: A Critical Biography*. New York: Knopf, 1953.

Butler's Lives of the Saints. Rev. ed. Ed. Herbert J. Thurston and Donald Attwater. 4 vols. London: Burns and Oates, 1981.

Campana, Michele. *European Carpets*. Trans. Margaret Grosland. London: Hamlyn, 1969.

The Canadian Encyclopedia. 2nd ed. Ed. James H. Marsh. 4 vols. Edmonton: Hurtig, 1988.

Cather, Willa. *On Writing: Critical Studies on Writing as an Art*. New York: Knopf, 1949.

The Catholic Encyclopedia: An International Work of Reference. Ed. Charles G. Hebermann et al. 15 vols. New York: Appleton, 1907–12.

Champlain, Samuel de. *Voyages of Samuel de Champlain, 1604–1618*. Ed. W. L. Grant. Trans. Charles P. Otis. New York: Scribner's, 1907.

Chapais, J. C. "Three Centuries of Agriculture." *Province of Quebec. Canada and Its Provinces*. Ed. Adam Shortt and Arthur Doughty. Edinburgh ed. 23 vols. Toronto: Publishers Assoc., 1914. 16: 505–27.

Charlevoix, Peter Francis Xavier (de). *History and General Description of New France*. 1744. Trans. John Gilmary Shea. 6 vols. 1866–72. Chicago: Loyola UP, 1962.

Choquette, Leslie. *Frenchmen into Peasants: Modernity and Tradition in the Peopling of French Canada*. Cambridge, Mass.: Harvard UP, 1997.

Colombo, John R., ed. *Colombo's Canadian Quotations*. Edmonton: Hurtig, 1974.

Culpeper, Nicholas. *Culpeper's Complete Herbal*. London: Foulsham, 1975.

De Brumath, A. Leblond. *Bishop Laval. The Makers of Canada*. Parkman edition. Ed. Duncan C. Scott and Pelham Edgar. 20 vols. Toronto: Morang, 1910. Vol. 2.

De Ligney, Francis. *Catholic Gems, or Treasures of the Church*. New York: Catholic Publications, 1887.

Demerliac, Alain. *La Marine de Louis XIV*. Nice: Omega, 1992.

Dictionary of Biblical Theology. Rev. ed. Ed. Xavier Leon-Dufour. New York: Seabury, 1973.

Dictionary of Canadian Biography. Ed. George W. Brown et al. Vol. 1 (1000 to 1700). Toronto: U of Toronto P, 1966. Corrected reprint, 1979.

——. Ed. David M. Hayne et al. Vol. 2 (1701 to 1740). Toronto: U of Toronto P, 1969.

Douville, Raymond, and Jacques Casanova. *Daily Life in Early Canada*. Trans. Carola Congreve. New York: Macmillan, 1967.

Drummond, Lewis. "The Church and the Colony." *New France, 1535–1760. Canada and Its Provinces*. 2: 379–442.

Duke, James A. *The Green Pharmacy*. Emmaus, Pa.: Rodale, 1997.

Eccles, W. J. *Frontenac: The Courtier Governor*. Toronto: McClelland & Stewart, 1959.

545

Eusebius. *The History of the Church*. Trans. G. A. Williamson. New York: Penguin, 1989.

Faillon, Étienne-Michel. *L'Héroine du Canada: ou Vie de Mlle Le Ber*. Montreal: Soeurs de La Congrégation, 1860.

Farmer, David Hugh. *The Oxford Dictionary of Saints*. New York: Oxford UP, 1982.

Flenley, Ralph. "Introduction." *A History of Montreal 1640–1672 from the French of Dollier de Casson*. 1871. Trans and ed. Ralph Flenley. London: Dent, 1928. 3–49.

Forman, Max L. *The World's Greatest Quotations*. Jericho, N.Y.: Exposition, 1970.

Funk & Wagnalls Standard Dictionary of Folklore, Mythology, and Legend. Ed. Maria Leach and Jerome Fried. New York: Harper & Row, 1984.

Gauthier, Nancy. *L'Évangélisation des pays de la Moselle*. Paris: Editions de Boceard, 1980.

Glasscheib, H. S. *The March of Medicine*. New York: Putnam, 1964.

Gosselin, Abbé A. E. "Education in Canada under the French Regime." *The Province of Quebec. Canada and Its Provinces*. 16: 323–93.

Hardon, John A. *Modern Catholic Dictionary*. Garden City, N.Y.: Doubleday, 1980.

Harris, Richard. "Willa Cather and Pierre Charron on Wisdom: The Skeptical Philosophy of *Shadows on the Rock*." *Willa Cather's Canadian and Old World Connections*. Ed. Robert Thacker and Michael A. Peterman. Lincoln: U of Nebraska P, 1999. 66–79.

Harvut, H. *Notices sur les rues, ruelles, promenades, quais, places, et fortifications de la ville de Saint-Malo*. Saint-Malo: n.p., 1884.

Herbst, Ron, and Sharon T. Herbst. *Wine Lover's Companion*. Hauppauge, N.Y.: Barron's, 1995.

Hough, Romeyn Beck. *Handbook of the Trees of the Northern States and Canada East of the Rocky Mountains.* Lowville, N.Y.: Hough, 1936.

Huschke, Ralph E. *Glossary of Meteorology.* Boston: American Meteorological Soc., 1970.

Jenness, Diamond. *The Indians of Canada.* 5th ed. Ottawa: National Museum of Canada, 1960.

The Jesuit Relations and Allied Documents: Travels and Explorations of the Jesuit Missionaries in New France, 1610–1791. Ed. Reuben Gold Thwaites. 73 vols. Cleveland: Burrows, 1896–1901. (See Kenton below.)

Juchereau [de la Ferté] de Saint-Ignace, Jeanne-Françoise, and Marie-Andrée Duplessis de Sainte-Hélène. *Les annales de l'Hôtel-Dieu de Québec, 1636–1716.* 1751. Ed. Albert Jamet. Quebec: Hôtel-Dieu, 1939.

Kates, George N. "Willa Cather's Unfinished Avignon Story." *Willa Cather: Collected Stories.* New York: Vintage, 1992. 464–93.

Kenton, Edna, ed. *The Jesuit Relations and Allied Documents.* New York: Boni, 1925. (Selections from the 73-volume series cited above.)

La Hontan, Louis Armand de Lom d'Arce, baron de. *New Voyages to North America.* 1703. Ed. Reuben Gold Thwaites. Chicago, 1905.

Lescarbot, Marc. *Novia Francia.* 1606. Trans. P. Erondelle. Intro. H. P. Biggar. New York: Harper, 1928.

Le Sueur, William D. *Count Frontenac. The Makers of Canada.* Parkman ed. Vol. 3. Toronto: Morang, 1910.

Lewis, Edith. *Willa Cather Living.* New York: Knopf, 1953.

Lodge, Anthony R. *French: From Dialect to Standard.* London: Routledge, 1993.

Lossky, Andrew. *Louis XIV and the French Monarchy*. New Brunswick, N.J.: Rutgers UP, 1994.

Madigan, Mark J. "Willa Cather and Dorothy Canfield Fisher: A Literary Correspondence." Thesis. U. of Vermont, 1987.

March, John. *A Reader's Companion to the Fiction of Willa Cather*. Ed. Marilyn Arnold. New York: Greenwood, 1993.

Marshall, Joyce, trans. and ed. *Word from New France: The Selected Letters of Marie de l'Incarnation*. Toronto: Oxford UP, 1967.

Martin Desgreves, Roger. *Navires de Saint-Malo, 17e–18e siècles*. Rennes: Association Parchemin, 1992.

Maurois, André. *A History of France*. Trans. Henry L. Binsse and Gerard Hopkins. New York: Farrar, 1956.

McKenzie, John L. *Dictionary of the Bible*. New York: Macmillan, 1965.

Montaigne, Michel Eyquem de. *The Complete Essays*. Trans. Donald M. Frame. Stanford, Calif: Stanford UP, 1958.

The New Encyclopedia Britannica. 15th ed. Ed. Philip W. Goetz. 32 vols. Chicago: Encyclopedia Britannica, 1988.

Osgood, William, and Leslie Hurley. *The Snowshoe Book*. 2nd ed. Brattleboro, Vt.: Greene, 1975.

Palou, Francisco. *Life of Fray Junípero Serra*. 1787. Trans. Maynard J. Geiger. Washington, D.C.: Academy of Franciscan History, 1955.

Parkman, Francis. *France and England in North America*. 1851–92. 2 vols. New York: Library of America, 1983.

Plutarch. "Alexander." *The Age of Alexander: Nine Greek Lives by Plutarch*. Trans. Ian Scott-Kilvert. New York: Penguin, 1973. 252–334.

Ragueneau, Paul. *La Vie de la Mère Catherine de Saint-Augustin*. 1671. Quebec: Hôtel-Dieu, 1923.

Saint-Simon, Louis de Rouvroy, duc de. *Mémoires*. 1788. Ed. Yves

Coirault. 8 vols. Paris: Gallimard, 1983–88. (Passages quoted in the notes translated by David Stouck.)

Schwartz, Marion. *A History of Dogs in the Early Americas*. New Haven: Yale UP, 1997.

Scott, Abbé H. A. *Bishop Laval. The Makers of Canada*. Anniversary edition. Ed. W. L. Grant. 12 vols. London: Oxford, 1926. Vol. 1 (with Dionne, N. E. *Champlain*).

Sergeant, Elizabeth Shepley. *Willa Cather: A Memoir*. 1953. Lincoln: U of Nebraska P, 1963.

Shea, John Gerald, and Paul Nolt Wagner. *Provincial Furniture*. New York: Bruce, 1938.

Thwaites, Reuben Gold. "Historical Introduction to The Jesuit Relations and Allied Documents." Reprinted in Kenton xix–liv.

Toulouse-Lautrec, Mapie de. *Good French Cooking*. Trans. Charlotte Turgeon. London: Hamlyn, 1966.

Les Ursulines de Québec, depuis leur établissement jusqu'à nos jours. 4 vols. Quebec, 1863–66; 2nd ed., 1866–78.

Voragine, Jacobus de. "Saint Mary of Egypt." *The Golden Legend*. Trans. William Granger Ryan. 2 vols. Princeton, N.J.: Princeton UP, 1993. 1: 227–29.

Weiser, Francis X. *Handbook of Christian Feasts and Customs: The Year of the Lord in Liturgy and Folklore*. New York: Harcourt, Brace & World, 1958.

Wheaton, Barbara. *Savoring the Past: The French Kitchen and Table from 1300 to 1789*. Philadelphia: U of Pennsylvania P, 1983.

Williams, Norman Lloyd. *Sir Walter Raleigh*. London: Eyre and Spottiswoode, 1962.

Wilson, P. Roy. *The Beautiful Old Houses of Quebec*. Toronto: U of Toronto P, 1975.

Woodress, James. *Willa Cather: A Literary Life*. Lincoln: U of Nebraska P, 1987.

549

Textual Apparatus

Textual Essay

THIS seventh volume of the Cather Edition presents a
critical text of Willa Cather's thirteenth book, *Shadows
on the Rock*, published by Alfred A. Knopf on 1 August 1931.
A late typescript of the novel is housed in the Division of
Manuscripts and Archives of the New York Public Library. A
carbon copy of this typescript is housed in Archives and Special Collections, Love Library, University of Nebraska–
Lincoln. The first British edition was published in London
by Cassell in January 1932, and the book is included in volume 10 of the Autograph Edition of Cather's fiction, which
appeared in 1938. A second Knopf edition, the text set line-
for-line in the same typeface, appeared in April 1946. No
other true editions were published during Cather's lifetime,
nor have proofs antedating or contemporary with these texts
been located. A four-page holograph fragment of what may
have been originally intended as a final chapter of the novel
was sold at a Sotheby's auction on 6 November 2001 to Drew
University; in it Auclair laments that he has made no provision for Cécile's future. Eventually, Cather concluded the

novel with an epilogue, and Auclair's lament was not used. No other manuscripts are known to exist.

The editorial procedure of the Cather Edition is guided by the protocols of the Modern Language Association's Committee on Scholarly Editions. We begin with a bibliographical survey of the history of the text, sorting out any problems it may present. Making a calendar of extant texts, we collect and examine examples of all texts published during Cather's lifetime, identifying those forms that may be authoritative (i.e., that involved or may have involved Cather's participation or intervention). These forms are then collated against a base text serving as a standard of collation.[1] The collations provide lists of substantive and accidental variations among these forms.[2] A conflation, constructed from the collations, then provides us with a list of all substantive pre- or post-copy-text changes in all relevant (authoritative) editions. After an analysis of this conflation, we choose a copy-text and prepare a critical text (an emended copy-text). The collations and their conflation also provide the materials for an emendations list that identifies changes the editors have made in the copy-text, and a Table of Rejected Substantives relevant to a history of the text as contained in its various authoritative forms. In a separate procedure, we make a list of end-hyphenated compounds with their proper resolution.[3]

This essay includes discussions of the composition of *Shadows on the Rock* and of the production and printing history of the text during Cather's lifetime; an analysis of the changes made in the text during this period; a rationale for the choice of copy-text for this edition; and a statement of the policy under which emendations have been introduced into the copy-text. All page and line references are to the text of the present edition, unless otherwise noted.

Composition

Shadows on the Rock sprang from a decision Cather and Edith Lewis made in June 1928 to go to Grand Manan Island, New Brunswick, by way of Quebec, "in order to try a new route and see some new country" (Lewis 153), and from the sudden illness of Lewis, who "was ordered to bed for ten days" after they arrived in Quebec (Brown 270). The visit brought back Cather's memories of France and French culture: Lewis notes that Cather was "overwhelmed by the flood of memory, recognition, surmise it called up" (153), and almost at once she began reading Parkman and other historians of the *ancien régime* in Canada, visiting sites and storing up impressions of the city and its past. She was so caught up in her enthusiasm that she revisited the city several times before the new novel was finished.

According to Lewis, Cather "began writing *Shadows on the Rock* that fall [1928] at the Grosvenor" (156), the hotel in New York City where she lived for some five years after being forced from her Bank Street apartment by new construction. Progress on the book was slow; Cather had to not only "work up her material" (Woodress 420) by reading extensively in historical materials but also deal with the aftermath of her mother's stroke in December 1928. Cather spent two months in the spring of 1929 with her paralyzed mother in California, but she was able to work on the book fairly steadily the following winter. She made another trip to Quebec at New Year's of 1930, visited her mother for six weeks thereafter, and on 14 May 1930 sailed with Lewis for France. There, "for two months we followed the trail of Count Frontenac in Paris" (Lewis 158) and other locations in France — Saint-Malo, Avignon, Aix-les-Bains. The travelers returned via Quebec, spending some time there in October 1930. Cather worked on her novel in Jaffrey, New Hampshire, for a month or so that fall. Lewis reports that when Cather "did finally start for Jaffrey, she could hardly wait to be at her writing-table again. She wrote the last part of *Shadows* very rapidly, part of it at Jaffrey, part at the Grosvenor, finishing it December 27th" (160).

The New York Public Library and Southwick Typescripts
Cather's customary practice was to write the first draft of her novels in longhand, then prepare or have prepared one or more typescripts, with carbons, always revising in the process. Final typescripts were ordinarily prepared by a professional typist.[4] Although Cather asked that setting copy be returned to her after production and wrote that such typescripts had been destroyed (Cather to Pat Knopf, 19 January 1936),[5] research has confirmed that a number of typescripts still exist, including one of *Shadows on the Rock* donated by Edith Lewis to the New York Public Library. A nearly com-

plete carbon copy of this typescript was recently discovered among papers belonging to Helen Cather Southwick; it now forms part of the Philip L. and Helen Cather Southwick Collection in Archives and Special Collections, Love Library, University of Nebraska–Lincoln.

The New York Public Library typescript (NT) comprises 250 text pages, numbered with occasional irregularities; the last page of the text, presumably corresponding to the last eleven lines of the first printing of the first book edition (K1.i), is missing, but the typescript is otherwise complete. Many page numbers are too blotted to be legible. Typed numbers run from pages [1] through 29. Beginning with page 30, the original typed numbers were crossed out and the pages renumbered by hand and underlined. The original numbers can often be read; page 30 was originally numbered 24, for example. This six-number gap widens to ten before page 50 and remains ten at least through page 86; thereafter only the handwritten, underlined sequence is visible (except on p. 100, where another number is crossed out). Pagination of text pages (excluding title leaves for books 3, 5, and 6), runs 1–46, 48–78, 78a, 79–237, 240–42, and 245–54. Page 35 is a pasted-up page made up of three different typed slips; pages 46, 49, 56, 77, 78, 93, 97, 98, 101, 102, 110, and 219 are also made up of parts of two or in some cases three typed sheets, and a printed version of the long quotation on page 75 is pasted over a typed version. There is only one sheet between page 45 and page 48, although the text is continuous; the resulting discrepancy in numbering is eliminated when page 78a follows page 78. Page numbers 238–39 and 243–44 are not used; the text, however, remains continuous. Title sheets for books 3, 5, and 6 appear between pages 101–2, 177–78, and 209–10. Pages 29 and 34 have less than half a page of text each; a line is drawn from the end of the text to the bottom of the page to indicate that the text is continuous. (In all references to the typescripts, we cite page numbers as they appear, ignoring all inconsistencies.)

These data show that the New York typescript was pieced together from parts of two or more earlier drafts, with some sections retyped and the whole renumbered. The result is by no means clean copy; there are numerous revisions throughout, both of substantives and accidentals, and at several points substantial passages are blotted or crossed out (these latter, so far as they are recoverable, are included in the Table of Rejected Substantives). Most of the substantive changes appear to be in Cather's hand; the numerous changes in red, especially to accidentals, were almost certainly made by a copy editor.

The New York typescript is marked into two sets of galley numbers. One sequence begins on page 163, where the job number 8681 is repeated (this number also appears on pages 102 and 209a); galley 17 is misnumbered 16. The numbers alone appear in the margins of typescript pages 169, 172, 183, 213, 217, and 230 and are often visible under the overwritten numbers of the other sequence, most obviously on typescript pages 220 (66/18) and 237 (71/23). The second sequence of galley numbers includes the whole typescript;

again, not all the numbers are legible, and there are anomalies. The number 67 appears twice, the second presumably a mistake for 68. The last three numbers are 73 (TS p. 245), 73 again (TS p. 248), and 74 (TS p. 252).

Despite the many additions, deletions, patched-together pages, and other changes throughout the New York Public Library typescript, the revised text of it (RNT) seems to have served as setting copy for *Shadows on the Rock*. We know that Cather characteristically wrote the first draft of one of her novels in longhand and revised constantly as she or, later, her typist produced one or more typescripts, followed by a "clean" copy on which Cather indicated further changes before sending it to her publisher (Bohlke 41, 76). If the red marks were made by a copy editor at Knopf to a Cather-revised typescript which, though by modern standards not at all clean, was indeed setting copy for K1 (and the marked division into galleys and the specific references to job number 8681 support this view), we have here another clear indication that Cather continued the process of revision in the proof stages. There are, for example, some 250 substantive variants between RNT and the first printing of the Knopf book edition (K1.i) — far more than can be accounted for by the correction of errors. Since the New York typescript is clearly authoritative, its readings are discussed below and included in the Table of Rejected Substantives.

The Southwick typescript (ST) is a nearly complete carbon copy of the New York Public Library typescript. It exhibits no copy-editing marks and is not marked into galleys.

Its substantive readings, in its revised form (RST), agree with those of RNT more than 80 percent of the time; in most cases where the readings differ, the reading of RNT agrees with the reading of K1.i. RST differs considerably from RNT in accidentals because the copy editor's alterations to RNT are not indicated on the carbon and because some changes indicated on RNT were not transferred to RST. The revisions indicated on RST seem mostly in Edith Lewis's hand; usually they result in readings identical to those of RNT, although they are not always indicated in the same way. Cather's hand is occasionally evident, sometimes on the same page as Lewis's. It is likely that Lewis transferred most of Cather's changes in RNT to the carbon.

The Southwick typescript comprises 230 text pages (not counting duplicates or unpaginated part-title pages), irregularly numbered; page numbers after 39 do not correspond to those of NT. Although there is no gap in ST's pagination sequence, the last pages of "The Long Winter," beginning at K1.i 162.23, are missing (pp. 146–48), as are pages 199–200. ST ends at K1.i 258.23; the last chapter of book 6 and the epilogue are missing. Pages numbered 35, 74, 100, 111, and 218 are long sheets; the rest are standard size. Pagination runs 1–46 (39 is numbered 39 & 40), 47, 47½, 48, 48½, 49–51, 51½, 52–74, 74½, 75–91, 98–100, 100½, 101–03, 104, 104, 105–75 [176 (title leaf for book 5)], 177–98, and 201–29.

The Southwick typescript shows no signs of piecing or paste-up, but it exhibits some variations from NT. For example, chapter numbers often differ in the two texts. ST page 100 is a long sheet beginning with a six-line paragraph that appears to have been typed in at the top of the page. The text of these lines in NT follows from the "There was" ending of page 96, but the text of ST drops all but the last word of line 1, and the resulting placement of the remaining text on the page is different in the two texts. The following page, numbered 100½ in ST and 98 in NT, is also different in its placement on the page. The last two lines of ST page 100 do not appear on NT 98 but at the top of page 99; ST repeats them at the top of page 99, bringing the two texts together again. "Mme." is circled at ST page 100½, lines 3 and 9, but spelled out on NT 98. "Jacques' " appears at ST line 19 instead of "Jacques's." These facts suggest that ST 100½ has been substituted for the original carbon.

Other anomalies exist as well. The placement of text on page 6 is one line higher on the page in ST than in NT (this could be the result of misalignment of the two sheets of paper). A second "a" in "monastaries" at page 6.7 is lined out and the correct letter "e" written above the line in RST; in RNT the original "a" has been erased and an "e" inserted. At page 18.2 the original "were" has been lined out on RNT and "was" written in; the correction is in red, presumably made by the copy editor. In RST the original reading has been erased and the correction typed in. At page 41.27, "of the" is typed in at the end of the line in RST. At NT 169.9/ST 167.9, "stuff" is lined out and "fill" written in above the line in RNT; on RST, the typed "tuff" of "stuff" has been erased and "stuff" written in the same space on the line. At NT 196.25/ST 195.25, the interlinear addition "with" is typed in on both RNT and RST, as is the "a" at NT 198.19/ST 197.19.

Because most of the revisions to RST are in Lewis's hand and most of those to RNT are in Cather's, we conclude that Cather revised the typescript before it was sent to Knopf and that Lewis and Cather transferred the changes to the carbon copy, not always indicating them in the same way (and in some cases altering or omitting them) before RNT was sent off. Cather may have gone over both original and carbon a second time. RNT is rather messy copy, and she was to make many additional revisions at the proof stages of production: more than a quarter of the substantive variants between the typescript and K1.i are unique to the Knopf first book edition text. RST remained with Cather and eventually came into the possession of her niece Helen Cather Southwick.

Production and Printing History

Cather sent the first two-thirds of the copy for *Shadows on the Rock* to Mr. Stimson at Knopf while the Knopfs themselves were in Europe, noting that Stimson praised the book highly at a time when she herself was feeling somewhat unsure about it (Cather to Ferris Greenslet, 26 November [1931]). In January and February 1931 Cather was in New York, awaiting galleys. In early March she left for California, taking at least some of the proofs with her. She seems to have read all of the galley proof during this period, but she asked Lewis to read the foundry proofs for her (Lewis 161). Knopf writes that "by mid-May she had seen and liked the copy that appeared over my name on the wrapper of 'Shadows on the Rock'" (Memoirs). Cather was again at Grand Manan when the novel was published on 1 August 1931.

The initial trade printing comprised 25,700 copies. Of these, 24,700 were bound in bright green cloth and 300 in library buckram for sale to institutions. The remaining 700 were bound in wrappers "made up of a trial dust jacket for distribution as advance review copies" (Crane 157). Crane, whose book is generally accurate, says that "The Canadian edition (Macmillan, 5,600 copies) is of the first trade printing sheets with altered title page imprint and copyright and with the Macmillan name stamped at the foot of the spine" (158). CE has not been able to locate a copy of this issue, and there is no information about it in the Knopf production record. Professor John J. Murphy has located two reviews of the novel, one in *Canadian Forum* and one in *Canadian Magazine* (January 1932), both of which list the Canadian source as Longmans, Green — not Macmillan. It seems possible, especially in the absence of the title in *A Bibliography of Macmillan Canada Imprints, 1906–1980* (Toronto: Dundurn Press, 1985), that in this case the copies shipped to Canada were copies of Knopf's trade printing and that there was no separate Canadian imprint.[6]

Knopf also offered a limited issue of the book, 199 copies on Shidzuoka Japan vellum and 619 copies on Croxley handmade paper, the two forms also having different bindings, appropriately different limitation notices, and somewhat different boxes. Copies belonging to these issues were numbered and signed. Knopf's advertisement for *Obscure Destinies* in *Publishers' Weekly* for 16 January 1932 says that "In keeping with the policy instituted with the limited edition of *Shadows on the Rock*, the exact number of copies printed will depend on orders received" (474). Crane, noting that Cather had her copies of the trade issue by 24 June 1931, concludes that "it is reasonably certain that a large part of the first printing of the trade issue had already come off the presses when the numbers of the limited issue were determined and put in work, especially as Knopf announced that 47,290 trade copies had been shipped before publication" (160–61).[7] Since both issues "were printed from the same setting of plates and frequently simultaneously, it is splitting hairs to make too fine a point of priority" (Crane 161). Both the trade and limited issues were set, electrotyped, and bound by Plimpton Press.

In support of her initial conclusion, Crane quotes part of a letter from Knopf's production chief, Sidney R. Jacobs: "Knopf never intended that the trade edition of any title, for which a limited number of copies were printed on special paper and numbered and signed, should be anything other than a first edition. In fact . . . different presses and make-readies were needed, and frequently the two printings were performed side by side with different sections of the text being on press at the same moment on the two presses. The trade edition was always considered a first edition, or at least part of a first edition" (157). This is an accurate description of Knopf's practice, but it does not follow that the copies of the limited issue were put in work after the majority of copies of the trade issue had been printed. Professor Herbert Johnson thinks that these copies may well have been "printed directly from the type, and bound and delivered while the trade edition was still in press" (letter to F. M. Link, 25 March 1996). In the absence of additional evidence, the question of priority becomes moot, and Professor Johnson's suggestion that a different criterion be used is reasonable: "Priority of first edition rank belongs to the edition with the fewest number of copies (really, the most expensive copies)."

As Crane notes, all of the advance review copies seen have "SECOND EDITION" on the copyright page. All seen also have a dropped letter "s" at 250.18 ("hay-bale$_x$").[8] The first reading was changed to "FIRST EDITION," in Crane's view, after the first 700 copies had been run off, but the dropped letter was not restored until the second printing, so copies of the trade, limited, and Canadian issues (if there was a separate Canadian issue) belong to state *a* of the first edition text.[9] Possibly to clarify the "SECOND EDITION" reading with booksellers, copies of the U.S. trade printing were sent out wrapped in cellophane. "Beneath the transparent wrap was inserted a printed note: 'This is a copy of the First Edition'" (Crane 156).[10]

There were also two issues of the second printing of the novel. The error at 250.18 is corrected in both, establishing state *b* of the text. The copyright page of the Knopf trade issue (40,000 copies, June 1931) reads "*First and Second Print-*

ings before Publication," and the colophon on page 282 has been altered to include the words "PRINTED AND BOUND BY THE HADDON CRAFTSMEN, INC." In copies belonging to the other issue, distributed by the Book-of-the-Month Club and Catholic Book Club (51,800 copies, July 1931), the copyright and colophon notices remain the same except that the double rules on pages ii and 282 (advertisement and colophon) are removed. The title page, however, is different: the shadowed capitals of the title, set in a single-rule panel within a rectangular double-rule frame in Knopf copies, are replaced by smaller italic letters set within a dark blue single-line arch topped by a line-and-diamond cross, this arch five-eighths of an inch inside a dark-blue scalloped decorative arch connected with it at six points by line-and-diamond lines. The effect is that of a church window or door with the letterpress information in the opening.

State *c* of the text is seen in copies of the fourth and subsequent printings, which correct the errors at 146.8 and 314.20, changing "linaments" to "liniments" and "1770" to "1700." Crane, citing Sidney R. Jacobs of Knopf as her source, writes that "one set of plates was expected to take care of BOMC's and Knopf's needs, and Knopf sent their plates to Haddon for their own later printings as well as the club's. . . . [T]he printings were either combined or run sequentially to share make-ready costs." Since the club copies did not carry a special notice on the copyright page, "subscribers were not to know whether their copies were part of the first printing or a later one" (161). CE has followed Knopf (and Crane) in treating the trade and book club versions as separate issues of the second printing of the novel. Knopf's production records provide no information about the book club version, but since its copyright notice, like that of the trade issue, reads *"First and Second Printings before Publication,"* Knopf also seems to have identified it as part of the second printing. This is consistent with the avowed interest in saving make-ready costs.

Information about the first twenty printings (those issued during Cather's lifetime) is shown in the following table: the information, except for that in the "state" column, is based on Crane (162–63),[11] checked against copies seen and Knopf production records:

Ptg/Issue	Descr.	State	Date	Number	Printer
i.a	Adv. Rev.	*a*	6/31	700	Plimpton
	Trade	*a*	6/31	19,400	Plimpton
i.b	Limited	*a*	6/31	818	Plimpton
i.c	Longman's?	*a*	6/31	5,600	Plimpton
ii.a	Trade	*b*	6/31	40,000	Haddon
ii.b	BOMC/CBC	*b*	7/31	51,800	Haddon
iii	Trade	*b*	8/31	10,000	Haddon
iv	Trade	*c*	8/31	10,000	Haddon
v	Trade	*c*	9/31	10,000	Haddon
vi	Trade	*c*	10/31	5,000	Haddon
vii	Trade	*c*	10/31	5,000	Haddon
viii	Trade	*c*	11/31	5,000	Haddon
ix	Trade	*c*	11/31	5,000	Haddon
x	Trade	*c*	12/31	5,000	Haddon
xi	Trade	*c*	12/31	5,000	Haddon
xii	Trade	*c*	10/32	5,000	Haddon
xiii	Trade	*c*	10/34	3,000	Haddon

Ptg/Issue	Descr.	State	Date	Number	Printer
xiv	Trade	c	2/36	2,500	Haddon
xv	Trade	c	4/37	3,000	Haddon
xvi	Trade	c	11/38	3,000	Plimpton
xvii	Trade	c	10/40	3,000	Plimpton
xviii	Trade	c	9/42	3,020	Plimpton
xix	Trade	c	12/43	2,000	Plimpton
xx	Trade	c	12/44	3,000	Plimpton

The book sold very well indeed, especially during the first six months after publication. Knopf's advertisement in the 16 January 1932 issue of *Publishers' Weekly* says that 167,679 copies were shipped in 1931 (the figure includes the Book-of-the-Month and Catholic Book Club issue). If the book club issue belongs to the second printing, as its copyright page suggests, more than 118,000 copies were produced prior to the official date of publication.

Knopf renumbered its trade impressions when new plates were made for what Crane calls the twenty-first printing, in April 1946. The five Vintage impressions (1971–76), issued in paper and produced by photo-offset from plates of the (second) trade edition, were not counted in the new sequence. If one follows Crane, all these impressions belong to the first edition of the novel because all are derived from the same setting of type. There is a question, however, about what Crane calls the twenty-first printing. It seems unlikely that Knopf would specifically advertise it as having been "reset" as well as printed from new plates if this were not the case. Although publishers often ignored the technical distinctions between issues, printings, and even editions, the word "reset" is less ambiguous. Although the copyright notice for the April 1946 printing reads in part "RESET AND PRINTED FROM NEW PLATES," Crane states that "these plates were electrotyped from the original plates of 1931" (159); this printing is "not a new edition, but [produced from] electrotype plates from the same setting" (163).[12]

Nevertheless, there is considerable evidence for considering the twenty-first and later printings as belonging to a second Knopf edition. As simple measurements and changes from swash to standard type for certain letters indicate, the preliminary matter has been wholly or partially reset: the half-title page and its verso advertisement, the title page and its verso copyright page, the contents page, the epigraph. The same tests will also show that the individual title pages preceding each of the six books have also been reset, as well as the running heads throughout. Errors previously uncorrected in the K1 text are newly corrected at 18.13 ("your" to "you"), 95.18 ("Auclaire's" to "Auclair"), and 158.21 ("*pré-/fére*" to "*pré-/fère*"); the last of these was not corrected in the Autograph Edition text. At 62.12, following the Autograph Edition reading, the "u" is added to "endeavored"; at 289.12, "*bléd*," becomes "*bléd*.", reverting to the typescript reading.

The letterpress text of the book is difficult to distinguish in the two printings; it was reset line for line using the identical fonts. Measurement of pages selected at random show insignificant differences of $\frac{1}{32}$ inch at most.[13] There are also minute differences in the type, at K1–2 82.7, for example. Crane may have based her judgment on this lack of apparent difference in the letterpress. However, a statement on the Knopf production record for the twentieth printing reads "new electros made see cost card 1st reset Edition" (22 March 1945); the record for the twenty-first printing contains the notes "OLD PLATES MELTED" (11 April 1951) and "CREDIT FOR METAL OF OLD SET OF PLATES" (with another 1951 date). New electrotypes would not usually be made from badly worn plates, nor is there evidence to suggest that two sets of plates were made originally. Moreover, there is also recorded, with a date in March 1945, a charge for "Comp and electros" ($648.48), and the "Miscellaneous" section of the record has a further note under "*Comp*": "12 pt. ad card, c/r [copyright page], contents, / quo[tation], 6 halftitles, 264 pp. text / (274 pp. [the remaining pages are blank]) @ $1.48 $405.52 / 2¾ pp. French @ $2.02 p. [$] 5.56 / 10 pt. footnotes—8 chapt. headings with rules and display type $27.00." A second note, under "*Electros*," lists a charge for 277 "beveled plates" at $.73 each.

The amount recorded as charged for composition is far too large to reflect the resetting of a few plates because of wear or damage, as may have been done when the plates were returned from Haddon to Plimpton for the sixteenth printing. New electrotypes were indeed made, but the production record confirms the statement on the copyright page that these electrotypes were made from a new setting of type.[14] What Crane calls the twenty-first and later trade printings, and also the five offset printings of the Vintage paperback, therefore belong to a third U.S. edition of *Shadows on the*

Rock, the Autograph Edition being the second. Hereafter, CE refers to printings after the twentieth as belonging to a new Knopf edition, K2. The matter is not of great consequence, however, so far as establishing the text is concerned because the only variants CE has noted involve the correction of obvious or perceived errors.

The first British edition of *Shadows on the Rock* was published in London by Cassell on 1 January 1932 and reprinted several times in the format of the Cassell Pocket Library (1936–61).[15] The "edition" published by Hamish Hamilton in 1961 was photo-offset from plates of the U.S. trade edition (Crane 166) and thus is not technically a new edition. There is no evidence that Cather was involved in the production or printing of these texts; we conclude that they are not authoritative and therefore exclude their readings from the Table of Rejected Substantives.

The Autograph Edition text of *Shadows on the Rock* was published in 1938 as volume 10 of that edition. Scribner's had wanted to publish a subscription edition of Cather's fiction as early as 1932, but Houghton Mifflin would not release rights to the four novels it had earlier published (Lewis 180; Ferris Greenslet to Cather, 1 July 1933; Knopf memoirs). When Houghton Mifflin itself took up Scribner's idea, Cather worked with Ferris Greenslet, who had been her editor there; after much negotiation, Cather agreed to the edition. She wanted W. A. Dwiggins, who had designed some of her Knopf books, as the designer, and she wanted the same type used in the Thistle edition of Robert Louis Stevenson (Cather to Greenslet, 18 December 1936). Greenslet did not agree (21 December 1936), and Bruce Rogers was chosen to design the edition. The Autograph Edition text was reissued in 1940 as the Library Edition and was reprinted in 1973 "from the original type of the Riverside Press" by the Rinsen Book Company, Kyoto, Japan (200 copies).

Changes in the Text

Five sets of changes are to be considered: those between the original text of the typescript (NT) and the revised and copy-edited text of that typescript in the New York Public Library (RNT); those between RNT and KI.i; those between RNT and the revised text of the Southwick carbon of that typescript (RST); those between KI.i and the Cassell text; and those between KI.i and the Autograph Edition text. Because the analysis that follows bears on the choice of copy-text, we present it in some detail, considering both substantive and accidental variants.

There are well over eight hundred accidental variants between NT and RNT. A high percentage of these are recorded in red ink, indicating the hand of a copy editor. The variants fall into the usual categories. "Auclaire" is changed to "Auclair," "Augustine" to "Augustin." Abbreviations in NT are normally expanded in RNT: "St." and "Ste." to "Saint" and "Sainte," "M." to "Monsieur," "Mgr." to "Monseigneur." Commas are frequently added or deleted. British spelling is adopted for such words as "colour" and "favour," which in

NT appear without the "u." "Gray" is changed to "grey," and forms of "inquire" are replaced by forms of "enquire." "Mass" usually becomes "mass," and the initial letter in words like "Mademoiselle" is usually reduced to lowercase when no name follows. There are numerous changes in word division and spelling. There are also a number of typographic changes — in paragraphing, for example.

There are more than six hundred substantive changes between NT and RNT. In more than 90 percent of these cases, the reading of RNT is that of K1.i; that is, there is far more change between NT and RNT than between RNT and K1.i, although K1.i does introduce some three hundred new readings. Most of the substantive variants between NT and RNT involve relatively small changes: "strangulation" to "suffocation" (11.9), "islands of gray" to "grey islands of" (180.20), "awaiting" to "expecting" (261.12), "right, all the same" to "right" (292.17). Others are more extensive, or more dramatic: "Racine" to "Plutarch" (23.5), "miraculously preserved from harm" to "not harmed" (113.18), "home, and other Christmases when they had plenty of Norman cider" to "home" (132.2), "wigwam to lie shuddering with disgust" to "wigwam" (176.7–8). In some cases the revision is extensive: RNT omits one or more sentences at 48.15, 52.25, 59.21, 61.5, 68.9–10, 69.2, 93.19, 111.17, 121.9, 123.17–18, 146.1, 149.7, 170.4, 188.22–24, and 285.8. One can sometimes follow Cather's revising hand from NT through RNT to K1.i: the process is evident in the three versions of 34.20–35.1, 38.3–4, 107.8–11, 142.13, 198.15–17, and 241.3, for example. Occasionally, a change suggests something more than a wish to eliminate unnecessary material or improve wording or style: at 115.14–16 a reference to miracles is deleted; at 121.23 a reference to Cécile's crèche as a "toy" is removed.

There are well over five hundred variant readings between RNT and K1.i. The accidental variants fall into the usual groups: changes in punctuation account for perhaps half of the total; changes in spelling and word division account for most of the rest, although there are many changes of case as well. The changes in punctuation are typical: commas are deleted, especially before dashes; semicolons are changed to colons and commas to semicolons; a few periods become exclamation points; a number of separate sentences are connected with semicolons. The most common change, one typical of Cather's revision, is the addition of a comma. Changes in spelling or accent often involve French names. "Clotilde" becomes "Clothilde" (17.18 and elsewhere), "Georgio" becomes "Giorgio" throughout. "Luth" is changed to "Lhut" (67.16), "Lalamant" to "Lalemant" (120.13), "Catharine" to "Catherine" (120.20). "Saint-Augustine" loses its final "e" (146.17); "*campagnard*" adds an "*e*" (215.25); *roche* occurs several times, always without the NT/RNT circumflex on the *o*. A few spelling changes correct spelling or typographical errors in NT: for example, "mantle" is corrected to "mantel" (285.24). Case changes include frequent examples of "palace," which is capitalized throughout in K1.i. Word-division changes are infrequent: for example, NT's "beaver dam" is hyphenated (63.5).

The substantive variants are more interesting, especially since they account for about half the total number of variants, a far higher percentage than one sees between the Cassell or Autograph Edition texts and K1.i. Even so, the great majority of the changes involve only a word or two. Many are quite minor: "that" to "which" (8.21 and elsewhere), "the proper" to "of the proper" (11.20–21), "greener" to "was greener" (24.7), "The Place" to "*La Place*" (55.18), "would" to "might" (147.19), "and the" to "but the" (167.14), "street" to "streets" (263.2), and "when" to "while" (305.14). Others make the reading more specific or precise: "the Count" becomes "Count Frontenac" (26.18), "stupid" becomes "bigoted" (37.14), "him" is specified as "Bichet" (107.12) and "her mother" as "Madame Auclair" (111.12), "vestry room" becomes "sacristy" (133.18), and "the Bishop" becomes "Saint-Vallier" (140.4). Many of these changes are unquestionably Cather's; taken together, they reveal her ongoing attention to detail.

Here and there, a change simplifies the RNT reading: "stories of cruelty and suffering" becomes "suffering" (112.15), "better, on the whole" is reduced to "better" (139.24), "wakened up" to "wakened" (166.15), and "people, red and white" to "people" (308.11). Often a word is replaced with a different word. "Soothing" becomes "mysterious" (125.5–6), "twist" becomes "sheath" (126.18), "beneficial" becomes "salutary" (295.22), "stupor" becomes "coma" (301.14), and "scarcely changed" becomes "little altered" (313.12–13). "Holy" becomes "Blessed" in K1 (153.13 and elsewhere). A few names are changed: "Nanette" to "Jeanette" (182.19), "Dinard" to "Dinan" (248.11), *"La Garonne"* to *"La Vengeance"* (274.25), and "Naömi" to "Noémi" in all four appearances on pages 282–83. RNT refers to the "Cathedral church," K1.i to the "Cathedral" (313.6 and elsewhere).

Nearly a quarter of the total number of substantive variants are accounted for by the change of "Archbishop" in its various forms to the equivalent forms of "Bishop." Cather had finished the novel on 27 December 1930. When she left to visit her mother in California in early March 1931, Lewis says that she asked her "to look over the foundry proofs when they came in," noting that Cather always "asked to see them" (161). While Lewis was reading them, she "got a telegram . . . saying that throughout the story *Archbishop* Laval and *Archbishop* de Saint-Vallier must be changed to *Bishop* Laval and *Bishop* de Saint-Vallier. It must have been through pure absent-mindedness that she made this mistake, for she knew the correct titles and had seen them hundreds of times in print — and so had I! But she had got used to writing the word Archbishop [*Death Comes for the Archbishop* had been published in 1927]. In San Francisco . . . she happened to show an old friend, a Catholic, some of the proofs she had with her; and this friend instantly noticed the error" (162). It is worth noting, however, that in some cases both NT and RNT read "Bishop" (e.g., at 13.3, 13.14, 28.16, 139.13, 140.8).

Some 20 percent of the substantive variants involve more than two or three words. A number of these are primarily stylistic. For example, RNT reads "In the afternoon he read Latin with a father at the Jesuits on the rue Saint-Antoine, just around the corner." In K1.i this becomes "Every afternoon he read Latin with a priest at the Jesuits on the rue Saint-Antoine" (34.20–35.1). The RNT reading "It was natural, Auclair felt" becomes "Auclair thought it natural" (62.18). The simplest sort of stylistic change may be seen in "with his lantern at the end of the bell-rope" (124.8), which replaces the RNT reading "at the end of the bell-rope with his lantern."

Several passages were more extensively revised:

RNT: "Yes, in the Récollet chapel." ¶ (These Franciscan brothers extended their charity even to the dead; they would say a mass for a departed soul very cheaply, — for whatever one felt able to give them, indeed.) ¶ "And will you take me with you?" ⟩ K1 90.14–17: "Yes, on the tenth of November, the day on which he was hanged." This mass Auclair had said at the Récollets' chapel where Count Frontenac heard mass every morning. ¶ "Please

RNT: But miracles happened repeatedly, even in behalf of the most depraved and those who died without having time to repent ⟩ K1 115.13–14: But there was always hope, even for the most depraved; and for those who died repentant.

RNT: Saint-Vallier; he felt something theatrical about him, and unstable. ⟩ K1 142.13: Saint-Vallier.

RNT: adopted that course of prudent piety by which she controlled ⟩ K1 143.21–22: become the grave and far-seeing woman who so greatly influenced

RNT: Who knows how soon we may be as cold as he? So we warm ⟩ K1 307.19: Let us cheer

The first, third, and fourth of these are typical: a parenthesis that could be seen as reflecting badly on the Franciscans and a description which suggests that Saint-Vallier is insincerely playing a role are eliminated, and the description of Mme de Maintenon is made more positive. One does not expect major revisions in a late typescript, and one does not get them here. Most of the changes either correct errors, deal with such niceties as the difference between "which" and "that," add description or delete redundancy and irrelevance, or introduce more accurate, precise, or specific word choices. A small number subtly alter the presentation of character or make changes in the syntax of a phrase or sentence.

The typographical variants between RNT and K1.i are frequent but slight. RNT often indicates a dash with a single typed dash instead of two consecutive ones; at times there are three. It sometimes inappropriately includes sentence punctuation as part of a word or phrase in italics; K1.i usually corrects to standard practice. Font changes are uncommon; most of the passages to be set in italics in K1.i are underlined in RNT or marked to be set in italics. Most of the typographical differences result from indentation establishing a new paragraph in K1.i, but there are many more examples of this typographical variant between K1.i and the Autograph Edition text.

Because the unrevised Southwick text (ST) is a carbon copy of the unrevised New York Public Library text, there are few differences between them; those that exist were discussed above. When Lewis and Cather copied the revisions made to

578

the original text onto the Southwick carbon, they of course did not transfer those made later by the RNT copy editor, most of which involve accidentals or typography. It is not surprising, however, that many accidental variants appear independently: "Auclaire" becomes "Auclair" and "Mass" becomes "mass" in both texts, for example. Both texts often make the same changes in spelling, especially to proper names. But RNT's changes to word division, its directions to spell out words like "Mgr.," and its insertion of the "u" into "color" or "favor" — to take only three examples — have no counterpart in RST.

There are more than one hundred substantive differences between RST and RNT. In about two-fifths of these cases, RST agrees with NT and RNT with K1; in another fifth of the cases, RST's reading is unique. RST readings that differ from those of RNT rarely appear in K1. In about half the variants, the RNT reading appears in red, which we interpret as indicating a change made by the copy editor. Many of the changes in red involve trivial sorts of "correctness": "will" to "shall," "would" to "should," "afterward" to "afterwards," "was" to "had been." Some correct simple errors or address conventional grammar: "Conte" to "Comte," "*es'*" to "*es- ce*," "their lives" to "his life" (following "everyone owed"). Some spell out abbreviations. The most striking copyediting changes are perhaps "But surely" for RST's "At any rate" (16.20), "life of" for "chapter on" (151.14), and "in time" for "and leave her" (205.10). Even here, the second change is a correction: Plutarch's book is divided by "lives" rather than chapters.

Other changes improve reference ("He" to "The cobbler" at 121.18), change "in which case" to "but then" (125.19) and "after" to "when" (126.24), substitute "anguish" for "torture" (188.25) and "West Indian" for "South American" (255.13). No change involves more than a few words.

Collations of the Cassell edition of 1932 show almost three hundred variants from K1.i. Of that total, some 85 percent are accounted for by typographical differences (changes from italics to roman or roman to italics, e.g. [30 percent]), which are probably to be ascribed to house styling, or by the following classes of accidentals: (a) changes in word division (25 percent), most of them involving the words "today," "tonight," and "tomorrow"; (b) changes from upper- to lowercase or vice versa (about 17 percent), most of them involving the words "mass" and "street"; and (c) changes in punctuation or the use of the apostrophe (13 percent). Many, if not most, of these accidental variants are also probably the result of Cassell's house style, but some correct errors in K1.i or substitute British for U.S. spellings. For example, "ax" is consistently spelled "axe" (e.g., 163.22), "Auclaire" (95.18) is properly spelled without the "e," the period required after "affair" (105.2) is supplied, a comma is added after "Father" when used in direct address (146.15), and a capital is used when the character nicknamed "the snail" is mentioned (235.19). The dropped "s" in "hay-bale" (288.7) is corrected, as are the spellings "linaments" (146.8) and "enterprize" (276.17).

There are fewer than a dozen substantive variants. Three are arbitrary: there is no reason to change K1.i's "rose" to "rode" (10.22), "New Year's" to "New Year's Day" (16.20–21, 171.20), or "Governor General" to "governor" (41.6). Three, all involving the change of "shingled" to "cropped" (14.19, 32.20, 300.4), seem to have resulted from Cassell's sense that "shingled" would not be clear in Britain.[16] Cassell changes "monastery" and "monastère" to "convent" (50.25, 51.12), possibly believing that the K1.i readings are incorrect or unclear when referring to a community of women, and misreads *"naivres"* as *"ravines"* (255.21). The other substantive variants correct errors in K1.i: "your" to "you" (18.13), "had" to "has" (291.10), and "1770" to "1700" (314.20).

It is of course possible that some or all of the changes, both of accidentals and substantives, were the result of communication between Knopf and Cassell, and possible also that Cather might have had a hand in them. However, CE has found no external evidence supporting either possibility, and a study of the variants shows none that could not easily result from the imposition of Cassell's house style, the desire of the British publisher to correct obvious errors in the setting copy, the desire to clarify or "improve" readings that were thought inaccurate or might not be clear to British readers, or simple misreading. It is relevant to note that the Autograph Edition text agrees with Cassell only in correcting errors in K1.i. Such Cassell variants as "rode" for "rose," "cropped" for "shingled," and "New Year's Day" for "New Year's" are in every case rejected. That the Autograph text agrees with Cassell in preferring "axe" to K1.i's "ax" merely indicates that Cather or her publisher preferred the more

British spelling in the 1938 edition. CE concludes that there is no evidence of authorial intervention in the Cassell edition, and therefore does not include its variants in the Table of Rejected Substantives.

The Autograph Edition text (A), however, is clearly authoritative. During 1936 Cather looked over the books included and made a number of changes, the number varying with the particular title. In the case of *Shadows on the Rock* there are more than six hundred changes. In addition, there are numerous typographical differences between the two texts. K1.i encloses speeches within double quotation marks whereas A uses single quotes; K1.i usually sets French titles and quotations in roman or italics without quotation marks whereas A tends to use both. A breaks the text some fifty times more with paragraph indentations than does K1.i. Most of these changes are probably due to Houghton Mifflin's house style or to the design for the edition. Although one cannot automatically rule out authorial intervention, other volumes in the Autograph Edition show many of the same changes: the use of single for double quotes, hyphenation of words like "to-day," the use of "although" and "afterwards" for "though" and "afterward." This suggests again that such variants result from house or edition style rather than authorial revision.

More than 95 percent of the variants involve accidentals or changes in font. Again, most are probably the result of house style or Rogers's design for the edition; more than a few of the accidental variants appear in other Autograph Edition texts. The accidentals may be divided into classes and conveniently shown in tabular form:

Variant Class	Approx. Percentage
Word division	16
Spelling	9
Accent	9
Punctuation	44
Case	10
Font (see below)	12

The number of *different* accidental variants is much smaller than the total number of accidentals would indicate; a great many are duplicates, involving words often repeated in the text. For example, the majority of changes in word division involve "today," "tonight," and "tomorrow," which are single words in K1.i but hyphenated compounds in A. Spelling variants include the forms of "enquire," which are always spelled with an "i" in K1.i but with an "e" in A. "Kebec," frequent in the text, is without an accent in K1.i but is always given one in A. The word "mass" is lowercase in K1.i but uppercase in A; this is also usually true of "street" when one is specifically named. "Afterwards" in K1.i becomes "afterward" in A, "Noël" is "Noel" in A. "Monsieur" in A replaces the "M." of K1.i when someone is being addressed.

Some of the variants result from the correction of errors or presumed errors in K1.i. "Thebais" is given an acute é in A (154.24); "Father," when used in direct address, is capitalized (189.13, 212.17); "Lalemant" (174.24) and "Tadousac" (231.8) become "Lalement" and "Tadoussac." The character referred to as "the snail" (235.19) is personalized as "the Snail" in A.

583

"Enterprize" is corrected to "enterprise" (276.17), and "*bléd*" is changed to "*blé*" (289.12). Other changes are minor. "Cardamon" becomes "cardamom" (68.1), pronouns referring to the deity are capitalized (188.11–12), "sirops" is changed to "syrups" (108.2, 244.13). A sometimes introduces errors or inconsistencies of its own, however: K 1.i's "Liège" is wrongly changed to "Liége," for example.

Changes in font are included in the above table. Although they are not accidentals, a large group of them is significant in this particular case. Both texts set quotations and substantial passages of French in italics. However, K 1.i usually sets common French words and phrases, or words and phrases that have English cognates or can easily be understood from their context, in the same roman type used for the English text; except for "salon," A sets such words and phrases in italic type. Examples include "crèche," "fête," "ménage," "béret," "bonjour," "pharmacie" and "pharmacien," "porte-cochère," "Merci beaucoup," "bien," "protégé," "paroisse," "Au revoir, monsieur," "la recluse de Ville-Marie," "messieurs les clients," "monastère," and even "poulet," "chirurgien," "réveillon," "flèche," "goûter," "déjeuner," and "allée." Many of these words appear more than once in the text ("goûter," "crèche," and "allée," e.g.). Keeping them in roman type in K 1.i emphasizes the indigenous nature of the French culture of Quebec, a sense that is markedly reduced in A when the use of a "foreign" language is underlined by the use of italic type. Since setting such words and phrases in italics is conventional, they may well have been the result of the typographical style used throughout the Autograph Edition.[17]

Fewer than 5 percent of the variants between к1.i and the Autograph Edition text are substantive, suggesting that Cather did not engage in any thoroughgoing revision. A few such variants correct errors in к1.i. "Your" is changed to "you" (18.13), "had been" to "has been" (291.10), and "1770" to "1700" (314.20). Pronouns are occasionally replaced with nouns, even when the referent is clear: "to her" is changed to "to Cécile" (23.16) and "He" to "Jacques" (84.5). Most of the changes involve no more than one or two words. "She got" becomes "she had got" (31.3), "dozens" becomes "dozen" (57.25), "said Jacques" becomes "Jacques said" (76.3–4). "Round" is changed to "around" (141.15), "though" to "although" (175.12), "gilt picture-frames" to "platters" (183.12), "Charron's" to "Pierre Charron's" (200.5), "pine" to "balsam" (217.17), and "beautiful" to "pleasant" (221.7). Of fewer than thirty substantive variants, only two can be considered significant revisions. The first comes at 199.16: A omits the phrase in к1.i about Pierre Charron's reputation "for a loyal friend and a relentless enemy," possibly because it suggests a negative element in an otherwise entirely positive characterization. The second, dropping the two references to the "little nuts" or "eucalyptus balls" that are used as mosquito repellents (219.11, 248.1) and instead referring to herbs, eliminates an anachronism.

Since there is both external and internal evidence of authorial intervention in the Autograph Edition text, its variant readings are included in the Table of Rejected Substantives.

The Choice of Copy-Text

The policy of the Cather Edition is to prefer as copy-text that printing of a given work which represents the text at the time of Cather's fullest creative engagement with it and closest editorial attention to it. However, the decision about copy-text comes only after we have completed and analyzed collations of all variants in the authoritative texts; it is always possible that such analysis will require a different decision.

Collation of copies of all potentially relevant texts of *Shadows on the Rock* demonstrates that five show evidence of Cather's hand and are, therefore, authoritative: those of the original and the two revised versions of the typescript, the text of K1.i, and the text of the Autograph Edition. All other editions during Cather's lifetime (including K2, discussed below) were either reprints, separate issues of K1.i, or derive from K1.i without evidence of authorial intervention. These include the Cassell edition of 1932, its later reprints in the Cassell Pocket Library series, and the Library Edition reprint of the Autograph Edition text, published in 1940.

Although the New York Public Library typescript of *Shadows on the Rock* is not dated, it obviously is roughly contemporary with K1.i, and it is unquestionably authoritative. An analysis of the variant readings between NT and RNT, between RST and RNT, and between RNT and K1.i, however, leads inevitably to the conclusion that both the original and the two revised versions of the typescript are way stations on the road to the K1.i text. K1.i does not merely correct misspelled words, wrong accents, and other errors in RST and

RNT; it introduces hundreds of other changes. Moreover, the changes are almost as often in substantives as in accidentals, and these changes are contemporary with the typescript but follow it in the sequence. Although RNT was evidently setting copy, it is clear from the many changes in K1.i that revision continued through the proof stages. Were the corrected galley and page proofs available, they would of course figure in the selection of copy-text, but we have not found any such texts.

The Autograph Edition text represents a somewhat later intention for the work, in this case one different in both accidentals and typography from that realized in K1.i. It corrects most of K1.i's errors, introducing a few of its own, but makes relatively few substantive changes. Moreover, many of both the accidental and the substantive variants appear to result from Houghton Mifflin's house style or from Rogers's design for the edition. These include many changes in punctuation and most of those affecting word division ("today" to "to-day," etc.), many changes in the handling of capitalization ("mass" to "Mass"), changes in the interest of more up-to-date word choices ("afterwards" to "afterward"). They also include the changes in font discussed above, which CE believes have some substantive force. Although only seven years elapsed between K1.i and A, the two forms of the text also have quite different "bibliographical" contexts: *Shadows on the Rock* is one volume of many in the Autograph Edition, which was produced for collectors and institutions, whereas K1.i offers the public a new work by its author.

There is no reason to use an advance review copy of the first edition as copy-text even if one accepts Crane's argument that the seven hundred copies containing the "SECOND EDITION" error were produced before those belonging to the remainder of the trade impression and to the limited issue. CE has chosen to use a later, corrected copy of the trade issue, produced for the general public. There seems little point in choosing an incorrect early copy from the same press run over a later corrected one, especially since the only textual difference is the dropped letter at 288.7.

The same argument applies to the text of the second edition of the Knopf text (K2, 1946). Collations have shown that there are only four variants between K1.iv and K2, all of them involving accidentals, all of them corrections or intended corrections. It is also unlikely that Cather had anything to do with the text of K2, although she may have known about it — CE has not found external evidence to help decide the question. Because the variants are few and affect only accidentals, and because the edition came late in Cather's life when the likelihood of her intervention was small, CE does not consider K2 to have independent authority.

The copy-text for this edition of *Shadows on the Rock* is thus a copy of the first printing of the first U.S. edition of the novel, trade issue, published on 1 August 1931 by Alfred A. Knopf (K1.i). The internal evidence analyzed above shows that the many differences between the original and revised texts of the typescript are paralleled by the many variants between the revised text of the typescript and K1.i; the process of revision continued (note "archbishop" ⟩ "bishop") until the novel was published in book form. Once that happened, few changes were made in Knopf's later printings and editions, and those correct errors in K 1.i. The texts of K 2 and Cassell have no independent authority. The Autograph Edition text arises from a later and different intention; its variants indicate the correction of a few errors in K 1, but most of them appear to reflect house style or the design for the edition, and most of them involve accidentals.

Emendation and Related Matters

C E has emended the copy-text of *Shadows on the Rock* under the following circumstances: (1) to correct a typographical error; (2) to resolve inconsistencies in capitalization, spelling, and punctuation when it is clear from other examples that a particular reading is anomalous or might distract the reader; (3) to correct a misspelled word or incorrect accent; and (4) to correct a substantive error when it is clear from other examples that a particular reading is a slip or a rare exception. C E does not emend merely to "improve" Cather's wording or grammar, to modernize her diction or usage or use of accidentals, to impose consistency where there is no evidence that consistency was desired or where inconsistency does not distract the reader, or to correct errors of fact that entail editorial revision as opposed to the simple substitution of one word or form of a word for another.

The fifty-seven emendations accepted into the copy-text by the present editors include six substantive changes (three of which correct what we deem typographical errors in K 1); three changes correcting typographical features such as dropped letters; and forty-eight changes in accidentals, including three changing punctuation, thirty-two altering spelling or accent marks (twenty-one of which involve one proper name), eleven altering case, and two changing word division. Notes on the emendations explain CE's choices when the explanation is not obvious. The textual apparatus lists all substantive variants, and some typical accidental and typographical variants, between the copy-text and the texts of RST, RNT, the four states of K 1.i, the Autograph Edition, and K2. Variants from the first British edition are not included, because CE does not consider this edition authoritative. In addition, the Table of Rejected Substantives includes a small number of accidentals which CE believes may affect meaning in specific instances ("!" ⟩ "." or vice versa), and a longer list of words and phrases set in roman in the copy-text but in italics in the Autograph Edition.

Records of Cather's direct involvement in the design and production of her works have led CE to take special care in the presentation of those works. We are particularly concerned with compositor error. By agreement with the University of Nebraska Press, we undertake proofreading in stages to meet the Committee on Scholarly Editions guidelines, which call for at least four readings.[18] Insofar as is feasible within the series format of a scholarly edition, the editors have cooperated with the designer to create a volume that reflects Cather's known wishes for the presentation of her works.

Notes

1. For this volume, CE conducted or supervised one independent solo hand collation of the unrevised typescript, a solo hand collation and a team collation of the original version of the typescript against the New York Public Library and Southwick revised versions, and two independent solo hand collations of the revised New York Public Library text against a copy of K1.i serving as the standard of collation. The K1.i standard of collation was solo hand collated against a copy of K2 (once), against a copy of the Autograph Edition (three times), and against a copy of the Cassell edition (once). One team collation of the K1.i standard of collation was also made against copies of the Autograph and Cassell editions. The copies listed below were spot-checked against the K1.i standard of collation. A conflation of the collations was made and checked three times; the listed variants were then checked against the K1.i standard of collation. The full record of the historical collations, including those of the Cassell edition, is on file and available in the Cather Project, Department of English, University of Nebraska–Lincoln.

The following copies were used in the preparation of this edition (UNL = Love Library, University of Nebraska–Lincoln; UNLS = Special Collections, Love Library, University of Nebraska–Lincoln; LCLH = Heritage Room collections, Bennett Martin Public Library, Lincoln NE):

Typescript, New York Public Library, Division of Manuscripts and Archives

Carbon of New York Public Library typescript, Philip L. and Helen Cather Southwick Collection, UNLS

K1.i, advance review issue: LCLH 3 3045 00707 1893

K1.i, trade issue: LCLH 3 3045 00852 0625, 2 2045 00782 8417, 3 3045 00782 8425, 3 3045 00782 8672; UNLS Faulkner PS3505 A87s5 1931; PS3505 A87s5, copies 4 & 5; UNLS Sullivan PS3505 A87s5 1931, copies 3 & 4; a copy owned by Frederick M. Link; 3 copies owned by Susan J. Rosowski; a copy owned by Judy Boss

K1.i, limited issue: LCLH 3 3045 00782 8615 (Croxley copy 442); UNLS PS3505 A87s5 1931, copy 2 (Croxley copy 118); UNLS PS3505 A87s8 1931bx (Shidzuoka copy 165)

K1.ii, trade issue: LCLH 3 3045 00782 8672; UNLS PS 3505 A87s5 1931, PS3505 A87s5 1931 & 1931b, PS3505 A87s5 1931, copy 3; a copy owned by Kari Ronning; two copies owned by the Estuary Bookstore, Lincoln NE

K1.ii, book club issue: LCLH 3 3045 00782 8623; a copy owned by Frederick M. Link

K1.iii: LCLH 3 3045 00782 86641

K1.iv: UNLS Slote PS3505 A87s5 1931; a copy owned by Susan J. Rosowski

K1.v: A copy owned by Susan J. Rosowski

K1.vii: A copy owned by Susan J. Rosowski

K1.xiii: Nebraska Wesleyan U PS 3505 A87s45

K1.xx: A copy owned by Kari Ronning

K2.i: A copy owned by Frederick M. Link

K2.iii: UNLS Faulkner PS3505 A87s5 1931, copy 2

Cassell (first British edition, 1932): LCLH 3 3045 00782 8656, 3 3045 00782 8649; UNLS Slote PS3505 A87s5 1932x, PS3505 A87s5 1932x, copies 1 & 2

Autograph Edition, 1938: LCLH 3 3045 00782 8631, volume 10, copy 450; UNLS PS3505 A87A15 1937x, volume 10, copy 294

Autograph Edition reprint, 1973 (Kyoto: Rinsen Book Co.):
UNLS Slote PS3505 A87A15 1973x, volume 10 (copy 129)

2. CE follows the usual distinction: substantive variants are changes
in wording (including morphemic variations); accidental variants include changes in spelling, case, punctuation, and word
division. Typographical changes (in paragraphing, font, spacing, etc.) are neither substantive nor accidental, although they
may be discussed; they represent part of what Jerome McGann
calls "bibliographical" as opposed to "linguistic" codes. The
basis of the distinctions here is the extent to which a class of
differences affects the meaning of the text: typography and accidentals often do not, substantives do. However, CE also recog-
nizes a class of variants, including some typographical and some
accidental variants, that *in a particular case* seem clearly to affect
meaning and thus have substantive force. There is a clear distinction, for example, between "she wanted to be *there*" and "she
wanted to be there," or between "You're hungry." and "You're
hungry?" See Bowers, Greg, McGann, and Tanselle, under
Works Cited, below. Discussions with Richard Rust concerning
the use of inflection as a basis for distinguishing accidentals that
affect meaning have also been of assistance.

3. CE has resolved end-line hyphenation in the copy-text to establish the form of the word or compound to be used in quotations
from this edition. The following criteria are applied in descending order: (1) majority rule, if one or more instances of the word
or compound appear elsewhere in the copy-text; (2) analogy, if
one or more examples of similar words or compounds appear
elsewhere in the copy-text; (3) example or analogy, if one or
more examples of the word or compound, or of similar words or
compounds, appear in the first editions of Cather's works

593

chronologically close to *Shadows on the Rock*; (4) in the absence of the above criteria, commonsense combinations of the following: (a) possible or likely morphemic forms; (b) examples of the word or compound, or of similar words or compounds, in the Autograph edition text; (c) the form given in *Webster's New International Dictionary* (1909); (d) the *Style Manual of the Department of State* (1937); (e) hyphenation of two-word compounds when used as adjectives.

4. Several descriptions of Cather's process of composition exist. See Bohlke 24, 76, 125; Lewis 127.

5. Alfred Knopf, interviewed in 1983 by Susan J. Rosowski, specifically mentioned Cather's requesting the return of her manuscripts and typescripts so that she could destroy them.

6. Macmillan Canada is now owned by CDG Books Canada, Inc. Ms. Stella Partheniou of that company, who kindly assisted our inquiries, has been unable to find any record of Macmillan's having issued the book under their imprint. It is also possible that Longmans, Green issued the book under their imprint rather than simply distributing Knopf trade printing copies, but we have been unable to find such a copy.

7. Since the production records show that there were 25,000 trade copies of the first printing and 40,000 trade copies of the second, Knopf's figure here refers to the number shipped prior to 1 August 1931, not to the number printed.

8. In one copy seen of the limited issue, the *s* of "hay-bales" is clearly visible, though faint. This is, however, insufficient evidence from which to conclude that the limited issue was run off before the trade issue.

9. The term "state" is used here to distinguish between copies belonging to the same edition but differing from other copies in

594

showing one or more accidental or substantive variants in the text. The term may be misleading in the case of books printed from electrotyped plates, since such plates can be — and in the case of *Shadows on the Rock* were — patched or even replaced in the course of printing a number of impressions over a period of time. The Knopf production records show numerous charges for patching plates over the twenty impressions that make up the first edition of the novel, and also many for correcting the plates of the second edition. Sometimes these changes establish states; for example, the records show charges for the corrections at 288.7 and at 146.8 and 314.20 (they show them on the records for the third and fifth printings, although the corrections were made in copies of the second and fourth printings). At other times the corrections were to typographic features of the plate that CE has not identified. The record for the sixteenth printing refers to "comp[osition]" as well as to plate correction, and new electrotypes were probably made for the pages mentioned (241, 243–44, 250–51, and 253). In this "typographical" sense there are many variant states of the plates of the two editions, states that might be recoverable by using the techniques of analytical bibliography. CE is concerned, however, only with those changes that lead to textual variants.

10. Crane's explanation of the "SECOND EDITION" reading is plausible, especially if one accepts her view that copies of the limited issues were printed after the majority of copies of the trade issue, but it is not the only one. Professor Herbert Johnson notes that "it was common book publishing practice for the printer to supply foundry proofs of all pages before electrotypes were made, and Knopf's proofreaders were responsible for checking the pages and approving them for plates and printing.

If it is possible that they missed 'SECOND EDITION,' would not this line also appear in the two limited editions? In other words, the proofreaders had already seen the manuscript, galley proofs, page proofs and foundry proofs, so where did 'SECOND EDITION' come from?" Johnson's answer is that the reading represents "a deliberate attempt by Knopf to lessen the market value of these free copies" so that they would compete less successfully with copies of the trade printing. He also notes that "the fact that the review copy wrapper is printed in one color of ink rather than two does not prove a trial jacket. These copies were to be made as cheaply as possible, so the wrappers were most likely printed directly from the type, possibly on a proof press" (letter to F. M. Link, 25 March 1996).

11. Crane (162–63) states that the presswork for "the second through sixteenth printings (November 1938) was done by the Haddon Craftsmen," but Knopf production records indicate that the sixteenth was done by the Plimpton Press. The production record for the 619 limited issue copies printed on Croxley handmade paper is missing from the set available to CE; here we rely on Crane. Note that the figure given for the Book-of-the-Month Club/Catholic Book Club issue is not mentioned in the production records; it comes from Knopf's advertising and refers particularly to copies shipped.

12. The copyright page of the fifth edition of *Death Comes for the Archbishop* also includes the statement "RESET AND PRINTED FROM NEW PLATES." In this case Crane agrees, presumably because the font in which the book is set is changed (interestingly, to that used for *Shadows on the Rock*) and there is correspondence between Knopf and Cather confirming the new edition. It is worth noting that Knopf did not in this case renumber

the printings to emphasize the new edition, but that he took this further step in April 1946 in the case of *Shadows on the Rock*.

13. CE followed McKerrow's suggestion (183), measuring the distance between points widely separated in the middle of a page. Professor Johnson notes that such a difference is not significant: "A single type point equals .01385″. Therefore, a single line equals 14 points x .01385″ or .1939″. If the Monotype casting machine operator was having a bad day, and misread his micrometer by ⅛ of a point (.0017″) in either direction, the result would be ⅛ point x 28 lines per page or 3.5 points per page. Normally 3.5 points is acceptable, so . . . ¹⁄₃₂″, which is less than 3.5 points, is also acceptable variation" (letter to F. M. Link, 7 March 1996).

14. CE assumes that the text was re-keyed and that a new paper tape was used to produce the type for the new edition. Had the original tape been preserved and reused, the typesetting would still have been a new one, but the distinction between "new edition" — what Professor Johnson terms a "reset edition" — and "new printing" would be even less obvious. Professor Johnson states: "As a general rule . . . no printer would keep the paper tapes after the book was printed. It would be easier and less expensive to make line or 'patch' corrections in the electrotypes than to re-run part of a paper tape and to correct the type as necessary. In a large Monotype plant, paper tapes add up rapidly, creating a severe storage problem" (letter to F. M. Link, 7 March 1996).

15. Until this point, Heinemann had been the British publisher for all of Cather's books except *Song of the Lark*. Alfred Knopf says that "We were negotiating, not very satisfactorily, with Heinemann to do the book in England. A little later, C. S. Evans of

597

Heinemann wrote: 'We all know that our loyalty and belief in [Cather] have been unflinching from the moment she first came to us.' This despite the fact that they had turned down 'One of Ours,' allowed us to sell it to Jonathan Cape, and then on Galsworthy's strong urging got us to get a release from Cape so that they could publish it. We were trying to get Heinemann to commit themselves to a collected edition, since they had all of [Cather's] books on their list except 'The Song of the Lark,' which we thought they could easily enough buy from Murray. Cassell were interested, and I wrote all details to Miss Cather asking her for instructions. She was disappointed with Heinemann and told us to go ahead with Cassell" (Memoirs). A little later, Knopf adds: "Note that when we started our London house we did not ask [Cather] to come over to us, but expected her to remain with Heinemann, which she would have done had Evans been reasonably enthusiastic about 'Shadows on the Rock,' for which he offered an advance of two hundred and fifty pounds."

16. See Matthew J. Bruccoli, "Some Transatlantic Texts: West to East," in Brack and Barnes 244–55.

17. CE has included these typographical variants in the Table of Rejected Substantives because of its belief that their cumulative effect bears on the meaning of the text. We do not consider an individual instance significant, and we do not regard these variants as either accidentals or substantives (see note 2).

18. The University of Nebraska Press sets the clear text directly into page proofs, running three sets. Two sets come to the CE editors, who read the clear text against the emended copy-text and the apparatus against the typescript setting copy, reading first as a team and then as individuals. At this stage, page and

line numbers are added to the materials comprising the apparatus, keying all references to the CE text. They also check end-
line hyphenation to ensure accurate resolutions and to gather
material for word-division list B. Also at this stage, the press
proofs the text of the new edition against the copy-text and
proofs the text of the apparatus against the typescript setting
copy. The editors collate their two sets of corrected proof and
the press collates all three sets, sending the final corrected proof
to the compositor for correction. When the corrected proofs
return from the press, the editors make a collation of the material, correcting any errors in page and line numbers, checking
to see that indicated corrections have been made, and compil-
ing word-division list B for the newly reset text of the novel.
The press, meanwhile, compares pages to corrected proof to
ensure that no text has been dropped, reading the lines that
have been corrected. The editors then make the same check.

Works Cited

Bohlke, L. Brent, ed. *Willa Cather in Person: Interviews, Speeches, and Letters.* Lincoln: U Nebraska P, 1986.

Bowers, Fredson. "The Problem of Semi-Substantive Variants: An Example from the Shakespeare-Fletcher *Henry VIII.*" *Studies in Bibliography* 43 (1990): 80–84.

Brack, O M, Jr., and Warner Barnes, eds. *Bibliography and Textual Criticism.* Chicago: U Chicago P, 1969. 244–55.

Brown, E. K. *Willa Cather: A Critical Biography.* Completed by Leon Edel. New York: Knopf, 1953.

Cather, Willa. Letters to Ferris Greenslet. Houghton Library, Harvard U, Cambridge, Mass.

———. *Shadows on the Rock.* Typescript. Division of Manuscripts and Archives, New York Public Library, New York.

——. *Shadows on the Rock*. Carbon copy of New York Public Library typescript. Philip L. and Helen Cather Southwick Collection. Archives and Special Collections, Love Library, U of Nebraska–Lincoln.

——. *Shadows on the Rock*. First trade edition, limited issues. New York: Alfred A. Knopf, 1931.

——. *Shadows on the Rock*. First trade edition, printings 1–4. New York: Alfred A. Knopf, 1931.

——. *Shadows on the Rock*. First trade edition, Book-of-the-Month Club/Catholic Book Club issue. New York: Alfred A. Knopf, 1931.

——. *Shadows on the Rock*. First British edition, 1st printing. London: Cassell, 1932.

——. *Shadows on the Rock*. Autograph edition. Boston: Houghton Mifflin, 1938.

——. *Shadows on the Rock*. Second trade edition, 1st printing. New York: Alfred A. Knopf, 1946.

Crane, Joan. *Willa Cather: A Bibliography*. Lincoln: U Nebraska P, 1982.

Greg, W. W. "The Rationale of Copy-Text." *Studies in Bibliography* 3 (1950–51): 19–36. Rptd. with minor revision in *The Collected Papers of Sir Walter Greg*. Ed. J. C. Maxwell. Oxford: Clarendon P, 1966. 374–91.

Johnson, Herbert H. Letters to F. M. Link, 7 and 25 March 1996.

Knopf, Alfred A. Memoirs. Typescript. Harry Ransom Humanities Research Center, U Texas–Austin.

——. Production records for Alfred A. Knopf, Inc. Knopf Collection. Harry Ransom Humanities Research Center, U Texas–Austin.

Lewis, Edith. *Willa Cather Living: A Personal Record*. New York: Knopf, 1953.

McGann, Jerome. *The Textual Condition*. Princeton UP, 1991.

McKerrow, Ronald B. *An Introduction to Bibliography for Literary Students*. Corr. imp. Oxford: Clarendon P, 1928.

Tanselle, G. Thomas. "Greg's Theory of Copy-Text and the Editing of American Literature." *Studies in Bibliography* 28 (1975): 167–229.

Webster's New International Dictionary. 1909 ed. Springfield, Mass. G. & C. Merriam & Co., 1927.

Whiteman, Bruce, Charlotte Stewart, and Catherine Funnell. *A Bibliography of Macmillan Canada Imprints, 1906–1980*. Toronto: Dundurn P, 1985.

Woodress, James. *Willa Cather: A Literary Life*. Lincoln: U Nebraska P, 1987.

Emendations

T HE following list records all substantive and accidental changes introduced into the copy-text, the first trade issue of the first printing of the first edition of *Shadows on the Rock*, published by Alfred A. Knopf in 1931. The reading of the present edition appears to the left of the bracket; to the right are recorded the source of that reading, followed by a semicolon; the copy-text reading and the abbreviation for the copy-text; and other variant readings (if any), followed by the abbreviations for the texts whose readings are cited. CE to the immediate right of the bracket indicates that an emendation is made on the authority of the present editors without a precedent in an authoritative text. When a text is not cited, its reading is that of the present edition. When a group of texts listed sequentially below share the same reading, the first and last are listed on either side of a hyphen (K1.i–iv, for example). The *c* state readings (see p. 566) persist through K1.xx, but we list only the first printing to show them (K1.iv). The decision to emend is made on the authority of the present editors, although most emendations are supported by readings from other authoritative texts. An asterisk preceding the page and line number(s) indicates that the reading is discussed in the Notes on Emendations. Page and line numbers refer to the CE text.

The following abbreviations are used:

NT   The original form of the typescript in the New York Public Library

RNT   The revised form of the New York Public Library typescript

RST   The revised form of the carbon copy of the New York Public Library typescript, Philip L. and Helen Cather Southwick Collection, Special Collections, Love Library, University of Nebraska–Lincoln

T   NT, RNT, and RST all have the indicated reading

K1.i   The trade issue of the first printing of the first edition, Knopf, 1931

K1.ii   The trade issue of the second printing of the first edition, Knopf, 1931

K1.iii   The trade issue of the third printing of the first edition, Knopf, 1931

K1.iv   The trade issue of the fourth printing of the first edition, Knopf, 1931

A   The Autograph Edition, vol. 10. Boston: Houghton Mifflin, 1938

K2   The trade issue of the first printing of the second edition, Knopf, 1946

604

18.13	you] T, A, K2; your K1.i–iv
*19.15, 20.18 & 21.6	ma'm'selle] CE; Ma'm'selle T–K1.iv, K2; *ma'm'selle* A
*43.7	Juchereau] CE; Juschereau T–K2
*62.12	endeavoured] A, K2; tried T; endeavored K1.i–iv
*70.16	Frog's] CE; frog's T–K2
*95.18	Auclair's] A, K2; Auclaire's T, K1.i–iv
*95.20, 146.2	Gervais] CE; Gervaise T–K2
105.2	affair.] T, A, K2; affair_x K1.i–iv
146.8	liniments] K1.iv, A, K2; linaments T–K1.iii
158.21	*préfère*] K2; *prefer* NT; *préfère* RST; *préfére* RNT–A
188.17	ma'm'selle] A; Ma'm'selle T–K1.iv, K2
*189.13, 212.24	Father] A; father T–K1.iv, K2
*217.14	Sainte-Pétronille] CE; St. Petronille NT, RST; Saint-Pétronille RNT–K2
*219.16	herbs] A; eucalyptus balls T–K1.iv, K2
226.15	*deux*"!] T, A; *deux!*" K1.i–iv, K2
231.8	Tadoussac] A; Tadousac T–K1.iv, K2
*235.19	Snail] A; snail T–K1.iv, K2
247.26	herbs] A; little nuts T–K1.iv, K2
*247.26	mosquitos] RNT, RST; mosquitoes NT, K1.i–K2

248.1   "Certainly] A; "Ah yes, the eucalyptus balls! Cer-
             tainly T, K1.iv, K2

*249.23, 24 mademoiselle] A; Mademoiselle T–K1.iv, K2

276.17   enterprise] A; undertaking T; enterprize K1.i–iv,
             K2

*288.7   hay-bales] RNT, A, K1.ii–K2; hay bales NT, RST;
             hay-bale_x K1.i

*289.12   *bléd.*] NT, RST, K2; *bléd,* K1.i–iv; *blé.* RNT, A

291.6   *préféreriez*] CE; *preferrez* T; *préférériez* K1.i–K2

*291.10   has] A; had T–K1.iv, K2

303.19   once,] NT, RNT, A, K2; once K1.i–iv

*304.13   muttered,] NT, RNT, A; muttered K1.i–iv, K2

309.5, 19   Governor General] CE; Governor-General NT,
             RNT–K2

314.20   1700] NT, RNT, K1.iv–K2; 1770 K1.i–iii

*320.13   bishop] CE; Archbishop NT; archbishop RNT;
             Bishop K1.i–K2

Notes on Emendations

With few exceptions, K1 sets "monsieur," "madame," and "made-moiselle" in lowercase unless a name follows. See also 188.17.   19.15 etc.

The name of the historical figure was "Juchereau." CE emends here   43.7
and at 44.6, 14; 45.5–6, 7, 19; 46.1, 13; 48.25; 49.5, 11; 50.5; 52.12;
137.13; 146.13; 147.1, 3, 12; 149.4, 6–7; and 215.20 on the grounds
that Cather wanted her French correct and took pains to use the
correct spelling of the names of her other historical personages.

The "u" is in other instances added; this appears to be a rare slip   62.12
rather than merely inconsistent.

The practice in most instances, followed by A at 205.14, is to cap-   70.16
italize the nickname; it is also clearer. See 205.14 below.

This is the only place where the original spelling "Auclaire" is not   95.18
in K1.i replaced by "Auclair." CE regards the reading as a rare slip.

The masculine form lacks the *e* in French. CE changes to the proper   95.20, 146.2
French form because of Cather's documented desire to have such
forms correct. We have also emended to correct French at 158.21
and 291.6.

212.24   In the many other instances in this text, K1 capitalizes in direct address, as also "Papa."

217.14   Petronilla was a woman, hence the correct French form is "Sainte."

219.16   As the explanatory note to this passage points out, the eucalyptus was not introduced into France until the nineteenth century. Although we have no direct evidence that the A reading is Cather's, it is not the sort of change an editor would make. We assume that at some point between 1931 and 1937–38 Cather was made aware of the anachronism and corrected K1 accordingly. We emend here and at 247.25 and 248.1 because the changes do not redefine the essential meaning of the passage or alter historical fact in the interests of fiction but rather correct a factual error.

235.19   See 70.16 above.

247.26   This word is spelled "mosquitos" in its other four appearances in the text, and it is specifically changed to this spelling in RST and RNT.

249.23, 24   The practice in the great majority of instances in this text is to set such appellations in lowercase when no name follows. See 14.4 above.

288.7   The final "s" of the word prints faintly in one copy of the limited edition CE has seen; it drops out completely in most copies of K1 but was patched in for K1.ii.

289.12   A comma following *bléd* does not complete the sentence properly; we substitute a period, following the practice in all texts except K1.i–iv.

608

The sense here either requires "has" or requires one to treat the 291.10
sentence as narration rather than as part of Cécile's speech. The
next sentence, however, eliminates the second option.

The comma is present in similar constructions in the text and was 304.13
also present in NT and RNT.

Lowercase is used throughout the text when no specific person is 320.13
mentioned. The NT reading is also corrected to lowercase in RNT.

Table of Rejected Substantives

THIS list records substantive and quasi-substantive variants between the copy-text (K1.i) and the texts of the other authoritative editions (the original [NT] and corrected [RNT and RST] forms of the typescript and the Autograph Edition [A]) that have been excluded from the present edition. The page, line number, and reading of the present edition text appear to the left of the bracket; to the right of the bracket appear, in chronological sequence, the variant readings and the abbreviations for their sources. Variants are separated by a semicolon. Ellipsis points indicate an omission made for the sake of brevity; they are not part of the CE text. If no reference is given, that text agrees with K1.i. When the reading of RNT or RST differs from that of NT or K1.i only in accidentals, the accidental variants are ignored. We also list the frequent French words and phrases set in roman type in K1.i–iv and K2 but in italics in A; we believe that their cumulative effect, at least, is substantive. For the same reason, we list the changes in the paragraphing of the various texts. We list one early example of recurring variant-spelling accidentals like "though"–"although," "ax"–"axe," "afterwards"–"afterward," and "inquire"–"enquire" and one instance of recurring variants in the spelling of proper names. Throughout the TS accent marks were added by hand; we have consistently regarded them as belonging to NT. A bracketed question mark indicates a typescript reading we are unsure of; a subscript "x" (ₓ) indicates a dropped or broken letter; a pointed bracket (⟨⟩) indicates a reading intermediate between NT and the final reading of RNT or RST, almost always one that has been entered and then canceled; braces indicate editorial interpolations. We have used the paragraph symbol without brackets to indicate variants in paragraphing; although such breaks are typographical rather than substantive, they sometimes have an effect on meaning.

The following abbreviations are used:

NT	The original form of the typescript in the New York Public Library
RNT	The revised form of the New York Public Library typescript
RST	The revised form of the carbon copy of the New York Public Library typescript, Southwick Collection, UNL
T	NT, RNT, and RST all have the indicated reading
A	The Autograph Edition, vol. 10. Boston: Houghton Mifflin, 1938

Note: In determining line numbers, only text lines are counted; chapter numbers and white spaces are not counted.

7.4	far beneath] beneath RST
7.6	splits] split NT
7.9	¶ As long as] All the morning, while NT; As long as RST, RNT

8.7 Montreal] Montreal with the news NT

8.8 lingered] still lingered NT

8.8 long after] after NT

8.20 rich] red NT

8.21 which] that T

8.22 Europe, and] Europe just then, the NT; Europe, just then) and RNT

9.1 as one of] as NT

9.15 grey stone with steep dormer roofs,] gray stone with steep dormer 〉 mansard {all canceled} roofs, RST

9.20 still stood] still, on a ledge sloping north, NT

9.21 facing] faced NT

10.2 Bishop's] Archbishop's T {This change from a form of "Bishop" to a form of "Archbishop" is also made at 26.19 (twice), 23; 27.24; 33.15, 17; 67.9, 11; 72.21; 82.10; 83.8; 84.9; 86.7; 87.3; 88.10; 91.1, 4; 92.8; 93.2; 111.19; 124.8; 133.7, 13, 16; 137.7; 141.5, 13, 25; 142.10, 25; 143.3; 145.22; 162.21; 188.9; 192.16; 201.20; 235.7; 238.8; 240.19; 253.2; 264.1, 23; 266.12; 267.2; 280.9; 282.6; 292.22, 24; 293.7; 296.7, 17; 300.18; 310.2, 18, 24; 311.3, 11, 15, 20, 25; 312.21; 313.16; 314.5, 13, 20; 316.9, 14; 318.5, 21; 319.23; 320.13; 321.6}

10.5 along] on RST

10.10   streets] street NT

10.23–24   which rose] bulking up T

10.25   d'Orléans,] d'Orléans lay T

10.25   was like] like T

11.1   lying] rising T

11.11   suffocation] strangulation NT

11.15   along] north and south, along T

11.16–17   a highway] an avenue NT

11.20   After all, the world] Ah, the world! It NT

11.21   *La*] the T

11.22–23   of the] the T

11.25   cut in a point] cut pointed NT

12.3   often had] had NT

12.5   inquiring] enquiring NT, A

12.5   everything] everything else NT

12.12–13   river. He was glancing] river and glanced NT

13.3   past] and past NT

13.3   and down] down NT

13.10   a mere] merely a NT

13.11–12   the French] French NT

13.13	stony] cobbled NT
13.14	Bishop's] new Bishop's T
13.16	Count] Count de NT
14.2	which was partly] partly T
14.3	a fire burned] there was a fire T
14.10	filling] filled T
14.20	*de*] *des* NT
14.22	*de*] *des* NT
14.25	Comte] Count NT; Conte RST
15.4	poulet] *poulet* A
15.10	ménage] *ménage* A
15.13	dined] had dinner ⟩ dined RST
15.22	was bringing] brought NT
16.6	la Rochelle] Rochelle NT
16.8	and] and {canceled and restored} RST
16.9	to Paris] in Paris NT
16.15	is sometimes] is NT
16.20	But surely] At any rate, NT, RST
16.21	one another] each other NT
16.22	béret] *béret* ⟩ béret RST; *béret* A

17.2	she] now she T
17.6	She] ¶ She A
17.16	should go] went NT
17.18	Clothilde] Clotilde A
17.19	means and] means, and who NT
18.4	a blank] blank NT
18.6	recall] catch NT
18.19	these] these wild NT
18.22	*tous*] *toutes* T
18.22	*jusqu'aux*] *jusqueau* NT; *jusqu'au* RST
19.3	an iron] the iron T
19.8	that] which RST
19.19	half-loaf] misshapen half-loaf NT
19.22	in his] on his NT
20.12	refuse] the refuse NT
20.16	very small] small RST
20.18	Merci, Ma'm'selle, merci beaucoup] *Merci, ma'm'selle, merci beaucoup* A
20.19	He] ¶ He A
20.19	sipped] drank NT

20.25   his glass] the glass NT

20.25   got up,] rose NT

21.3   and] so that T

21.6   Bon soir] *Bonsoir* A

21.21   rocky cliff] rock wall of Mountain Hill T

22.7–8   adventurers who disliked] fellows who preferred adventure to NT

22.12   fell] in felling NT

22.13   for firewood] to feed the ovens NT

22.18   and tortured by] by T

22.21–22 goûter] *goûter* A

22.21–22 goûter. Breakfast was a] goûter, the breakfast a NT; goûter, breakfast a RNT; goûter, and breakfast a goûter. Breakfast was a goûter, breakfast a RST

22.23   and a fresh loaf which] with the fresh loaf ⟩ K I RST

22.24   Auclair] he NT

23.4   She] It was then she NT

23.4–5   the fables of La Fontaine] La Fontaine NT

23.5   Plutarch] Racine NT

23.12   publish] write NT

23.16   her] Cécile A

23.19   was only] was not T

24.1   across it] across R S T

24.2–3   street and faced upon its own court] street and faced
             its own court N T; street R S T

24.7   was greener] greener T

25.6   recall it] remember N T; recall R S T, R N T

25.18   grandparents] grandfather N T

25.23   got up] got N T

26.4   grandmother] Grandfather N T

26.18   Count Frontenac] the Count T

26.22   him!] him. T

26.23   had] had now T

26.25   diocese] parish T

27.1   landed] had landed N T

27.11   candles] lights N T

27.13   the Count] he N T

27.22   back with him] home T

28.1   seemed to be] seemed T

28.14   was] were ⟩ was R N T

28.16   Bishop's] new Bishop's T

29.13 comfortable sitting-room] sitting-room T

29.17 apothecary] personal apothecary NT

30.1 stuffed] skeleton of a NT

30.11 a similar] the same T

31.3 got] had got A

31.4 ménage] *ménage* A

32.14 her red] the red NT

33.20 had asked] asked NT

33.22 carried] had carried NT

34.12 *Qu'est-ce*] *Qu'es* [?] NT, RST

34.20–35.1 shop. Every . . . Saint-Antoine] shop and reading Latin with a Sulpitian Father NT; shop. In the afternoon he read Latin at the Jesuits on the Rue St. Antoine just around the corner RST; shop. In the afternoon he read Latin with a father at the Jesuits on the rue Saint-Antoine, just around the corner RNT; {same as K I.i except "Jesuits' "} A

35.18 off than he] off NT

35.21 was] was quite NT

35.24 tenants, the Auclairs] tenants NT

36.1 ¶ The Count] The Count T

36.2 always] had always T

36.11   lived] had lived NT

36.15–16   sometimes paid] used sometimes to pay NT

37.3   content with] devoted to NT

37.8   period] time NT

37.9   deep] deeply NT, RST

37.12   further] farther A

37.14   considered Fagon] believed Faguet NT

37.14   a bigoted] to be a stupid NT; a stupid RST, RNT

37.20   prescribed] tried to get NT

38.2–3   that the . . . for him] important NT

38.3–4   Versailles it . . . household] Versailles, one after another of the King's household had been bled at the
feet NT; Versailles it was regularly practised on the
King's household RNT

38.9   pharmacien] druggist NT; *pharmacien* RST, A

38.25   Moreover, he] He NT

39.5–6   the Innocents . . . Saint-Paul] Saint Innocents while
NT; the Innocents . . . St. Paul's RST

39.8   the Count] her husband NT

39.20   ever] had ever NT

40.8   the wrongs] outrages NT

40.11	always] constantly NT
40.17	palace] palaces NT
40.17	Versailles] Versailles and Marley NT; Versailles and Marly ⟩ Versailles RST
40.20	less] better NT
40.24	prisons of Paris] prisons NT
40.24–25	boyhood] father's time, NT
41.1	put to death] executed NT
41.7	wished] would like NT
41.9	as eager] eager NT
41.13	the one] that NT
41.19	might] would NT
42.9	allée] *allée* A
42.15	allée] *allée* A
43.19	Auclair] he NT
43.21	it] you know it NT
43.22	ships sail] ship sails T
43.22	many] so many NT
43.23	examine] have to examine T
43.24	shall] will NT, RST

43.24	boats] boat NT
44.11	from her] on her T
44.19	at this] in this NT
45.9	on] upon NT
45.10	hospital] house NT
46.3	to] left to NT
46.9	I have had to sit here with] I had NT
46.14–15	*qu'elle ait quitté*] elle a quitté NT
46.20	the town] Dieppe NT
47.11	¶ Twelve] Twelve A
48.12	to repent] repent NT
48.15	abridged, and now] abridged, and wiping out by the intensity of my sufferings a debt which would otherwise have taken many years to clear away. Now NT
49.4	*en supplie*] implore T
49.9	Yes] Yes, yes NT
49.10	day.] day, when I have thought about it. NT; day! RST; day. after 〉 day. RNT
49.25	She] Juschereau NT
50.18	Jesuit missionaries] Jesuits NT
51.8	an] a RNT

51.12   monastère] *monastère* A

51.16   permission] consent T

51.20   her father's consent] the consent of her father NT

51.25   where she first] when first she NT

52.7–8   Father Brébeuf, the martyr] Pere Bréboeuf, the most genial and engaging of all the martyrs NT

52.9–10   for all her] for her RST

52.11   communicated to] given NT

52.14   many people] many NT

52.16–17   nervous,] nervous, exalte NT

52.23   hardy] humble-born, hardy NT

52.24   Canada.] Canada. ¶ Mother Juschereau was a shrewd judge of human nature, and this little girl of Auclaire's puzzled her. She suspected the child of having ideas which she did not communicate to her elders. Cécile was not reserved, on the contrary, she was impulsive and outspoken, with no small vanities as to dress or person. Yet there was something, very much alive, which she kept within herself. Mother Juschereau sometimes wondered if she were not addicted to {end of page} NT

55.9   church] church, with a narrow street to right and left NT

55.12	had been] was NT, RST
55.14	was] had been NT, RST
55.16	houses with walls] walls T
55.17	steep, slated] steep, RST
55.17	and dormers] with jutting dormers NT; with dormers RST, RNT
55.18	*La Place*] The Place T; La Place A
56.3	middle] centre NT
56.3	plot (pitifully small, indeed)] plot, pitifully small, indeed NT
56.9	laid] hung T
56.22	the] this T
57.1	carrots, pumpkins,] carrots, NT
57.2	salads] salad NT
57.12–13	got through the winter] lived the winter through NT
57.23	dozens] dozen A
58.5	carried] had NT
58.5	over] sent over NT
58.9	extremely] very A
58.15–16	I must . . . today] The market is full of wood doves T

59.10 both of us] both NT

59.10 who] that RST

59.21 stone] stone, with a clumsy spire. The King had given the new Archbishop money to build it ten years ago NT

60.2 the Place] La Place A

60.4 meditating in] enjoying NT

60.14 look at] notice NT

61.6 worst. She] worst. The poor Savoyard who had selected her out of the lot offered him, afterward drank himself to death in revenge for his bad choice. They NT

61.6 daughter] child NT

61.10 reform] reformation NT

61.10 *Gironde*] *Garonne* NT

61.12 for France] in the autumn NT; for France in the autumn RST

61.12 After] When NT

61.14 work] work much NT

61.17 she] 'Toinette NT

61.18 shipmates] old captain NT; old shipmates RST

61.18 had] had taken pity on him, T

61.19   on board *La Gironde* and taken] on *La Garonne* and shipped NT

61.24   the ships] ships NT

61.24   they stuck] the stuck {error} NT

62.12   endeavoured] tried T

62.16   had first noticed] first began to notice NT; had first began to noticed {*sic*} RST

62.17   and begun to] and to NT

62.17–18   her, wash] her to wash NT

62.18   Auclair thought it natural] It was natural, Auclaire felt T

62.20   to care] care NT

62.22   La] Le NT

62.22   was] watched Jacques carefully, NT

62.23   saw] showed NT

62.24   closely] so closely ⟩ closely RST

63.2   goûter] *goûter* A

63.25–64.1   Grenouille. Likely] Grenouille, and likely NT

64.2   night, and the] night. The NT

65.2   "Papa"] ¶ 'Papa' A

65.9   Giorgio] Georgio T

626

66.2   Picard] Gaspard NT

66.3   Giorgio and to ask] Georgio, asked NT; Georgio
            and ask RST, RNT

66.4   were] was NT

66.6   Georges Million] Georges NT

66.10   as a] as NT

67.16   Lhut] Luth T

68.1   the drummer boy] Georgio NT

68.5   one] one often T

68.5   Picard] Gaspard NT

68.9–10   apartment in . . . wing. ¶ The] apartment on the
            second floor of the south wing. Gaspard opened the
            door and asked her to wait in the hall while he spoke
            to his master. The NT

68.12   study. The] study. ¶ The NT

68.14   and his] and the NT

68.15   bed] bed, which stood imposingly in the angle of the
            two walls without windows NT

68.20–21   Picard] Gaspard NT

68.21   laid down his pen, beckoned] put down his pen,
            turned in his chair, and beckoned NT; put down his
            pen, beckoned RNT; beckoned RST

68.22   forefinger,] forefinger. He NT

68.24   As] When NT

69.1   lips] lips. The Count had a strange mouth for an old
             man; his lips were not hard and set like old Bishop
             Laval's. They were full and muscular, and could ruf-
             fle up with rage like a turkey gobbler's comb NT

70.15   into] in NT

70.17   Picard] Gaspard NT

71.8   above] behind NT

71.11   the Saracens] some Moor, they have a great many
             secrets about glass NT; a Saracens RNT

71.17   should] would NT, RST

71.22   She] ¶ She A

71.23   Picard] Gaspard NT

72.8   which] that NT

73.1   happily] twice NT

73.2–3   world. Only . . . become] world, before she became
             NT

73.5   that] which T

73.6   when] whenever NT

73.13   school] convent NT

73.16   enjoy] console herself with R S T

73.17   she] Cécile R S T

73.18   river so thick] river so thick the river so thick N T
             {duplication due to patched pages}

73.21   flèche] *flèche* A

74.4–5   It was . . . own house] It was on days like this that
             Cecile loved her town best, when one could not see
             the people one passed, or the river, or one's own
             house. It was like walking in a dream N T

74.7–8   from everything . . . way, she] from the world and
             living in a twilight of miracles and dreams. She
             loitered on her way, and after she had delivered the
             packet of lime flowers to Sister Agatha she N T

74.10   ¶ Cécile] She N T

74.22   came] got N T

75.4–5   in there . . . wind] one was out of the wind there T

76.3–4   said Jacques] Jacques said A

76.4   She] ¶ She A

76.8   church* {footnote: "*The charm . . . of 1929."}]
             church {no footnote number or text} N T; church[1]
             {but no footnote text} R N T

76.11   had] has N T

76.23   greatly] quite R S T

629

77.5   as] at N T

78.11   Blessed] Holy T

78.23   fête] *fête* A

78.25   savoir-faire] *savoir-faire* A

79.18   later] after while N T

81.7   wouldn't] shouldn't R N T

81.14   *Garonne*] *Seine* N T, R S T

81.23   going] getting T

82.2   déjeuner] *déjeuner* A

83.19–20   walls. Long veils of smoky fog were] walls, long veils
            of smoky fog T

83.20   were caught] caught T

83.21   how fresh the air smelled!] the air smelled so fresh.
            T

84.4   He] Jacques A

84.20   overhead] over the Isle d'Orleans T

84.23–24   trees . . . ice. It] trees. It T

85.3   afterwards] afterward N T, R S T

85.4   up the] up N T

86.10   which] that N T, R S T

630

88.12   ¶ "No] 'No A

88.21   The] ¶ The A

89.9   he was left] left him NT, RST

89.11   cloak] coat NT

89.17   which] that T

89.24   measures] measure NT

89.25   had been] was NT

90.7   guides] guide NT

90.15   before] long before NT

91.4   Bishop] Archbishop RNT

91.24   bonne] *bonne* A

93.2   Bishop. If] Archbishop, and if T

93.16–17   shoulders; his head was] shoulders, his head T

93.18   his fleshy face was] a fleshy face, T

93.19   creases] creases. The two deep lines that curved
               from the base of his nose to his chin divided that
               part of his face into a separate oval, like a little egg
               standing against a big egg NT

94.1   Bonjour] *Bonjour* A

94.7   He] ¶ He A

94.14   woman] lady NT

94.19   about much] about NT

94.22   Oui, madame] *Oui, madame* A

95.2   Madame] ¶ Madame A

95.9   see her mother] their house NT

95.15   this Noël] Noel A

95.20   chirurgien] *chirurgien* A

96.1   had found] found NT

96.1   the crutch] her crutch NT

96.5   runners] runner NT

96.6   over the snow to the Cathedral] to the Cathedral over the snow NT

96.9   leather,] leather and NT

96.11   she loved to watch] and she loved to see NT

96.21   Cécile] ¶ Cécile A

97.8   he] be NT

98.3   down] up T

98.25   Tonti] Tonty T

98.25–99.1   Robert de La Salle has] He used to NT; He Robert de La Salle has RNT

99.4–5   It is always like that] That is the way NT; It is always that RST

99.10   from Pommier] in Pommier NT

100.8   teeth] ones T

100.13   oui, monsieur] oui NT; oui, Monsieur 〉 oui, mon-
          sieur RNT; *oui, monsieur* A

101.20   fellow] boy NT

103.7   something that] that NT; something which RST

103.22   white] glass NT

104.5   had suggested that he] suggested he should NT

104.16   tightly wrapped] wrapped NT

104.18   The] ¶ The A

105.1–2   Je . . . savez!] *Je suis mère, vous savez!* A

105.8   Bien] *Bien* A

105.12   "The] ¶ 'The A

105.13   different] very different NT

105.19   "Do] ¶ 'Do A

106.4–5   Au revoir, monsieur] *Au revoir, monsieur* A

106.13   Auclair] M. Auclaire NT

107.1   among] with NT

107.6–7   Cécile . . . always?"] Cécile, tomorrow is All Souls'
          Day; shall you have a mass said for poor Bichet?" T

107.8–12 "Yes, on . . . "Please] "Yes, in the Récollet chapel."
          These Franciscan brothers extended their charity to

the dead; they would say a mass for a departed soul very cheaply, — for whatever one felt able to give them, indeed. ¶ "And will you take me with you? Please NT; "Yes, in the Récollet chapel." ¶ (These Franciscan brothers extended their charity even to the dead; they would say a mass for a departed soul very cheaply, — for whatever one felt able to give them, indeed.) ¶ "And will you take me with you? Please RST, RNT

107.12   Bichet] him T

107.19   ¶ "Poor] "Poor NT

107.21   and he] now and then he NT; and RST

108.21   on the rue du Figuier stood] there was on the rue NT; on the rue des Jardins stood RST; on the rue des Jardins stood ⟩ du Figuier stood RNT

109.6   ¶ One] One T

109.22   house . . . done] house NT, RST

110.18   except by] except NT

110.25   thief] thieves NT

111.3   every year] tomorrow T

111.4   should] would NT, RST

111.7   the day he died] All Souls' Day T

111.9–10   long; in the . . . Dieu] long. In the morning to the Récollets', with her father, to hear the Mass said for poor Bichet, then to the Ursuline chapel to pray with the nuns for the souls of the founders and early Superiors. In the afternoon she went to the Hôtel Dieu to pray for Mother Catherine de St. Augustine T

111.12   Madame Auclair] her mother T

111.17   was.] was. Not so sorrowful but that she could enjoy the beautiful golden ceiling at the Recollets' chapel, where she seldom went, and feel the comfort of getting back to her own little church in the Lower Town, like returning to one's own fireside after a pilgrimage. NT

112.14   on] if it is T

112.15   the] all the T

112.16   suffering] stories of cruelty and suffering T

112.17   value, — seem] value. They appeal to a child as they do to an artist, and NT

112.19   ¶ On] On T

112.23   fog;] fog, and T

113.3   Catherine] Catharine T

113.3   her] all her T

113.3–4   rose up before one] had come to life again NT

113.6   ¶ At] At T

113.13   with the] with NT

113.14   hidden in] taken to NT

113.18   not harmed] miraculously preserved from harm NT

114.7   ships] ships. The post-bags always brought grief to
                  someone T

114.11   Kebec] Quebec NT; Kébec A

114.19   glorious] goodly NT

114.25   realities] important realities T

115.14–15   but there . . . repentant] but miracles happened re-
                  peatedly, even in behalf of the most depraved; and
                  for those who died without having time to repent T

115.22   good] excellent ⟩ good {*stet*} RNT

115.23   exquisite] lovely NT

116.4   remote and savage] savage RST

116.14   morning] the morning T

117.2   hill] street NT

117.3   protégé] *protégé* A

117.4   déjeuner] *déjeuner* A

117.8   unfastened] took off NT

117.25   goûter] *goûter* A

118.5   shot] went NT

119.4   in] in from the kitchen NT

119.20   stooped] stopped NT

119.22   hill] street NT

120.1   out for] after NT

120.6   where the] where NT

120.9   they] that they T

120.13   Lalemant] Lalamant T

120.16   tortures] unimaginable tortures which NT

121.8   crèche] *crèche* A

121.8   shall] will NT, RST

121.9   too. And] too. We are going to arrange it on the very day before Christmas, as my Aunt directed, and NT

121.10   Monsieur] M. NT, RST

121.18   The cobbler] He RST

121.19   blaze] fire NT

121.23   on] down on T

121.23   weight] weight. But she must see your creche; she likes toys NT, RST {except "crêche"}

121.24   like] like even better NT

121.24   house again] house NT

121.25	it] it. I used to go there so often NT
122.5	was then] was NT
122.9	friend] friend again NT
122.13	Jacques and Cécile] the two children NT
122.15	softly] softly out into the blue NT; softly in the blue dusk RST; softly in the blue RNT
122.20	fiery vapours] vapor NT
122.20	clouds] clouds; red and gold and orange and lavender NT
123.3	She] ¶ She A
123.7	tender, burning] flaming NT
123.17–18	sea. VIII {centered; white space before and after}] sea. IX {centered; white space before and after} ¶ Marie Louise Pigeon, the baker's third daughter, was still a day pupil at the Ursulines, and one evening she brought a note {text discontinuous} her teacher fancied, had been given some such invisible token. A circle of glowing admirations, a jewel box full of legends that never lost their radiance. IX {centered; white space after} NT
124.1	crunch] craunch T
124.8	with . . . bell-rope] at the end of the bell-rope with his lantern T

124.16	would] could NT
124.17	de Laval] Laval T
124.21–22	which rang in the] in the NT
125.1	The punctual bell and the] The bell and the rope and the NT
125.2	rang] pulled NT
125.5–6	mysterious] soothing T
125.8	Cécile] she NT
125.9–10	wood. Today they would unpack] wood, to decorate NT
125.10	crèche] *crèche* A
125.11	had lain] that had stood NT
125.17	crèche] *crèche* A
125.19	but then] in which case NT, RST
125.20	This] But this T
126.8	home. ¶] home. A
126.9	¶ Cécile] Cécile A
126.11	waylaid] found NT
126.18	sheath] twist T
126.24	When] After NT, RST

127.2   would be] was NT

127.3   when he] he RST

127.4   away. She] away, and T

127.7   fête] *fête* A

127.9–10   was so . . . and was] seemed a little bewildered and NT

127.17   Blessed Virgin] Virgin T

127.23   Those] They T

128.4   down by] down NT

128.5   here] there T

128.21–22   another listener, by the fireplace behind her, and she had entirely] entirely {does not follow from p. 96, which ends "There was"} RST; another listener by the fireplace, behind her, and she had entirely RNT

129.6   crèche] *crèche* A

129.6   to bid] bid T

129.14   after] when NT

129.17   paroisse] *paroisse* A

129.17–18   réveillon] *réveillon* A

129.21   does that] does NT

129.23   here. Such] here, such T

131.7	crèche] *crèche* A
131.11	crèche] *crèche* A
132.2	home] home, and other Christmases when they had plenty of Norman cider NT
132.4	was] was quite NT, RST
132.4	crèche] *crèche* A
132.7	Before] ¶ Before A
132.11	him] him here NT
132.13–14	Non . . . toujours] *Non . . . toujours* A
132.14	toujours] toujour NT
132.20	C'est . . . ça] *C'est . . . ça* A
133.1	out-of-doors] out-of-door NT
133.7	say] perform T
133.7	Bishop would be present] Archbishop would be in the choir T
133.9	music] chants T
133.16	Bishop Laval] the old Archbishop T
133.17	sacristy] vestry room T
133.22–23	chapel . . . difficult] chapel was a little difficult, over fresh snow that had not packed NT, RST
133.24–134.1	alight. Across] alight, and across NT, RST

641

134.5	ruddy] lighted R S T
137.7	young Bishop's] Archbishop's T
137.9	come] been N T
137.12	boxes] boxes of lemon peel R S T
138.12	Saint-Vallier's] The Bishop's T
138.13	conciliatory] wearied N T
139.2	away from] from N T
139.7	de Laval's] Laval's T
139.13	Bishop] young Bishop N T
139.14	which] that N T
139.18	de Laval] Laval N T
139.19	that he] that the N T, R S T
139.20	white] glass N T
139.21	"You] ¶ 'You A
139.24	better] better, on the whole, T
140.4	Saint-Vallier] The Bishop T
140.23	be reduced] be doubled or reduced N T
141.4	¶ These] These T
141.10–11	to take away] taking away R S T, R N T
141.11	transfer] transfering R S T, R N T

141.14   Priests' House] porter's lodge NT

141.15   round] around A

141.25   new Bishop] young Archbishop NT; new Archbishop RST, RNT

142.10   forty-four; he] forty-four, though he NT

142.11   twelve] ten NT

142.11–12   years, — . . . France] years NT

142.13   Saint-Vallier.] Saint-Vallier; he felt something theatrical about him, and something untrustworthy, unstable, rather NT; Saint-Vallier; he felt something theatrical about him, and something unstable RST; Saint-Vallier; he felt something theatrical about him, and unstable RNT

142.23   charities] charities, his gifts to poor parishes and to poor people T

143.1   this debt] this NT

143.1   years] year NT

143.5–6   de Saint-Vallier . . . Rome] St. Vallier out of many to be his successor T

143.7   predecessor] co-adjutor T

143.18   had little] not had much NT

143.18–19   follies . . . world.)] follies that were not in line of business NT

643

143.19–20   one day . . . Bishop] to become second Archbishop T

143.21–22   become . . . influenced] adopted that course of pru-
             dent piety by which she controlled T

144.1   secured] he secured T

144.7   Saint-] ¶ Saint- A

144.17   special permission] permission NT; especial permis-
             sion RST; especial ⟩ special permission RNT

145.4   piety] bigotry T

145.23   age, he] age of {discontinuous text} he NT

146.1   After] The long part of the Canadian winter was the
             stretch between New Year's and Easter, — no matter
             how late Easter came, it was winter still. After NT

146.2   chirurgien] *chirurgien* A

146.5   was much] was NT

146.6   and from] from NT, RNT

146.7   or he was] or NT

146.13   that] which NT

147.12   Mother] how angry Mother NT

147.12   be horrified] be NT

147.14   cures] miracles NT

147.19   might] would NT, RNT; would ⟩ might {canceled} RST

147.21   I think it probable] Absolutely T

147.22   jar] glass jar NT

147.23   is sometimes] is NT

147.24   in small doses for] in very small doses NT; for RST

147.24   certain] God knows what NT

147.25   still to be] {word illegible} to be NT

147.25   many] some NT

148.2   remedy] horrible remedy NT

148.10   that was] it was NT

148.15   died in agony] died NT; died in agony {canceled &
              restored} RNT

148.17   bones] those NT

148.20   relics] bones NT

149.5   Her father must be] She knew her father was NT

149.8   bone.] bone. While she washed the dishes she was
              thinking that there were two kinds of cures in the
              world, and that it was very hard to make them agree.
              NT

150.3   likely hear] hear T

150.9   soup] soup and because of his bad jaw he could not
              eat and talk at the same time NT

150.10   Cécile] ¶ Cécile A

150.17   light] bright light NT

150.21   ¶ "Did] Cécile was beginning to see the picture.
                "Did NT

151.14   life of] chapter on NT, RST

151.21   blew] put T

151.21–22   himself got] got NT

152.1   In her . . . whole] The whole NT

152.2   Montreal] Montreal took on new life in her mind,
                kindled by this marvelous incident NT

152.3   Le Ber, the recluse,] Le Ber NT

152.4–5   Montreal. When] Montreal, and when NT, RST

152.10   saw] had seen T

152.12   had told] used to tell NT

152.20   her] the Le Bers' NT

152.25–153.1   convent, returned] convent, and returned A

153.3   society and] society, NT

153.10   from school] home T

153.13   Blessed] Holy T

153.16   of the] of that T

153.17	When] ¶ When A
153.23	there were many] many were the NT
153.24	said] whispered NT
154.3	childhood] infancy NT
154.5	brief] short NT
154.19	Upon] Before NT
154.24	Thebais] Thebiad NT, RST; Thébais A
155.12	exceptional] exception NT
155.17	her daughter's] that NT
155.19	dish] food NT
156.7	the kiss] a kiss NT
156.14–15	Behind] At the back of it, behind NT
156.15	altar of this chapel] alter, NT
156.16	At] When she was thirty-two years of age, at NT
156.18	had been] was NT, RST
156.20	were] had long been NT
156.22	still, after two years] still NT
157.10	Blessed] Holy T
157.20	admiration] his admiration NT

157.21	or when] or NT
157.23	with a] and a NT
158.2	sometimes] often NT
158.15	urged] had urged NT
158.18	*ma*] *mon* NT
159.1	little Jacques] Jacques NT
159.9	wind] wind from Montreal NT
159.17	parishes. Wherever] parishes, and wherever NT
159.17	pleasure, as] pleasure. It was as NT
159.21	gift. In] gift; even the most needy habitants would not have bartered it for food or clothing. In T
160.3	desire] wish and desire NT
160.15	moccasins, with] moccasins and T
161.15	snow] snow. I have not seen my sister yet NT
161.15	I came] I have come RST
162.18	a little cordial for himself] himself a little cordial at this good news NT
163.25	some] in some NT
164.19	stand] stand up NT
165.13	go] come RST

165.14   Blessed Sacrament] Sacrament T

166.15   wakened] wakened up T

166.17   Ave Maria] *Ave Maria* A

167.2   blowing] blowing from the southwest NT

167.14   but the] and the RST, RNT

167.21   Blessed Sacrament] Sacrament T

168.1   weak] weak from hunger and eating snow NT; weak, RST

168.17–18   after that] afterward NT, RST; afterwards RNT

169.4   more] quite T

169.11   heed] hear NT

170.4   Frichette."] Frichette." ¶ Cecile waited until her father had given the man some medicine and seen him out of the door, when ⟩ then she came into the shop. ¶ "Father, will he really never be well again?" ¶ "Not very well, my dear, — not for his kind of work. But we must remember that he has come off better than poor Michel, after all, and we will find something here for him to do. And he has brought us the good news that Father Hector is coming." NT

170.8   out] then with the sick doctor, Gervaise Beaudoin NT

170.21–171.1   Aix-en-Provence] Isle de France NT

171.13	it] that it was NT
171.16–17	the wood] their last wood NT
171.20	scarcely ate] could scarcely eat NT
171.21	their guest] Father Hector T
171.22–23	up to Father Hector] up NT
171.23	he] Father Hector had NT
172.2	that we] we NT
172.7	enjoy] appreciate NT
172.8–11	this." He . . . ¶ She] this. How I wish you could keep her from growing up, Euclide." ¶ He reached out and put his hand lightly on Cécile's head and she NT
172.20	live over] enjoy NT
172.21	Cécile.] Cécile! A
173.1	a teacher in the college] a parish priest NT; still teacher in a college RST; a teacher in a college RNT
173.2	young] little NT
173.8–9	forehead, with] forehead, clean cut like the head of a statue, with NT
173.9	a sweep] the sweep A
173.9	above] over NT
173.10–11	"And now . . . Hector] "You may bring the Chartreuse, too, Cecile," said her father. ¶ "And we will tell him NT

173.12   go] shall go NT

173.13   enough;] enough, and T

173.17   smiled . . . his head] took the liqueur glass offered to
                him, smiled, and set it down. NT

173.20   glass] cordial NT

173.20   set it down] held it there NT

173.25   He] Let us drink to the vanquished!" He NT

174.10   Is it] It is NT

174.23   Chabanel, Euclide] Chabanal NT

174.23–24   He was not so great a figure] He is not so celebrated
                T

174.24   Lalemant] Lalement A

175.4   only] but NT

175.6   that gracious city.] that gentle country. We of the
                north have something harder in us, Auclaire. NT

175.7   ¶ Chabanel] Chabanal NT, RST

175.9   From] In his father's house he had been surrounded
                by scholars and artists. From T

175.12   though] although A

176.11   in the snow] in the the snow RST

176.13   wigwam] wigwam to lie shuddering with disgust NT

176.17	the women] them T
176.21	were] were utterly NT
178.2	Blessed] Holy T
178.4	he sent] sent NT, RST
178.12	not surely] never T
178.22	and am] and I am NT
179.9	lodged] lodging NT
179.10	not take] take NT
179.14	bound] richly bound RST, RNT
179.21–22	medicines for my mission] medicines NT
180.4	missions] mission NT, RNT
180.16	ground] dark ground T
180.20	grey islands of] islands of gray NT
181.6	the] this NT
181.24	hot mustard] mustard NT
182.5	Raleigh, he said] Raleigh T
182.6	when] after NT
182.8	and continued] continued T
182.11	occasional] small NT
182.19	Jeanette] Nanette T

182.20	asking] getting T
182.21	*tranquilles*] *tranquille* T
182.23	even when] when NT
183.2	about] of NT
183.11	and the] and NT
183.12	gilt picture-frames] platters A
183.23	would] should NT
184.1	had, one evening,] one evening had NT
184.16	should] would NT, RST
184.18	drooped] dropped A
185.3	"Monsieur] ¶ 'Monsieur A
185.7	¶ "Well] 'Well A
185.12	him, for] him, NT
185.17	Then something] Something T
186.1–2	often thrashed] used to thrash NT
186.24	he had put to] under NT
187.9	Le Havre] Havre NT
187.14–15	washerwoman's] wash woman's NT
187.23	Kebec] Quebec A
188.2	Blinker] ¶ Blinker A

188.10 afterwards] after that NT; afterward RST, A

188.14 Sébastien] Joseph NT

188.22–24 trade." Blinker . . . had begun] trade." ¶ Blinker's face was so pale under his read {*sic*} hair, so twisted by his disfigurement and by his anguish of mind, his poor crooked eyes were so full of suffering, that Auclaire felt almost afraid of him. Moreover, the miserable man began NT; A = K1 {except no ¶ after "sleeve"}

188.25 anguish. Auclair] torture. Auclaire NT, RST; anguish. ¶ Auclair A

189.1 the twisted] this NT

189.6–7 measure out a dose] get Blinker his bottle NT

189.7 laudanum. After Blinker] laudanum, and after the poor fellow NT; laudanum. ¶ After Blinker A

189.16 "He] ¶ 'He A

189.17 my dear] dear NT

189.20 Sébastien] Joseph NT

191.1 She] ¶ She A

191.2 He] ¶ He A

192.13–14 Monseigneur] Monsieur NT

195.1 It was the] The NT

195.1	June] June, golden, glorious NT
195.3–4	clear weather] the weather NT
195.13–14	slender man in buckskins] slender man NT; man in buckskins RST
195.16	fellow] man NT, RST
195.17	coureurs de bois] *coureurs de bois* A
196.1	When] ¶ When A
196.14	so well] as well T
196.14–15	stayed at home] stayed NT
196.17	But I must] I must NT
196.18	and first] but first NT
197.1	¶ "Oh] 'Oh A
197.8	"Oh] ¶ 'Oh A
197.12	big beaver towns] red trees, and the beavers T
197.16	The] ¶ The A
197.17	here] there NT
197.18	up] down NT
197.18	shallop] sloop T
197.25	waters] water NT, RNT
197.25	To both] Both to NT

655

198.4   forests which] forests NT

198.16   like the . . . rapids upon] like the bright rapids on
               NT; like the sunlight on the bright rapids upon RST,
               RNT

198.18   father,] father had been NT

198.19   had] who had NT

198.19   built himself] built NT

198.20   dwelling] dwelling for himself NT

199.3   was thought to have] had NT

199.10–11   disappointment] his disappointment T

199.16   dealing . . . enemy.] dealing. A

199.21   mother] mother, whom he adored NT

199.24–25   boots, — he was wearing moccasins] boots NT

200.2   her his] her NT

200.5   Charron's] Pierre Charron's A

200.7   in] out in T

200.21   Versailles] the Court NT

201.14   and] and the NT

201.21   It was] His was T

201.22   of] of slim NT

201.24–25   quince-tree] pear-tree T

202.7   and of the] and the NT

202.8   Bourgeoys] de Bourgeoys T

203.1   should] would NT, RST

203.1–2   it better] it NT

203.5   liked to have children] liked children to NT

204.6   bottle or two] bottle T

204.7   Gaillac] Sauterne NT

204.7   presently] finally NT

204.20   Bourgeoys] de Bourgeoys T

205.14   in time] and leave her NT, RST

205.15   This] It NT

205.19   his] his supple T

206.6   allée] *allée* A

206.19   should] would NT, RST

208.5   was alarmed] felt startled NT; was disturbed RST

208.6   the sad] that sad NT

208.11   ¶ "It was] "It was T

208.12   this year I] I NT

208.19   No] Ah T

208.25	dog] little dog NT
209.24	Pierre's] ¶ Pierre's A
210.16	aloud, . . . My] aloud. She said the litany to the Blessed Virgin, I remember. Then more — but my T
211.12	church] chapel NT
212.10	her] her about NT
212.10–11	farmers lived over there] farmer lived NT
212.11	eel-fishings] eel fishing NT
212.11–12	autumn] spring T
213.2	such] so good NT
213.11–12	so distracted I cannot] too surprised to NT
213.22	¶ "Are] 'Are A
213.22	presently called] called NT
213.24	am not sure] don't know NT
214.3	waiting, seated] sitting NT
214.6	him. Cécile] Pierre. She NT
214.7	wished them] said NT; wished her RST
214.14	boat] sloop ⟩ boat {canceled, then marked *stet*} RNT
214.14	shallop] one NT; sloop RST; sloop ⟩ shallop RNT
215.14	to] up to NT

215.15   those] those little NT

215.19   saw] noticed NT

216.3   partridge] pheasant NT

216.6   *campagnarde*] *campagne* NT; *campagnard* RST, RNT

216.17   they let] let NT

216.23   when everything] everything NT

217.2   sat] sit NT

217.21   seemed to stir] stirred NT

217.23   pine] balsam A

218.19   stuffed] skeleton of the NT

218.22   fill] stuff NT, RST

219.10   the genial] the NT

219.19   felt uneasy] began to feel uneasy A

220.2   all the four] all four of the T

220.4   to give] they must give NT

220.8   only wore] wore NT

220.14   sheets. The] sheets, and the NT

220.20   spreading] putting NT

220.22   put] lay NT

221.12   beautiful] pleasant A

221.22   ¶ Cécile] Cécile A

222.23   living] living, had left them behind her NT

223.2   indeed] somehow NT

223.11   they] that they NT

223.14   wood; as] wood, and as T

223.15   These children] The little girls T

224.11   things] things together NT

224.13   satisfactory] entertaining NT

225.2   He] ¶ He A

225.5   used to dream] used to like to dream NT

225.18   He] But he NT

225.20   Soon] Now NT

225.21   then] now NT

226.10   on] upon NT

226.11   seem so] seem NT

227.10   As she began] This afternoon, as she was NT

222.14   taught] told NT

228.6   beautiful] lovely NT

231.7   ¶ Word] Word NT

231.9   head] adverse NT

233.1   "You] ¶ 'You A

234.6   the early] the NT

235.10   cannon] cannons NT

235.16   ¶ All] All NT, RST

235.18   fresh and handsome] very handsome T

235.19   her hair] hair NT

235.24   him] him today NT

236.3   with] and T

236.13   stand] stand up T

237.11   Le Havre] La Havre NT

237.13   new shouts] more shouting NT; shouts RST, RNT

237.18   came] himself came NT

237.24   young Duc] Duc NT

237.25   was married to] was soon to marry NT; had married RST

238.8   ¶ The] The NT

238.11   Sometimes] Some years T

238.13   succession. By] formation, and by NT; formation. By RST, RNT

239.10   wondered] used to wonder NT

239.12   wracked and broken, and] so wracked and broken
           that T

239.14   And all] All NT

241.1   freezing gales] ice-cold winds T

241.3–4   The colony owed its life to these] Everyone in the
           colony owed their lives NT, RST; Everyone in the
           colony owed his life RNT

241.4   whatever] and whatever NT

241.9   in the] every NT

241.16–17 share in] watch T

242.4–5   of course] certainly NT

242.11   such luxuries] them NT

242.14   which] that T

242.18   alcohol and borax] camphorated alcohol T

244.7   pharmaciens] *pharmaciens* A

244.13   sirops] syrups A

244.14   Madame] Mère A

244.21   here] in NT

244.22   pharmacie] *pharmacie* A

245.12   Auclair] He T

246.14   like herself again] more at ease RST; more at ease
           {lined out & original reading marked *stet*} RNT

247.6 which] that T

247.14 jumped] sprang NT

248.11 Dinan] Dinard T

248.25 cooks] two cooks NT

249.7 and a] and a very NT

249.13–14 at his ease] cheerful RST; cheerful ⟩ "at his ease" {canceled, then marked *stet* = K I} RNT

250.3–4 Le Havre] La Havre NT

250.4 The] ¶ The A

250.6–7 Le Havre] La Havre NT

250.15 should] would NT, RST

250.21 reason!] reason. T

251.10 very much] so much NT

251.11 was] was very much NT

251.16–17 tail-feathers] tail feather NT

251.21 a] a polite NT

251.23 if you please] please NT

252.15 Cécile] ¶ Cécile A

253.14 ¶ "Not] 'Not A

253.19 Jacques] ¶ Jacques A

254.5   "You] ¶ 'You A

254.10   Jacques] ¶ Jacques A

255.1   warm] hot T

255.13   West Indian] South American NT, RST

255.14   Should] Would NT, RST

255.22–23   perfectly] musically NT, RST

255.23   his] his liquid NT, RST

255.23   was very musical, sounded] sounded NT, RST

256.3   they] that they NT, RNT

256.8   relating] telling NT

256.10   the story] a story T

256.11   Indian] India T

256.19   a house] one T

257.9   should] would NT, RST

257.13   sets] set T

257.15   him] him that T

258.6   Provence] *pays* NT

258.22–23   young . . . hollows] young NT, RNT

259.4   ¶ Down] Down NT

259.21   ¶ "Papa] 'Papa A

260.4	¶ "Ah] 'Ah A
260.15	two] two closed N T
261.5	Three] Two 〉 Three R N T
261.6–7	*Garonne, Le Duc de Bretagne*] *Garonne, La Reine du Nord* N T, R S T; *Garonne, La Reine du Nord* {last name canceled, then marked *stet*} R N T
261.12	expecting] awaiting N T
261.23	sometimes] even T
261.24	market. So] market, so N T
262.6–7	had turned] were all N T
262.22	which] that T
262.23	that] which T
262.24	The] That T
263.2	streets] street N T, R N T
263.10	those] what T
263.14	Récollets] Récollets' R N T
263.16	Cathedral,] Cathedral church T
264.7	ground was] ground N T, R S T
264.13	Monseigneur] Monsieur T
265.6	mon père] *mon père* A

265.10   Blessed] Holy T

265.15   Monseigneur] Monsieur T

266.19   He] ¶ He A

266.22   Blessed] Holy T

267.3   thoughts. His] thoughts, because his NT

267.3   and] and so NT

267.12   should] would NT, RST

267.17   already] quite T

268.1   at] of light at NT

268.3   coming up] coming NT

268.3   out] up out NT

268.15   arm] hand NT

268.17   very far] away NT

268.21   home] back NT

269.4   flèche] *flèche* A

273.1   at the] at his NT

273.2   room] room full of sunlight NT

273.6   smouldering, — it] smouldering, for it T

274.7   ¶ It] It NT, RST

274.11   Count] man NT

274.24	should] would NT, RST
274.25	*Vengeance*] Gironde NT; *Garonne* RST, RNT
275.5	of my] my T
275.7	¶ The] The NT
277.19	creatures] brutes NT
278.4	The] Here the NT; ¶ The A
278.8	judged] knew T
278.15	should] would NT, RST
279.10	was] were NT; were ⟩ were RNT
279.16	Paris] the town T
279.17	either were] were either NT, RST
279.17	or] or they NT, RST
279.21	houses] house NT
281.13	stuck] stuck fast T
282.19	Noémi] Naömi T
282.21	Noémi] Naömi T
283.2	Noémi] Naömi T
283.3–4	had done] had NT
283.4	felt] felt anything NT

283.7 Noémi] Naömi T

283.11 in] in his N T

283.12 farm-house] little property T

283.25–284.1 Madame de la Grange Frontenac] certainly N T

284.2 the little property he had] whatever he had left R S T

284.3 Once] His N T

284.5 which] that N T

284.7 feel any] feel R S T

284.20–22 something . . . honour. The] something that their lives and their appetites did not explain. Conceptions of courage, duty, honor did not come out of the appetites, — and the N T; something in life that did not come out of their appetites; conceptions of courage, duty, honor. The R S T

285.7 the Count] he N T

285.8 hospitality.] hospitality. Long ago the Count had been much in the company of the Duc d'Orleans, a vehement atheist. In his last letter from his wife, Madame de la Grange Frontenac, (she wrote him once a year all the gossip of Paris) he had learned it was now common talk that the Duc d'Orleans had corrupted his own daughter, who was barely twelve years old. On the whole the Count had a low opinion of unbelievers. N T

285.10	Count Frontenac] he NT
285.15–16	Monsieur Auclair] Auclair T
285.16	o'clock] o'clock today NT
285.20–21	find myself so comfortable] like it so well NT
285.23	gave] made NT
286.8	sober] so uncomfortable NT
286.10	arrange] wish NT
286.11	personal belongings as I wish] own property NT; own property as I wish RST, RNT
286.14	remedies. A] remedies, but a NT
286.18	sleep, however] sleep T
286.24	time.] time, seeming comfortable in mind and body T
287.2	asleep. But suddenly he] asleep, when he suddenly NT
287.7	Many] A number NT
287.9	should] would NT, RST
287.25	at the] to the NT
288.7	boatmen] boatman NT
288.7–8	tarpaulins] tarpaulin NT
288.9	Célestins'] Célestins NT, RST

288.16	hardly] first NT
288.20	one] me {?} NT
288.21	it] it was NT
288.22	wood-supply . . . Paris] wood supply NT
289.18	together,] together and T
290.16	poêle] *poêle* A
290.18	messieurs les clients] *messieurs les clients* A
290.19	pharmacien] *pharmacien* A
291.8	*plaît*] *plaites* NT, RST
291.16	each] every NT
291.23	But he] He T
292.8	Father] Father, dear NT
292.14	call here] call NT
292.17	right] right, all the same NT
293.5	should] would NT, RST
293.5	serious] very serious NT
293.14	probably] likely NT
293.15	man] man to be in T
294.18	which] that T
294.18–19	denounced his policy] spoken NT

TABLE OF REJECTED SUBSTANTIVES

294.20	noted] have noted NT, RST
294.20	present in the church] in the audience T
295.12	impress] to impress T
295.12	and] and the RST, RNT
295.22	salutary] beneficial T
296.10	"It] ¶ 'It A
296.16–17	the Bishop's] this NT; the Archbishop's RST, RNT
296.17	him] the Archbishop NT
296.23	everything] nothing NT
296.25	Her father] "And we will continue to keep them away!" her father T
297.1	hungry!" he declared.] hungry! T
297.4	cheerful.] cheerful. Now why is that? NT; cheerful. How can that be? RST, RNT
297.5	That] It T
297.8	he] the man NT
298.19	took the] took NT
299.16	week] week, and he had laid by no provisions this fall NT, RNT
299.23	in two days] tomorrow NT, RNT
299.24	this] that NT

671

300.3   upon] on NT

301.6   them] them both, and asked for more NT

301.14   coma] stupor NT, RNT

301.20   Auclair] the apothecary NT, RNT

301.22   the Count's] his NT, RNT

301.24   why his privacy was] an explanation of his privacy's being NT

301.25   in] from NT

302.2   praying. He] knees, in prayer, and NT; knees, praying, and RNT

302.12   Merci] *Merci* A

302.12–13   word he spoke] sound he made NT

302.14–15   wondering . . . face] wondering at his calm face that NT

302.16   suffering. He] suffering, he NT

302.20–21   there all was still] all was still there NT

302.23   the hard] these hard NT

303.9   They would indeed have] She had been happy to be sure of NT

303.10   but] but now NT

303.16   their little world] the little world of Quebec NT

304.5   She] But she NT

304.11   quick] swift NT

305.5   I'm] But I'm NT

305.14   while] when NT, RNT

306.8   Detestable] I detest them NT

306.8   I] a poor woodsman NT

306.13   have some] have NT

306.18   leave] lief NT

307.18   Not] Think a moment; not NT, RNT

307.20   now. Let us cheer] now. Who knows how soon we
           may be as cold as he? So we warm NT, RNT

307.24   would] he would NT, RNT

308.10   authority, and a power] authority; and he had a new
           kind of power NT; authority; and he had a certain
           power RNT

308.11   people] people, red and white NT, RNT

308.12   passion. His] passion, She {illegible words} thought
           of him as a rov-{illegible} and, usually on his way to
           some far distant land or cataract or island merely
           because he wanted to see it {illegible} because he
           found those places irresistable {sic}. He would say
           {illegible} She used to think those {illegible} he, his
           secrets! That was why his NT; {passage heavily lined
           through in RNT}

673

309.3–4   St. Lawrence] river NT, RNT

310.4   Cathedral] Cathedral church NT, RNT

310.7   Hill] Way NT, RNT

310.9   sailed] had sailed NT

310.25   Saint-Vallier] he NT

312.9   befriended] liked NT

312.11   diocese] bishopric NT, RNT

312.15–16   Cathedral] Cathedral church NT, RNT

313.6   Cathedral] Cathedral church NT, RNT

313.9   He] ¶ He A

313.12–13   little altered] scarcely changed NT, RNT

313.19   His once] His NT

313.20   thin and grey] white and thin NT

314.18–19   un petit appartement] *un petit appartement* A

314.20   *Some] Note: Some NT; ¹Some RNT

314.24   unchanged] still unchanged NT, RNT

315.20   common] mutual NT

316.8   saw] say NT

316.10   attend] should attend NT, RNT

317.4   nodded] sighed NT, RNT

317.10   remains] is still NT

318.18   winds] wind A

319.21   should] would NT

320.23   the feeling] a happy feeling NT, RNT

            {last page of TS missing = 11 lines of K1}

Word Division

L IST A records compounds or possible compounds hyphenated at the ends of lines in the copy-text and resolved by the editors as one word, as hyphenated, or as two words. Page and line references are to the present edition. See the Textual Essay for a discussion of the criteria for resolving these forms. List B contains the end-of-line hyphenations that are to be retained as hyphenations in quotations from the present edition. Page and line references are to the present edition. Note that hyphenated words that are obviously to be resolved as one word ("com-/pound," for example) are not included in either list.

List A

9.18	well-sheltered
10.1	staircase
13.12–13	watercourse
24.14	care-taker
30.10–11	cotton-velvet

35.1	Saint-Antoine
41.5	reappearances
46.1–2	warm-hearted
57.1–2	beet-root
57.18	makeshifts
57.19	cold-frames
66.10	Haute-Savoie
68.10–11	dressing-cabinet
69.8	lavender-water
70.1–2	eye-sockets
70.22	yard-arms
71.4	yellow-green
74.23–24	brownish-lilac
74.24–25	lead-coloured
85.10	Dog-sledging
93.4	self-important
100.17	cough-syrup
109.5	care-taker's
109.7–8	ironmonger
117.17–18	rose-colour

122.14	candlelight
130.14	arm-chair
150.1	dog-sledges
154.3	playfellow
159.20	rose-tree
163.24	deer-gut
164.11	snowshoes
187.14–15	washerwoman's
220.6	night-gown
241.9	Saint-Paul
253.4	*Saint-Antoine*
262.15–16	goldsmith's
279.14	re-entrance
279.20	gate-keepers
280.7	bed-curtains
281.16	rust-flakes
282.25	bed-curtains
289.21	chair-claws
290.1	counterpane
290.13	wood doves

298.21	door-step
304.23–24	Ville-Marie
305.4	belly-band
309.5	Governor General
309.8	long-expected

List B

14.7–8	low-roofed
21.12–13	ill-favoured
30.10–11	cotton-velvet
31.14–15	rain-water
40.1–2	city-dweller
46.1–2	warm-hearted
57.1–2	beet-root
68.10–11	dressing-cabinet
70.1–2	eye-sockets
74.23–24	brownish-lilac
74.24–25	lead-coloured
77.6–7	gold-work
84.16–17	snow-covered
86.13–14	Saint-Vallier

92.16–17	half-way
94.9–10	foot-gear
102.22–23	window-panes
108.9–10	spending-money
109.1–2	coach-house
117.17–18	rose-colour
133.11–12	Saint-Sulpice
143.25–144.1	Saint-Vallier
144.1–2	Saint-Vallier's
149.1–2	Saint-Augustin
150.13–14	work-room
154.8–9	soldier-priest
169.8–9	brother-in
170.21–171.1	Aix-en
176.15–16	corn-meal
179.23–24	bed-curtains
195.2–3	cliff-side
201.8–9	Ville-Marie
201.24–25	quince-tree
211.6–7	half-facing

222.4–5	night-cap
227.21–22	cabinet-work
234.16–17	ear-rings
234.17–18	market-women
237.11–12	anchor-chains
245.15–16	self-forgetful
251.14–15	bird-like
251.16–17	tail-feathers
256.13–14	house-tops
274.2–3	seventy-eighth
280.15–16	farm-house
281.1–2	boot-tops
287.3–4	Nicholas-des
290.4–5	fire-light
298.15–16	barber-surgeon
304.23–24	Ville-Marie
309.14–15	Saint-Vallier
311.12–13	Saint-Vallier
314.20–21	Saint-Vallier
321.3–4	twenty-four